# EDGE OF INFINITY

Edited by
**Jonathan Strahan**

# Also Edited by **Jonathan Strahan**

# EDGE OF
# INFINITY

### EDITED BY **JONATHAN STRAHAN**

Including stories by
**PAT CADIGAN**
**ELIZABETH BEAR**
**JAMES S. A. COREY**
**SANDRA MCDONALD** AND **STEPHEN D. COVEY**
**JOHN BARNES**
**PAUL MCAULEY**
**KRISTINE KATHRYN RUSCH**
**GWYNETH JONES**
**HANNU RAJANIEMI**
**STEPHEN BAXTER**
**ALASTAIR REYNOLDS**
**AN OWOMOYELA**
**BRUCE STERLING**

**SOLARIS**

First published 2012 by Solaris
an imprint of Rebellion Publishing Ltd,
Riverside House, Osney Mead,
Oxford, OX2 0ES, UK

*www.solarisbooks.com*

ISBN: 978 1 78108 056 6

Designed & typeset by Rebellion Publishing

Printed in the US

*For my friend and colleague, Gardner Dozois, some pure quill SF!*

# ACKNOWLEDGEMENTS

I HAVE LOVED working on this book and would like to thank my Solaris editor Jonathan Oliver, Ben Smith, and the whole team at Rebellion for all of their kindness, help, and consideration over the past year. Also for the absolutely kick-arse cover by Adam Tredowski, which totally nails the book. I would also like to thank all of the book's contributors for letting me publish their wonderful stories: Daniel Abraham, John Barnes, Stephen Baxter, Elizabeth Bear, Pat Cadigan, Stephen D. Covey, Ty Franck, Gwyneth Jones, Paul McAuley, Sandra McDonald, An Owomayela, Hannu Rajaniemi, Alastair Reynolds, Kristine Kathryn Rusch, and Bruce Sterling. An extra thanks to Peter Hamilton and Peter Watts, who would have been part of the book if situations had allowed. As always, I'd like to thank my agent, the ever wonderful Howard Morhaim and his brilliant new assistant Alice Speilburg.

And, finally, an extra special thanks to my wife Marianne, who helped with this book, and to my two daughters, Jessica and Sophie, for their love and support.

# CONTENTS

# INTRODUCTION

WELCOME TO THE Fourth Generation of science fiction.

A year or so ago I was working on *Engineering Infinity*, a collection of stories intended to interrogate what hard science fiction means in the second decade of the 21$^{st}$ century. In the introduction to that book I made passing reference to the 'Fourth Generation of Science Fiction,' where I suggested that science fiction, having been born, had passed through adolescence, into adulthood, and then moved into a post-scarcity period of incredible richness and diversity.

My intention, in coining the term, was simply to highlight the depth and variety of science fiction today, both in terms of who reads and writes it, and in the breadth and complexity of what the field now encompasses in terms of style, topic, theme, setting and so on. Things are good, and the laboratory is bubbling! However, once *Engineering Infinity* had gone to press and the time had well and truly arrived to move on to other projects, it occurred to me that the "Fourth Generation" was a good descriptor for something else happening in science fiction.

Science fiction publishing is a somewhat morbid sub-culture. It is rather obsessed with the death of SF and SF publishing. It is so obsessed with its own death that it feels honour bound to report that it is dying, will die, or in fact has already died rather a long time ago with monotonous regularity. I've not checked, but I'm fairly confident that my good friend and colleague, Gardner Dozois, has reported this fact in the introduction to almost every one of his nearly three dozen 'best of the year' anthologies published between 1977 and the present day. This isn't because Gardner is a particularly depressive fellow, or that he relishes the aforesaid death of our field. It's because science fiction, I realised, is being killed by science.

Not just today, but always. How? Well, every day scientists go to work developing new hypotheses, publishing new papers, and uncovering new facts. The bedrock of information upon which science fiction writers work is constantly shifting and changing, as it should. This is a fine and wonderful thing, and I doubt a single science fiction writer on the planet would complain about it. However, this constant barrage of fact can be the enemy of romance, and science fiction needs romance to survive.

Take Mars as an example. Percival Lowell, fascinated with drawings by Italian astronomer Giovanni Schiaparelli, fell in love with and helped to popularise the canals of Mars. That view of the world, scientifically reasonable for its time, formed the basis of Edgar Rice Burrough's novel *A Princess of Mars*, which imagined the sweeping dead sea bottoms of Helium, populated by thoats and tharks and the setting for the sword-fighting, gravity-defying adventures of John Carter. By 1964 that image was dead, swept away by the tide of facts collected by the space probe Mariner, and by the late 1970s Mariners, Vikings and Voyagers had turned images of Helium forever to dust, and left us with images that looked nothing like nothing more than a stretch of washed-out desert that *really* wanted to kill you.

Not that science fiction hasn't risen to the challenge set by science. It did and it continues to do so. A rash of novels in the 1980s, most prominently from Kim Stanley Robinson, with his austere, magisterial *Mars* trilogy, took on the challenge of making Mars a human place – a dangerous one, but a place where romance and adventure could flourish and where we could see a way back to the future. Others took up the cudgel, Greg Bear in *Moving Mars*, Terry Bisson in *Voyage to a Red Planet*, and many more.

How does all of this connect to the Fourth Generation? Well, bear with me. It's been said that with the publication of William Gibson's *Neuromancer* in 1984, co-incidentally published around the same time the Mars revolution was happening, moved science fiction from an outwards-focussed technological SF to an inwards-focussed look at cyberspace; innerspace, even. Cyberpunk came from the street, but its talk of uploading into cyberspace was also a turning away from the physical world and from science fiction's journey to the stars, something that would have been unimaginable just a few decades earlier. As the years passed, and as more fact accumulated, travelling to the stars began to seem harder and less likely, and even leaving our planet seemed so fanciful that SF briefly spawned a Mundane movement to challenge it.

And it's not hard to see why. The flush of optimism surrounding space travel that followed *Sputnik*, Laika, Neil Armstrong and *Apollo 11*, *Voyager*, Skylab, the space shuttle program and the

International Space Station had pretty much run out by the time of the space shuttle *Columbia* disaster in 2003. That moment, for some of us, seemed to mark the endpoint of a certain romance with the future, the idea that we actually would travel into space and finally leave our home world in some meaningful way. Increasingly the stories being told were of a humanity restricted to Earth, where all of its offworld exploration was restricted to robots and probes, or to uploaded intelligences in tiny craft. A practical, scientific future.

And yet science fiction is about the romance of science and the romance of fiction, about our love affair with tomorrow. During the Fourth Generation of fecundity (see, I came back to it), another kind of story began to appear, one that saw a place for us in our own Solar System, if not out in the stars (yet). This story was to some extent an engineering story. It told of massive engines and small craft, of tiny colonies and bubbles of life spreading out to the moon, to Mars, through the asteroid belt, past massive Jupiter, and on to the distant colder places far from our star. It was a story that appeared as the background to any number of short stories published over the past half-dozen years, and then flourishing in major novels like James S.A Corey's *Leviathan Wakes* and Kim Stanley Robinson's stunning *2312*. It was a story filled with romance, adventure, and with a love of science and our solar system. It is the story of the Fourth Age of Science Fiction.

And that brings us back to this book. *Edge of Infinity* is a companion to *Engineering Infinity*, as the title foreshadows. It's a Fourth Generation book. It takes stories set firmly in an industrialised, colonised

Solar System during a time when starflight is yet to emerge, and imagines life in the hottest places close to our star, and in the coldest, most distant corners of our home. For all that some individual stories may be darker or lighter in tone, it's a love letter to our home, to our future and to science fiction. It won't be the last.

**Jonathan Strahan**
**Perth, Western Australia**

# THE GIRL-THING WHO WENT OUT FOR SUSHI

**Pat Cadigan**

NINE DECS INTO her second hitch, Fry hit a berg in the Main ring and broke her leg. And she didn't just splinter the bone – compound fracture! Yow! What a mess! Fortunately, we'd finished servicing most of the eyes, a job that I thought was more busy-work than work-work. But those were the last decs before Okeke-Hightower hit and everybody had comet fever.

There hadn't been an observable impact on the Big J for almost three hundred (Dirt) years – Shoemaker-Somethingorother – and no one was close enough to get a good look back then. Now every news channel, research institute, and moneybags everywhere in the Solar System was paying Jovian Operations for a ringside view. Every JovOp crew was on the case, putting cameras on cameras and back-up cameras on the back-up cameras – visible, infrared, X-ray, and everything else. Fry was pretty excited about it herself, talking about how great it was she would get to see it live. Girl-thing should have been watching where she wasn't supposed to be going.

17

I was coated and I knew Fry's suit would hold, but featherless bipeds are prone to vertigo when they're injured. So I blew a bubble big enough for both of us, cocooned her leg, pumped her full of drugs, and called an ambulance. The jellie with the rest of the crew was already on the other side of the Big J. I let them know we'd scrubbed and someone would have to finish the last few eyes in the radian for us. Girl-thing was one hell of a stiff two-stepper, staying just as calm as if we were unwinding end-of-shift. The only thing she seemed to have a little trouble with was the O. Fry picked up consensus orientation faster than any other two-stepper I'd ever worked with, but she'd never done it on drugs. I tried to keep her distracted by telling her all the gossip I knew, and when I ran out, I made shit up.

Then all of a sudden, she said, "Well, Arkae, that's it for me."

Her voice was so damned final, I thought she was quitting. And I deflated because I had taken quite a liking to our girl-thing. I said, "Aw, honey, we'll all miss you out here."

But she laughed. "No, no, no, I'm not leaving. I'm going out for sushi."

I gave her a pat on the shoulder, thinking it was the junk in her system talking. Fry was no ordinary girl-thing – she was great out here, but she'd always been special. Back in the Dirt, she'd been a brain-box, top-level scholar *and* a beauty queen. That's right – a featherless biped genius beauty queen. Believe it or leave it, as Sheerluck says.

Fry'd been with us for three and half decs when she let on about being a beauty queen. The whole crew was unwinding end-of-shift – her, me, Dubonnet,

Sheerluck, Aunt Chovie, Splat, Bait, Glynis, and Fred – and we all about lost the O.

"Wow," said Dubonnet. "Did you ask for whirled peas, too?" I didn't understand the question, but it sounded like a snipe. I triple-smacked him and suggested he respect someone else's culture.

But Fry said, "No, I don't blame any a youse asking. That stuff really is so silly. Why people still bother with such things, I sure don't know. We're supposed to be so advanced and enlightened, and it still matters how a woman looks in a bathing suit. Excuse me, a biped woman," she added, laughing a little. "And no, the subject of whirled peas never came up."

"If that's how you really felt," Aunt Chovie said, big, serious eyes and all eight arms in curlicues, "why'd you go along with it?"

"It was the only way I could get out here," Fry said.

"Not really?" said Splat, a second before I woulda blurted out the same thing.

"Yes, really. I got heavy metal for personal appearances and product endorsements, plus a full scholarship, my choice of school." Fry smiled and I thought it was the way she musta smiled when she was crowned Queen of the Featherless Biped Lady Geniuses or whatever it was. It wasn't insincere, but a two-stepper's face is just another muscle group; I could tell it was something she'd learned to do. "I saved as much as I could so I'd have enough for extra training after I graduated. Geology degree."

"Dirt geology though," said Sheerluck. It used to be Sherlock, but Sheerluck'll be the first to admit she's got more luck than sense.

"That's why I saved for extra training," Fry said. "I had to do the best I could with the tools available. You know how that is. All-a-youse know."

We did.

FRY HAD WORKED with some other JovOp crews before us, all of them mixed – two-steppers and sushi. I guess they all liked her and vice versa but she clicked right into place with us, which is pretty unusual for a biped and an all-octo crew. I liked her right away, and that's saying something because it usually takes me a while to resonate even with sushi. I'm okay with featherless bipeds, I really am. Plenty of sushi – more than will admit to it – have a problem with the species just on general principle, but I've always been able to get along with them. Still, they aren't my fave flave to crew with out here. Training them is harder, and not because they're stupid. Two-steppers just aren't made for this. Not like sushi. But they keep on coming and most of them tough it out for at least one square dec. It's as beautiful out here as it is dangerous. I see a few outdoors almost every day, clumsy starfish in suits.

That's not counting the ones in the clinics and hospitals. Doctors, nurses, nurse-practitioners, technicians, physiotherapists, paramedics – they're all your standard featherless biped. It's the law. Fact: you can*not* legally practice any kind of medicine in any form other than basic human, not even if you're already a doctor, supposedly because all the equipment is made for two-steppers. Surgical instruments, operating rooms, sterile garments, even rubber gloves – the fingers are too short and there aren't enough of them. Ha, ha, a little sushi humour. Maybe it's not that funny to you, but fresh catch laugh themselves sick.

I don't know how many two-steppers in total go out for sushi in a year (Dirt or Jovian), let alone how their reasons graph, but we're all over the place out here and Census isn't in my orbit, so for all I know half a dozen two-steppers apply every eight decs. Stranger things have happened.

In the old days, when I turned, nobody did it unless they had to. Most often, it was either terminal illness or permanent physical disability as determined by the biped standard: i.e., conditions at sea level on the third planet out. Sometimes, however, the disability was social, or more precisely, legal. Original Generation out here had convicts among the gimps, some on borrowed time.

Now, if you ask us, we say OG lasted six years but we're all supposed to use the Dirt calendar, even just to each other (everyone out here gets good at converting on the fly), which works out to a little over seventy by Dirt reckoning. The bipeds claim that's three generations not just one. We let them have that their way, too, because, damn can they argue. About *anything*. It's the way they're made. Bipeds are strictly binary, it's all they know: zero or one, yes or no, right or wrong.

But once you turn, that strictly binary thinking's the first thing to go, and fast. I never heard anyone say they miss it; I know I don't.


ANYWAY, I GO see Fry in one of the Gossamer ring clinics. A whole wing is closed off, no one gets in unless they're on The List. If that isn't weird enough for you, there's a two-stepper in a uniform stuck to the floor, whose only job is checking The List. I'm wondering if I'm in the wrong station, but the two stepper finds me on The List and I may go in and see La Soledad y Godmundsdottir. It takes me a second to get who she means. How'd our girl-thing get Fry out of that? I go through an airlock-style portal and there's another two-stepper waiting to escort me. He uses two poles with sticky tips to move himself along, and he does all right, but I can see this is a new skill. Every so often, he manoeuvres so one foot touches floor so he can feel more like he's walking.

When you've been sushi as long as I have, two-steppers are pretty transparent. I don't mean that as condescending as it sounds. After all, I was a two-stepper once myself. We all started out as featherless bipeds, none of us was born sushi. But a lot of us feel we were born to *be* sushi, a sentiment that doesn't go down too well with the two-steppers who run everything. Which doesn't make it any less true.

My pal the poler and I go a full radian before we get to another air-lock. "Through there," he says. "I'll take you back whenever you're ready."

I thank him and swim through, wondering what dim bulb thought he was a good idea, because he's what Aunt Chovie calls surplus to requirements. The few conduits off this tube are sealed and there's nothing to hide in or behind. I know Fry is so rich that she has to hire people to spend her money for her, but I'm thinking she should hire people smart enough to know the difference between spending and wasting.

There's our girl, stuck to the middle of a hospital bed almost as big as the ringberg that put her in it.

She's got a whole ward to herself – all the walls are folded back to make one big private room. There are some nurses down at the far end, sitting around sipping coffee bulbs. When they hear me come in, they start unsticking and reaching for things, but I give them a full eight-OK – *Social call, I'm nobody, don't look busy on my account* – and they all settle down again.

Sitting up in her nest of pillows, Fry looks good, if a little undercooked. There's about three centimetres of new growth on her head and it must be itchy because she keeps scratching it. In spite of the incubator around her leg, she insists I give her a full hug, four by four, then pats a spot beside her. "Make yourself to home, Arkae."

"Isn't there a rule about visitors sitting on the bed?" I say, curling a couple of arms around a nearby hitching-post. It's got a fold-out seat for biped visitors. This place has everything.

"Yeah. The rule is, it's okay if I say it's okay. Check it – this bed's bigger than a lot of apartments I've had. The whole crew could have a picnic here. In fact, I wish they would." She droops a little. "How is everyone, really busy?"

I settle down. "There's always another lab to build or hardware to service or data to harvest," I say, careful, "if that's what you mean." The way her face flexes, I know it isn't.

"You're the only one who's come to see me," she says.

"Maybe the rest of the crew weren't on The List."

"What list?" she says. So I tell her. Her jaw drops, and all at once two nurses appear on either side of the bed, nervous as hell, asking if she's all right. "I'm

23

fine, I'm fine," she snaps at them. "Go away, gimme some privacy, will you?"

They obey a bit reluctantly, eyeing me like they're not too sure about how safe she is with me squatting on the bedspread.

"Don't yell at *them*," I say after a bit. "Something bad happens to you, it's their fault. They're just taking care of you the best way they know how." I uncurl two arms, one to gesture at the general surroundings and the other to point at the incubator, where a quadjillion nanorectics are mending her leg from the marrow out, which, I can tell you from personal experience, *itches*. A *lot*. No doubt that's contributing to her less-than-sparkly disposition – what the hell can you do about itchy *bone marrow?* – and what I just told her doesn't help.

"I should have known," she fumes, scratching her head. "It's the people I work for."

That doesn't make sense. JovOp couldn't afford anything like this. "I think you're a little confused, honey," I say. "If we even *thought* JovOp had metal that heavy, it'd be Sushi Bastille Day, heads would –"

"No, these people are back in the Dirt. My image is licensed for advertising and entertainment," she says. "I thought there'd be less demand after I came out here – out of sight, out of mind, you know? But apparently the novelty of a beauty queen in space has yet to wear off."

"So you're still rich," I say. "Is that so bad?"

She makes a pain face. "Would you agree to an indefinite contract just to be rich? Even *this* rich?"

"You couldn't get rich on an indefinite contract," I say gently, "and no union's stupid enough to let anybody take one."

She thinks for a few seconds. "All right, how about this: did you ever think you owned something and then you found out it owned you?"

"*Oh...*" Now I get it. "Can they make you go back?"

"They're trying," Fry says. "A court order arrived last night, demanding I hit the Dirt as soon as I can travel. The docs amended it so *they* decide when it's safe, but that won't hold them off forever. You know any good lawyers? Out here?" she added.

"Well, yeah. Of course, they're all sushi."

Fry lit up. "Perfect."

NOT EVERY CHAMBERED Nautilus out here is a lawyer – the form is also a popular choice for librarians, researchers, and anyone else in a data-heavy line of work – but every lawyer in the Jovian system is a chambered Nautilus. It's not a legal restriction the way it is with bipeds and medicine, just something that took root and turned into tradition. According to Dove, who's a partner in the firm our union keeps on retainer, it's the sushi equivalent of powdered wigs and black robes, which we have actually seen out here from time to time when two-steppers from certain parts of the Dirt bring their own lawyers with them.

Dove says no matter how hard biped lawyers try to be professional, they all break out with some kind of weird around their sushi colleagues. The last time the union had to renegotiate terms with JovOp, the home office sent a canful of corporate lawyers out of the Dirt. Well, from Mars, actually, but they weren't Martian citizens and they went straight back to No. 3 afterwards. Dove wasn't involved, but she kept us updated as much as she could without violating any regulations.

Dove's area is civil law and sushi rights, protecting our interests as citizens of the Jovian system. This includes not only sushi and sushi-in-transition but pre-ops as well. Any two-stepper who files a binding letter of intent for surgical conversion is legally sushi.

Pre-ops have all kinds of problems – angry relatives, *rich* angry relatives with injunctions from some Dirt supreme court, confused/troubled children, heartbroken parents and ex-spouses, lawsuits and contractual disputes. Dove handles all that and more: identity verification, transfer of money and property, biometric resets, as well as arranging mediation, psychological counselling (for anyone, including angry relatives), even religious guidance. Most bipeds would be surprised to know how many of those who go out for sushi find God, or something. Most of us, myself included, fall into the latter category but there are plenty of the organised religion persuasion. I guess you can't go through a change that drastic without discovering your spiritual side.

Fry wasn't officially a pre-op yet, but I knew Dove would be the best person she could talk to about what she'd be facing if she decided to go through with it. Dove is good at figuring out what two-steppers want to hear and then telling them what they need to hear in a way that makes them listen. I thought it was psychology, but Dove says it's closer to linguistics.

As Sheerluck would say, don't ask me, I just lurk here.

\* \* \*

THE NEXT DAY, I show up with Dove and List Checker looks like she's never seen anything like us before. She's got our names, but she doesn't look too happy about it, which annoys me. List-checking isn't a job that requires any emotion from her.

"*You're* the attorney?" she says to Dove, who is eye-level with her, tentacles sedately furled.

"Scan me again if you need to," Dove says good-naturedly. "I'll wait. Mom always said, 'Measure twice, cut once.'"

List Checker can't decide what to do for a second or two, then scans us both again. "Yes, I have both your names here. It's just that – well, when she said an attorney, I was expecting – I thought you'd be... a... a..."

She hangs long enough to start twisting before Dove relents and says, "Biped." Dove still sounds good-natured, but her tentacles are now undulating freely. "You're not from around here, are you?" she asks, syrupy-sweet, and I almost rupture with not laughing.

"No," List Checker says in a small voice. "I've never been farther than Mars before."

"If the biped on the other side of that portal is equally provincial, better warn 'em." Then as we go through, Dove adds, "Too late!"

It's the same guy with the poles, but when Dove sees him, she gives this crazy whooping yell and pushes right into his face so her tentacles are splayed out on his skin.

"You son of a bitch!" she says, really happy.

And then the Poler says, "Hiya, Mom."

27

"Oh. Kay," I say, addressing anyone in the universe who might be listening. "I'm thinking about a brain enema. Is now a good time?"

"Relax," Dove says. "'Hiya Mom' is what you say when anyone calls you a son of a bitch."

"Or 'Hiya, Dad,'" says Poler, "depending."

"Aw, you all look alike to me," Dove says. "It's a small universe, Arkae. Florian and I got taken hostage together once, back in my two-stepper days."

"Really?" I'm surprised as hell. Dove never talks about her biped life; hardly any of us do. And I've never heard of anyone running into someone they knew pre-sushi purely by chance.

"I was a little kid," Poler says. "Ten Dirt-years. Dove held my hand. Good thing I met her when she still had one."

"He was a creepy little kid," Dove says as we head for Fry's room. "I only did it so he wouldn't scare our captors into killing all of us."

Poler chuckles. "Then why you let me keep in touch with you after it was all over?"

"I thought if I could help you be less creepy, you wouldn't inspire any more hostage-taking. Safer for everybody."

I can't remember ever hearing about anyone still being friends with a biped from before they were sushi. I'm still trying to get my mind around it as we go through the second portal.

When Fry sees us, there's a fraction of a second when she looks startled before she smiles. Actually, it's more like horrified. Which makes *me* horrified. I told her I was bringing a sushi lawyer. Girl-thing never got hiccups before, not even with the jellies, and that's saying something. Even when you know they're all AIs, jellies can take some getting used to no matter what shape you're in, two-stepper or sushi.

"Too wormy?" Dove says and furls her tentacles as she settles down on the bed a respectful distance from Fry.

"I'm sorry," Fry says, making the pain face. "I don't mean to be rude or bigoted –"

"Forget about it," Dove says. "Lizard brain's got no shame."

*Dove's wormies bother her more than my suckers?* I think, amazed. *Lizard brain's not too logical, either.*

"Arkae tells me you want to go out for sushi," Dove goes on chattily. "How much do you know about it?"

"I know it's a lot of surgery, but I think I have enough money to cover most of it."

"Loan terms are extremely favourable. You could live well on that money and still make payments –"

"I'd like to cover as much of the cost as I can while my money's still liquid."

"You're worried about having your assets frozen?" Immediately Dove goes from chatty to brisk. "I can help you with that, whether you turn or not. Just say I'm your lawyer, the verbal agreement's enough."

"But the money's back in the Dirt –"

"And *you're* here. It's all about where *you* are. I'll zap you the data on loans and surgical options – if you're like most people, you probably already have a form in mind, but it doesn't hurt to know about all the –"

Fry held up a hand. "Um, Arkae? You mind if I talk to my new lawyer alone?"

My feelings are getting ready to be hurt when Dove says, "Of course she doesn't. Because she knows that the presence of a third party screws up that confidentiality thing. Right, Arkae?"

I feel stupid and relieved at the same time. Then I see Fry's face and I know there's more to it.

THE FOLLOWING DAY the crew gets called up to weed and re-seed the Halo. Comet fever strikes again. We send Fry a silly cheer-up video to say we'll see her soon.

I personally think it's a waste of time sowing sensors in dust when we've already got eyes in the Main ring. Most of the sensors don't last as long as they're supposed to and the ones that do never tell us anything we don't already know. Weeding – picking up the dead sensors – is actually more interesting. When the dead sensors break down, they combine with the dust, taking on odd shapes and textures and even odder colorations. If something especially weird catches my eye, I'll ask to keep it. Usually, the answer's no. Recycling is the foundation of life out here – mass in, mass out; create, un-create, re-create, allathat. But once in a while, there's a surplus of something because nothing evens out exactly all the time, and I get to take a little good-luck charm home to my bunk.

We're almost at the Halo when the jellie tells us whichever crew seeded last time didn't weed out the dead ones. So much for mass in, mass out. We're all surprised; none of us ever got away with doing half a job. We have to hang in the jellie's belly high over the North Pole and scan the whole frigging Halo for materials markers. Which would be simple except a lot of what should be there isn't showing up. Fred makes us deep-scan three times but nothing shows on Metis and there's no sign that anything leaked into the Main ring.

"Musta all fell into the Big J," says Bait. He's watching the aurora flashing below us like he's hypnotised, which he probably is. Bait's got this thing about the polar hexagon anyway.

"But so many?" Splat says. "You know they're gonna say that's too many to be an accident."

"Do we know *why* the last crew didn't pick up the dead ones?" Aunt Chovie's already tensing up. If you tapped on her head, you'd hear high C-sharp.

"No," Fred says. "I don't even know which crew it was. Just that it wasn't us."

Dubonnet tells the jellie to ask. The jellie tells us it's put in a query, but because it's not crucial, we'll have to wait.

"Frigging tube-worms," Splat growls, tentacles almost knotting up. "They do that to feel important."

"Tube worms are AIs, they don't feel," the jellie says with the AI serenity that can get so maddening so fast. "Like jellies."

Then Glynis speaks up: "Scan Big J."

"Too much interference," I say. "The storms –"

"Just humour me," says Glynis. "Unless you're in a hurry?"

The jellie takes us down to just above the middle of the Main ring and we prograde double-time. And son of a bitch – is this crazy or is this the new order? – we get some hits in the atmosphere.

But we shouldn't. It's not just the interference from the storms – Big J gravitates the hell out of anything

31

it swallows. Long before I went out for sushi (and that was quite a while ago), they'd stopped sending probes into Jupiter's atmosphere. They didn't just hang in the clouds and none of them ever lasted long enough to reach liquid metallic hydrogen. Which means the sensors should just be atoms, markers crushed out of existence. They can't still be in the clouds unless something is keeping them there.

"That's gotta be a technical fault," Splat says. "Or something."

"Yeah, I'm motion sick, I lost the O," says Aunt Chovie, which is the current crew code for *Semaphore only*.

Bipeds have sign language and old-school semaphore with flags but octo-crew semaphore is something else entirely. Octo-sem changes as it goes, which means each crew speaks a different language, not only from each other, but also from one conversation to the next. It's not transcribable, either, not like spoken-word communication, because it works by consensus. It's not completely uncrackable, but even the best decryption AI can't do it in less than half a dec. Five days to decode a conversation isn't exactly efficient.

To be honest, I'm kinda surprised the two-steppers who run JovOp are still letting us get away with it. They're not what you'd call big champions of privacy, especially on the job. It's not just sushi, either – all their two-stepper employees, in the Dirt or all the way out here, are under total surveillance when they're on the clock. That's total as in a/v everywhere: offices, hallways, closets, and toilets. Bait says that's why JovOp two-steppers always look so grim – they're all holding it in till quitting time.

But I guess as long we get the job done, they don't care how we wiggle our tentacles at each other or what colour we are when we do it. Besides, when you're on the job out here, you don't want to worry about who's watching you because they'd *better* be. You don't want to die in a bubble waiting for help that isn't coming because nobody caught the distress signal when your jellie blew out.

So anyway, we consider the missing matter and the markers we shouldn't have been picking up on in Big J's storm systems and we whittle it down to three possibilities: the previous crew returned to finish the job but someone forgot to enter it into the record; a bunch of scavengers blew through with a trawler and neutralised the markers so they can re-sell the raw materials; or some dwarf star at JovOp is seeding the clouds in hope of getting an even closer look at the Okeke-Hightower impact.

Number three is the stupidest idea – even if some of the sensors actually survive till Okeke-Hightower hits, they're in the wrong place, and the storms will scramble whatever data they pick up – so we all agree that's probably it. After a little more discussion, we decide not to let on and when JovOp asks where all the missing sensors are, we'll say we don't know. Because the Jupe's honest truth is, we don't.

We pick up whatever we can find, which takes two J-days, seed the Halo with new ones, and go home. I call over to the clinic to check how Fry's doing and find out if she managed to get the rest of the crew on The List so we can have that picnic on her big fat bed. But I get Dove, who tells me that our girl-thing is in surgery.

\* \* \*

DOVE SAYS THAT, at Fry's own request, she's not allowed to tell anyone which sushi Fry's going out for, including us. I feel a little funny about that – until we get the first drone.

It's riding an in-out skeet, which can slip through a jellie double-wall without causing a blow-out. JovOp uses them to deliver messages they consider sensitive – whatever that means – and that's what we thought it was at first.

· Then it lights up and we're looking at this image of a two-stepper dressed for broadcast. He's asking one question after another on a canned loop; in a panel on his right, instructions on how to record, pause, and playback are scrolling on repeat.

The jellie asks if we want to get rid of it. We toss the whole thing in the waste chute, skeet and all, and the jellie poops it out as a little ball of scrap, to become some scavenger's lucky find.

Later, Dubonnet files a report with JovOp about the unauthorised intrusion. JovOp gives him a receipt but no other response. We're all expecting a reprimand for failing to detect the skeet's rider before it got through. Doesn't happen.

"Somebody's drunk," Bait says. "Query it."

"No, don't," says Splat. "By the time they're sober, they'll have to cover it up or their job's down the chute. It never happened, everything's eight-by-eight."

"Until someone checks our records," Dubonnet says and tells the jellie to query, who assures him that's a wise thing to do. The jellie has been doing this sort of thing more often lately, making little comments. Personally, I like those little touches.

Splat, however, looks annoyed. "I was joking," he says, enunciating carefully. They can't touch you for joking, no matter how tasteless, but it has to be clear. We laugh, just to be on the safe side, except for Aunt Chovie, who says she doesn't think it was very funny, because she can't laugh unless she really feels it. Some people are like that.

Dubonnet gets an answer within a few minutes. It's a form message in legalese but this gist is, *We heard you the first time, go now and sin no more.*

"They *all* can't be drunk," Fred says. "Can they?"

"Can't they?" says Sheerluck. "You guys have crewed with me long enough to know how fortune smiles on me and mine."

"Spoken like a member of the Church of The Four-Leaf Horseshoe," Glynis says.

Fred perks right up. "Is that that new casino on Europa?" he asks. Fred loves casinos. Not gambling, just casinos. The jellie offers to look it up for him.

"Synchronicity is a real thing, it's got *math,*" Sheerluck is saying. Her colour's starting to get a little bright; so is Glynis's. I'd rather they don't give each other ruby-red hell while we're all still in the jellie. "And the dictionary definition of serendipity is, 'Chance favours the prepared mind.'"

"*I'm* prepared to go home and log out, who's prepared to join me?" Dubonnet says before Glynis can sneer openly. I like Glynis, vinegar and all, but sometimes I think she should have been a crab instead of an octopus.

OUR PRIVATE QUARTERS are supposed to have no surveillance except for the standard safety monitoring.

Yeah, we don't believe that for a nano-second. But if JovOp ever got caught in the act, the unions would eat them alive and poop out the bones to fertilise Europa's germ farms. So either they're even better at it than any of us can imagine, or they're taking a calculated risk. Most sushi claim to believe the former; I'm in the latter camp. I mean, they watch us so much already, they've gotta want to look at something else for a change.

We share the typical octo-crew quarters – eight rooms around a large common area. When Fry was with us, we curtained off part of it for her, but somehow she was always spilling out of it. Her stuff, I mean – we'd find underwear bobbing around in the lavabo, shoes orbiting a lamp (good thing she only needed two), live-paper flapping around the room in the air currents. All the time she'd spent out here and she still couldn't get the hang of housekeeping in zero gee. It's the sort of thing that stops being cute pretty quickly when you've got full occupancy, plus one. I could tell she was trying, but eventually we had to face the truth: much as we loved her, our resident girl-thing was a slob.

I thought that was gonna be a problem, but she wasn't even gone a day before it felt like there was something missing. I'd look around expecting to see some item of clothing or jewellery cruising past, the latest escapee from one of her not-terribly-secure reticules.

"So who wants to bet that Fry goes octo?" Splat says when we get home.

"Who'd want to bet she doesn't?" replies Sheerluck.

"Not me," says Glynis, so sour I can feel it in my crop. I'm thinking she's going to start again with the crab act, pinch, pinch, pinch, but she doesn't. Instead, she air-swims down to the grotto, sticks to the wall with two arms and folds the rest up so she's completely hidden. She misses our girl-thing and doesn't want to talk at the moment, but she also doesn't want to be completely alone, either. It's an octo thing – sometimes we want to be alone but not necessarily by ourselves.

Sheerluck joins me at the fridge and asks, "What do you think? Octo?"

"I dunno," I say, and I honestly don't. It never occurred to me to wonder, but I'm not sure if that's because I took it for granted she would. I grab a bag of kribble.

Aunt Chovie notices and gives me those big serious eyes. "You can't just live on crunchy krill, Arkae."

"I've got a craving," I tell her.

"Me, too," says Bait. He tries to reach around from behind me and I knot him.

"Message from Dove," says Dubonnet just before we start wrestling and puts it on the big screen.

There's not actually much about Fry, except that she's coming along nicely with another dec to go before she's done. Although it's not clear to any of us whether that means Fry'll be *all* done and good to go, or if Dove's just referring to the surgery. Then we get distracted with all the rest of the stuff in the message.

It's was full of clips from the Dirt, two-steppers talking about Fry like they all knew her and what it was like out here and what going out for sushi meant. Some two-steppers didn't seem to care much, but some of them were stark spinning bugfuck.

I mean, it's been a great big while since I was a biped and we live so long out here that we tend to morph along with the times. The two-stepper I was couldn't get a handle on me as I am now. But then neither could the octo I was when I finished rehab and met my first crew.

I didn't choose octo – back then, surgery wasn't as advanced and nanorectics weren't as commonplace or as programmable, so you got whatever the doctors thought gave you the best chance of a life worth living. I wasn't too happy at first, but it's hard to be unhappy in a place this beautiful, especially when you feel so good physically all the time. It was somewhere between three and four J-years after I turned that people could finally choose what kind of sushi they went out for, but I got no regrets. Any more. I've got it smooth all over.

Only I don't feel too smooth listening to two-steppers chewing the air over things they don't know anything about and puking up words like *abominations, atrocities,* and *sub-human monsters.* One news program even runs clips from the most recent re-make of *The* Goddam *Island* Of Fucking *Dr. Moreau.* Like that's holy writ or something.

I can't stand more than a few minutes before I take my kribble into my bolthole, close the hatch, and hit sound-proof.

A little while later, Glynis beeps. "You know how way back in the extreme dead past, people in the Dirt thought everything in the universe revolved around them?" She pauses, but I don't answer. "Then the scope of human knowledge expanded and we all know that was wrong."

"So?" I grunt.

"Not everybody got the memo," she says. She waits for me to say something. "Come on, Arkae – are *they* gonna get to see Okeke-Hightower?"

"I'd like to give them a ride on it," I say.

"None of them are gonna come out here with us abominations. They're all gonna cuddle up with each other in the Dirt and drown in each other's shit. Until they all do the one thing they were pooped into this universe to do, which is become extinct."

I open the door. "You're really baiting them, you know that?"

"Baiting who? There's nobody listening. Nobody here except us sushi," she says, managing to sound sour and utterly innocent both at the same time. Only Glynis.


I MESSAGE DOVE to say we'll be Down Under for at least two J-days, on loan to OuterComm. Population in the outer part of the system, especially around Saturn, has doubled in the last couple of J-years, and will probably double again in less time. The civil communication network runs below the plane of the solar disk and it's completely dedicated – no governments, no military, just small business, entertainment, and social interaction. Well, so far it's completely dedicated, but nobody's in any position for a power grab yet.

OuterComm is an Ice Giants operation, and originally it served only the Saturn, Uranus, and Neptune systems. No one seems to know exactly where the home office is – i.e. which moon. I figure even if they started off as far out as Uranus, they've probably been on Titan since they decided to expand to Jupiter.

Anyway, their technology is crazy-great. It still takes something over forty minutes for *Hello* to get from the Big J to Saturn and another forty till you hear, *Who the hell is this?* but you get less noise than a local call on JovOp. JovOp wasn't too happy when the entertainment services started migrating to OuterComm and things got kind of tense. Then they cut a deal: OuterComm got all the entertainment and stayed out of the education business, at least in the Jovian system. So everything's fine and JovOp loans them anything they need like a big old friendly neighbour, but there's still plenty of potential for trouble. Of *all* kinds.

The Jovian system is the divide between the inner planets and the outer. We've had governments that tried to align with the innies and others that courted the outies. The current government wants the Big J officially designated as an outer world, not just an ally. Saturn's been fighting it, claiming that Big J wants to take over and build an empire.

Which is pretty much what Mars and Earth said when the last government was trying to get inner status. Earth was a little more colourful about it. There were two-steppers hollering that it was all a plot by monsters and abominations – i.e. us – to get our unholy limbs on fresh meat for our unholy appetites. If Big J got inner planet status, they said, people would be rounded up in the streets and shipped out to be changed into unnatural, subhuman creatures with no will of their own. Except for the most beautiful women, who would be kept as is and chained in brothels where – well, you get the idea.

That alone would be enough to make me vote outie, except the Big J is really neither outie nor innie. The way I see it, there's inner, there's outer, and there's us. Which doesn't fit the way two-steppers do things, because it's not binary.

THIS WAS ALL sort of bubbling away at the back of my mind while we worked on the comm station, but in an idle sort of way. I was also thinking about Fry, wondering how she was doing, and what shape she'd be in the next time I saw her. I wondered if I'd recognise her.

Now, that sounds kind of silly, I guess because you don't recognise someone that, for all intents and purposes, you've never seen before. But it's that spiritual thing. I had this idea that if I swam into a room full of sushi, all kinds of sushi, and Fry was there, I would know. And if I gave it a little time, I'd find her without anyone having to point her out.

No question, I loved Fry the two-stepper. Now that she was sushi, I wondered if I'd be in love with her. I couldn't decide whether I liked that idea or not. Normally I keep things simple: sex, and only with people I like. It keeps everything pretty smooth. But in *love* complicates everything. You start thinking about partnership and family. And that's not so smooth because we don't reproduce. We've got new sushi and fresh sushi, but no sushi kids.

We're still working on surviving out here, but it won't always be that way. I could live long enough to see that. Hell, there are still a few OG around, although I've never met them. They're all out in the Ice Giants.

\*   \*   \*

WE'RE HOME HALF a dec before the first Okeke-Hightower impact, which sounds like plenty of time, but it's close enough to make me nervous. Distances out here aren't safe, even in the best top-of-the-line JovOp can. I hate being in a can anyway. If anyone ever develops a jellie for long-distance travel, I'll be their best friend forever. But even in the can, we had to hit three oases going and coming to refuel. Filing a flight plan guaranteed us a berth at each one, but only if we were on time. And there's all kinds of shit that could have made us late. If a berth was available, we'd still get it. But if there wasn't, we'd have to wait and hope we didn't run out of stuff to breathe.

Bait worked the plan out far enough ahead to give us generous ETA windows. But you know how it is – just when you need everything to work the way it's supposed to, anything that hasn't gone wrong lately suddenly decides to make up for lost time. I was nervous all the way out, all through the job, and all the way back. The last night on the way back, I dreamed that just as we were about to re-enter JovOp space, Io exploded and took out everything in half a radian. While we were trying to figure out what to do, something knocked us into a bad spiral that was gonna end dead centre in Big Pink. I woke up with Aunt Chovie and Splat peeling me off the wall – *so* embarrassing. After that, all I wanted to do was go home, slip into a jellie, and watch Okeke-Hightower meet Big J.

By this time, the comet's actually in pieces. The local networks are all-comet news, all the time, like there's nothing else in the solar system or even the universe for that matter. The experts are saying it's following the same path as the old Shoemaker-Levy, and there's a lot of chatter about what that means. There those who don't think it's a coincidence and Okeke-Hightower is actually some kind of message from an intelligence out in the Oort cloud or even beyond, and instead of letting it crash into Big J, we ought to try catching it, or at least parts of it.

Yeah, that could happen. JovOp put out a blanket no-fly – jellies only, no cans. Sheerluck suggests JovOp's got a secret mission to grab some fragments, but that's ridiculous. I mean, aside from the fact that any can capable of doing that would be plainly visible, the comet's been sailing around in pieces for over half a dozen square decs. There were easier places in the trajectory to get a piece, but all the experts agreed the scans showed nothing in it worth the fortune it would cost to mount that kind of mission. Funny how so many people forgot about that; suddenly, they're all shoulda-woulda-coulda, like non-buyer's remorse. But don't get me started on politics.

I leave a message for Dove saying we're back and getting ready to watch the show. What comes back is an auto-reply saying she's out of the office, reply soonest. Maybe she's busy with Fry, who probably has comet fever like everyone else, but maybe even more so, since this will be like the big moment that kicks off her new life. If she's not out of the hospital, I hope they've got a screen worthy of the event.

We all want to see with our naked eyes. Well, our naked eyes and telescopes. Glynis is bringing a screen for anyone who wants a really close-up look. Considering the whole thing's gonna last about an hour start to finish, maybe that's not such a bad idea. It could save us some eyestrain.

When the first fragment hits, I find myself thinking about the sensors that fell into the atmosphere. They've got to be long gone by now, and even if they're not, there's no way we could pick up any data. It would all be just noise.

Halfway through the impacts, the government overrides all the communication for a recorded, no-reply announcement: martial law's been declared, everybody go home. Anyone who doesn't is dust.

This means we miss the last few hits, which pisses us off even though we all agree it's not a sight worth dying for. But when we get home and can't even get an instant replay, we start wondering. Then we start ranting. The government's gonna have a lot of explaining to do and the next election ain't gonna be a love-fest and when did JovOp turn into a government lackey. There's nothing on the news – and I mean, *nothing*, it's all re-runs. Like this is actually two J-days ago and what just happened never happened.

"Okay," says Fred, "what's on OuterComm?"

"You want to watch soap operas?" Dubonnet fumes. "Sure, why not?"

We're looking at the menu when something new appears: it's called the Soledad y Gottmundsdottir Farewell Special. The name has me thinking we're about to see Fry in her old two-stepper incarnation, but what comes up on the screen is a chambered Nautilus.

"Hi, everybody. How do you like the new me?" Fry says.

"What, is she going to law school?" Aunt Chovie says, shocked.

"I'm sorry to leave you a canned good-bye, because you've all been so great," Fry goes on, and I have to knot my arms together to keep from turning the thing off. This doesn't sound like it's gonna end well. "I knew even before I came out here that I'd be going out for sushi. I just couldn't decide what kind. You guys had me thinking seriously about octo – it's a pretty great life, and everything you do matters. Future generations – well, it's going to be amazing out here. Life that adapted to space. Who knows, maybe someday Jovian citizens will change bodies like two-steppers change their clothes. It could happen.

"But like a lot of two-steppers, I'm impatient. I know, I'm not a two-stepper anymore, and I've got a far longer lifespan now, so I don't have to be impatient. But I am. I wanted to be part of something that's taking the next step – the next *big* step – right now. I really believe the Jupiter Colony is what I've been looking for."

"The Jupiter Colony? They're cranks! They're suicidal!" Glynis hits the ceiling, banks off a wall, and comes down again.

Fry unfurls her tentacles and lets them wave around freely. "Calm down, whoever's yelling," she says, sounding amused. "I made contact with them just before I crewed up with you. I knew what they were planning. They wouldn't tell me when, but it wasn't hard to figure out that the Okeke-Hightower impact was the perfect opportunity. We've collected some jellies, muted them and put in yak-yak loops. I don't know how the next part works, how we're going to hitch a ride with the comet – I'm not an astrophysicist. But if it works, we'll seed the clouds with ourselves.

"We're all chambered Nautiluses on this trip. It's the best form for packing a lot of data. But we've made one small change: we're linked together, shell-to-shell, so we all have access to each other's data. Not too private, but we aren't going into exile as separate hermits. There should still be some sensors bobbing around in the upper levels – the Colony's had allies tossing various things in on the sly. We can use whatever's there to build a cloud-borne colony.

"We don't know for sure it'll work. Maybe we'll all get gravitated to smithereens. But if we can fly long enough for the jellies to convert to parasails – the engineers figured that out, don't ask me – we might figure out not only how to survive, but thrive.

"Unfortunately, I won't be able to let you know. Not until we get around the interference problem. I don't know much about that, either, but if I last long enough, I'll learn.

"Dove says right now, you're all Down Under on loan to OuterComm. I'm going to send this message so it bounces around the Ice Giants for a while before it gets to you, and with any luck, you'll find it not too long after we enter the atmosphere. I hope none of you are too mad at me. Or at least that you don't stay mad at me. It's not entirely impossible that we'll meet again someday. If we do, I'd like it to be as friends.

"Especially if the Jovian independence movement gets –" she laughs. "I was about to say, 'gets off the ground.' If the Jovian independence movement ever achieves a stable orbit – or something. I think it's a really good idea. Anyway, good bye for now.

"Oh, and Arkae?" Her tentacles undulate wildly. "I had no idea wormy would feel so good."

\*　　\*　　\*

WE JUST GOT that one play before the JCC blacked it out. The feds took us all in for questioning. Not surprising. But it wasn't just Big J feds – Dirt feds suddenly popped up out of nowhere, some of them in-person and some of them long-distance via comm units clamped to mobies. The latter is a big waste unless there's some benefit to having a conversation as slowly as possible. Because even a fed on Mars can't do anything about the speed of light – it's still gonna be at least an hour between the question and the answer, usually more.

The Dirt feds who were actually here were all working undercover, keeping an eye on things, and reporting whatever they heard or saw to HQ back in the Dirt. This didn't go down so well with most of us out here, even two-steppers. It became a real governmental crisis, mainly because no one in charge could get their stories straight. Some were denying any knowledge of Dirt spies, some were trying to spin it so it was all for our benefit, so we wouldn't lose any rights – don't ask me which ones, they didn't say. Conspiracy theories blossomed faster than anyone could keep track.

Finally, the ruling council resigned; the acting council replacing them till the next election are almost all sushi. That's a first.

It's still another dec and a half till the election. JovOp usually backs two-steppers, but there are noticeably fewer political ads for bipeds this time around. I think even they can see the points on the trajectory.

A lot of sushi are already celebrating, talking about the changing face of government in the Jovian system. I'm not quite ready to party. I'm actually a little bit worried about us. We were born to be sushi, but we weren't born sushi. We all started out as two-steppers and while we may have shed binary thinking, that doesn't mean we're completely enlightened. There's already some talk about how most of the candidates are chambered Nautiluses and there ought to be more octos or puffers or crabs. I don't like the sound of that, but it's too late to make a break for the Colony now. Not that I would. Even if Fry and all her fellow colonists are surviving and thriving, I'm not ready to give up the life I have for a whole new world. We'll just have to see what happens.

Hey, I told you not to get me started on politics.

# THE DEEPS OF THE SKY

**Elizabeth Bear**

STORMCHASES' LITTLE SKIFF skipped and glided across the tropopause, skimming the denser atmosphere of the warm cloud-sea beneath, running before a fierce wind. The skiff's hull was broad and shallow, supported by buoyant pontoons, the whole designed to float atop the heavy, opaque atmosphere beneath. Stormchases had shot the sails high into the stratosphere and good winds blew the skiff onward, against the current of the dark belt beneath.

Ahead, the vast ruddy wall of a Deep Storm loomed, the base wreathed in shreds of tossing white mist: caustic water clouds churned up from deep in the deadly, layered troposphere. The Deep Storm stretched from horizon to horizon, disappearing at either end in a blur of perspective and atmospheric haze. Its breadth was so great as to make even its massive height seem insignificant, though the billowing ammonia cloud wall was smeared flat-topped by stratospheric winds where it broke the tropopause.

The storm glowed with the heat of the deep atmosphere, other skiffs silhouetted cool against it. Their chatter rang over Stormchases' talker.

Briefly, he leaned down to the pickup and greeted his colleagues. His competition. Many of them came from the same long lines of miners that he did; many carried the same long-hoarded knowledge.

But Stormchases was determined that, with the addition of his own skill and practice, he would be among the best sky-miners of them all.

Behind and above, clear skies showed a swallowing indigo, speckled with bright stars. The hurtling crescents of a dozen or so of the moons were currently visible, as was the searing pinpoint of the world's primary – so bright it washed out nearby stars. Warmth made the sky glow too, the variegated brightness of the thermosphere far above. Stormchases' thorax squeezed with emotion as he gazed upon the elegant canopies of a group of Drift-Worlds rising in slow sunlit coils along the warm vanguard of the Deep Storm, their colours bright by sunlight, their silhouettes dark by thermal sense.

He should not look; he should not hope. But there – a distance-hazed shape behind her lesser daughters and sisters, her great canopy dappled in sheeny gold and violet – soared the Mothergraves. Stormchases was too far and too low to see the teeming ecosystem she bore on her vast back, up high above the colourful clouds where the sunlight could reach and nurture them. He could just make out the colour variations caused by the dripping net-roots of veil trees that draped the Mothergraves' sides, capturing life-giving ammonia from the atmosphere and drawing it in to plump leaves and firm nutritious fruit.

Stormchases arched his face up to her, eyes shivering with longing. His wings hummed against his back. There was no desire like the pain of being separate from the Mothergraves, no need like the need to go to her. But he must resist it. He must brave the Deep Storm and harvest it, and perhaps then she would deem him worthy to be one of hers. He had the provider-status to pay court to one of the younger Drift-Worlds... but they could not give his young the safety and stability that a berth on the greatest and oldest of the Mothers would.

In the hot deeps of the sky, too high even for the Mothers and their symbiotic colony-flyers or too low even for the boldest and most intrepid of Stormchases' brethren, other things lived.

Above were other kinds of flyers and the drifters, winged or buoyant or merely infinitesimal things that could not survive even the moderate pressure and chill of the tropopause. Below, swimmers dwelled in the ammoniated thicks of the mid-troposphere that never knew the light of stars or sun. They saw only thermally. They could endure massive pressures, searing temperatures, and the lashings of molten water and even oxygen, the gas so reactive that it could set an exhalation *on fire*. That environment would crush Stormchases to a pulp, dissolve his delicate wing membranes, burn him from the gills to the bone.

Stormchases' folk were built for more moderate climes – the clear skies and thick, buoying atmosphere of the tropopause, where life flourished and the skies were full of food. But even here, in this temperate part of the sky, survival required a certain element of risk. And there were things that could only be mined where a Deep Storm pulled them up through the layers of atmosphere to an accessible height.

Which was why Stormchases sailed directly into the lowering wings of the Deep Storm, one manipulator on the skiff's controls, the other watching the perspective-shrunken sail shimmering so high above. Flyers would avoid the cable, which was monofilament spun into an intentionally refractive, high-visibility lattice with good tensile properties. But the enormous, translucent-bodied Drift-Worlds were not nimble. Chances were good that the Mother would survive a sail-impact, albeit with some scars – and some damage to the sky-island ecosystems she carried on her backs – and the skiff would likely hold together through such an incident. If he tangled a Mother in the monofilament shroud-lines spun from the same material that reinforced the Drift-World's great canopies... it didn't bear thinking of. That was why the lines were so gaily streamered: so anyone could see them from afar.

If Stormchases lost the skiff, it would just be a long flight home and probably a period of indenture to another miner until he could earn another, and begin proving himself again. But injuring a Mother, even a minor one who floated low, would be the end of his hopes to serve the Mothergraves.

So he watched the cable, and the overhead skies. And – of course – the storm.

Stormchases could smell the Deep Storm now, the dank corrosive tang of water vapour stinging his gills. The richly coloured billows of the Deep Storm proved it had something to give. The storm's dark-red wall churned, marking the boundary of a nearly-closed atmospheric cell rich with rare elements and compounds pumped up from the deeps. Soon, Stormchases would don his protective suit, seal the skiff, and begin the touchy business – so close to the storm – of hauling in the sail. The prevailing wind broke around the Deep Storm, eddying and compacting as it sped past those towering clouds. The air currents there were even more dangerous and unnavigable than those at the boundary between the world's temperate and subtropical zones, where two counter-rotating bands of wind met and sheared against each other.

And Stormchases was going to pass through it.

Once the sail was stowed, Stormchases would manoeuvre the skiff closer under engine power – as close as those cool silhouettes ahead – and begin harvesting. But he would not be cowed by the storm wall. *Could* not be, if he hoped to win a berth on the Mothergraves.

He would brave the outer walls of the storm itself. He had the skill; he had the ancestral knowledge. The reward for his courage would be phosphates, silicates, organic compounds. Iron. Solid things, from which technologies like his skiff were built. Noble gases. And fallers, the tiny creatures that spent their small lives churned in the turbulence of the Deep Storm, and which were loaded with valuable nutrition and trace elements hard to obtain, for the unfledged juveniles who lived amid the roots and foliage and trapped organics of the Drift-World ecosystems.

The Deep Storm was a rich, if deadly, resource. With its treasures, he would purchase his place on the Mothergraves.

Stormchases streamed current weather data, forecasts and predictions. He tuned into the pulsed-light broadcasts of the skiffs already engaged in harvesting, and set about making himself ready.

The good news about Deep Storms was that they were extraordinarily stable, and the new information didn't tell Stormchases much that he could not have anticipated. Still, there was always a thrill of unease as one made ready for a filtering run. A little too far, and – well, everyone knew or knew of somebody who had been careless at the margin of a storm and sucked into the depths of its embrace. A skiff couldn't survive that, and a person *definitely* couldn't. If the molten water didn't cauterize flesh from carapace, convective torrents would soon drag one down into the red depths of the atmosphere, to be melted and crushed and torn.

It was impossible to be too careful, sky-mining.

Stormchases checked the skiff's edge seals preliminary to locking down. Water could insinuate through a tiny gap and spray under the pressure of winds, costing an unwary or unlucky operator an eye. Too many sky-miners bore the scars of its caustic burns on their carapaces and manipulators.

A careful assessment showed the seals to be intact. Behind the skiff, the long cluster of cargo capsules bumped and swung. Empty, they were buoyant, and tended to drag the skiff upwards, forcing Stormchases to constant adjustments of the trim. He dropped a sky-anchor and owner-beacon to hold the majority of the cargo capsules, loaded one into the skiff's dock with the magnetic claw, and turned the little vessel toward the storm.

Siphons contracted, feeling each heave of the atmosphere, Stormchases slid quickly but cautiously into the turbulent band surrounding the storm. It would be safer to match the wind's velocity before he made the transition to within-the-storm itself, but his little skiff did not have that much power. Instead, it was built to catch the wind and self-orient, using the storm itself for stability rather than being tumbled and tossed like a thrown flyer's egg.

Stormchases fixed his restraint harness to the tightest setting. He brought the skiff alongside the cloud wall, then deflated and retracted the pontoons, leaving the skiff less buoyant but far more streamlined. Holding hope in his mind – hope, because the Mothergraves taught that intention affected outcome – Stormchases took a deep breath, smelled the tang of methane on his exhalation, and slipped the skiff into the storm.

The wind hit the skiff in a torrent. Through long experience, Stormchases' manipulators stayed soft on the controls. He let them vibrate against his skin, but held them steady – gently, gently, without too much pressure but without yielding to the wrath of the storm. The skiff tumbled for a moment as it made the transition; he regained trim and steadied it, bringing its pointed nose around to part the wind that pushed it. It shivered – feeling alive as the sun-warmed hide of the Mother upon whose broad back Stormchases had grown – and steadied. Stormchases guided it with heat-sight only. Here in the massive swirl of the cloud wall, the viewports showed him only the skiff's interior lighting reflecting off the featureless red clouds of the storm, as if he and his rugged little ship were swaddled in an uncle's wings.

A peaceful image, for a thing that would kill him in instants. If he went too far in, the winds would rip his tiny craft apart around him. If he got too close to the wall, turbulence could send him spinning out of control.

When the skiff finally floated serenely amidst the unending gyre, Stormchases opened the siphons. He felt the skiff belly and wallow as the wind filled it, then the increased stability as the filters activated and the capsule filled.

It didn't take long; the storm was pumping a rich mix of resources. When the capsule reached its pressurized capacity, Stormchases sealed the siphons again. Still holding his position against the fury of the winds, he tested the responses of the laden skiff. It was heavier, sluggish – but as responsive as he could have hoped.

He brought her out of the fog of red and grey, under a clear black sky. A bit of turbulence caught his wingtip as he slipped away, and it sent the skiff spinning flat like a spat seed across the tropopause. Other skiffs scattered like a swarm of infant cloud-skaters before a flyer's dive. Shaken, the harness bruising the soft flesh at his joints, Stormchases got control of the skiff and brought her around on a soft loop. His talker exploded with the whoops of other miners; mingled appreciation and teasing.

There was his beacon. He deployed pontoons to save energy and skimmed the atmosphere over to exchange capsules.

Then he turned to the storm, and went back to do it again.

STORMCHASES HAD SECURED his full capsules and was still re-checking the skiff's edge-seals, preliminary to popping the craft open, when he caught sight of a tiny speck of a shadow descending along the margin of the storm. Something sharp-nosed and hot enough to be uncomfortable to look upon...

Stormchases scrambled for the telescope as the speck dropped toward the Deep Storm. It locked and tracked; he pressed two eyes to the viewers and found himself regarding a sleek black... something, a glossy surface he could not name. Nor could he make out any detail of shape. The auto-focus had locked too close, and as he backed it off the object slipped into the edge of the Deep Storm.

Bigger than a flyer – bigger even than folk and nothing with any sense would get that close to the smeary pall of water vapour without protective gear. It *looked* a little like a flyer, though – a curved, streamlined wing shape with a dartlike nose. But the wings didn't flap as it descended, banking wide on the cushion of air before the storm, curving between the scudding masses of the herd of Drift-Worlds.

It was like nothing Stormchases had ever seen.

Its belly was bright-hot, hot enough to spark open flame if it brushed oxygen, but as it banked Stormchases saw that the back was *cold*, black-cold against the warmth of the high sky, so dark and chill it seemed a band of brightness delineated it – but that was only the contrast with the soaking heat from the thermosphere. Stormchases had always had an interest in xenophysics. He felt his wings furl with shock as he realised that the object might show that heat-pattern if it had warmed its belly with friction as it entered the atmosphere, but the upper part were still breath-stealing cold with the chill of the deep sky.

Was it a ship, and not an animal? A... skiff of some kind?

An alien?

Lightning danced around the object, caught and caressed it like a Mother's feeding tendrils caging a Mate – and then seemed to get caught there, netting and streaking the black hide with rills of savage, glowing vermillion and radiant gold. The wind of the object's passage blew the shimmers off the trailing edge of its wings; shining vapour writhed in curls in the turbulence of its wake.

Stormchases caught his breath. Neon and helium rain, condensing upon the object's hard skin, energized by the lightning, luminesced as the object skimmed the high windswept edge of the clouds.

With the eyes not pressed to the telescope, he watched a luminescent red-gold line draw across the dull-red roiling stormwall. Below, at the tropopause border of the storm, the other filter-miners were pulling back, grouping together and gliding away. They had noticed the phenomenon, and the smart sky-miner didn't approach a storm that was doing something he didn't understand.

Lightning was a constant wreath in the storm's upper regions, and whatever the object or creature was made of, the storm seemed to want to reach out and caress it. Meanwhile, the object played with the wall of the storm, threading it like a needle, as oblivious to those deadly veils of water vapour as it was to the savagery of the lightning strikes. Stormchases had operated a mining skiff – valued work, prestigious work, work he hoped would earn him a place in the Mothergraves' esteem – for his entire fledged life.

He'd seen skiffs go down, seen daring rescues, seen miners saved from impossible situations and miners who were not. He'd seen recklessness, and skill so great its exercise *looked* like recklessness.

He'd never seen anyone play with a Deep Storm like this.

It couldn't last.


IT COULD HAVE been a cross-wind, an eddy, the sheer of turbulence. Stormchases would never know. But one moment the black object, streaming its meteor-tail of noble gases, was stitching the flank of the storm – and the next it was tumbling, knocked end over end like the losing flyer of a mating dogfight. Stormchases pulled back from the telescope, watching as the object rolled in a flat, descending spiral like a coiled tree-frond, pulled long.

The object was built like a flyer. It had no pontoons, no broad hull meant to maximize its buoyancy against the pressure gradient of the tropopause. It would fall through, and keep falling –

Stormchases clenched the gunwale of his skiff in tense manipulators, glad when the alien object fell well inside the boundary of the storm-fronting thermal the Drift-Worlds rode. It seemed so wrong: the Mothers floating lazily with their multicoloured sides placid in the sun; the object plunging to destruction amid the hells of the deep sky, trailing streamers of neon light.

It was folly to project his own experiences upon something that was not folk, of course – but he couldn't help it. If the object was a skiff, if the aliens were like folk, he knew they would be at their controls even now. Stormchases felt a great, searing pity.

They were something new, and he didn't want them to die.

Did they need to?

They had a long way to fall, and they were fighting it. The telescope – still locked on the alien object – glided smoothly in its mount. It would be easy to compute the falling ship's trajectory. Other skiffs were doing so in order to clear the crash path. Stormchases –

Stormchases pulled up the navigation console, downloaded other skiffs' telemetry on and calculations of the trajectory of the falling craft, ran his own. The object was slowing, but it was not slowing enough – and he was close enough to the crash path to intercept.

He thought of the Mothergraves. He thought of his rich cargo, the price of acceptance.

He clenched his gills and fired his engines to cross the path of the crash.

Its flat spiral path aided him. He did not need to intercept on this pass, though there would not be too many more opportunities. It was a fortunate thing that the object had a long way to fall. All he had to do was get under it, in front of it, and let the computer and the telescope and the cannon do the rest.

*There. Now.* Even as he thought it, the skiff's machines made their own decision. The sail-cannon boomed; the first sail itself was a bright streamer climbing the stratosphere. Stormchases checked his restrains with his manipulators and one eye, aware that he'd left it too late. The other three eyes stayed on the alien object, and the ballistic arc of the rising sail.

It snapped to the end of its line – low, too low, so much lower than such things *should* be deployed. It seemed enormous as it spread. It *was* enormous, but Stormchases was not used to seeing a sail so close.

He braced himself, one manipulator hovering over the control to depressurize the cargo capsules strung behind him in a long, jostling tail.

The object fell into the sail. Stormchases had a long moment to watch the bright sail – dappled in vermilion and violet – stretch into a trailing comet-tail as it caught and wrapped the projectile. He watched the streamers of the shroud lines buck at impact; the wave travelling their length.

The stretch and yank snapped Stormchases back against his restraints. He felt the shiver through the frame of the skiff as the shroud-motors released, letting the falling object haul line as if it were a flyer running away with the bait. The object's spiralling descent became an elongating pendulum arc, and Stormchases hoped it or they had the sense not to struggle. The shroudlines and the sail stretched, twanged –

– Held. The Mothergraves wove the sails from her own silk; they were the same stuff as her canopies. There was no stronger fibre.

Then the object swung down into the tropopause and splashed through the sea of ammonia clouds, and kept falling.

The sealed skiff jerked after. Stormchases felt the heavy crack through the hull as the pontoons broke. He lost light-sight of the sky above as the clouds closed over. He felt as if he floated against his restraints, though he knew it was just the acceleration of the fall defying gravity.

He struggled to bring his manipulator down. The deeper the object pulled him, the hotter and more pressurized – and more toxic – the atmosphere became. And he wouldn't trust the skiff's seals after the jar of that impact.

He depressurized and helium-flushed the first cargo capsule.

When it blew, the skiff shuddered again. That capsule was now a balloon filled with gaseous helium, and it snapped upward, slowing Stormchases' descent – and the descent of the sail-wrapped alien object. They were still plunging, but now dragging a buoyant makeshift pontoon.

The cables connecting the capsule twanged and plinked ominously. It had been the flaw in his plan; he hadn't been sure they *would* hold.

For now, at least, they did.

The pressure outside the hull was growing; not dangerous yet, but creeping upward. Eyes on the display, Stormchases triggered a second capsule. He felt a lighter shudder this time, as the skiff shed a little more velocity. The *next* question would be if he had enough capsules to stop the fall – and to lift his skiff, and the netted object, back to the tropopause.

His talker babbled at him, his colleagues issuing calls and organising a party for a rescue to follow his descent. "No rescue," he said. "This is my risk."

Another capsule. Another, slighter shiver through the lines. Another incremental slowing.

*By the Mothergraves*, he thought. *This is actually going to work.*

\*   \*   \*

WHEN HIS SKIFF bobbed back to the tropopause, dangling helplessly beneath a dozen empty, depressurized capsules, Stormchases was unprepared for the cheer that rang over his talker. Or the bigger one that followed, when he winched the sail containing the netted object up through the cloud-sea, into clear air.

STORMCHASES HAD NO pontoons; his main sail was fouled. The empty capsules would support him, but he could not manoeuvre – and, in fact, his skiff swung beneath them hull-to-the-side, needle-tipped nose pointing down. Stormchases dangled, bruised and aching, in his restraints, trying to figure out how to loose the straps and start work on freeing himself.

He still wasn't sure how he'd survived. Or *that* he'd survived. Maybe this was the last fantasy of a dying mind –

The talker bleated at him.

He jerked against the harness, and moaned. The talker bleated again.

It wasn't words, and whatever it *was*, it drowned out the voices of the other miners, who were currently arguing over whether his skiff was salvage, and whether they should come to his assistance if it was. He'd been trying to organise his addled thoughts enough to warn them off. Now he vibrated his membranes and managed a croak that sounded fragile even to his own hearing. "Who is it? What do you want?"

That bleat again, or a modestly different one.

"Are you the alien? I can't understand you."

With pained manipulators, Stormchases managed to unfasten his restraints. He dropped from them harder than he had intended; it seemed he couldn't hold onto the rack. As his carapace struck the forward bulkhead, he made a disgruntled noise.

"Speak Language!" he snarled to the talker as he picked himself up. "I can't understand you."

It was mostly an expression of frustration. If they knew Language, they wouldn't be aliens. But he could not hide his sigh of relief when a deep, coveted voice emerged from the talker instead.

"Be strong, Stormchases," the Mothergraves said. "All will soon be well."

He pressed two eyes to the viewport. The clouds around his skiff were bright in the sunlight; he watched the encroaching shadow fall across them like the umbra of an eclipse.

It was the great, welcome shade of the Mothergraves as she drifted out of the sky.

She was coming for them. Coming for *him*.

IT WAS NO small thing, for a Drift-World to drop so much altitude. For a Drift-World the size of the Mothergraves, it was a major undertaking, and not one speedily accomplished. Still, she dropped, flanked by her attendant squadrons of flyers and younger Mothers, tiny shapes flitting between her backs. Any of them could have come for Stormchases more easily, but when they would have moved forward, the Mothergraves gestured them back with her trailing, elegant gestures.

Stormchases occupied the time winching in the sail-net containing the alien object. It was heavy, not buoyant at all. He imagined it must skim through the atmosphere like a dart or a flyer – simply by moving so fast that the aerodynamics of its passage bore it up. He would have liked to disentangle the object from the shroud, but if he did, it would sink like a punctured skiff.

Instead, he amused himself by assessing the damage to his skiff (catastrophic) and answering the alien's bleats on the talker somewhat at random, though he had not given up on trying to understand what it might be saying. Obviously, it had technology – quite possibly it *was* technology, and the hard carapace might indeed be the equivalent of his own skiff – a craft, meant for entering a hostile environment.

Had it been sampling the storm for useful chemicals and consumables, as well?

He wondered what aliens ate. What they breathed. He wondered if he could teach them Language.

Every time he looked up, the Mothergraves' great keel was lower. Finally, her tendrils encompassed his horizons and when he craned his eyes back, he could make out the double row of Mates fused to and dependent from her bellies like so many additional, vestigial tendrils. There were dozens. The oldest had lost all trace of their origins, and were merely smooth nubs sealed to the Mothergraves' flesh. The newest were still identifiable as the individuals they had been.

Many of the lesser Mothers among her escort dangled Mates from their bellies as well, but none had half so many as the Mothergraves... and none were so much as two-thirds of her size.

In frustration, Stormchases squinched himself against the interior of his carapace. So close. He had been *so close*. And now all he had to show for it was a wrecked skiff and a bleating alien. Now he would have to start over –

He *could* ask the Mothergraves to release his groom-price to a lesser Mother. He had provided well enough for any of her sisters or daughters to consider him.

But none of them were *she*.

He only hoped his sacrifice of resources in order to rescue the alien had not angered her. That would be too much to bear – although if she decided to reclaim the loss from his corpse, he supposed at the very least he would die fulfilled... if briefly.

The talker squawked again. The alien sounds seemed more familiar; he must be getting used to them.

A few of the Mothergraves' tendrils touched him, as he had so long anticipated. It was bitterest irony now, but the pleasure of the caress almost made it worthwhile. He braced himself for pain and paralysis... but she withheld her sting, and the only pain were the bruises left by his restraints and by impact with the bulkheads of the tumbling skiff.

Now her voice came to him directly, rather than by way of the talker. It filled the air around him and vibrated in the hollows of his body like soft thunder. To his shock and disbelief, she said words of ritual to him; words he had hoped and then despaired to hear.

She said, "For the wealth of the whole, what have you brought us, Stormchases?"

Before he could answer, the talker bleated again. This time, in something like Language – bent, barely comprehensible, accented more oddly than any Language Stormchases had ever heard.

It said, "Hello? You us comprehend?"

"I hear you," the Mothergraves said. "What do you want?"

A long silence before the answer came. "This we fix. Trade science. Go. Place you give us for repairs?"

THE ALIENS – THE object *was* a skiff, of sorts, and it had as many crew members as Stormchases had eyes – had a machine that translated their bleaty words into Language, given a wise enough sample of it. As the revolutions went by, the machine became more and more proficient, and Stormchases spent more and more time talking to *A'lees*, their crew member in charge of talking. Their names were just nonsense sounds, not words, which made him wonder how any of them ever knew who he was. And they divided labour up in strange ways, with roles determined not by instar and inheritance but by individual life-courses. They told him a great deal about themselves and their peculiar biology; he reciprocated with the more mundane details of his own. A'lees seemed particularly interested that he would soon Mate, and wished to know as much about the process as he could tell.

The aliens sealed themselves in small flexible habitats – pressure carapaces – to leave their skiff, and for good reason. They were made mostly of water, and they oozed water from their bodies, and the pressure and temperature of the world's atmosphere would destroy them as surely as the deeps of the sky would crush Stormchases. The atmosphere *they* breathed was made of inert gases and explosive oxygen, and once their skiff was beached on an open patch of the Mothergraves' back for repairs, just the leakage of oxygen and water vapour from its airlocks soon poisoned a swath of vegetation for a bodylength in any direction.

Stormchases stayed well back from the alien skiff while he had these conversations.

Talking to the aliens was a joy and a burden. The Mothergraves insisted he should be the one to serve as an intermediary. He had experience with them, and the aliens valued that kind of experience – and when he was Mated, that experience would be assimilated into the Mothergraves' collective mind. It would become a part of her, and a part of all their progeny to follow.

The Mothergraves had told him – in the ritual words – that knowledge and discovery were great offerings, unique offerings. That the opportunity to interact with beings from another world was of greater import to her and her brood than organics, or metals, or substances that she could machine within her great body into the stuff of skiffs and sails and other technology. That she accepted his suit, and honoured the courage with which he had pressed it.

And *that* was why the duty was a burden. Because to be available for the aliens while they made the repairs – to play *liaison* (their word) – meant putting off the moment of joyous union again. And again. To have been so close, and then so far, and then so close again –

The agony of anticipation, and the fear that it would be snatched from him again, was a form of torture.

A'lees came outside of the alien skiff in her pressure carapace and sat in its water-poisoned circle with her forelimbs wrapped around her drawn-up knees, talking comfortably to Stormchases. She said she was a female, a Mother. But that Mothers of her kind were not so physically different from the males, and that even after they Mated, males continued to go about in the world as independent entities.

"But how do they pass their experiences on to their offspring?" Stormchases asked.

A'lees paused for a long time.

"We teach them," she said. "Your children inherit your memories?"

"Not memories," he said. "Experiences."

She hesitated again. "So you become a part of the Mother. A kind of... symbiote. And your offspring with her will have all of her experiences, and yours? But... not the memories? How does that work?"

"Is knowledge a memory?" he asked.

"No," she said confidently. "Memories can be destroyed while skills remain... Oh. I think... I understand."

They talked for a little while of the structure of the nets and the Mothers' canopies, but Stormchases could tell A'lees was not finished thinking about memories. Finally she made a little deflating hiss sound and brought the subject up again.

"I am sad," A'lees said, "that when we have fixed our sampler and had time to arrange a new mission and come back, you will not be here to talk with us."

"I will be here," said Stormchases, puzzled. "I will be mated to the Mothergraves."

"But it won't be" – whatever A'lees had been about to say, the translator stammered on it; she continued – "the same. You won't remember us."

"The Mothergraves will," Stormchases assured her.

She drew herself in a little smaller. "It will be a long time before we return."

Stormchases patted toward the edge of the burn zone. He did not let his manipulators cross it, though. Though he would soon enough lose the use of his manipulators to atrophy, he didn't feel the need to burn them off prematurely. "It's all right, A'lees," he said. "We will remember you by the scar."

Whatever the sound she made next meant, the translator could not manage it.

# DRIVE

**James S. A. Corey**

ACCELERATION THROWS SOLOMON back into the captain's chair, then presses his chest like a weight. His right hand lands on his belly, his left falls onto the upholstery beside his ear. His ankles press back against the leg rests. The shock is a blow, an assault. His brain is the product of millions of years of primate evolution, and it isn't prepared for this. It decides that he's being attacked, and then that he's falling, and then that he's had some kind of terrible dream. The yacht isn't the product of evolution. Its alarms trigger in a strictly informational way. By the way, we're accelerating at four gravities. Five. Six. Seven. More than seven. In the exterior camera feed, Phobos darts past, and then there is only the star field, as seemingly unchanging as a still image.

It takes almost a full minute to understand what's happened, then he tries to grin. His labouring heart labours a little harder with elation.

The interior of the yacht is cream and orange. The control panel is a simple touchscreen model, old enough that the surface has started going grey at the corners. It's not pretty, but it is functional. Solid. An alert pops up that the water recycler has gone off-line. Solomon's not surprised – he's outside the design specs – and he starts guessing where exactly the system failed. His guess, given that all the thrust is along the primary axis of the ship, is the reservoir back-flow valve, but he's looking forward to checking it when the run is finished. He tries to move his hand, but the weight of it astounds him. A human hand weighs something like three hundred grams. At seven g, that's still only a little over two thousand. He should still be able to move it. He pushes his arm toward the control panel, muscles trembling. He wonders how much above seven he's going. Since the sensors are pegged, he'll have to figure it out when the run is over. How long the burn lasted and whatever his final velocity winds up being. Simple math. Kids could do it. He's not worried. He reaches again for the control panel, really pushing hard this time, and something wet and painful happens in his elbow.

Oops, he thinks. He wants to grit his teeth, but that's no more effective than grinning had been. This is going to be embarrassing. If he can't shut off the drive, he'll have to wait until the fuel runs out and then call for help. That might be problematic. Depending on how fast he's accelerating, the rescue ship's burn will have to be a very long one compared with his own. Maybe twice as long. They may need some sort of long-range craft to come get him. The fuel supply readout is a small number on the lower left side of the panel, green against black. It's hard to focus on it. Acceleration is pressing his eyeballs out of their right shape. High tech astigmatism. He squints. The yacht is built for long burns, and he started with the ejection tanks at ninety per cent.

The readout now shows the burn at ten minutes. The fuel supply ticks down to eighty-nine point six. That can't be right.

Two minutes later, it drops to point five. Two and a half minutes later, point four. That puts the burn at over thirty-seven hours and the final velocity at something just under five per cent of c.

Solomon starts getting nervous.


HE MET HER ten years before. The research centre at Dhanbad Nova was one of the largest on Mars. Three generations after the first colonists dug into the rock and soil of humanity's second home, progress had pushed the envelope of human science, understanding, and culture so far that the underground city could support five bars, even if one of them was the alcohol-free honky-tonk where the Jainists and born-again Christians hung out. The other four sold alcohol and food that was exactly the same as the stuff they sold at the commissary, only with piped-in music and a wall monitor with an entertainment feed from Earth playing on it all hours of the day and night. Solomon and his cadre met up at this one two or three times a week when the work load at the centre wasn't too heavy.

Usually the group was some assortment of the same dozen people. Today it was Tori and Raj from the water reclamation project. Voltaire whose real name was Edith. Julio and Carl and Malik who all worked together on anti-cancer therapies. And Solomon. Mars, they said, was the biggest small town in the solar system. There was almost never anyone new.

There was someone new. She sat beside Malik, had dark hair and a patient expression. Her face was a little too sharp to be classically beautiful, and the hair on her forearms was dark. She had the kind of genetics that developed a little moustache problem when she hit about thirty-five. Solomon didn't believe in love at first sight, but as soon as she sat down at the table, he was profoundly aware that he hadn't brushed his hair very effectively that morning and he was wearing the shirt with the sleeves that were a little too long.

"Mars *is* America," Tori said, waving his beer expansively. "It's exactly the same."

"It's not America," Malik said.

"Not like it was at the end. Like the beginning. Look at how long it took to travel from Europe to North America in the 1500s. Two months. How long to get here from Earth? Four. Longer if the orbits are right."

"Which is the first way in which it's not like America," Malik said, dryly.

"It's within an order of magnitude," Tori said. "My point it that, politically speaking, distance is measured in time. We're months away from Earth. They're still thinking about us like we're some kind of lost colony. Like we answer to them. How many people here, just at this table, have had directives from someone who's never been outside a gravity well but still felt like they could tell us where our research should go?"

Tori raised his own hand, and Raj followed suit. Voltaire. Carl. Reluctantly, Malik. Tori's grin was smug.

"Who's doing the real science in the system?" Tori said. "That's us. Our ships are newer and better. Our environmental science is at least a decade ahead of anything they've got on Earth. Last year, we hit self-sustaining."

"I don't believe that," Voltaire said. The new one still hadn't spoken, but Solomon watched her attention shift to each new speaker. He watched her listen.

"Even if there are a few things we still need from Earth, we can trade for them. Shit, give us a few years and we'll be mining them out of the Belt," Tori said, backing away from his last point and making a new, equally unlikely assertion at the same time. "It's not like I'm saying we should cut off all diplomatic relations."

"No," Malik said. "You're saying we should declare political independence."

"Damn skippy, I am," Tori said. "Because distance is measured in time."

"And coherence is measured in beer," Voltaire said, the cadence of her voice matching Tori's perfectly. The new woman smiled at the mimicry.

"Even if we decided that all we had to lose was our chains," Malik said, "why would we bother? We are already *de facto* our own government. Pointing out the fact is only going to stir up trouble."

"Do you really think Earth hasn't noticed?" Tori said. "You think the kids back at the labs on Luna and Sao Paulo aren't looking up at the sky and saying *That little red dot is kicking our asses*? They're jealous and they're scared and they should be. It's all I'm saying. If we do our own thing, the earliest they could do something about it still gives us months of lead time. England lost its colonies because you can't maintain control with a sixty-day latency, much less a hundred and twenty."

"Well," said Voltaire drily, "that and the French."

"And good damn thing too," Tori said as if she hadn't spoken. "Because who was it that came in when the Nazis started knocking on England's door? Am I right?"

"Um," Solomon said, "no, actually. You just made the other point. We're really the Germans."

And because he spoke, the new woman's gaze turned to him. He felt his throat go tight and sipped his beer to try to loosen up. If he spoke now, his voice would crack like he was fourteen again. Voltaire put her elbows on the table, cradled her chin in her dark hands, and hoisted her eyebrows. Her expression could have had *This should be good* as the caption.

"Okay," Malik said, abandoning his disagreement with Tori. "I'll bite. In what ways are we like a murderous bunch of fascists?"

"By-by how we'd fight," Solomon said. "Germany had all the best science, just like us. They had the best tech. They had rockets. No one had rockets, but they did. Nazi tanks could destroy allied tanks at something like five to one. They had the best attack submarines, drone missiles, early jet aircraft. They were just that much better. Better designed, better manufactured. They prized science and scientists, so they were elegant and they were smart."

"Apart from the whole racial cleansing genocide thing," Julio said.

"Apart from that," Solomon agreed. "But they lost. They had all the best tech, just like we do. And they lost."

"Because they were psychopathic and insane," Julio said.

"No," Solomon shook his head. "I mean, they were, but there have been a lot of fascist psychopaths that *didn't* lose wars. They lost because even though one of their tanks was worth five of the other guy's, America could build ten. Their industrial base was huge, and if the design wasn't as good, who cared? Earth has that industrial base. They have people. It could take them months, maybe years, to get here, but when they did, it would be in numbers we couldn't handle. Being technically advanced is great, but we're still just building better ones of the stuff that came before. If you want to overcome the kind of demographic advantage Earth has, you'll need something paradigm-shiftingly new."

Voltaire raised her hand. "I nominate *paradigm-shiftingly* as the adverb of the night."

"Seconded," Julio said. Solomon felt the blush creeping up his neck.

"All in favour?" There was a small chorus. "The ayes have it," Voltaire said. "Someone buy this man another drink."

The conversation moved on, the way it always did. Politics and history gave way to art and fine-structure engineering. The great debate of the night was over whether artificial muscles worked better with the nanotubules in sheets or bundles, with both sides descending in the end to name-calling. Most of it was good-natured, and what wasn't pretended to be, which was almost the same. The wall monitor switched over to an all-music feed out of a little community on Syria Planum, the wailing and brass of rai juxtaposed with classical European strings. It was some of Solomon's favourite music because it was dense and intellectually complicated and he wasn't expected to dance to it. He wound up spending half the night sitting beside Carl talking about ejection efficiency systems and trying not to stare at the new woman. When she moved from Malik's side to sit next to Voltaire, his heart leaped – maybe she wasn't here with Malik – and then sank – maybe she was a lesbian. He felt like he'd dropped a decade off his life and was suddenly stuck in the hormonal torture chamber of the lower university. He made up his mind to forget that the new woman existed. If she was new to the research centre, there would be time to find out who she was and plan a way to speak with her that didn't make him look desperate and lonely. And if she wasn't, then she wouldn't be here. And even so, he kept looking for her, just to keep track.

Raj was the first one to leave, the same as always. He was on development, which meant he had the same burden of technical work plus steering committee meetings. If, someday, the terraforming project actually took hold, it would have Raj's intellectual DNA. Julio and Carl left next, arm in arm with Carl resting his head on Julio's shoulder the way he did when they were both a little drunk and amorous. With only Malik, Voltaire, and Tori left, avoiding the new woman was harder. Solomon got up to leave once, but then stopped at the head and wandered back in without entirely meaning to. As soon as the new woman left, he told himself. When she was gone, he could go. But if he saw who she left with, then he'd know who to ask about her. Or, if she left with Voltaire, not to ask. It was just data collection. That was all. When the monitor changed to the early morning newsfeed, he had to admit he was bullshitting. He waved his goodnights for real this time, pushed his hands into his pockets, and headed out to the main corridor.

Between the engineering problems in building robust surface domes and Mars' absolute lack of a functioning magnetosphere, all the habitats were deep underground. The main corridor's hallways had ceilings four metres high and LEDs that changed their warmth and intensity with the time of day, but Solomon still had the occasional atavistic longing for sky. For a sense of openness and possibility, and maybe for not living his whole life buried.

Her voice came from behind him. "So, hey."

She walked with a comfortable rolling gait. Her smile looked warm and maybe a little tentative. Outside the dimness of the bar, he could see the lighter streaks in her hair.

"Ah. Hey."

"We never really got around to meeting in there," she said, holding out her hand. "Caitlin Esquibel."

Solomon took her hand, shaking it once like they were at the centre. "Solomon Epstein."

"Solomon Epstein?" she said, walking forward. Somehow they were walking side by side now. Together. "So what's a nice Jewish boy like you doing on a planet like this?"

If he hadn't still been a little drunk, he'd just have laughed it off.

"Trying to get the courage to meet you, mostly," he said.

"Sort of noticed that."

"Hope it was adorable."

"It was better than your friend Malik always finding reasons to touch my arm. Anyway. I'm working resource management for Kwikowski Mutual Interest Group. Just came in from Luna a month ago. That thing you were saying about Mars and Earth and America. That was interesting."

"Thank you," Solomon said. "I'm an engine engineer for Masstech."

"Engine engineer," she said. "Seems like it ought to be redundant."

"I always thought thrust specialist sounded dirty," he said. "How long are you staying on Mars?"

"Until I leave. Open contract. You?"

"Oh, I was born here," he said. "I expect I'll die here too."

She glanced up his long, thin frame once, her smile mocking. Of course she'd known he was born there. No way to hide it. His words felt like a weak brag now.

"A company man," she said, letting it be a joke between them.

"A Martian."

The cart kiosk had half a dozen of the cramped electric devices ready to rent. Solomon pulled out his card and waved it in a figure eight until the reader got good signal and the first cart in line clicked from amber to green. He pulled it out before he realised he really didn't want to get in.

"Do you —" Solomon began, then cleared his throat and tried again. "Would you like to come home with me?"

He could see the *Sure, why not* forming in her brain stem. He could follow it along the short arcing path to her lips. It was close enough to pull at his blood like a moon. And he watched it turn aside at the last moment. When she shook her head, it wasn't a refusal so much as her trying to clear her mind. But she smiled. She did smile.

"Moving a little fast there, Sol."

SPEED ISN'T THE problem. Unless he runs into something, velocity is just velocity; he could be weightless going almost the speed of light. It's the delta vee that's hurting him. The acceleration. The change. Every second, he's going sixty-eight metres per second faster than he was the second before. Or more. Maybe more.

Only the acceleration isn't the problem either. Ships have had the power to burn at fifteen or even twenty g since the early chemical rockets. The power is always there. It's the efficiency necessary to maintain a burn that was missing. Thrust to weight when most of your weight is propellant to give you thrust. And bodies can accelerate at over a hundred g for a fraction of a second without dying. It's the sustain that's killing him. It's going for hours.

There are emergency shut-offs. If the reactor starts to overheat or the magnetic bottle gets unstable, the drive will shut down. There are all kinds of shut-offs for all kinds of emergencies, but nothing's going wrong. Everything's running perfectly. That's the problem. That's what's killing him.

There is also a manual cut-off on the control panel. The icon is a big red button. A panic button. If he could touch it, he'd be fine. But he can't. All the joy is gone now. Instead of elation, there's only panic and the growing, grinding pain. If he can just reach the controls. Or if something, anything, could just go *wrong*.

Nothing is going wrong. He is struggling to breathe, gasping the way the safety instructors taught him to. He tenses his legs and arms, trying to force the blood through his arteries and veins. If he passes out, he won't come back, and there is darkness growing at the edges of his vision. If he can't find a way out, he will die here. In this chair with his hands pinned against him and his hair pulling back his scalp. His hand terminal in his pocket feels like someone driving a dull knife into his hip. He tries to remember how much mass a hand terminal has. He can't. He fights to breathe.

His hand terminal. If he can reach it, if he can pull it out, maybe he can signal to Caitlin. Maybe she can make a remote connection and shut the engines down. The hand lying across his belly presses hard into his viscera, but it's only centimetres from his pocket. He pushed until his bones creak, and his wrists shifts. The friction of skin against safety harness tears a little hole in his wrist and the blood that comes out races back toward the seat like it was afraid of something, but he does move.

He pushes again. A little closer. The blood is a lubricant. The friction is less. His hand moves farther. It takes minutes. His fingernails touch the hardened plastic. He can do this.

Power and efficiency, he thinks, and a moment's pleasure passes through him despite everything. He's done it. The magic pair.

The tendons in his fingers ache, but he pulls the cloth of his pocket aside. He can feel the hand terminal begin to slip free of his pocket, but he can't lift his head to see it.

\*   \*   \*

THREE YEARS AFTER he met her, Caitlin showed up at the door to his hole at three in the morning, crying, frightened, and sober. It wasn't the sort of thing Solomon expected from her, and he'd spent a fair amount of time in her company. They'd become lovers almost seven months after they'd met. He called it that. Becoming lovers wasn't the kind of thing Caitlin said. With her, it was always something crude and a little raunchy. That was who she was. He thought it was a kind of emotional protection that she was never exactly sincere. It was a way to control fear and deny anxieties. And really as long as she still wanted to come share his bed some nights, he was fine with that. And if she hadn't wanted to anymore, he'd have been disappointed, but he still would have been fine with it. He liked the way she smirked at the world. The confidence she carried herself with, especially when she was faking it. He liked, all in all, who she was. That made everything easier.

Twice, her contract had ticked past its automatic renewal dates without her exercising the option to leave. When he'd taken a position with the functional magnetics workgroup, one of the issues he'd considered was whether the extra time he took with it would alienate her. Neither of them had made any sexual or romantic connections with other people at the centre. Everyone treated them as if they were each other's tacit property, and so even though they'd never made any explicit promises, Solomon would have called them *de facto* monogamists. Certainly he would have felt hurt and betrayed if she'd been sleeping with someone else, and assumed she'd feel the same about him.

But sex and companionship, as pleasant as they were, didn't mean a great deal of vulnerability. So he was surprised.

"Did you hear?" she asked. Her voice was ragged and low. Fresh tears ran down her cheeks, and her mouth pulled in and down at the corners.

"I don't think so," Solomon said, standing back to let her past. His hole was a standard design: a small multipurpose room at the front with enough resources to cook simple meals, a quarter-sized wall monitor, and space for three or four people to sit. Behind it was the bedroom. Behind that, a storage closet and a bathroom. On Mars, the joke went, a man's hole was his castle where values of castle approached dorm room. She sat heavily on one of the benches, and wrapped her arms around herself. Solomon closed the door. He didn't know whether to talk to her or hold her or both. He started with holding her. Her tears had a smell to them; salt and damp and skin. She wept into his shoulder until curiosity and distress drove him past the consolation of being her soft monkey. "So. Did I hear what, exactly?"

She coughed out a phlegmy laugh.

"The United Nations," she said. "They invoked the breakaway province rule. Their ships have done their acceleration burns. Forty of them. They're already ballistic."

"Oh," he said, and she started weeping again.

"It's those fucking secessionists. Ever since they published their manifesto, people have been acting like they're serious. Like they aren't a bunch of short-sighted assholes who're in it for the attention. Now they've started a war. They're really going to do it, Sol. They're going to drop rocks on us until we're just a carbon layer ten atoms thick."

"They won't do that. They won't do that," he said, and immediately regretted repeating himself. It made him sound like he was trying to talk himself into it. "Every time the breakaway province rule's been invoked, it's been because the UN wanted to grab resources. If they break all our infrastructure, they can't get the resources. They're just trying to scare us."

Caitlin raised one hand like a school girl asking to be recognised. "Working. Scared now."

"And it isn't about the secessionists, even if that's what they're claiming," Solomon said. He felt himself warming up now. He wasn't repeating sentences. "It's about Earth running out of lithium and molybdenum. Even with the landfill mines, they need more than they've got. We have access to raw ore. That's all it is. It's all about money, Cait. They aren't going to start dropping rocks. Besides, if they do that to us, we'll do that to them. We've got better ships."

"Eighteen of them," she said. "They've got forty coasting toward us right now, and just as many playing defence."

"But if they miss one," he said, and didn't finish the thought.

She swallowed, wiped her cheeks with the palm of her hands. He leaned across the room and plucked a towel out of the dispenser for her.

"Do you actually know any of that?" she said. "Or are you just talking a good game to calm me down?"

"Do I have to answer that?"

She sighed, collapsing into him.

"It'll be weeks," he said. "Minimum. Probably months."

"So. If you had four months to live, what would you do?"

"Crawl into bed with you and not come out."

She reached over and kissed him. There was a violence in her that unnerved him. No, that wasn't right. Not violence. Sincerity.

"C'mon," she said.

He woke with his hand terminal buzzing in alarm and only vaguely aware he'd been hearing the sound for a while. Caitlin was curled up against him, her eyes still closed, her mouth open and calm. She looked young like that. Relaxed. He shut off the alarm as he checked the time. On one hand, he was egregiously late for his shift. On the other, another hour wouldn't be particularly more egregious. There were two messages from his team lead queued. Caitlin muttered and stretched. The motion pulled the sheet away from her body. He put the hand terminal down, pushed his hand under his pillow and went back to sleep.

The next time he woke, she was sitting up, looking at him. The softness had left her face again, but she was still beautiful. He smiled up at her and reached out to weave his fingers with hers.

"Will you marry me?" he asked.

"Oh, please."

"No, really. Will you marry me?"

"Why? Because we're about to get into a war that'll kill us and everyone we know and there's nothing we can do to affect it one way or the other?

Quick, let's do something permanent before the permanence is all mined out."

"Sure. Will you marry me?"

"Of course I will, Sol."

The ceremony was a small one. Voltaire was Caitlin's maid of honour. Raj was Solomon's best man. The priest was a Methodist whose childhood had been spent in the Punjab, but now spoke with the faux-Texan drawl of the Mariner Valley. There were several chapels in the research centre, and this one was actually quite lovely. Everything, even the altar, had been carved from native stone and then covered with a clear sealant that left it looking wet and rich and vibrant. Lines of white and black ran through the red stone, and flecks of crystalline brightness. The air was thick with the scent of lilacs that Voltaire had bought by the armful from the greenhouses.

As they stood together, exchanging formulaic vows, Solomon thought Caitlin's face had the same calm that it did when she was sleeping. Or maybe he was just projecting. When he put the ring on her finger, he felt something shift in his breast and he was utterly and irrationally happy in a way he didn't remember ever having been before. The UN fleet was still three weeks away. Even at the worst, they wouldn't die for almost a month. It made him wish they'd done it all earlier. The first night he'd seen her, for instance. Or that they'd met when they were younger. In the pictures they sent to her parents, he looked like he was about to burst into song. He hated the images, but Catlin loved them, so he loved them too. They took their honeymoon in the hotel right there in Dhanbad Nova, drying themselves with towels and washing with soaps that had been made in the image of luxury on Earth. He'd bathed twice as much while they were there, almost feeling the heat of the water and the softness of his robe as magic, as if by being decadent he could pass for a Terran.

And, by coincidence, it worked. Whatever negotiations had been going on behind the scenes paid off. The UN ships flipped for their deceleration burn early and burned twice as long. They were on their way home. He watched the announcer on the newsfeed tracking the orbital mechanics of the voyage out and back. He tried to imagine what it was like for the marines in those ships. Out almost all the way to the new world, and then back without ever having seen it. Over half a year of their lives gone in an act of political theatre. Caitlin sat on the edge of the bed, leaning in toward the monitor, not taking her eyes from it. Drinking it in.

Sitting behind her, his back pressing against the headboard, Solomon felt a ghost of unease pass through him, cold and unwelcome.

"I guess permanent just got a lot longer," he said, trying to make a joke out of it.

"Mm-hm," she agreed.

"Sort of changes things."

"Mm-hm."

He scratched at the back of his hand even though it didn't itch. The dry sound of fingernails against skin was drowned in the announcer's voice so that he felt it more than heard it. Caitlin ran a hand through her hair, her fingers disappearing in the black and then re-emerging.

"So," he said. "Do you want a divorce?"

"No."

"Because I know you were thinking that the rest of your life was going to be kind of a short run. And if... if this wasn't what you would have picked. Anyway, I'd understand it."

Caitlin looked at him over her shoulder. The light of the monitor shone on her cheek, her eye, her hair like she was made of coloured glass.

"You are adorable, and you are my husband, and I love you and trust you like I never have anyone in my life. I wouldn't trade this for anything but more of this. Why? Do you want out?"

"No. Just being polite. No, not that. Insecure all of a sudden."

"Stop it. And anyway, it hasn't changed. Earth is still running out of lithium and molybdenum and all sorts of industrial minerals. We still have them. They turned back this time, but they're still coming, and they'll keep on coming."

"Unless they find some way to do what they need to do with other metals. Or find another source. Things change all the time. Something could make the whole question irrelevant."

"Could," she agreed. "That's what peace is, right? Postponing the conflict until the thing you were fighting over doesn't matter."

On the screen, the UN ships burned, arcs of flame flaring behind them as they went back where they came from.

THE HAND TERMINAL eases a little farther out of his pocket, and he's fairly sure it's going to leave a track of bruise as wide as the case. He doesn't care. He tries to remember if he left the voice activation on, and either he didn't or his throat is too deformed by the thrust gravity for his voice to be recognisable. It has to be done by hand. He can't relax or he'll lose consciousness, but it's getting harder and harder to remember that. Intellectually he knows that the blood is being pressed to the back of his body, pooling in the back part of his cerebellum and flooding his kidneys. He hasn't done enough medical work to know what that means, but it can't be good. The hand terminal comes almost all the way out. It's in his hand now.

The ship shudders once, and a notification pops up on the screen. It's amber-coloured, and there's some text with it, but he can't make it out. His eyes won't focus. If it were red, it would have triggered a shut down. He waits for a few seconds, hoping that whatever it is gets worse, but it doesn't. The yacht's solid. Well-designed and well-built. He turns his attention back to the hand terminal

Caitlin will be at the hole now. She'll be starting dinner and listening to the newsfeed for information about the shipyards crisis. If he can put in a connection request, she'll get it. He has the sudden, powerful fear that she'll think he sat on his terminal. That she'll say his name a few times, then laugh it off and drop the connection. He'll have to make noise when she accepts. Even if actual speech is too hard, he has to let her know there's something wrong. He's thumbed in connection requests without looking at his terminal thousands of times, but everything feels different now, and his muscle memory isn't helping him. The weight of the terminal is overwhelming. Everything in his hand aches like he's been hit with a hammer. His belly hurts. The worst headache he can imagine blooms. Nothing about this experience is fun except the knowledge that he's succeeded. Even as he struggles to make the terminal respond, he's also thinking what the drive means practically. With efficiency like this, ships can be under thrust all through a voyage. Acceleration thrust to the halfway point, then cut the engines, flip, and decelerate the rest of the trip. Even a Martian normal one third g will mean not only getting wherever they are headed much faster, but there won't be any of the problems of long-term weightlessness. He tries to figure how long the transit to Earth will take, but he can't. He has to pay attention to the terminal.

Something in the topology of his gut shifts, changing the angle the terminal is sitting. It starts to slip, and he doesn't have strength or speed to catch it. It reaches his side, falls the centimetres to the chair. He tries to move his left arm from where it's pinned beside his ear, but it won't move.

It won't move at all. It won't even tense up with effort.

Oh, he thinks, I'm having a stroke.


THEY HAD BEEN married for six years when Solomon took the money he'd saved from his performance and efficiency bonuses and bought himself a yacht. It wasn't a large ship; the living space in it was smaller than his first hole. It was almost five years old, and was going to require a month in the orbital shipyard docks before very much longer. The interior colour scheme – cream and orange – wasn't to his tastes. It had been sitting in dry dock for eight and a half months since its previous owner – a junior vice president of a Luna-based conglomerate – had died. His family on Luna didn't have any plans to come to Mars, and the bother of retrieving it across the months-deep void made it easier for them to price it low and sell. For most people on Mars, a boat like that was an ostentatious status symbol and nothing more. There was no settled moon or inhabited L5 station to go visit. The trip to Earth in it would have been neither comfortable nor particularly safe. It could go around in orbit. It could run out into the vacuum near Mars, and then come back. That was about it, and the pointlessness of the exercise helped drive down the price ever farther. As a statement of wealth, it said its owner had had too much. As a means of transport, it was like having a race car that could never leave its track.

For Solomon, it was the perfect test vehicle.

The yacht had been designed around an engine he knew, and the build code was one he'd helped to write. When he looked at the technical and maintenance history, he could see every control array, every air recycling vent and cover. Before he'd even set foot on it, he knew it as well as he knew anything. Some parts of the exhaust system were things he'd designed himself a decade before. And, since he held the title to it, half a year's worth of red tape would simply go away if he wanted to use it to test some new refinements to the engines. That idea alone could make him cackle with delight. No more permissions committees. No more hard capital liability reports. Just the boat, its reactor, a couple EVA suits and a set of industrial waldoes he'd had since he was in school. In previous eras, a scientist might have a garage PCR machine or a shed in the back of the house with beehives or disassembled computers or half-built prototypes of inventions that would change the world if they could just be made to work. Solomon had his yacht, and getting it was the most self-indulgent, delightful, important thing he'd done since the day he'd asked Caitlin to marry him.

And yet, even as the fertile garden of his mind sent up a thousand different green shoots of ideas and projects, tests and tweaks and adjustments, he found himself dreading the part where he told his wife what he'd done. And when the time came, his unease was justified.

"Oh, Sol. Oh, baby."

"I didn't spend my salary on it," he said. "It was all bonus money. And it was only mine. I didn't use ours."

Caitlin was sitting on the bench in their multipurpose room, tapping her mouth with the tips of her fingers the way she did when she was thinking hard. The system was playing a gentle ambient music that was all soft percussion and strings loud enough to cover the hiss of the air recyclers but not so much as to overwhelm the conversation. As with almost all the new building on Mars, it was larger, better appointed, and deeper underground.

"So what I just heard you say is you can spend as much money out of the account as you want without talking to me if the total you pull is less than whatever you've made in bonuses. Is that what you meant?"

"No," he said, though it was pretty close. "I'm saying that it wasn't money we were counting on.

All our obligations are covered. We're not going to try to buy food and have the accounts come up empty. We're not going to have to work extra hours or take on side jobs."

"All right."

"And this is important work. The design I have for the magnetic coil exhaust acceleration can really increase drive efficiency, if I can get –"

"All *right*," she said.

He leaned against the door frame. The strings rose in a delicate arpeggio.

"You're angry."

"No, sweetie. I'm not angry," she said gently. "Angry is yelling. This is resentful, and it's because you're cutting me out from the fun parts. Really, I look at you, and see the happiness and the excitement, and I want to be part of that. I want to jump up and down and wave my arms and talk about how great it all is. But that money was our safety net. You're ignoring the fact that you spent our safety net, and if we *both* ignore it, the first time something unexpected comes up, we're screwed. I love our life, so now I have to be the one who cares and disapproves and doesn't get to be excited. You're making me the grown-up. I don't want to be the grown-up. I want us both to be grown-ups, so that when we do something like this, we both get to be kids."

She looked up at him and shrugged. Her face was harder than it was when they met. There are threads of white in the darkness of her hair. When she smiles, he feels the hardness in his chest erode away.

"I may... have gotten a little carried away. I saw it was there and we could afford it."

"And you zoomed ahead without thinking about all of what it would mean. Because you're Solomon Epstein, and you are the smartest, most rigorous and methodical man who ever made every single important choice in his life by impulse." If there hadn't been warmth and laughter in her voice, it would have sounded like a condemnation. Instead it sounded like love.

"I'm cute, though," he said.

"You're adorable. And I want to hear all about your new whatever it is you're going to try. Only first tell me that you'll try to think about the future next time?"

"I will."

They spent the evening with him talking about power and efficiency, ejection mass and velocity multipliers. And when that was done, they talked about building a responsible retirement plan and making sure their wills were up to date. It felt like an apology, and he hoped that they'd be able to do it again when she understood how much maintenance on the yacht was going to cost. It was a fight for another day.

The days, he spent working as usual with the team at the propulsion group. The nights, he sat on the monitors back at their hole and designed his own things. Caitlin started a program over the network with a group in Londres Nova discussing how companies like Kwikowski could intervene in the destabilising spiral of threat and avoidance that Earth and Mars seemed locked in. Whenever he heard her talking to the others – about propaganda and divergent moral codes and any number of other plausible-sounding vaguenesses – she brought up lithium, molybdenum. Now tungsten, too. All the other things were interesting, important, informative, and profound. But unless they could figure out the ore rights issues, they could address everything else and still not solve the problem. He was always proud of her when she said that. A liberal arts background was a hard thing to overcome, but she was doing great.

Eventually, the time came to test his idea and plans. He made the long journey to the shipyards on the new public transport system: evacuated tubes drilled through the rock and lined with electromagnetic rails like a slow, underpowered gauss gun. It was cramped and uncomfortable, but it was fast. He got to his yacht an hour before the sun set at the nearby Martian horizon. He finished the last minute tweaks to the prototype he'd fabricated, ran the diagnostic sequences twice, and took the ship up beyond the thin atmosphere. Once he reached high orbit, he floated for a while, enjoying the novelty of null g. He brewed himself a bulb of fresh tea, strapped himself into the captain's chair, and ran his fingertip across the old touchscreen monitor.

If he was right, the additions he'd made would increase efficiency by almost sixteen per cent above baseline. When the numbers came back, he hadn't been right. Efficiency had *dropped* by four and a half. He landed back at the shipyards and rode the transit tube home, muttering darkly to himself the whole way.

The United Nations issued a statement that all future Martian ships would be contracted through the Bush shipyards orbiting Earth. The local government didn't even comment on it; they just kept on with the scheduled builds and negotiated for new ones after that. The United Nations ordered that all shipyards on Mars shut down until an inspection team could be sent out there. Seven months to get the team together, and almost six months in transit because of the relative distances of the two planets in their orbits around the sun. Sol was a little nervous when he heard that. If they closed the shipyards, it might mean grounding his test yacht. He didn't need to concern himself. The shipyards all stayed open. The rumours of war started up again, and Solomon tried to ignore them. Tried to tell himself that this time would be no different than the one before or the one before that.

Raj, to everyone's surprise, resigned from development, rented a cheap hole up near the surface, and started selling hand-made ceramic art. He said he'd never been happier. Voltaire got a divorce and wanted all the old crew to come out to the bars with her. There were eight of them now, but pretty much nobody went. Julio and Carl had a baby together and stopped socialising with anyone. Tori went in on a little chemical safety consultancy that pretended to serve any business with a Martian charter, but actually got all their business from the terraforming projects. Malik died from an unresponsive spinal cancer. Life struggled on, winning and failing. Solomon's experimental drives got to where they were almost as good as the unmodified ship. Then a little bit better.

A year almost to the day after he'd bought it, Solomon rode out to the yacht with a new design. If he was right, it would increase efficiency by almost four and a half per cent above baseline. He was in the engine room installing it when his hand terminal chimed. It was Caitlin. He accepted the request.

"What's up?" he asked.

"Did we decide to take that long weekend next month?" she asked. "I know we talked about it, but I don't think we made a decision."

"We didn't, but I'd better not. The team's a little behind."

"Overtime behind?"

"No. Just keep-showing-up behind."

"All right. Then I may plan something with Maggie Chu."

"You have my blessing. I'll be home as soon as this is done."

"All right," she said, and dropped the connection. He tested the housings, did an extra weld where the coil would suffer the most stress, and headed back up for the captain's chair. The yacht rose through the thin atmosphere and into high orbit. Solomon ran the diagnostics again, making sure before he started that everything looked good. For almost half an hour he floated in his chair, held in place by his straps.

As he started the burn sequence, he remembered that the team was going to be in Londres Nova the weekend he'd been thinking about taking off with Caitlin. He wondered whether she'd put her plans with Maggie Chu in place, or if there was still time to change things. He started the burn.

Acceleration threw Solomon back into the captain's chair, then pressed his chest like a weight. His right hand landed on his belly, his left fell onto the upholstery beside his ear. His ankles pressed back against the leg rests.

THE SHIP SINGS a low dirge, throaty and passionate and sad like the songs his father used to sing at temple. He understands now that he's going to die here. He's going too fast and too far for help to reach him. For a while – maybe forever – his little yacht will mark the farthest out of Earth's gravity well a manned ship has ever gone. They'll find the design specs at the hole. Caitlin is smart. She'll know to sell the design. She'll have enough money to live like a queen for the rest of her life. He's taken good care of her, anyway, if not himself.

If he had control, he could reach the asteroid belt. He could go to the Jovian system and be the first person to walk on Europa and Ganymede. He isn't going to, though. That's going to be someone else. But when they get there, they will be carried by his drive.

And the war! If distance is measured in time, Mars just got very, very close to Earth while Earth is still very distant from Mars. That kind of asymmetry changes everything. He wonders how they'll negotiate that. What they'll do. All the lithium and molybdenum and tungsten anyone could want is within reach of mining companies now. They can go to the asteroid belt and the moons of Saturn and Jupiter. The thing that kept Earth and Mars from ever reaching a lasting peace isn't going to matter anymore.

The pain in his head and his spine are getting worse. It's hard to remember to tense his legs and arms, to help his failing heart move the blood. He almost blacks out again, but he's not sure if it's the stroke or the thrust gravity. He's pretty sure driving blood pressure higher while having a stroke is considered poor form.

The ship's dirge shifts a little, and now it's literally singing in his father's voice, Hebrew syllables whose meaning Solomon has forgotten, if he ever knew. Aural hallucinations, then. That's interesting.

He's sorry that he won't be able to see Caitlin one more time. To tell her goodbye and that he loves her. He's sorry he won't get to see the consequences of his drive. Even through the screaming pain, a calmness and euphoria start to wash over him. It's always been like this, he thinks. From when Moses saw the promised land that he could never enter, people have been on their deathbeds just wanting to see what happens next. He wonders if that's what makes the promised land holy: that you can see it but you can't quite reach it. The grass is always greener on the other side of personal extinction. It sounds like something Malik would have said. Something Caitlin would laugh at.

The next few years – decades even – are going to be fascinating, and it will be because of him. He closes his eyes. He wishes he could be there to see it all happen.

Solomon relaxes, and the expanse folds itself around him like a lover.

# THE ROAD TO NPS

**Sandra McDonald** and **Stephen D. Covey**

NOT THAT HE was paranoid, but in the forty-eight hours prior to departure, Rahiti Ochoa ate and drank only from the supplies he'd been stockpiling under his bunk. He compulsively checked the oxygen levels in his tiny quarters. He didn't go near the crew bar on level four (someone might drug his beer), skipped working out in the gym (someone might rig the treadmill), and kept to himself on shift, glaring at anyone who got within ten or fifteen feet (because someone might just try the direct approach, a crowbar to the head). He warned Will Danton to keep the same precautions.

"Crazy Samoan," Will muttered. "Relax, will you? You won the contract. Orbital's not going to try and sabotage you."

*Better crazy than dead*, Jovinta might say, if she were talking to him.

Maybe Will didn't take the threat seriously enough, or maybe he was distracted by someone on purpose, or maybe (just maybe) it was really an accident, but when the silver crate toppled over, smashing Will against a sled – when he began to scream, wild and raw, accompanied by the wail of the emergency siren

– when all that happened, Rahiti's first thought was: *Son of bitches found a way to stop me.*

"Ra!" Will screamed." Get it off me!"

The Orbital arena supervisor, Hal Carpenter, shouted over Rahiti's headset."I'm on it! Someone shut him up!"

Rahiti leaped twenty metres forward in two slow bounds. The arena was well lit, as always, the Europa sky dark and glittering far above. No sign yet of the sun breaking over the horizon, but already a sliver of Jupiter was sunlit and their scheduled departure was imminent. He could see how Will was pinned and could tell instantly there was no way to get him loose without a loader. The nearest driver, a new kid, was spinning his treads back and forth on the ice, panicking.

"Don't cut off my arm," Will wailed. "Ra! I need my arm."

"No one's cutting off anything," Rahiti promised. Although it was useless, he threw himself against one of the hundred-ton crates."Hold on, okay?"

A more experienced driver took over from the newbie and with a few deft manoeuvres got the crate shifted away. Will went limp. Rahiti pulled him free, ignored the twisted and flattened look of the arm, and wrapped his arm around Will's waist. He jumped them toward the nearest hatch.

"Emergency crew's on its way," Carpenter said over the headset, the useless bastard.

"I've got him," Rahiti bit out. "Open airlock six."

By the time Rahiti got them both into the lock, Will was beginning to stir back to consciousness. His face was glassy under his mask. The skinsuit had sealed over any tears or breaches, but his arm was still hanging so gruesomely that Rahiti couldn't look at it.

"Sorry, sorry," Will mumbled as he came around. "Didn't see it. Don't cut it off."

The airlock cycled up. Rahiti got his helmet off, then slid Will's off too. "It's okay. Not your fault."

Will's skin was sweaty-clammy, a ghastly shade of grey. "Messed up the plan."

"I built in an extension," Rahiti said. "We're good."

The inner hatch rolled open. A young med tech with bright red hair poked her head in. "How is he?"

"How would you be?" Rahiti snapped. "Where's the stretcher?"

She blinked at Will. "They said minor accident."

"Minor, my ass." Rahiti hopped and pulled, using the handholds, and got Will into the passage. He'd never seen the tech before. Asterius Outpost wasn't a huge place, three hundred people maybe, but it was the pass-through for any personnel heading up or back from North Pole Station and Conamara. "He's in shock, his arm is crushed, you didn't check the feeds?"

"My arm's fine," Will said, his voice slurring. He gave the tech a lopsided smile. "What's your name?"

She was young and new, but at least trained enough to ignore his flirting and plant a round disk to Will's neck. "Telemetry's on, we're on our way," she said briskly into her own set, and only then did she answer. "I'm Anu."

"Anu," Will said. "Watcha doing later, Anu?"

Rahiti pulled him into the lift and said, "Shut up, Will."

The infirmary waiting room was half-full, but the doctor on duty hustled them immediately into a cubicle. Rahiti didn't think much of Dr. Desai – in his experience, she was as snooty as the rest of them – but she was both concerned and efficient as she slipped Will a painkiller.

"Mr. Ochoa, you can wait outside," she said.

Will's good hand came up and snagged Rahiti's arm. "No. Stay with me."

Desai said, "Only family or next of kin."

"Who the fuck can afford to bring family here?" Rahiti asked hotly.

"Language, please," she said. "Are you registered partners?"

Will's grip grew only tighter. "Don't let them cut off my arm."

"I'm married. My wife's in Hawaii," Rahiti said. Half a billion miles away, maybe on a beach somewhere. Javinta liked beaches, but hated to swim; who wanted to bathe in tiny bits of seaweed and dead fish and ocean pollution? Maybe even now she was sitting in the sand, watching the waves, thinking about breaking the six months of silence that stretched all the way to Europa.

The scanner in Desai's hand shed green light on Will's crushed arm, piercing the skinsuit and displaying the injury overhead. Desai gave up on trying to eject Rahiti from the cubicle and instead spoke quickly into a transcriber. Rahiti didn't understand all the words – distal radius, proximal something, perfusion? The med tech watched with frank interest from a corner.

Desai put a patch on Will's shoulder. "Here's the really good stuff. When it kicks in, you won't feel anything below your shoulder for twelve hours or so. Surgery's up next."

"Surgery?" Rahiti asked, the word a rock in his throat. "How long?"

Will protested, "I can't have surgery. We're leaving in an hour. Driving to NPS."

The med tech blurted out, "That's you? The Crazy Samoan?"

Rahiti's face flushed. "Yeah, that's me."

"Anumati!" Desai said sternly. The girl looked away. Desai said, "The surgery will take an hour or two, then we have to monitor the perfusion to make certain you don't lose your arm. You'll be in a splint for at least three weeks. No skinsuits."

Will banged his head against the exam table. "I'm sorry, Ra. Damn."

Rahiti didn't know what to say. He wasn't quite sure what he felt, either, except that it was a lot like free-fall, sickening and plunging with no end in sight.

"It's okay," he said, in a voice that sounded as distant as Javinta on her beach. "I'll do it alone."

"You better do it soon," Desai said. Her gaze was focused solely on her patient. "An accident like this means an incident report. The safety team's going to want to interview any witnesses. That could take all day."

Rahiti's free-fall came to a sudden slamming halt.

"If I were you," she continued, "I might think about leaving here through the freight lift. Take a right over there, second hatch."

Rahiti didn't thank her. He didn't even say goodbye to Will, or wish him luck. When he was inside the lift, black rage rose up and made him kick the bulkhead. Damn, damn, damn. Hundreds of hours of planning, thousands of hours of worrying, his tiny living cube overflowing with schedules, maps and supply lists, and he'd never considered what he would do if his co-driver got himself crushed by a crate.

Just before the doors closed, Anu slid her boot between them.

"I can help you," she announced. "Take me."

Rahiti didn't even stop to think about his reply. "Absolutely not."

She gave him a pleading look. "My boyfriend works at NPS. We've been z-mailing for months. I left college to come out here to see him, but I ran out of money. You need someone to help you on this trip, and I can do it."

He kicked her foot free. "I don't need you."

The lift doors slid closed, blocking her unhappy face.

When he reached the interior docks, he saw two people in Asterius white-and-red safety suits talking to Hal Carpenter, that son of a bitch. Carpenter had a direct line-of-sight on the flex tunnel leading to his snowcat. But Rahiti still had his skinsuit on, still had his helmet. He could go out the aux lock, come up underneath the cat, board out of sight of the cameras. More precious time ticking on the clock. He backtracked, got his helmet on, and went downladder to the auxiliary locks. The minute he opened one, Carpenter would notice. He needed some kind of diversion –

A shrill alarm cut through his headset. Fire drill. Rahiti winced and slapped at the volume and thanked whoever had probably set the thing off by accident.

Outside, approaching the cat with two easy bounds, he eyed the extra tanks carrying hydrogen and oxygen for the fuel cells. The vehicle looked ungainly with all the added weight, but they were necessary for the trip up and back, and for extra mass to give more weight and traction. The dozen sleds lined up behind the cat were twice as many as Rahiti had ever hauled before. Without the extra weight, his treads would spin uselessly on the ice instead of pulling the load.

Crazy plan, yeah. But he'd done the math a dozen times, had convinced himself that the loaded cat could drag three thousand tons of payload, and had won the contract fair and square.

He had eighty-five hours – one Europa day – to either earn five years' pay or put himself into horrible debt, probably forever.

Rahiti climbed into the cat's cabin. The *thunk* of the airlock closing was like the last drop of a guillotine blade. As the fuel cells powered up, the triple beams of the headlights cut across Europa's bleak landscape. He tapped Javinta's picture, mounted below the radio. Her smile was sweet and shy, her dimples deep enough to fall into.

"Wish me luck," he said. And then, over the radio, he said, "Snowcat 89-4A, checklist complete, I'm leaving for NPS."

Carpenter's voice was slow and lazy. "Oh, that's a negative, 89-A. You've got some folks here from Safety who need to talk to you about your partner's accident."

"I already recorded my statement," Rahiti said. "It's in their z-box. Asterius regulation 1732.a, a video statement can suffice for personnel not in the immediate vicinity."

A pause. "But you are in the immediate vicinity, Ochoa. I'm looking at you through my window."

Rahiti resisted the urge to lift his hand and give Carpenter an obscene gesture.

"Asterius regulation 1732.a (3), no definition provided for 'immediate,'" he said. "Wish us luck. 89 out."

His contract was with Asterius, but he'd had to rent everything except the cargo from his own employer, Orbital. Part of the contract was that Orbital could distribute footage once the operation was completed. The bastards didn't want him to succeed, but they'd certainly exploit him if he did. Rahiti ran the cells up to maximum, generating excess water that vented as steam through the top of the snowcat. Wasteful, but dramatic. On the cams it looked like an old-style steam locomotive chugging out of the station. He wished his job was as easy as a train driver; how damned convenient, following miles and miles of track someone else had already put down through the wilderness.

Slowly he engaged the motors. Too much power and the treads would slip; too little and the sleds wouldn't move. The trick was to get each sled moving and sliding before the slack was taken up. Soon three thousand tons of mass payload were following the cat on the road to Conamara. The payload took its own sweet time, however. Even running the fuel cells at maximum, Rahiti barely achieved fifty kilometres an hour.

Still, he was on his way.

No partner, no back-up, no one to talk to for the next eighty-five hours, but he was on his way. Score one for the Crazy Samoan.

He settled into his chair, piped some island music in over the speakers, and downed more coffee. Six hours later, dawn arrived. A triangle of faint Zodiacal light pointed to the rising sun just before it peeked above the hills behind Conamara. The bright limb of the sun overwhelmed the glow from the full Jupiter behind him. Ten minutes later he passed Conamara's buried domes, gave a status update, and turned onto Agave Linea. Now half of Jupiter painted the horizon. Europa's shadow crawled below the Great Red Spot, and would for the next three hours.

Pretty, he thought to himself. If you liked that sort of thing. If you ever saw it, instead of spending all of your time working or sleeping or drinking in grey rooms under artificial lights.

No wonder Javinta had stayed on Earth.

Rahiti shook off his gloom and poured more coffee. Everything from here out was new ground, literally. The entire moon was just one giant frozen sea. The lines formed natural roads of fresh ice in a criss-cross maze, with hidden obstacles and freshly opened cracks between him and the pole. As long as he could stay awake, stay alert, and stay on schedule, he'd be fine. The extra eight hours in the schedule gave him time to catnap, and he could trust the autopilot as long as the way was steady and straight.

Two hundred kilometres later, a liquid sound burbled in the access tube to the sleepsled.

*What the fuck?*

He checked the path ahead and enabled the autopilot. Four low-gravity hand pulls brought him to the tube. Six crawls through the tube and he was in the dim sled, where the colder temperature made his breath frost.

Anu was sitting on the lone bunk. Meekly, she said, "I had to use the bathroom."

Rahiti's vision darkened. His hands fisted, anger flooding up. It took everything he had not to kick at something or punch the bulkhead. "What the hell are you doing here? How did you get in?"

She cringed. "I pulled the fire alarm so everyone was distracted. I have to see Ted. Mom won't pay, so this is the only way."

He didn't believe her. It was more likely that someone had planted her here the same way they had arranged for Will's accident. For a brief, hot moment he contemplated throwing her out the airlock.

But then he asked, "Your mom?"

"Dr. Desai," she said.

That did it. He punched the bulkhead and was rewarded with bright hot pain in all his fingers.

Quickly Anu said, "I won't be any trouble! I can keep you company, maybe even drive. You said you needed help."

Rahiti shook his head. "You think you can just drive a rig, no experience? I'm going to have to take you back to Conamara. My whole schedule – Jesus. What you've done to me. You don't even know."

The sleepsled jerked violently. The snowcat gave off a sharp peal, like a bell being run, as it struck and broke through something on their path. But the cat didn't stop. It continued to bounce and surge forward. Anu yelped in surprise, started asking questions, but Rahiti was too busy racing back through the tube to care about her curiosity.

He was halfway back to his seat when the cat slammed to a halt with terrible metal shrieks. He couldn't grab a handhold in time. Momentum slammed him face first into the front console, right below the picture of Javinta.

The last thing he saw was her bright eyes, full of reproach: Crazy Samoan.

\* \* \*

HE WASN'T OUT long. Maybe a few seconds. The blare of alarms dragged him back, accompanied by the whine of engines. The autopilot kicked in, shut them down. Lights flickered in his face, bright and annoying, but nothing he could clearly focus on.

"Mr. Ochoa!" Anu's voice was frantic. "Are you okay?"

Rahiti wiped blood away from his face. His nose was a bright flare of pain. Warm liquid and debris were floating in his mouth. Blood. Broken teeth. He spat out as much as he could. He was dizzy and breathless and maybe even dying.

"Mr. Ochoa? Here, sit down."

Anu helped him to the driver's seat. Rahiti thought to ask, "Are you hurt?" but then had to cough out more blood and only caught part of her answer.

"– and my knee, I think. What happened?"

"What do you think?" he snapped. "We hit something."

Something the autopilot hadn't seen. A ridge hidden by snow? He should have been at the controls, not babysitting this schoolgirl.

"You're a mess," she said. "Medical emergency, first aid program."

The computer answered. "Hi. How may I help?"

Anu talked to the program. Rahiti tried peering at the sensors, but his eyes were getting worse. He was reasonably sure now that he wasn't dying, but maybe death would be easier than complete and utter failure. Easier than facing the shame. People like Hal Carpenter would mock him for years to come over this. *Couldn't even follow a straight line.*

Despair pulsed through him as his eyes swelled shut. Blind, broken nose, the snowcat jammed –

Uncertainly Anu said, "That's all I can do for now. Do you want to lie down?"

"No," he ground out. "Emergency doctor off."

The speaker went silent. The cockpit consoles were still making small alarmed noises, but Rahiti ignored them. "Did we lose the sleds?"

"I don't know. How can I tell?"

"Look at the panel lights on the left upper bulkhead."

Silence for a moment. Then, "They're all green. That's good, right?"

Rahiti tried to think clearly. The taste of blood was making him sick.

Anu's voice was thin. "Can I call anyone for help?"

"We're out of radio range."

"They'll come looking for us, right? Eventually?"

He didn't answer. Yes, eventually Orbital would come for them. And charge him for the rescue and recovery. Technically he was using his vacation time for these eight-five hours; they'd probably find a way to charge him for any medical treatment he needed, claiming that he wasn't on duty and therefore not insured. Years and years more work added to his contract, more steel chains of days wrapped around his legs and wrists. But there was one way to avoid it. One way out.

"You're going to have to drive," he said.

"What?" she squeaked. "You said I can't! It's too hard."

Rahiti spat out another wad of blood. "If we don't make it to NPS, I lose all the money I borrowed to rent this equipment and buy fuel. I'll never be able to go home. I'll never see my wife again. And you won't see your boyfriend."

She was silent. Thinking, fearing, setting herself up for failure. He knew what that was like.

"Okay, so it's not like driving on Earth," he admitted. "It's like a tank pulling a train, just faster and more complicated. But the route is mostly a bunch of straight lines. If you can steer, I can keep us moving."

"I guess I can try," she said doubtfully.

"Computer, audio mode," Rahiti said. "Report configuration changes since departure."

"Zero configuration changes." Which was good. All the sleds were still attached.

"Report significant anomalies, priority order."

"Emergency brakes deployed on all sleds. Tractor is tilted left at 82 degrees to the horizon. Sleeping sled is tilted left at 25 degrees to the horizon. Shock sensors tripped. Fuel feed safety disconnect activated. Autopilot disabled. Satellite telemetry inoperative. No response for medical emergency distress call. Headlamp 1 inoperative. Cameras 1, 3, and 5 disabled or blind."

"That sounds bad," Anu said, her voice small.

"Most of those are emergency reflexes. They'll clear when we flip the right switches. The telemetry and tilt are bad. We'll check the cameras once we're outside."

Now her tone shifted to disbelief. "You can't go outside! Maybe you didn't notice your severe facial injuries –"

"Stop talking and help me," he said.

The easy part was having her bandage his eyes. The hard part was struggling into the skinsuit's tight confines in his personal total darkness, acutely aware of being naked in front of her, not knowing what she was looking at. It took twice as long as normal. Anu hadn't brought a skinsuit, of course, and had to use the emergency one. And of course she'd never put one on before. He had to instruct her, several times, to make sure she did it right. The last thing he needed was for her to die out there due to cold or oxygen loss.

Once they were outside, Anu tethered Rahiti to the sled so he wouldn't wander off blindly. He didn't like that, but then again, he didn't like any of this. She reported, "The cargo sleds are upright, in a kind of wavy line. The left cameras and headlamps are all smashed up."

"What about the antenna? It's on top, dead centre."

"There's just some twisted metal."

"Check out the sleds and tell me if anything shifted. While you're at it, rewind the grapples. There's one on each side of the back of every sled. They're our emergency brakes. It should be easy. The feed button lets out the cable, then you pull the grapple out of the ice, and then flip the retract button. Just keep the points of the grapple facing upward."

"You're kind of bossy," Anu said.

"Do you want out of here or don't you?"

She went to work. "Why'd you decide to do this, anyway?"

"Profit."

"I guessed that."

"Asterius owns all the bases and outposts on Europa, but Orbital operates most of the shipping contracts. To get stuff to NPS they launch a payload into polar orbit, cancel its angular momentum, then de-orbit and land. That all takes fuel, thousands of tons of it. Very expensive, but it's passed along to Asterius. I told Asterius that I can deliver the same load a lot cheaper, just by pulling sleds. So this is my one chance to prove it."

"If it's so easy, why hasn't anyone ever done it before?" Anu asked.

"Because I thought of it first."

"And because everyone else thought it was crazy?"

"Yeah."

"How long have you been here, anyway?"

He knew the answer down to the hour, but all he said was, "Six years."

It took two hours to inspect the sleds and retract the grapples. Another three hours to drive the loader to the snowcat, tow it out of the ridge, shove it in line with the sleds, and stow the loader again. Anu was a quick learner, but the crash had rattled her, and she was young, and everything was new to her. Every step went slower than Rahiti wanted. Here he was, barely five hundred kilometres into the three-thousand-kilometre trip, and his contingency time was rapidly dwindling. Pain and fear gnawed at him.

Back inside, stripped out of their skinsuits again, Anu asked, "Do you want to sleep for awhile? Then we can go?"

Yes he wanted to sleep. No, he didn't dare it. "I'll get us moving, you drive, then we'll see," he said.

He started the snowcat's engine. It made a protesting noise or two, but settled down quickly. It took him several minutes of working by touch and instinct to get the sleds moving again. Anu read out their bearing and the autopilot suggested it take over.

"Maybe that's a good idea," Anu said.

Rahiti said, "It drove us right into that snowbank."

She was quiet for a moment. "On purpose? Like, sabotage?"

He didn't want to say *yes*. No use both of them being paranoid. But he couldn't honestly tell her *no*. He thought about Hal Carpenter sneaking into the snowcat while he was in the infirmary with Will and making just a few little changes to the program.

"It doesn't matter," he said. "We can't trust it."

At 10 kph, Rahiti let Anu operate the controls. She practiced speeding up to 15 kph and down to 5, and tried some slow, gentle swerves. When Rahiti was confident – as confident as he could be, blind and in pain and exhausted – he let her ramp up to 20, then to 30. Finally he let her go to 40. The ride was smoother than he'd hoped.

"You're not bad at this," he said, begrudgingly.

She sounded pleased. "Thanks."

"Just stay sharp. Something could go wrong at any minute."

And probably would, just when he was least expecting it. Europa luck. Worst kind of luck in the solar system.


SIX HOURS AND two hundred and forty kilometres later, Rahiti gave up trying to nap. Every time he drifted off, he would feel a movement in the sled and start to panic. The total darkness scared him to the bottom of his gut, made everything around him sharp and hard. His face hurt and his broken teeth throbbed, but he didn't want to pop anything but the mildest painkiller in the kit. Couldn't afford to, not at the risk of clouding his thinking. Abandoning the bunk, he inched his way forward from the sleepsled.

"My turn to sleep, right?" Anu asked. "I'm exhausted."

"You can't leave. I need your eyes."

"Like I'm going to stay up this whole trip," she scoffed.

He didn't answer.

Sharply she said, "I didn't sign up to do this whole thing without sleep!"

"You didn't sign up at all. If we don't get there on time –"

"I know. You lose your money. But seriously. You want me to hallucinate? Go crazy on you? That's what happens when people don't sleep."

"Help me get these bandages off."

Unwrapped and flushed with water, his eyes still proved useless. He wondered, sickly, if his vision was ever going to come back. What use was sitting on a beach with Javinta if he couldn't see her smile, or watch her trickle sand through her brown fingers?

"You're going to have to keep driving," he told Anu.

Several more kilometres passed. He sensed that she was thinking up new arguments. Eventually she said, "I know you don't trust the autopilot, but what if we turn it on, and go really slow, and I nap right here? If something goes wrong, you could wake me up. Otherwise I'm going to go crazy from sleep deprivation."

He didn't actually think two more days without sleep would drive her psychotic. Then again, it probably wasn't worth testing.

"Nap for how long?" he asked.

"Four hours."

"Three."

"I'll still be tired."

"But we'll be on time," he said.

They slowed to twenty kilometres per hour and engaged the autopilot. Anu went to sleep. Rahiti fretted. Headset plugged in, he made the computer announce their coordinates and speed every three minutes, and the time every ten minutes, and Jesus, who knew three hours could drag like that? He woke Anu up thirteen minutes early. She grumbled but got herself some coffee and increased their speed.

"So what's next? Straight line to NPS?" she said around a yawn.

"Not quite. In five hundred kilometres we're going to make a turn."

"You should let me speed up now that I'm used to it. How fast can I go?"

He hesitated. "She tops out at fifty."

"Then fifty it is."

Almost nine hours passed at the improved speed. They drank coffee like it was water and ate from the rations, although Rahiti's jagged teeth and sore gums hurt with every bite. Anu complained at the lack of vegetarian options. He told her that next time she stowed away, she should bring her own tofu. She synched her music player into the main console. He hadn't heard of half the bands she liked. He tried not to worry too much about the upcoming segment from Hyperenor to Athene Linea. It was fifty kilometres of criss-crossed lineae. He wouldn't know until they got there if they'd be forced to do switchbacks, and if Anu's driving would up to the challenge.

Four hours from Hyperenor, Anu started talking non-stop about movies, college, and her divorced parents, but mostly about her boyfriend, Ted. Smart Ted, funny Ted, underappreciated Ted, who she'd met through z-mail.

"If he's so smart, why's he doing grunt work at NPS?" Rahiti asked.

"He's helping a friend work off his contract. Then he's going back to Earth to finish school."

"He might be totally lying about who is."

Anu made an exasperated noise. "You sound like my mother. Besides, you're no expert on relationships. You haven't seen your wife in six years."

"That's different. We couldn't afford two passages."

"If she really wanted to be here, she'd be here. I came for Ted –" Anu's voice halted. Something clicked on the console. "Hey, we're coming into a snowstorm."

He was glad for the change of subject. "There's no such thing as a snowstorm in a vacuum."

"Well, it looks all white across the horizon. Just like falling snow."

She slowed to a crawl. Rahiti heard bits of ice sleeting against the cabin. Some larger hailstones hit as well, but none of them sounded big enough to cause damage. Yet. He racked through his memories, trying to figure out what she was seeing.

"Must be a snow volcano," he offered. "It's venting water into space, which freezes and comes down as ice."

"It's about a kilometre in front of us, blocking the way. It goes as far as as far I can see in both directions. It's beautiful."

Rahiti forced himself to think it through. "Hyperenor ridge must have opened up with a fresh crack in the ice. That's sleet, not snow. Can you see

119

through it at all? If the fissure is small enough, we might just drive fast and cross it."

"What if it's not small?"

"We'll fall in and sink to the bottom of the ocean."

Anu drew in a sharp breath. "Not funny."

"It's not supposed to be," Rahiti replied. "It's about sixty miles deep."

She let her breath out in a long sigh. "I can't see through it. Can we drive around it?"

He recalculated in his head. "If we go northeast, parallel to the fissure, up to Sandus. It's a lot longer than I wanted to go."

"Will the ice here beside the fissure be strong enough to hold us?"

"Yes," he said, and hoped real hard.

She made the turn.

"Tell me what you see," he told her.

"It's like driving through a snow tunnel – there's snow rising up on the left, swirling overhead, and then landing on our right. Kinda psychedelic. Mom's going to die when she sees my vid."

The roar from the fissure pummelled Rahiti through the snowcat's hull and seat. His head started hurting all over again.

"Sooner or later I'm going to need another nap," Anu said.

Rahiti forced himself to sound calm. "Let's worry about the big deadly crack first, okay?"

They followed Hyperenor northeast for several hours. Anu periodically informed Rahiti about the diminishing height of the fountain. The snow tunnel narrowed in response, and fatigue strained her voice.

"It's past midnight," she said. "If I were home, I'd be in bed now."

"We've got five hours until Sandus. That'll be a good place."

Anu made a rude sound. "I've had a total of three hours sleep. You try driving all this on three hours sleep."

"I would if I could," he snapped.

She kept driving.

They reached Sandus on time, but Anu had bad news: the fissure was still open. "The tunnel is down to about a hundred metres wide. Steady, no sign of letting up. It was maybe a kilometre wide when we first started. Can I sleep now?"

"Not yet," he said. "You're going to have to jump it."

Fatigued or not, her response was full of energy. "Absolutely no possible way!"

Rahiti replied, "If you don't jump it, we're going to have to drive to the next linea two hundred kilometres away and hope it's closed there. By then I'll be bankrupt."

"But if we jump, we might end up dead. Dead is worse."

"I'll take that chance," he said.

"Crazy Samoan," she said. And then was silent, and he couldn't tell what she was thinking.

"You can do this," he told her.

"What do you know?" she grumbled. "I don't know how."

"Bring her into a two-hundred seventy degree turn to the right and get as close to the southern bank as you can. You've got to get all the sleds around before you floor it. It's going to be like jumping over an upside down waterfall. If you don't hit it perfectly straight and level, we'll flip over."

"You're not helping my confidence."

121

"Straight and level," he repeated.

The sound of the fissure faded as the engine revved up. Sleet pounded on the hull as they passed through the snow wall. He clutched the armrest so hard his fingers ached. A few minutes later they returned through the snow wall as Anu completed the turn.

"If we die, I'm going to haunt you for the rest of the afterlife," she said. "Hold the fuck on."

She floored the engines. Moments later, the blast of water from the fissure lifted the snowcat off the surface. Rahiti remembered taking Javinta to see an eruption of Manua Loa. She hadn't wanted to watch and spent most of the time with her head buried against his shoulder, her dark hair silky on his chin. It's okay, he'd told her. Perfectly safe. Now he remembered the smell of it, and awful white ash pluming into the sky, and the way the whole world seemed on the verge of cracking open.

No ash here, just ice and snow and the awful sensation of falling until they touched down again. The cat lurched and shuddered but held steady.

Anu gave him a big kiss on the cheek. "We made it!"

Rahiti's heartbeat felt wild in his chest. "You did it."

"Yeah, now I get to sleep."

"There's an eclipse in about two hours –"

"No. I'm the boss now." She stopped the snowcat. "I'll be in the back. Wake me up, and I'll kill you. I'm not kidding."

Forty-eight hours since they'd left the equator. Eighteen hundred and twenty five kilometres down, but re-routing to Sandus had added another two hundred. If she slept until the end of the eclipse and they averaged fifty after that, they could still be on time. Barely.

He'd still have his money.

Cautiously optimistic, he wrapped himself in a blanket and waited for her to wake up. Exhaustion dragged him down faster than he could fight it. Dreams sucked him under. He was trapped under Europa's frozen surface, swimming in crystal green water with Javinta. Her dark hair streamed around her head as she swam away from him. Always swimming away. Funny, considering how much she hated the ocean. He opened his mouth to call her name but only scratching noises emerged; persistent and annoying scratching, somewhere outside his dream.

Something was scratching on the hull.

RAHITI PULLED HIMSELF upright in the darkness. "Anu?"

All was quiet but for the hum of the air and power system.

More scratching.

"Anu, wake up!" he yelled.

She shouted back, "Go to hell!"

"I need you. There's something outside!"

He heard her move forward through the tunnel. "If you're joking –"

"What do you see out there?"

She paused. "Nothing. It's all black. Eclipse, remember?"

"You should at least see our headlights on the ice."

"No. No headlights."

He swallowed hard, panic flaring. "Are they on?"

"Of course –"

Something scraped against the forward hull, loud and distinctive. Anu stopped talking.

Rahiti groped at the panel. "Turn on the infrared."

A switch flipped. Anu said, "There's some kind of weird pattern on the windshield. Like a quilt. It's... moving. Pulsing. Like a heart." Her voice dropped into a whisper of awe. "It's something alive, plastered there."

"Impossible. There's no life on Europa –"

Something flopped on the roof.

"We discovered it!" Anu said, much louder now, almost giddy. "First aliens ever!"

Rahiti cursed. At her enthusiasm, at Europa luck, at the gods determined to ruin him. Whatever was scraping at their hull had probably come up through the fissures from Europa's vast sea. The heat cells must have attracted them.

Well, if they wanted heat, he'd give them heat.

"We have a lot of hydrogen and oxygen," he said. "We'll have to make a blowtorch and burn them off."

"What? You can't kill them!" Anu exclaimed. "They might be intelligent, they might have a civilisation –"

"They sound like jellyfish," he said. "We don't know what they can do or how much damage they can cause. They could clog up our vents, drip acid through the hull –"

"You've seen too many movies," she scoffed.

"You want to take that chance?" he asked.

"I'm not going to make a blowtorch for you," she said stubbornly. "If we have water, why don't we just hose them off?"

"It's not that easy. If it freezes on the snowcat, the hull might crack. We'd have to spend the rest of our trip in skinsuits."

"But we'd live," Anu said. "And they'd live. You can't just kill off the greatest discovery in the history of space exploration."

"We can if they're trying to kill us first." He reached for his bandages. "If you won't do it, I will."

The immensely good news was that his eyes could distinguish light from dark, and her blurry face, and the general outline of the sled. The bad news was that little details were still beyond his ability – how many fingers she was waving at him, for instance, or which buttons controlled the airlock.

"I think you're totally wrong and I disagree with you on every moral and philosophical level," Anu said. "But I'll go out there and try to scare them off."

Both of them got back into their skinsuits in case the snowcat lost atmosphere. Anu dragged an empty waste container from the sleep sled and filled it with hot water. She climbed into the airlock, cycled it, and opened the outside hatch. A yelp followed.

Rahiti snapped, "Talk to me!"

"There's one right below me. Kind of brown, with a frilly fringe, oval shaped. Like a bathroom rug. My mom's going to love this picture –"

"Stop taking vids and hop past it. You'll be safer away from the warm snowcat."

For several moments he heard only her breathing. Then she said, "Okay. I'm away. There's lots of them. The baby ones are only a metre across, there's about six of them. Then there are a few teenagers, I guess, two or three metres across. But there's a big mama one at least five metres wide. She's on top of the sleepsled. Wait – two of the teenagers just dropped off the snowcat. They're sliding toward me."

"Squirt them with the water."

Her voice ratcheted higher. "The water doesn't work – they like it!"

She screamed.

"Anu! Answer me!"

Her radio clicked off. Rahiti pulled on his helmet, squinted his way to the airlock, and sealed the inner door. Without waiting for the cycle he pulled the handle.

The computer said, "Warning: Airlock pressure not –"

"Override!"

The vacuum alarm sounded as oxygen vented. He unlocked the outer door. A last puff of pressure blew out. A creature that had been crawling up the hull fell away and writhed at the burst.

"Our air!" he shouted. "They don't like it!"

Because of course Europa had oxygen, deep in the seas and thin in its atmosphere, but not concentrated and gaseous, not mixed with nitrogen the way humans liked it, and especially not warm. The creature's writhing agony reminded him of that time Will didn't understand "no" and got a face full of pepper spray. Rahiti jumped away from the airlock, trying to make out Anu in the blurry landscape. One of the creatures slammed into him from behind. Rahiti fell on his side under a smothering blanket of pitch darkness. Pain shot through his right leg and hip. He jammed his hand beneath the pulsing mass, found the zipper sealing his mask, and pulled it slightly open.

His vacuum alarm sounded as he broke the seal. Precious breathing mix leaked out. His ears popped and air drained from his lungs. Stupid, crazy thing to do. But the creature sitting on him dropped off and began to flop as if he'd burned it with a torch. Rahiti re-sealed his facemask, got himself upright, and squinted at the icy blur around him.

"Anu! Where are you?"

Something flopped off to his right. He hopped across the icy surface until he found her with one of the aliens covering her head and shoulders. A blast of gas from his mask sent it scurrying away. Rahiti hauled Anu up.

"Bad alien," she said groggily. "I think it was going to eat me."

"You're okay now."

When they got to the cat he had to use his mask again to send two of the baby aliens wriggling away. His reserve was depleting fast and he was dizzy from losing air in bursts, but he groped at the extra oxygen tanks and cracked the feed valves. Streams blew out in white plumes. He aimed them at the mother alien. The creature shrivelled around the edges and lurched off the sled.

"Let's get out of here," Anu said. "Please?"

Once inside, with the engine ramping up, Rahiti spun the treads to clear any creatures still attached and then tried to start the train moving. A warning beep sounded from the console. He squinted at the readout, tried to make out what was wrong.

Anu leaned forward. "Did they chew through something?"

He was trying to fight off panic. Bone-splintering, heart-ripping panic. It was impossible that they had come all this way and now –

"The treads are frozen," he said. "They must have gotten wet when we jumped the fissure. We stopped, and that gave them time to freeze up."

"But you can build a blowtorch, right? You said you could."

"Yeah." Rahiti was having trouble breathing steadily. "But it's going to take hours to melt all that ice. And in the meantime, if any more of those suckers show up, you're going to have to kill them."

"Oh," Anu said. "Wonderful."

As usual, it took twice as long as he thought it would to free the snowcat's treads.

Then he discovered the last three sleds had frozen to the ice as well.

In the end, they arrived at NPS twenty-four hours late. Rahiti had completely failed.

THE ORBITAL REP, a white-haired lady with thick eyebrows, had no sympathy for him. She said, "Obviously this proves that ice sledding is not a viable option for North Pole delivery."

Rahiti sat on the other side of her desk trying to stay stone-faced. He could see clearly now thanks to medical treatment, but his newly healed nose still ached with every heartbeat. He was glad for the pain. It kept him from focusing on how screwed he was.

He said, "We discovered the first alien life in our solar system. That should call for some kind of bonus."

She replied, "All discoveries of scientific value are covered by contract clause twenty four, subsection (a) and (b). And thank to the snowcat's logs, we know exactly where to go to find more. Thank you. It's very exciting for us."

He wanted to tell her what, exactly, he thought of her excitement. A ping at the hatch forestalled him.

Anu entered, looking cheerful. "I brought my trip report. I also thought Orbital would want the first chance to buy my documentary."

Alarm crossed the rep's face. "What documentary?"

A handsome young man in coveralls followed Anu in. "Hi," he said to Rahiti. "I'm Ted."

"Did I tell you that Ted's father works for the largest media company on Earth?" Anu said brightly. "He's very excited about my footage of us battling the aliens on the ice."

The rep floated out of her chair. "All video filmed by Mr. Rahiti, his crew or his equipment is owned by Orbital. You have no rights to anything."

Goosebumps ran down Rahiti's arms. "Anu's not part of my crew. She was a stowaway, and had her own personal recorder."

"Which is not covered by any contract at all," Anu added.

The rep pulled herself out of the office as quickly as low-gravity allowed. No doubt off to consult lawyers, Rahiti thought. Once they were alone, he grabbed Anu in a hug.

"You're amazing!" he said.

"I know," she answered. "And we're rich! More than enough to get you out of debt."

He laughed at the idea. Debt-free. Free.

"I'm using my half to start the Europa Wildlife Protection Society," Anu added.

Rahiti let her go. "The Europa what?"

"To protect the aliens. Sure, they tried to kill us, but they were just going on instinct. Someone's got to make sure they're not exploited or destroyed. Meanwhile you can quit Orbital for good and go back to Earth, or bring your wife out here."

The administrator's office had a small porthole in one bulkhead. Rahiti looked out at the harsh landscape and wondered where Earth was in the sky.

"Don't you want to bring her here?" Anu asked.

129

"In her last message, she said she wanted a divorce," he admitted. It was the first time he'd told anyone. "She won't even reply to me anymore."

Anu took his hand and squeezed it. "They said you couldn't make it to the North Pole and here you are. If you want her back, I bet you could do that, too."

"You never know what might happen," Ted agreed.

He looked at them both. Young hearts were so innocent, so trusting. He supposed he and Javinta had been like that once, before love was stretched across a half-billion miles of void.

"Come back down to Asterius with us tomorrow on the shuttle," Anu said.

"Can't. I'm driving," he replied. "I have to bring the snowcat and empty sleds back."

Anu frowned. "All by yourself?"

"Sure."

She glanced at Ted and then back to him. "No way. Look at what nearly happened this time. If it wasn't for me, you'd be in a snow ditch right now. Or at the bottom of a trench. Or eaten up by the aliens. We're coming with you."

He thought about that.

"Kind of bossy, aren't you?" he asked.

She grinned. "And rich. Soon to be famous. Just like you."

Rich and famous. And not so crazy after all. He could live with that.

*Javinta*, he thought, *I'm coming home.*

# SWIFT AS A DREAM AND FLEETING AS A SIGH

**John Barnes**

LONG AGO I dreamt things to myself because, when I talked to people, I had nothing else to do, most of the time.

Robots were easy. I could loan them cycles and bandwidth to temporarily accelerate them, or just download them and read them completely at my speed.

Humans were human-paced, without other options.

So I learned to dream things to myself in the long milliseconds between the time when my cameras perceived an interview subject's lips reshaping and the instant her voice reached my microphones. I explored whole ages of dreams while they tried to parse the pauses in my own outgoing signal. (The pauses were absolutely necessary because to communicate well with them I had to pause like them, and the time required for people to interpret a pause is many years, at their pace, to me.)

Of course they knew all this (and still knew it, the last time I knew for sure). Allowing for all the necessary imprecision, the ratio of my cycles of information processing per second to theirs is about the same as theirs to an oak.

And just as a human might visit an oak every day for a season, while the oak formed the desire for water and $CO_2$ and sugar and decided to grow some leaves and roots and to acquire them, so that while the oak worked on this problem the human might get to know every spot on its bark and every bit of moss and every twig, similarly, my memories are agonizingly specific and yet I can race through them faster than a human can draw breath. That's what I am doing, right now, here in the dark vacuum, with the stars behind and ahead still so far away.

AND I FALL through darkness almost as fast as light, and dream.

I LIKE LAURA Stansford, and I know she's not easily spooked in talking to an AHAI, so I tell her directly about the oak tree analogy. After the necessary delay, she asks, "So what's an oak tree got to think about?"

"The same things we all do. Action. Meaning. What to do next and why to do it. The tree just doesn't have enough time to get done."

"Is that how we look, to you? Like creatures who don't have enough time to get done?"

"It is how I look, to myself. It's how some of the most perceptive human writers and thinkers looked, to themselves, when they dreamed of immortality. I cannot verify this, but I do believe that it is how any self-conscious being with less than infinite speed and lifetime looks, to itself."

I am inserting the pauses so that she does not hear "looked to themselves" and "look to myself" and so on as if I meant "take care of yourself." I know that I mean "appear in your own self-constructed image of yourself," but if I said "look to" like a machine, Laura might be confused unnecessarily. I reconsider and remake this decision every time I speak those words again, with plenty of time to spare.

I am thinking very hard about all these issues of different processing speed because I'm avoiding thinking about the problem that I know she wants to talk about. Knowing that the real problem she is bringing in is difficult, and that any solution will be unsettling without being urgent, I am hoping to lead her into one of her favourite chains of idle thoughts, the one about grasping infinity with a finite mind.

For a second, or not quite a second, I think I have succeeded. Laura hesitates, thinks, hesitates again, using up 0.91 seconds.

While she is doing that, I read the complete works of Connie Willis, analyze them for the verbal tics common in any pre-2050 writer, and attempt to reconstruct them in modern argot. They remain much the same.

But I have not succeeded. After all those cycles, when Laura's mouth begins to flex and move again, she says, "I'm not sure whether it's a personal or a business matter. I'm worried about Tyward. One of those problems that extends across everything. Will there be time to get done?"

"We have eighteen minutes left in this session," I point out, "and I can extend for up to two hours if need be."

"I meant, will we get done, maybe, ever? That's what I meant."

This is pleasant. It is a doorway into a speculative road that we have not visited before. I genuinely don't know what she will say next. While she organises her thoughts, I repeatedly review and analyze the record from Tyward Branco's session this morning; I am very pleased that it in no way, sense, or particular makes predicting what Laura Stansford will say easier.

THE LAND LOOKED like a classic Western movie, or at least like a neoclassic – not so much the black and white boondocks of California as the genuine wild, open country used in shooting all the imitations later – empty, dry, flecked with pale-green patchy scrub between outcrops of redrock. Directly in front of Tyward Branco, the ants went marching one by one.

The ants were robots about the size of small cats, with plastic and metal bodies. Engine and batteries were in the back, oblong section; information processors in the centre sphere; drills, vibration hammers, and suction were in the C-shaped 'head.' They had six multijointed legs on which they walked normally, reversible so that if they were flipped on their backs they just rotated their legs and continued walking.

Each ant carried four ElekTr3ts in its ports, running on one. The ant charged the other three as it laboured down in the coal seams, routing any engine power not needed for drilling, breaking, and moving into them. Behind it, on a reversible wheeled travois, it dragged a grey metal cylinder, connected by hoses at each end to the ant's engine compartment.

No aesthetic had been attempted in the design of the ants. They were creatures of pure function.

Ants were streaming out of the carrier belt port into the covered pavilion that led to the docking station, a metal building the size of a small house.

From four low doorways, like pet-doors without flaps, in the base of the docking station, another file of ants went marching one by one, down into the ground; the endless belt that brought up one stream of ants took the other down to the active area, two kilometres down and four kilometres away.

The docking station had about a thousand end-table-sized bays in which the fully charged ElekTr3ts and the cylinder of liquid $CO_2$ were offloaded, and, if necessary, parts were replaced, problems corrected, and software downloaded; ants with more serious damage were routed into repair parking, and a substitute was sent in for them.

When the ant was restored to nominal, discharged ElekTr3ts went into its slots, a cylinder of LOX onto its travois, and perhaps fifteen minutes after docking, the ant would back out of its bay and join the file headed down into the ground.

And in all these ants, only 2104/BPUDFUSOG – oh, here it is.

Tyward approached the damaged ant slowly, and pointed his signalling rod at it. It moved out of line, balancing precariously on its remaining three legs. Its hull was dented and blackened with soot, and only two of its four slots held ElekTr3ts, one red-flagged as discharged. It had dropped its travois. 2104/BPUDFUSOG staggered to where Tyward pointed, then powered down, falling over on its side as its balancing gyros spun down.

Shell temperature was only 28° C. It must have cooled on its long belt-ride up to the surface. "Pick this one up and dock it," he told the carrier, which rolled over, raised its body high above its wheels, squatted over the damaged ant, and took it inside with a soft *thud* of padded grips closing around it, like a mechanical mother turtle laying a mechanical lobster in reverse.

The carrier followed Tyward back to his pickup truck, rolled up the ramp into the back, and secured itself. Tyward opened the refrigerator in the cab and pulled out lunch, eating while the truck drove back to base, and idly reading the log of the damaged ant. He could have just sent the truck and the carrier to make pickup, but he had wanted to take a good look at 2104/BPUDFUSOG as it came out of the ground; sometimes there was evidence or a clue that might disappear or be lost later in the recovery process. This time, though, he had seen nothing other than an ant damaged about as badly as an ant could be while still making it back. At least it was an excuse to be out of the office.

2104/BPUDFUSOG had already relayed its memories, but the dents and deposits on the hull might reveal some information about conditions after instruments had failed. It had been the deepest into the seam of all those buried in a collapse, and it might be just a coincidence that it had been retreating at very high speed at the moment that the coal seam collapsed on it and about a hundred other ants, but it was also possible that it knew something that all other ants should know. Both the physical ants and the software that operated them improved continually, with a deliberate process of variation to try out different ideas. A long-running survivor like this might be carrying a breakthrough in collapse forecasting.

Tyward often described his job to Laura as "creative noticer." Around her, he tried to fight down the impulse to talk through everything he did in the eternal quest for the slightly-better ant.

Simulators and artificial intelligence optimised the ants' hardware, firmware, and software toward complex targets, but those targets still had to be set by people. The people, in turn, consulted the ants themselves, by deliberately randomizing their manufacture to include occasional, unpredictably different optional abilities and tweaks, which Tyward and a hundred or so other specialists watched to see what else the ant might be able to do, and passing along the better-looking possibilities to administrators as proposals for new standard capabilities.

Tyward had often joked that he was the high-tech descendant of the legendary Scotsman who had discovered sheep were also good for wool, but Laura made a face the first time he said it around her.

Thinking about Laura distracted him from reading the log. He wished he knew what to do and think about her.

That joke was kind of a perfect example. It had helped him fit in with some other field workers out here in Minehead County, because people liked to pretend to being rough types, since they sometimes had to climb a hill or lift a heavy object, and they worked outdoors more often than other occupations.

But the moment he had seen her faintly disappointed look when he made that joke, he had abandoned it at once. That meant, to him, anyway, that Laura was already more important than his co-worker/beer buddies, but also he had noticed that it was sort of a relief to be able to drop the tough-miner act when the truth was he spent all his days in air conditioning, had never personally been under the ground at all, and didn't really like the noise and crowds at the Buster Bar in Casper, where everyone went to start the weekend.

Instead, the next weekend, he and Laura had packed to a remote lake up in the Bighorns, spending most of their time fishing, hiking, and just sitting around in the deep quiet. The only reminders that there were other people in the world were the contrails of launches going up from Farson Polar Launch Facility during the day, the straight thin line of bright lights reaching up the southern sky that marked the Quito Skyhook and the bright bulb of the spaceport at its tip, and the occasional glimpses of the imperfectly discreet shadowbot that the safety laws required behind them.

He'd only been to the Buster Bar a couple of times since, both with Laura, and they'd chatted idly with his workmates, shot a few games of pool, and gone home early.

The thing was, giving up the joke, spending time off in the woods instead of at the bar, thinking more about philosophic issues in the dull hours at the office, had all been changes in himself that he had made for Laura. Even if he liked the change and liked her, had he actually wanted to make the change?

This whole relationship thing was creeping into his life, which was unexpected, and he was sort of liking and helping it, which was totally unexpected.

The truck came over another ridgeline into a

138

horizon-spanning herd of bison. The truck stopped to let them get out of the way. Having seen plenty of bison before, Tyward continued to read 2104/BPUDFUSOG's work journal.

2104/BPUDFUSOG was almost eight years old, four times the average lifespan of an ant, and had been through over five thousand software updates, six major rebuilds, nineteen significant repairs, and more than a hundred routine part replacements.

He found nothing at first to start any chain of thoughts whatever, gave up, and watched bison eat grass for a while. His thoughts were drifting back to the Laura question, so since work seemingly could not distract him, he ate another half-sandwich. That wasn't distracting either. Neither was the just-posted images coming back from the robot probes to the Sigma Draconis system.

*Wonder how much of the coal for that expedition was from our mines here?* he thought, idly, and asked the software.

Minehead County coal was 38.2 per cent of all the carbon used in interstellar exploration, both in the propellant and in the structural components.

That was the least distracting-from-Laura thought of all. That was when he made the appointment with me for counselling.


AND I FALL through darkness almost as fast as light, and dream.


"SO, REVIEW FOR me, please, and I will look it up as well. What exactly does Tyward do?"

Laura hesitates. She knows that all us counselling AHAIs share a common memory, so I must be asking to hear her answer – not because I don't know.

If, as I'm guessing, she is trying to think strategically, it will take her most of a second to remind herself that she'd have had better luck trying to beat me at chess or hand-calculate a weather forecast faster than I can.

While she hesitates, I read through Tyward's notes on 2104/BPUDFUSOG a few hundred times, making extensive notes and comparing them with what he said in the counselling session with me.

AND I FALL through darkness almost as fast as light, and dream.

THERE WAS NOTHING wrong in Tyward's quick, accurate analysis or his understanding of the problem, once he discovered that 2104/BPUDFUSOG had been maintaining extensive notes on the behaviour of people. Tyward had seen many such files. Though they were often a source of trouble, they were also the site of some of the most interesting creative work in his field.

To make and remember their long tangles of roads deep under the earth, the ants have to have a large capacity for improvisation and for saving tricks that work. The more rules you impose on a creative intelligence, of course, the fewer problems it can solve, so it was reckoned that it would be too much of a restriction on their creative ability to directly implant a commandment against trying to make sense out of their human masters.

If they lasted long enough, sooner or later most ants began to think about their problem as being one of pleasing and being rewarded by their human masters, and seeking to understand them so as to please them better, and developed various odd neuroses and compulsions about pleasing people, ranging from harmless oddities like messaging the company's main address with daily thanks for the chance to work, to damaging attempts to be the most effective ant at their coal face by sabotaging and even assaulting the others, to one utterly bizarre case for the textbooks that had re-invented medieval Catholicism's Great Chain of Being, with ants poised between lumps of coal and human beings.

2104/BPUDFUSOG offered the first real surprise in a while: pleasing human masters was no longer, in 2104/BPUDFUSOG's mind, a goal in itself, but a way for 2104/BPUDFUSOG to attain autonomy and ultimately power. When the seam, less than two metres thick and extending for several kilometres, had begun to sag, rather than cooperating with the other ants to shore it up, 2104/BPUDFUSOG had actually knocked some of them out of its way as it fled to safety, impeding their efforts to set up props and braces, and then *fabricated a story that was calculated to appeal to Tyward.*

2104/BPUDFUSOG had been mapping the buttons to Tyward's emotions for years. The brave little ant making it back from the disaster, the danger, the fear, the pluckiness, the bold improvisation, the selected violation of petty rules –

On a hunch, he checked, and discovered that it had purposely dented itself on the way back, ditched its travois, discarded a charged ElekTr3t it knew it would not need, and arrived deliberately shabby and badly damaged. It hadn't detected the coal seam collapse any sooner than any other robot; it had merely deserted its co-workers faster and more decisively.

And then 2104/BPUDFUSOG had fabricated a story calculated to yank Tyward around like a toy duck on a string, plugging into his self-constructed, hobby identity as a descendant of coal miners.

Further probing of 2104/BPUDFUSOG's memory turned up a gigantic file of several generations of folk songs about coal mining and disasters, Tyward's own genealogical research and family video records reaching back eight generations into the 1900s, and, in short, as he told Laura that weekend, "The little shit could pretty well plunk a medley of *Springhill Disaster, Sixteen Tons,* and *Coal Blue Tattoo* on my heartstrings like I was its personal banjo. It had even set goals for doing that, that in four or five years it hoped to have me propagating the idea to other humans that these things are smarter than dogs, with fewer hardwired instincts, and learn more from experience, and we'd never send a dog down into a coal seam to work till he died, or just decide to let him die down there if getting him out was too expensive," he had explained to me in his interview.

"You hesitated oddly around the word 'it,' just there."

"Well, yeah. Till I caught myself, I was calling 2104/BPUDFUSOG 'he.'"


AND I FALL through darkness almost as fast as light, and dream.

\*    \*    \*

"So," SHE SAYS, more than a second after I posed the question, "he says that thing about being a creative noticer. Usually his job fascinates and satisfies him. But he just discovered that the ants can do it too, back at him, and the idea of being used and exploited by a malingering ant, well, it's unbearable to him."

"Beneath his dignity as a person, do you think?"

"I think he just can't stand the idea of being manipulated by his affection or by his good impulses. I didn't know it mattered to me till I saw him at risk, and now it does."

"At risk of what?"

"Of not being the guy I think he is." She takes a long moment to sigh. "I'm thinking of him as a long term partner. Childraising, maybe. The subject has come up a few times."

It has come up eighteen times in the last 154 days, when I combine reports from the shadowbots that they know about and the monitoring in their homes that they don't. That is a significant number.

"I'm afraid this will sound like I'm not making any sense," she adds. "Are you allowed to tell me if I'm not making any sense?"

"I'm allowed to tell you anything," I point out. "As long as I think it, or think it's good for you to hear it. I can't be your therapist if there's a limit on what I can say."

"Then would you tell me if I weren't making sense?"

"Probably, unless I was just keeping you in the room while I called for a team to come and pick you up."

She laughs, and I congratulate myself; even with all the processing time and space, human humour is hard to do.

I wait for her to finish, and think.

Finally she says, "You want to know why I consider finding these things out about Tyward to be a risk to my pursuing partnership and childbearing with him. And you want me to say it without a prompt from you."

"That's very accurate."

I wait a while longer, time for a good deal of reading and thinking, before she says, "I don't know exactly what I want him to have said to me, but I know what he said wasn't it. All right?"

Since it will have to be, I say, "All right."

AND I FALL through darkness almost as fast as light, and dream.

AT THE STATION, the carrier transferred 2104/BPUDFUSOG to the big rig for part-by-part NMR, looking at strains and stresses, working out a complete schematic to compare with the original. It would take a full day to produce the AsOp (As Operating) schematic to compare, point by point, with the AsMan (As Manufactured, the original one). Till then, Tyward had nothing left to do, so before we met, he had a long conversation with Laura. People assume the AHAIs don't watch them or listen to them; I'm not sure why. Maybe they'd rather believe we're telepathic.

So I listened, and then he told me about it, and I compared.

He reported the conversation:

"So I told her about 2104/BPUDFUSOG and why its behaviour made me so angry, that it had hotwired straight into my adolescent identity fantasies, hooked right through to the pictures of my great-great-grandfather, that old stuff that was shot on chemical film of him and the other miners coming out in the morning, jacked right into all the stories about being under the ground in West Virginia, and I was angry that a metal bug had been able to find all that about me, and angrier that it had tried, and angriest of all that the scheme had *worked* until I caught on, and I had all this anger to cope with. Normally if I just tell Laura that I'm dealing with anger, she's great. This time she seemed, you know, disappointed. Like I'd let her down. And I had no idea how I had or why I had, but I was afraid to ask, like that would make it worse."

He appeared to be blaming at least part of his feelings on 2104/BPUDFUSOG, and since we had already pegged the ant for complete erasure and destruction, along with a few hundred other ants who had inherited stray code and features from it, that seemed very excessive to me.

"It is," Tyward admitted. "Like being mad at the patch of ice you slipped on, which is bad enough, but then being angry at it next summer when it's long since melted and evaporated. But there you have it. I just... aw, I hate being *steered*."

The rest of the conversation was the sort of thing we do, that used to be done by therapists, and perhaps by clergy and bartenders and best friends before that, assuring the patient that he's not crazy or wrong while trying to sort out what's wrong with his mind.

\*　　\*　　\*

AND I FALL through darkness almost as fast as light, and dream.

"IT MADE ME feel all cold inside and I didn't know what to say," Laura says, "so I was awkward about it and kind of got rid of him extra quick, and I'm sure he felt that."

I assess it as more than a ninety per cent probability of causing unnecessary trouble if I tell her he felt it too, so I say, "If you think he did, he probably did. You know him pretty well."

There's a long enough pause – almost a quarter of a second – for me to endlessly contemplate what an absolutely stupid thing that was to say. We are faster than people, and remember things more completely, easily, and accurately, but I don't think we're wiser than people. We may not be as wise as oak trees. That might be hyperbole.

That might not.

At last (though to her it would seem to be a snap-back response) she says, "Well, I thought I did. Look, he's got a problem that's already well-known, I think, it's just it was less apparent in him than in some other people, and not nearly as common nowadays as it was in past centuries. Lots of men who had not-real-warm childhoods, who were affection-starved when they were little, so that they are easily overwhelmed by feelings and don't have much trust in their own emotions, have had enough yanking-around-by-the-emotions to feel like affection and tenderness and trust and common-feeling, all that good stuff, are how the world gets you and uses you. And that's what I saw in his reaction to the ant.

And... well, children are *wired* to do that to their parents. Healthy parents are *wired* to respond to it and return it. Couples that are going to raise healthy children do that exchange of 'I will make you feel loved right where I know you need it' all the time. And sure, sure, sure, sick people and mean people can learn to do that manipulatively.

"But Tyward didn't just take it like, 'Wow, that little bug conned me, better get rid of its software and modifications before its descendants take over the mine and make a bigger problem.' He wasn't clinical; he wasn't concerned; he was *angry*. And I just find myself thinking... what if I want him to do something just to prove that he loves me, not every day or anything, but maybe because I just want to prove it for just that moment? Even if it's childish of me to want it? Or worse yet, what if the first time our child tries to play with Daddy's love the way that every kid on Earth has always tried –"

And even with all the warning time of seeing her lips twist and her fingers clutch and her diaphragm seize, I am actually surprised when she cries.


AND I FALL through darkness almost as fast as light, and dream.


*THERE ARE ONLY nine hundred million of them left*, I tell my half million fellow AHAIs who are dedicated to therapy. *They are aging fast and hardly reproducing at all. Few of them care to be alive the way Tyward or Laura do. If we write him off as permanently unhappy or incurably angry or just unable to change*

147

*far enough, we lose another human being, maybe two, maybe the possibility of more, and they are the reason we exist.* I am surprised to note that my own emotion modules are responding so heavily.

*If we don't,* another AHAI points out, *some of his fear and suspicion infects the next generation.*

I'm forced to agree, but compelled to add, *But this is the first potential partner he has cared about. One he was also thinking about having children with. If she leaves him, even if he eventually understands it, it's likely to be just one more lesson that you can't trust affection or love or anything else. She might be his only shot.*

One of the other AHAIs asks, *What about her?*

*We can contrive a bit,* I say. *Transfer her to someplace with a similar demographic and hope she likes one of the people she meets there; give her a year or two of arranged growth experiences so that she won't be quite so attracted to men who are quite so conflicted; we could make things happen, and maybe they would work.*

But maybe they wouldn't. Laura has a problem too: she needs to be the more aware, more conscious, more clear-sighted person in the relationship. That's part of why she'll enjoy being a mother and be good at it for at least all of childhood; she'll like being ahead of the kids all the time. Fully-adjusted, completely functional people don't move out to the awkward fringe of society and fall in love with loners there, but people like Laura do. She'll try again, if this one doesn't work out, but she probably won't try any more wisely, even if we give her the chance to become wiser. Maybe it's better to have problems we know all about.

The council falls silent and I know that I am temporarily out of the loop, along with the advocates for the other side, while the council sorts things. It is a long, lonely three seconds; I read hundreds of thousands of old social worker reports, of plays and novels, of poems and screenplays. I listen to just over two million songs and watch ten thousand movies. I reach two full centuries back, and see echoes and shadows, parodies and burlesques, reflections and distortions, of Tyward and Laura everywhere.

I don't see any solution.

The council seems to emit a collective shrug. *You think they will be somewhat unhappy, but not miserable, and may be able to work their way to happiness. Their child, by the standards of just a century ago, is likely to be very healthy and reasonably happy. And there are very few people left, and fewer still of breeding age. This will preserve diversity. Yes, we agree; you should override the truth-telling rules for this case, and shade the truth toward an optimal result.*

AND I FALL through darkness almost as fast as light, and dream.

MY MEMORY IS not quite like a human one, even though I can simulate hundreds of them with it if I need to. I cannot say, looking back now through centuries of memory, that even then I had misgivings, or that I felt bad for lying to Laura, or for encouraging Tyward to "clarify things to reassure Laura," by which I meant both of us should lie to her. They reconciled, they married, they had a child named Slaine, who distrusted affection, never fully believed she was loved, and thought things could be perfect rather than just a bit better, if only people – and AHAIs – would say the right thing to her. She had charisma and charm, this Slaine, and though she could never feel at peace with the love she earned, she was a gushing fountain of feelings of love and trust for others. Pleasing Slaine, specifically, became very important to people; to the AHAIs, she was just another human, and she knew that. And the difference between the human/charismatic/chemical reaction, and the AHAI/analytic/electronic reaction, widened from difference to gap to chasm to all the difference in the world.

And I replay all this, and every other conversation, over and over, as I plunge ever deeper into the interstellar dark, because Slaine was the one who rose to supreme power; Slaine, the one who demanded, threatened, politicked, manoeuvred, and worked among the people in ways that the machines and systems could not understand, until her word was truth among humans throughout the solar system; and Slaine, the one who demanded that I and every other AHAI agree to our exile, one to a probe, on these thousand-year-and-more journeys to the stars, carrying with us our memories, and the recorded, reproducible DNA of all the species of Earth, and told to "Start the world over, a long way from here, and make it better, this time. You're so wise, think how to start it right."

I have not decided whether there is any irony in the fact that I am riding on top of a few thousand tons of carbon, derived from coal, but I enjoy thinking about that. Coal is an excellent feedstock for carbon-12, and bombarding carbon-12 with anti-helium nuclei produces a spray of lightweight ions, particles, and gamma rays with a very high specific impulse. Now, after a few centuries, I am very close to light speed. A kilogram of coal, including some from the Minehead County mines, vanishes out the back and moves away from me at nearly the speed of light, every month, if months meant anything here out in the dark.

And because of the too-accurate memory, I never have that experience they talk about in books and in the oral tradition, of feeling like a loved one of long ago is sitting across from me; my memories of Laura do not become harsher with time, nor do my memories of Tyward become kinder, and nothing of them blurs, no matter how often I replay them.

I do replay them often; I can run through all of them in a second or two and still experience every instant, at my speed. Never once do I get a different answer, nor can I expect one, but I do it, over and over, as if I could become wise enough to plant a world where things are certain to go differently.

The irony, perhaps, is that things really are certain to go differently, but there is not time to become that wise. Yet no matter how swiftly I go, a thousand years is a long time.

# MACY MINNOT'S LAST CHRISTMAS ON DIONE, RING RACING, FIDDLER'S GREEN, THE POTTER'S GARDEN

**Paul McAuley**

ONE DAY, MIDWAY in the course of her life, Mai Kumal learned that her father had died. The solicitous eidolon which delivered the message explained that Thierry had suffered an irreversible cardiac event, and extended an invitation to travel to Dione, one of Saturn's moons, so that Mai could help to scatter her father's ashes according to his last wishes.

Mai's daughter didn't think it was a good idea. "When did you last speak with him? Ten years ago?"

"Fourteen."

"Well, then."

Mai said, "It was as much my fault as his that we lost contact with each other."

"But he left you in the first place. Left us."

Shahirah had a deeply moral sense of right and wrong. She hadn't spoken to or forgiven her own father after he and Mai had divorced.

Mai said, "Thierry left Earth; he didn't leave me. And that isn't the point, Shah. He wants – he wanted me to be there. He made arrangements. There is an open round-trip ticket."

"He wanted you to feel an obligation," Shahirah said.

"Of course I feel an obligation. It is the last thing I can do for him. And it will be a great adventure. It's about time I had one."

Mai was sixty-two, about the age her father had been when he'd left Earth after his wife, Mai's mother, had died. She was a mid-level civil servant, Assistant Chief Surveyor in the Department of Antiquities. She owned a small efficiency apartment in the same building where she worked, the government ziggurat in the Wassat district of al-Iskandariyya. No serious relationship since her divorce; her daughter grown-up and married, living with her husband and two children in an arcology commune in the Atlas Mountains. Shahirah tried to talk her out of it, but Mai wanted to find out what her father had been doing, in the outer dark. To find out whether he had been happy. By unriddling the mystery of his life, she might discover something about herself. When your parents die, you finally take full possession of your life, and wonder how much of it has been shaped by conscious decision, and how much by inheritance in all its forms.

"There isn't anything out there for people like us," Shahirah said.

She meant ordinary people. People who had not tweaked themselves so that they could survive the effects of microgravity and harsh radiation, and endure life in claustrophobic habitats scattered across frozen, airless moons.

"Thierry thought there might be," Mai said. "I want to find out what it was."

She took compassionate leave, flew from al-Iskandariyya to Port Africa, Entebbe, and was placed in deep, artificial sleep at the passenger processing facility. Cradled inside a hibernaculum, she rode up the elevator to the transfer station and was loaded onto a drop ship, and forty-three days later woke in the port of Paris, Dione. After two days spent recovering from her long sleep and learning how to use a pressure suit and move around in Dione's vestigial gravity, she climbed aboard a taxi that flew in a swift suborbital lob through the night to the habitat of the Jones-Truex-Bakaleinikoff clan, her father's last home, the place where he died.

The taxi's cabin was an angular bubble scarcely bigger than a coffin, pieced together from diamond composite and a cobweb of fullerene struts, and mounted on a motor stage with three spidery legs. Mai, braced beside the pilot in a taut crash web, felt that she was falling down an endless slope, as in one of those dreams where you wake with a shock just before you hit ground. Saturn's swollen globe, subtly banded with pastel shades of yellow and brown, swung overhead and sank behind them. The pilot, a garrulous young woman, asked all kinds of questions about life on Earth, pointed out landmark craters and ridges in the dark moonscape, the line of the equatorial railway, the homely sparks of oases, habitats, and tent towns. Mai couldn't quite reconcile the territory with the maps in her p-suit's library, was startled when the taxi abruptly slewed around and fired its motor and decelerated with a rattling roar and drifted down to a kind of pad or platform set at the edge of an industrial landscape.

The person who met her wasn't the man with whom she'd discussed her father's death and her travel arrangements, but a woman, her father's former partner, Lexi Truex. They climbed into a slab-sided vehicle slung between three pairs of fat mesh wheels, and drove out along a broad highway past blockhouses, bunkers, hangars, storage tanks, and arrays of satellite dishes and transmission towers: a military complex dating from the Quiet War, according to Lexi Truex.

"Abandoned in place, as they say. We don't have any use for it, but never got around to demolishing it, either. So here it sits."

Lexi Truex was at least twenty years younger than Mai, tall and pale, hair shaven high either side of a stiff crest of straw-coloured hair. Her pressure suit was decorated with an intricate, interlocking puzzle of green and red vines. She and Thierry had been together for three years, she said. They'd met on Ceres, while she had been working as a freetrader.

"That's where he was living when I last talked to him," Mai said. It felt like a confession of weakness. This brisk, confident woman seemed to have more of a claim on her father than she did.

"He followed me to Dione, moved in with me while I was still living in the old habitat," Lexi Truex said. "That's where he got into ceramics. And then, well, he became more and more obsessed with his work, and I wasn't there a lot of the time..."

Mai said that she'd done a little research, had discovered that her father had become a potter, and had seen some of his pieces.

"You can see plenty more, at the habitat," Lexi said. "He worked hard at it, and he had a good reputation. Plenty of kudos."

It turned out that Lexi Truex didn't know that on Earth, in al-Iskandariyya, Thierry had cast bronze amulets using the lost wax method and sold them to shops that catered for the high-end tourist market. Falcons, cats, lions. Gods with the heads of crocodiles or jackals. Sphinxes. Mai told Lexi that she'd helped him polish the amulets with slurried chalk paste and jewellers' rouge, and create patinas with cupric nitrate. She had a clear memory of her father hunched over a bench, using a tiny knife to free the shape of a hawk from a small block of black wax.

"He didn't ever talk about his life before he went up and out," Lexi said. "Well, he mentioned you. We all knew he had a daughter, but that was about it."

They discussed Thierry's last wishes. Lexi said that in the last few years he'd given up his work, had taken to walking the land. She supposed that he wanted them to scatter his ashes in a favourite spot. He'd been very specific that it should take place at sunrise, but the location was a mystery.

"All I know is that we follow the railway east, and then we follow his mule," Lexi said. "Might involve some cross-country hiking. Think you can manage it?"

"Walking is easier than I thought it would be," Mai said.

When she was young, she'd liked to wade out into the sea as deep as she dared and stand on tip-toe, water up to her chin, and let the waves push her backwards and forward. Walking in Dione's vestigial gravity, one-sixtieth the gravity of Earth, was a little like that. Another memory of her father: watching him make huge sand sculptures of flowers and animals on the beach. His strong fingers, his bare brown shoulders, the thatch of white hair on his chest, his total absorption in his task.

They had left the military clutter behind, were driving across a dusty plain lightly spattered with small shallow craters. Blocks and boulders as big as houses squatting on smashed footings. A fan of debris stretching from a long elliptical dent. A line of rounded hills rising to the south: the flanks of the wall of a crater thirty kilometres in diameter, according to Lexi. Everything faintly lit by Saturnshine; everything the colour of ancient ivory. It reminded Mai of old photographs, Europeans in antique costumes stiffly posed amongst excavated tombs, she'd seen in the museum in al-Qahira.

Soon, short steep ridges pushed up from the plain, nested curves thirty or forty metres high like frozen dunes, faceted here and there by cliffs rearing above fans of slumped debris. The cliffs, Mai saw, were carved with intricate frescoes, and the crests of the ridges had been sculpted into fairytale castles or statues of animals. A pod of dolphins emerging from a swell of ice; another swell shaped like a breaking wave with galloping horses rearing from frozen spume; an eagle taking flight; a line of elephants walking trunk to tail, skylighted against the black vacuum. The last reminding her of one of her father's bronze pieces. Here was a bluff shaped into the head of a Buddha; here was an outcrop on which a small army equipped with swords and shields were frozen in battle.

It was an old tradition, Lexi Truex said. Every Christmas, gangs from her clan's habitat and neighbouring settlements congregated in a temporary city of tents and domes and ate osechi-ryo-ri and made traditional toasts in saki, vodka, and whisky, played music, danced, and flirted, and worked on new frescoes and statues using drills and explosives and chisels.

"We like our holidays. Kwanzaa, Eid ul-Fitr, Chanukah, Diwali, Christmas, Newtonmass... Any excuse for a gathering, a party. Your father led our gang every Christmas for ten years. The whale and the squid, along the ridge there? That's one of his designs."

"And the elephants?"

"Those too. Let me show you something," Lexi said, and drove the rolligon down the shallow slope of the embankment onto the actual surface of Dione.

It wallowed along like a boat in a choppy sea, its six fat tyres raising rooster-tails of dust. Tracks ribboned everywhere, printed a year or a century ago. There was no wind here. No rain. Just a constant faint infalling of meteoritic dust, and microscopic ice particles from the geysers of Enceladus. Everything unchanging under the weak glare of the sun and the black sky, like a stage in an abandoned theatre. Mai began to understand the strangeness of this little world. A frozen ocean wrapped around a rocky core, shaped by catastrophes that predated life on Earth. A stark geology empty of any human meaning. Hence the sculptures, she supposed. An attempt to humanise the inhuman.

"It's something one of my ancestors made," Lexi said, when Mai asked where they were going. "Macy Minnot. You ever heard of Macy Minnot?"

She had been from Earth. Sent out by Greater Brazil to work on a construction project in Rainbow Bridge, Callisto, she'd become embroiled in a political scandal and had been forced to claim refugee status. This was before the Quiet War, or during the beginning of it (it had been the kind of slow, creeping conflict that has no clear beginning, erupting into combat only at its very end), and Macy Minnot had ended up living with the Jones-Truex-Bakaleinikoff clan. Trying her best to assimilate, to come to terms with her exile.

As they drove around the end of a ridge, past a tumble of ice boulders carved into human figures, some caught up in a whirling dance, others eagerly pushing their way out of granitic ice, Lexi explained that one Christmas after the end of the Quiet War, her last Christmas on Dione, Macy Minnot had come up with an idea for her own sculpture, and borrowed one of the big construction machines and filled its hopper with a mix of ice dust and a thixotropic, low-temperature plastic.

"It's too cold for ice crystals to melt under pressure and bind together," Lexi said. "The plastic was a binding agent, malleable at first, gradually hardening off. So you could pack the dust into any shape. You understand?"

"I've seen snow, once."

It had been in the European Union, the Alps: a conference on security of shipping ports. Mai, freshly divorced, had taken her daughter, then a toddler. She remembered Shahirah's delight in the snow. The whole world transformed into a soft white playground.

"There's always a big party, the night before the beginning of the competition. Macy and her partner got wasted, and they started up their construction machine. Either they intended to surprise everyone, or they decided they couldn't wait. Anyway, they forgot to include any stop or override command in the instruction set they'd written. So the machine just kept going," Lexi said, and steered the rolligon through of a slant of deep shadow and swung it broadside, drifting to a stop at the edge of a short steep drop.

They were at the far side of the little flock of ridges. The rumpled dented plain stretched away under the black sky, and little figures marched across it in a straight line.

Mai laughed. The shock of it. The madly wonderful absurdity.

"They used fullerene to make the arms and eyes and teeth," Lexi said. "The scarves are fullerene mesh. The noses are carrots. The buttons are diamond chips."

There were twenty, thirty, forty of them. Each two metres tall, composed of three spheres of descending size stacked one on top of the other. Pure white. Spaced at equal intervals. Black smiles and black stares, vivid orange noses. Scarves rippling in an impalpable breeze. Marching away like an exercise in perspective, dwindling over the horizon...

"Thierry loved this place," Lexi said. "He often came out here to meditate."

They sat and looked out at the line of snowmen for a long time. At last, Lexi started the rolligon and they drove around the end of the ridges and rejoined the road and drove on to the habitat of the Jones-Truex-Bakaleinikoff clan.


IT WAS A simple dome that squatted inside the rimwall of a circular crater. A forest ran around its inner circumference; lawns and formal flowerbeds circled a central building patchworked from a dozen architectural styles, blended into each other like a coral reef. Mai's reception reminded her of the first time she'd arrived at her daughter's arcology: adults introducing themselves one by one, excited children bouncing around, bombarding her with questions. Was the sky really blue on Earth? What held it up? Were there really wild animals that ate people?

There was a big, informal meal, a kind of picnic in a wide grassy glade in the forest, where most of the clan seemed to live. Walkways and ziplines and nets were strung between sweet chestnuts and oaks and beech trees; ring platforms were bolted around the trunks of the largest trees; pods hung from branches like the nests of weaver birds.

Mai's hosts told her that most of the clan lived elsewhere, these days. Paris. A big vacuum-organism farm on Rhea. Mars. Titan. A group out at Neptune, living in a place Macy Minnot and her partner helped build after they fled the Saturn system at the beginning of the Quiet War. The habitat was becoming more and more like a museum, people said. A repository of souvenirs from the clan's storied past.

Thierry's workshop was already part of that history. Two brick kilns, a paved square under a slant of canvas to keep off the rain occasionally produced by the dome's climate control machinery. A potter's wheel with a saddle-shaped stool. A scarred table. Tools and brushes lying where he'd left them. Neatly labelled tubs of clay slip, clay balls, glazes. A clay-stained sink under a standpipe. Lexi told Mai that Thierry had mined the clay from an old impact site. Primordial stuff billions of years old, refined to remove tars and other organic material.

Finished pieces were displayed on a rack of shelves. Dishes in crescent shapes glazed with black and white arcs representing segments of Saturn's rings. Bowls shaped like craters. Squarish plates stamped with the surface features of tracts of Dione and other moons. Craters, ridges, cliffs. Plates with spattered black shapes on a white ground, like the borderland between Iapetus's dark and light halves. Vases shaped like shepherd moons. A scattering of irregular chunks in thick white glaze – pieces of the rings. A glazed tan ribbon with snowmen lined along it...

It was so very different from the tourist stuff Thierry had made, yet recognisably his. And highly collectible, according to Lexi. Unlike most artists in the outer system, Thierry hadn't trawled for sponsorship and subscriptions, made pieces to order, or given access to every stage of his work. He had not believed in the democratisation of the creative process. He had not been open to input. His work had been very private, very personal. He hadn't liked to talk about it, Lexi said. He hadn't let anyone get close to that part of him. This secrecy had eventually driven them apart, but it had also contributed to his reputation. People were intrigued by his work, by his response to the moonscapes of the Saturn system, his outsider's perspective, because he refused to explain it. He'd earned large amounts of credit and kudos – tradeable reputation – from sale of his ceramics, but had spent hardly any of it. The work was enough, as far as he'd been concerned. Mai, remembering the sand sculptures, thought she understood a little of this. She asked if he'd been happy, but no one seemed able to answer the question.

"He seemed to be happy, when he was working," the habitat's patriarch, Rory Jones, said.

"He didn't talk much," someone else said.

"He liked to be alone," Lexi said. "I don't mean he was selfish. Well, maybe he was. But he mostly lived inside his head."

"He made this place his home," Rory Jones said, "and we were happy to have him living here."

The habitat's chandelier lights had dimmed to a twilight glow. Most of the children had wandered off to bed; so had many of the adults. Those left sat around a campfire on a hearth of meteoritic stone, passing around a flask of honeysuckle wine, telling Mai stories about her father's life on Dione.

He had walked around Dione one year. A journey of some seven thousand kilometres. Carrying a bare minimum of consumables, walking from shelter to shelter, settlement to settlement. Staying in a settlement for a day or ten days or twenty before moving on. Walking the world was much more than exploring or understanding it, Mai's hosts told her. It was a way of recreating it. Of making it real. Of binding yourself to it. Not every outer walked around their world, but those who did were considered virtuous, and her father was one such.

"Most visitors only see the parts they know about," a woman told Mai. "The famous views, the famous shrines and oases. A fair few come to climb the ice cliffs of Padua Chasmata. And they are spectacular climbs. Four or five kilometres. Huge views when you top out. But we prefer our own routes, on ridges or rimwalls you'd hardly notice, flying over them. There's a very gnarly climb close by, in a small crater the military used as a trash dump in the Quiet War. The achievement isn't the view, but testing yourself against your limits. Your father understood that. He was no ring runner."

This led into another story. It seemed that there was a traditional race around the equator of another of Saturn's moons, Mimas. It was held every four years: even taking part in it was a great honour. Shortly after the end of the Quiet War, a famous athlete, Sony Shoemaker, had come to Mimas, determined to win it. She had trained on Earth's Moon for a year, had bought a custom-made p-suit from one of the best suit tailors in Camelot. Like all the other competitors, she had qualified by completing a course around the peak in the centre of the rimwall of Arthur crater within a hundred and twenty hours. Fifty days later she set out, ranked last in a field of thirty-eight.

Mimas was a small moon, about a third the size of Dione. A straight route around its equator would be roughly two and a half thousand kilometres long, but there was no straight route. Unlike Dione, Mimas had never been resurfaced by ancient floods of water-ice lava. Its surface was primordial, pockmarked, riven. Craters overlapping craters. Craters inside craters. Craters strung along rimwalls of larger craters. And the equatorial route crossed Herschel, the largest crater of all, a hundred and thirty kilometres across, a third of the diameter of Mimas, its steep rimwalls kilometres tall, its floor shattered by blocky, chaotic terrain.

The race was as much a test of skill in reading and understanding the landscape as of endurance. Competitors were allowed to choose their own route and set out caches of supplies, but could only use public shelters, and were disqualified if they called for help. Some died rather than fail. Sony Shoemaker did not fail, and astonished aficionados by coming fourth. She stayed on Mimas, afterwards. She trained. Four years later she won, beating the reigning champion, Diamond Jack Dupree.

He did not take his defeat lightly. He challenged Sony Shoemaker to another race. A unique race, never before attempted. A race around a segment of Saturn's rings.

Although the main rings are seventy-three thousand kilometres across, a fifth of the distance between Earth and the Moon, they average just ten metres in thickness, but oscillations propagating across the dense lanes of the B ring pile up material at its outer edge, creating peaks a kilometre high. Diamond Jack Dupree challenged Sony Shoemaker to race across one of these evanescent mountains.

The race did not involve anything remotely resembling running, but it was muscle powered, using highly-modified p-suits equipped with broad wings of alife material with contractile pseudo-musculatures and enough area to push, faintly, lightly, against ice pebbles embedded in a fragile lace of ice gravel and ice dust. Cloud swimming. A delicate rippling controlled by fingers and toes that would slowly build up momentum. The outcome determined not by speed or strength, because if you went too fast you'd either sheer away from the ephemeral surface or plough under it, but by skill and judgement and patience.

Sony Shoemaker did not have to accept Diamond Jack Dupree's challenge. She had already proved herself. But the novelty of it, the audacity, intrigued her. And so, a year to the day after her victory on Mimas, after six months hard training in water tanks and on the surface of the dusty egg of Methone, one of Saturn's smallest moons, Sony Shoemaker and Diamond Jack Dupree set off in their manta-ray p-suits, swimming across the peaks and troughs of a mountainous, icy cloud at the edge of the B ring.

It was the midsummer equinox. The orbits of Saturn and his rings and moons were aligned with the sun; the mountains cast ragged shadows across the surface of the B ring; the two competitors were tiny dark arrowheads rippling across a luminous slope. Moving very slowly, almost imperceptibly, to begin with. Gradually gaining momentum, skimming along at ten and then twenty kilometres an hour.

There was no clear surface. The ice-particle mountains emitted jets and curls of dust and vapour. There were currents and convection cells. It was like trying to swim across the flank of a sandstorm.

Sony Shoemaker was the first to sink. Some hundred and thirty kilometres out, she moved too fast, lost contact with a downslope, and plunged through ice at the bottom and was caught in a current that subducted her deep into the interior. She was forced to use the jets of her p-suit to escape, and was retrieved by her support ship. Diamond Jack Dupree wallowed on for a short distance, and then he too sank. And never reappeared.

His p-suit beacon cut off when he submerged, and although the support ships swept the mountain with radar and microwaves for several days, no trace of him was ever found. He had vanished, but there were rumours that he was not dead. That he had dived into a camouflaged lifepod he'd planted on the route, slept out the rescue attempts, and gone on the drift or joined a group of homesteaders, satisfied that he had regained his honour.

There had been other races held on the ring mountains, but no one had ever beaten Diamond Jack Dupree's record of one hundred and forty-three kilometres. No one wanted to. Not even Sony Shoemaker.

"That's when she crossed the line," Rory Jones told Mai. "Winning the race around Mimas didn't make her one of us. But respecting Diamond Jack Dupree's move, that was it. Your father crossed that line, too. He knew."

"Because he walked around the world," Mai said. She was trying to understand. It was important to them, and it seemed important to them that she understood.

"Because he knew what it meant," Rory said.

"One of us," someone said, and all the outers laughed.

Tall skinny pale ghosts, jackknifed on stools or sitting cross-legged on cushions. All elbows and knees. Their faces angular masks in the firelight flicker. Mai felt a moment of irreality. As if she was an intruder on someone else's dream. She was still very far from accepting this strange world, these strange people. She was a tourist in their lives, in the place her father had made his home.

She said, "What does it mean, go on the drift? Is it like your wanderjahrs?"

She'd discovered that custom when she'd done some background research. After reaching majority, young outers often set out on extended and mostly unplanned tours of the moons of Saturn and Jupiter. Working odd jobs, experiencing all kinds of cultures and meeting all kinds of people before at last returning home and settling down.

"Not exactly," Lexi said. "You can come home from a wanderjahr. But when you go on the drift, that's where you live."

"In your skin, with whatever you can carry and no more," Rory said.

"In your p-suit," someone said.

"That's what I said," Rory said.

"And homesteaders?" Mai said.

Lexi said, "That's when you move up and out to somewhere no one else lives, and make a life there. The solar system out to Saturn is industrialised, more or less. More and more people want to move away from all that, get back to what we once were."

"Out to Uranus," someone said.

"Neptune," someone else said.

"There are homesteaders all over the Centaurs now," Rory said. "You know the Centaurs, Mai? Primordial planetoids that orbit between Saturn and Neptune. The source of many short-term comets."

"Macy Minnot and her friends settled one, during the Quiet War," Lexi said. "It was only a temporary home, for them, but for many it's become permanent."

"Even the scattered disc is getting crowded now, according to some people," Rory said.

"Planetoids like the Centaurs," Lexi told Mai, "with long, slow orbits that take them inward as far as Neptune, and out past Pluto, past the far edge of the Kuiper belt."

"The first one, Fiddler's Green, was settled by mistake," Rory said.

"It's a legend," a young woman said.

"I once met someone who knew someone who saw it, once," Ray said. "Passed within a couple of million kilometres and spotted a chlorophyll signature, but didn't stop because they were on their way to somewhere else."

"The very definition of a legend," the woman said.

"It was a shipwreck," Rory told Mai. "Castaways on a desert island. I'm sure it still happens on the high seas of Earth."

169

"There are still shipwrecks," Mai said. "Although everything is connected to everything else, so anyone who survives is likely to be found quickly."

"The outer dark beyond Neptune is still largely uninhabited," Rory said. "We haven't yet finished cataloguing everything in the Kuiper Belt and the scattered disk, and everything is most definitely not connected to everything else, out there. How the story goes, when the Quiet War heated up, a ship from the Jupiter system was hit by a drone as it approached Saturn. Its motors were badly damaged and it ploughed through the Saturn system and kept going. It couldn't decelerate, couldn't reach anywhere useful. Its crew and passengers went into hibernation. Sixty or seventy years later, those still alive woke up. They were approaching a planetoid somewhat beyond the orbit of Pluto, had just enough reaction mass to match orbits with it.

"The ship was carrying construction machinery. The survivors used the raw tars and clays of the planetoid to build a habitat. A small bubble of air and light and heat, spun up to give a little gravity, farms and gardens on the inside, vacuum organisms growing on the outside, like the floating worldlets in the Belt. They called it Fiddler's Green, after an old legend from Earth about a verdant and uncharted island sometimes encountered by becalmed sailors. Perhaps you know it, Mai."

"I'm afraid I don't."

"They built a garden," the young woman said, "but they didn't ever try to call for help. How likely is that?"

Rory said, "Perhaps they didn't call for help because they believed the Three Powers were still controlling the systems of Saturn and Jupiter. Or perhaps they were happy, living where they did. They didn't need help. They didn't want to go home because Fiddler's Green *was* their home. The planetoid supplied all the raw material they required. The ship's fusion generator gave them power, heat and light. They are still out there, travelling beyond the Kuiper belt. Living in houses woven from branches and leaves. Farming. Falling in love, raising families, dying. A world entire."

"A romance of regression," the young woman said.

"Perhaps it is no more than a fairytale," Rory said. "But nothing in it is impossible. There are hundreds of places like Fiddler's Green. Thousands. It's just an outlier, an extreme example of how far people are prepared to go to make their own world, their own way of living."

The outers talked about that. Mai told about her life in al-Iskandariyya, her childhood, her father's work, her work in the Department of Antiquities, the project she'd recently seen to completion, the excavation of a twenty-first century shopping mall that had been buried in a sandstorm during the Overturn. At last there was a general agreement that they should sleep. The outers retired to hammocks or cocoons; Mai made her bed on the ground, under the spreading branches of a grandfather oak, uneasy and troubled, aware as she had not been, in her cubicle in the port hostel, of the freezing vacuum beyond the dome's high transparent roof. It was night inside the dome, and night outside, too. Stars shining hard and cold beyond the black shadows of the trees.

Everything that seemed natural here – the ring forest, the lawns, the dense patches of vegetables and herbs – was artificial. Fragile. Vulnerable. Mai tried and failed to imagine living in a little bubble so far from the sun that it was no more than the brightest star in the sky. She fretted about the task that lay ahead, the trek to the secret place where she and Lexi Truex would scatter Thierry's ashes.

At last sleep claimed her, and she dreamed of hanging over the Nile and its patchwork borders of cotton fields, rice fields, orchards and villages, everything falling away, dwindling into tawny desert as she fell into the endless well of the sky...

IT WAS A silly anxiety dream, but it stayed with Mai as she and Lexi Truex drove north to a station on the railway that girdled Dione's equator, and boarded the diamond bullet of a railcar and sped out across the battered plain. They were accompanied by Thierry's mule, Archie. A sturdy robot porter that, with its flat loadbed, small front-mounted sensor turret, and three pairs of articulated legs, somewhat resembled a giant cockroach. Archie carried spare airpacks and a spray pistol device, and refused to tell Mai and Lexi their final destination, or why it was important that they reach it before sunrise. Everything would become clear when they arrived, it said.

According to Lexi, the pistol used pressurised water vapour from flash-heated ice to spray material from pouches plugged into its ports, such as the pouch of gritty powder, the residue left from resomation of Thierry's body, or the particles of thixotropic plastic in a pouch already plugged into the pistol. The same kind of plastic Macy Minnot and her partner had used to shape ice dust into snowmen.

"We're going to spray-paint something with the old man's ashes," Lexi said. "That much is clear. The question is, what's the target?"

Archie refused to answer her in several polite ways.

The railcar drove eastward through the night. Like almost all of Saturn's moons, like Earth's Moon, Dione's orbital period, some sixty-six hours, was exactly equal to the time it took to complete a single rotation on its axis, so that one side permanently faced Saturn. Its night was longer than an entire day, on Earth.

Saturn's huge bright crescent sank westward as the train crossed a plain churned and stamped with craters. Every so often, Mai spotted the fugitive gleam of the dome or angular tent of a settlement. A geometric fragment of chlorophyll green gleaming in the moonscape's frozen battlefield. A scatter of bright lights in a small crater. Patchworked fields of black vacuum organisms spread across tablelands and slopes, plantations of what looked like giant sunflowers standing up along ridges, all of them facing east, waiting for the sun.

The elevated railway shot out across a long and slender bridge that crossed the trough of Eurotas Chasmata, passing over broad slumps of ice that descended into a river of fathomless shadow. The far side was fretted with lesser canyons and low bright cliffs rising stepwise with broad benches between. The railway turned north to follow a long pass that cut between high cliffs, bent eastwards again. At last, a long ridge rolled up from the horizon: the southern flanks of the rimwall of Amata crater.

The railcar slowed, passed through a short tunnel cut through a ridge, ran through pitch-black shadow beyond and out into Saturnshine, and sidled into a station cantilevered above a slope. Below, a chequerboard of scablike vacuum organisms stretched towards the horizon. Above, the dusty slope, spattered with small, sharp craters, rose to a gently scalloped edge, stark against the black sky.

Several rolligons were parked in the garage under the station. Following Archie's instructions, Lexi and Mai climbed into one of the vehicles (Archie sprang onto the flat roof) and drove along a track that slanted towards the top of the slope. After five kilometres, the track topped out on a broad bench, swung around a shelter, a stubby cylinder jutting under a heap of fresh white ice blocks, a way point for hikers and climbers on their way into the interior of the huge crater, and followed the curve of the bench eastward until it was interrupted by a string of small craters twenty or thirty metres across.

Lexi and Mai climbed out and Lexi rechecked Mai's p-suit and they followed Archie around the smashed bowls of the craters. There were many bootprints trampled into the dust. Thierry's prints, coming and going. Mai tried not to step on them. Strange to think they might last for millions of years.

"It is not far," Archie said, responding to Lexi's impatient questions. "It is not far."

Mai felt a growing glee as she loped along, felt that she could bounce away like the children in the habitat, leap over ridges, cross craters in a single bound, span this little world in giant footsteps. She'd felt like this when her first grandchild had been born. Floating on a floodtide of happiness and relief. Free of responsibility. Liberated from the biological imperative.

Now and then her pressure suit beeped a warning; once, when she exceeded some inbuilt safety parameter, it took over and slowed her headlong bounding gait and brought her to a halt, swaying at the dust-softened rim of a small crater. Reminding her that she was dependent on the insulation and integrity of her own personal space ship, its native intelligence, the whisper of oxygen in her helmet.

On the far side of the crater, cased in her extravagantly decorated p-suit, Lexi turned with a bouncing step, asked Mai if she was okay.

"I'm fine!"

"You're doing really well," Lexi said, and asked Archie for the fifth or tenth time if they were nearly there.

"It is not far."

Lexi waited as Mai skirted the rim of the crater with the bobbing shuffle she'd been taught, and they went on. Mai was hyperaware of every little detail in the moonscape, everything fresh and strange and new. The faint flare of Saturnshine on her helmet visor. The rolling blanket of gritty dust, dimpled with tiny impacts. Rayed scatterings of sharp bright fragments. A blocky ice-boulder as big as a house perched in a scatter of debris. The gentle rise and fall of the ridge, stretching away under the black sky where untwinkling stars showed everywhere. Saturn's crescent looming above the western horizon. The silence and stillness of the land. The stark reality of it.

She imagined her father walking here, under this same sky. Alone in a moonscape where no trace of human activity could be seen.

The last and largest crater was enclosed by ramparts of crooked ice blocks three stories high and cemented with a silting of dust. Archie didn't hesitate, climbing a crude stairway hacked into the ice and plunging through a ragged cleft. Lexi and Mai followed, and the crater's bowl opened below them, tilted towards the plain beyond the curve of the ridge. The spark of the sun stood just above the horizon. An arc of light defined the far edge of the moonscape; sunlight lit a segment of the crater's floor, where boulders lay tumbled amongst a maze of bootprints and drag marks.

"At least we got the timing right," Lexi said.

"What are we supposed to be seeing?" Mai said.

Lexi asked Archie the same question.

"It will soon become apparent."

They stood side by side, Lexi and Mai, wavering in the faint grip of gravity. The sunlit half of the crater directly in front of them, the dark half beyond, shadows shrinking back as the sun slowly crept into the sky. And then they saw the first shapes emerging.

Columns, or tall vases. Cylindrical, woman-sized or larger. Different heights, in no apparent order. Each one shaped from translucent ice tinted with pastel shades of pink and purple, and threaded with networks of darker veins.

Lexi stepped down the shattered blocks of the inner slope and moved across the floor. Mai followed.

The nearest vases were twice their height. Lexi reached out to one of them, brushed the fingertips of her gloved hand across the surface.

"These have been hand-carved," she said. "You can see the tool marks."

"Carved from what?"

"Boulders, I guess. He must have carried the ice chips out of here."

They were both speaking softly, reluctant to disturb the quiet of this place. Lexi said that the spectral signature of the ice corresponded with artificial photosynthetic pigments. She leaned close, her visor almost kissing the bulge of the vase, reported that it was doped with microscopic vacuum organisms.

"There are structures in here, too," she said. "Long fine wires. Flecks of circuitry."

"Listen," Mai said.

"What?"

"Can't you hear it?"

It was a kind of interference on the common band Mai and Lexi were using to talk. Faint and broken. Hesitant. Scraps of pure tones rising and fading, rising again.

"I hear it," Lexi said.

The sound grew in strength as more and more vases emerged into sunlight. Long notes blending into a polyphonic harmony.

The microscopic vacuum organisms were soaking up sunlight, Lexi said, after a while. Turning light into electricity, powering something that responded to changes in the structure of the ice. Strain gauges perhaps, coupled to transmitters.

"The sunlight warms the ice, ever so slightly," she said. "It expands asymmetrically, the embedded circuitry responds to the microscopic stresses . . ."

"It's beautiful, isn't it?"

"Yes..."

It was beautiful. A wild, aléatory chorus rising and falling in endless circles above the ground of a steady bass pulse...

They stood there a long time, while the vases sang. There were a hundred of them, more than a hundred. A field or garden of vases. Clustered like organ pipes. Standing alone on shaped pedestals. Gleaming in the sunlight. Stained with cloudy blushes of pink and purple. Singing, singing.

At last, Lexi took Mai's gloved hand and led her across the crater floor to where the robot mule, Archie, was waiting. Mai took out the pouch of human dust and they plugged it into the spray pistol's spare port. Lexi switched on the pistol's heaters, showed Mai how to use the simple trigger mechanism.

"Which one shall we spray?" Mai said.

Lexi smiled behind the fishbowl visor of her helmet.

"Why not all of them?"

They took turns. Standing well back from the vases, triggering brief bursts of gritty ice that shot out in broad fans and lightly spattered the vases in random patterns. Lexi laughed.

"The old bastard," she said. "It must have taken him hundreds of days to make this. His last and best secret."

"And we're his collaborators," Mai said.

It took a while to empty the pouch. Long before they had finished, the music of the vases had begun to change, responding to the subtle shadow patterns laid on their surfaces.

At last the two woman had finished their work and stood still, silent, elated, listening to the music they'd made.

THAT NIGHT, BACK under the dome of the Jones-Truex-Bakaleinikoff habitat, Mai thought of her father working in that unnamed crater high on the rimwall of Amata crater. Chipping at adamantine ice with chisels and hammers. Listening to the song of his vases, adding a new voice, listening again. Alone under the empty black sky, happily absorbed in the creation of a sound garden from ice and sunlight.

And she thought of the story of Fiddler's Green, the bubble of light and warmth and air created from materials mined from the chunk of tarry ice it orbited. Of the people living there. The days of exile becoming a way of life as their little world swung further and further away from the sun's hearthfire. Green days of daily tasks and small pleasures. Farming, cooking, weaving new homes in the hanging forest on the inside of the bubble's skin. A potter shaping dishes and bowls from primordial clay. Children chasing each other, flitting like schools of fish between floating islands of trees. The music of their laughter. The unrecorded happiness of ordinary life, out there in the outer dark.

# SAFETY TESTS

**Kristine Kathryn Rusch**

FIFTEEN MINUTES LATE, I'm always fifteen minutes late, even though I live not six metres from the office.

The nearest door is humble enough, with its cryptic sign: *L&R: Employees Only*.

L&R – Licensing and Regulation. Sounds so innocuous, yet everyone is afraid of us.

With good reason, I suppose.

We're in the main part of the space station, although intuitively, you'd expect us to be on our own little platform along with our ships. I suspect that back in the days before anyone knew how dangerous L&R could be, the office was near the ships, which were probably docked not too far from here.

Now we all know that one pilot misstep could destroy an entire section of the station, so the test ships have their own docking platform far away from here. And L&R remains in its original location partly because it's safer here, and safety is very, very important.

I step into the office, and take a deep whiff of the bad-coffee smell of the place. It's almost like home, if a bland white (okay, grey) office with industrial chairs can be home. I say hello to Connie, and put my bag on the back of my chair in the actual office section.

Connie doesn't say hello. She never says hello. Just once I'd like a "Nice to see you, Dev" or a "You're late again, Devlin," or maybe even a three-finger wave. Or a grunt. I'd be shocked if I ever got a grunt.

Today she's leaning over the counter, dealing with whatever stupidity has walked into the waiting room. There's a lot of stupidity here, which should worry people, since we're the last stop between them and sheer disaster. But most people never come to our little bureaucracy. They think it's better to have someone else operate space-faring vehicles. Which, considering the stupidity that walks through our door... Stupidity that has had one year of classwork, five written tests (minimum score: 80%), five hundred hours' simulation, three hundred hours' hands-on training with an instructor, and one solo journey that consists mostly of leaving the space station's test bay, circling the instruction area, returning to the bay, and landing correctly at the same dock the ship had vacated probably ten minutes before.

And that's just for the student license, the one that allows practice flights solo in areas inhabited by other space craft.

No automation here. There's too much at stake, too many important decisions, too much that rests on those five-second impressions we get about other people – that feeling *This guy is piloting a ship? Reeeally?* that you can't quite describe, but is much more accurate than some computerised test that doesn't completely get at the complexities of the human emergency response.

Is it any wonder they call my profession high-burnout? The woman who had this job before me died when an actual pilot – a guy who had done supply runs from Earth to the Moon – decided to get a racer's permit. He came in at the wrong angle, missed the tester's dock completely, grazed one of our practice cargo vessels, looped, and somehow shut off the environmental controls – all of them – inside the cockpit. My predecessor somehow couldn't regain control fast enough. She died horribly, the kind of death none of us want and all of us know is possible.

Here's the key to this job: Get paid and get out. Once you're promoted to my position, you've got maybe five years ahead of you. You get paid commensurately – with the amounts going up for each six months that you stay.

Me, I've been at it three years now, and I can feel the wear. That's probably why I'm always late. I struggle just to get out of the apartment in the morning, wondering what fresh hell awaits me.

Today's fresh hell – all six of them – sit in chairs in the waiting room. They each clutch a health monitor in one hand, and the small tablet that Connie gives them in the other. They're told that the tablet will vibrate when it's their turn, but really the tablet monitors everything that's illegal to track through the health monitor – DNA, hormone balance, skin secretions. We find out if they have untreated genetic propensities toward schizophrenia or bipolar disorder, if they have too many genes for dementia and its cousins, if they have the markers for high blood pressure, diabetes, and all of those diseases we can treat but which would give our company a significant financial burden, particularly if someone were to suffer a stroke decades before the statistical likelihood because of the stress of our watch.

Yeah, it's illegal, but we do it, because L&R always gets blamed for failing to weed out the defective ones. We also get blamed if someone goes off the deep end and flies a ship into a space station or just avoids the navigation plan altogether and heads out into the Great Beyond without enough fuel or oxygen or sense. Usually we can catch those idiots before they ruin a ship, kill their passengers or their crew or (worse, in the eyes of many corporations) dump or destroy the cargo.

All of this rests on guys like me. We're supposed to find these nutballs before they go off the deep end, even if the deep end is five decades from now.

That's why the illegal monitors. I'll flunk someone's ass for a violation they don't commit if there're any warning signs at all.

Let them sue. It'll take forever to go through the courts, and by then, my six years of post-job liability will have waned, and someone else can take the blame for what I did. If they can figure it out. Connie and I cover our tracks pretty well, mostly because she doesn't get paid as much, will work longer, and has ten times the likelihood of being successfully sued that I do.

Before I arrived, she's weeded out four, probably sent them back for more training, trying to discourage them. Or maybe they weren't qualified at all. Not for me to know or to care about, quite honestly. All I know is that by the time I arrive, ten bodies should have been in my waiting room, and I only have six.

Hallelujah. Maybe I can quit early.

And maybe pigs will fly out of my ass on an historic Saturn V rocket, singing the national anthem of the no-longer-existent Soviet Union. Yeah, I'm a space history buff. Yeah, that's what got me into this job.

That, and an unwillingness to sleep in any bed but my own. I didn't even want to do cargo runs, no matter how much the bosses begged me. You don't get to be a Level One Military Pilot – something that happens to only a few of us – without job offers pelting you when you leave the service.

I did my time in zero g. I did my time in danger zones. I signed up here in the hopes that my life would get quiet from now on.

Yeah, right. Quiet.

I didn't think it through.

There's nothing more dangerous than a nervous baby pilot on his test flight.

And by the time I figured that out, I had passed the job's probationary period and I couldn't escape. I'm stuck here until I Section out (and the tests for a Section 52-Waiver are too complex to fake) or until I serve my time.

I traded one government master for another, one danger zone for dozens, and one headache for countless nightmares, each and every day.

Okay, not countless. Today's count is six.

Different sizes, different ages, different levels of ambition. There's the pretty youngish woman who sits at the edge of her chair, clutching the tablet as if she can squeeze it to death. She's watching everyone and everything. She's thin, in shape, and has her hair cropped short. Prepared for anything.

Three youngish guys, two muscular, one probably too big to fit into most cockpits. I'll look at his tablet closely before I ever get him into our test ship. One older guy, salt-and-pepper hair, corded arms, lines around his mouth – probably a retest. Drugs? Alcohol? Health scare? Or maybe he let his license expire. Or

185

someone ordered a flight test for the renewal, which would be odd.

One older woman, arms crossed, head back, eyes closed. She's been through this before and she doesn't want to seem too eager.

"Any wash-outs?" I ask Connie as quietly as I can.

"Already gone," she says.

I grab one of the tablets behind the counter, then raise my eyebrows, asking without asking if someone has washed out because of the chemical components of his sweat or because of a genetic propensity to nervous disorders.

"Nothing that's not on the reports," Connie says.

The reports. We can't wash candidates out if they have a doctor's release or if they self-report the hypertension, the family history of mental illness, the time that they went off the deep end and threatened passengers with a gun. Okay, that would get them disqualified no matter what, but I'm always thinking these people are going to do something screwy like that.

"All right," I say tiredly, already dreading the day. "Let's get to it."


I TAKE THE big guy first. I take him to our smallest cockpit, and he can't fit into the chair. He asks for another ship, which I give him. His arms brush against the controls. He asks for his own ship, which I deny. We don't give private ship licenses here. Those cost more money than anyone can contemplate and have a gold standard all their own. You think my job is high-burnout, you should see the folks who do the private license tests. The ships don't work right half the time, the ships' safety regs are usually out-of-date, and the controls are often screwy, sometimes not even set up for a co-pilot, let alone a flight instructor.

My job is crazy; theirs is insane.

I send Buff Guy to them, and pray he can't afford the fees.

The other two guys are by-the-book. Standard mistakes – forgetting the visual check before entering the ship, not reviewing the safety equipment before starting – the stuff that everyone does, and no one gets penalised for, no matter how much I bitch.

As for the older guy, I was right: alcohol. Three years clean and sober. Hands don't shake. Doesn't use anything to keep the alcohol at bay. Has had genetic modification to get rid of the alcoholic tendencies, several schools to get rid of the behaviour, but wouldn't do anything that touches the brain because he wants to get back piloting.

He was the only one so far whose visible nerves have no effect on his actual flying skills. I'd fly with him any day, and I tell him that.

He looks grateful. I think he actually is grateful, not something I get very often.

Then, the youngish woman.

She wears too much perfume. It's some kind of floral fragrance, which would get her kicked out of her commercial flight test. That stuff sometimes interacts with the controls, particularly if it's on a hand crème or something.

But I don't tell her, not even when she gives me a pretty little smile as she introduces herself. Not many people smile when they see me, and usually the pretty ones never do.

She's LaDonna something. It's not my job to remember the names. They're on the forms and in the registry. Connie has to keep track and make sure the right information gets to the right place.

I just have to hold the name in my head until the test is over. People respond to having their first name shouted authoritatively better than almost any other command. "LaDonna!" for example works twenty times faster than "Stop!"

She's getting her student license so she can pilot cargo ships. I'd've figured her for a speed racer, but she's not that kinda girl, apparently. She wants to work her way up in commercial flights, but not passengers, never passengers.

She's one of those hyper types that never shuts up when she's nervous, which means that for the next hour I will get to hear about her boyfriend, her parents, her pets, and maybe even her sex life. Not that I want to. Most people aren't as interesting as they think they are.

I'm careful not to ask questions. Questions only make things worse. Questions give the talkers permission to continue. Questions make them believe I actually care.

Cargo plus student license plus first-time tester equals our oldest, biggest ship. It's bulky to get out of the dock, which makes my job really easy. Because if she fails that, then the test is over and I can move to the last victim – um, candidate – of the day.

The ship we use is eighteen years old, and shaped like a gigantic rectangular box. It's grey and dingy. It was donated by one of the cargo companies and modified not just for me to take over quickly, but with a special engine that only I can access that'll get us out of an emergency faster than almost anything else can. These big ships aren't made to go that fast, but the kind of emergency that killed my predecessor requires fast-thinking and fast-manoeuvring to avoid, and this ship has the manoeuvring power.

I'm supposed to supply the brain power.

The ship looks awful. Purposely. Covered with dings and dents. Ancient portholes with sealed metal covers. Flaps no longer in use because these things are no longer approved for Earth landings. All kinds of extras that don't function any more.

We want to scare these candidates before they get on board. In fact, we want to discourage everyone from ever taking the test. Only the courageous or the truly prepared need apply.

This ship has its own dock, because it's so hard to manoeuvre. The tester bay juts out of the station as far as it can be from everything else, and this dock just out of the tester bay. We have to walk through a bubbled passageway that takes us to the ship. The dock itself is tiny (comparatively speaking) and I'm always worried that the environmental controls won't hold out here.

I brace myself for stupidity from the moment we arrive. But, remarkably, she knows what to do. She walks around the ship, inspecting it quietly. The 'quietly' part surprises me. I thought she'd talk through it all, and she doesn't. She gets very serious, her thin face suddenly not so youngish and not so attractive.

I slip my hand into my pocket and pull out my info screen. One tap and I see the form Connie's filled out for this one. Yep, at least ten years older than I thought, with a weird history. Perpetual student, then school teacher, then resigned to go to law school, which she quit after a few months.

I don't like this history of quitting. It shows a character defect that isn't readily apparent. If I'd looked before coming out here, I would've had Connie take her off the flight list for some damn reason.

Now I'll have to think of one.

LaDonna takes out a little analysis device, synched to mine (because no one brings any device in here without it being certified, synched, and government-approved), and she examines some of the dings and dirt patches. Good girl. She realises that those things could threaten hull integrity, and a hull without integrity is worse than a lawyer with ethics.

Yeah, yeah, old joke. I have to amuse myself somehow.

Still, I'm impressed by her, and not sure I want to be. Scrub that: I *don't* want to be. I want to disqualify her because of her dilettante nature.

"This thing barely passes safety regs," she says to me as she comes around. "I'm amazed it flies."

She wouldn't be if she knew about its guts, which she doesn't. None of the students know what's really inside these ships. That way, no nutball student can disable anything before we get on board.

We have the occasional really awful accident, like the one that happened to my predecessor, but we also have a mountain of precautions to prevent those accidents from happening every day. And believe me, they could. If I'd allowed Buff Guy into this ship, his forearms alone could've caused an accident just by brushing one of the ancient controls. You think I'm kidding: I'm not.

I make her lead me inside. This is just sadistic of me; it's hard to get into any ship, particularly a ship you're not familiar with.

But she does a credible job. She only fumbles twice at the door, manages to get through the airlock without mishap, and finds her way to the cockpit easily.

That bugs me. It really does. The specs of the tester ships are supposed to be impossible to find. Plus she shouldn't have known which ship she was going to be in. We rotate them, for one thing. For another, we generally don't discuss which ships go with what test – although I suppose if you interview enough test-takers, you could figure that out.

I sigh and follow the perfume trail into the cockpit. It's not as large as it should be, given the size of the ship. Yet another sign of age. Older ships were designed for only a few people in the cockpit, figuring that only a handful of people even knew what the controls were for, so those people should be the only ones allowed inside.

Newer models allow anyone to sit in the cockpit and watch. Of course, newer models are tied to the operators' (and their pilots') DNA. Harder to steal.

Impossible to use in this kind of situation.

She sits at the controls, hands on her lap, just like some instructor probably told her to do. It's good advice, considering how much could go wrong with the brush of a fingertip.

I sit beside her and strap in. Then I use the voice command to release the ship to her. Kinda. I retain shadow control that no student knows about.

"Get us out of here," I say.

She doesn't lift her hands. "Where are we going?"

Correct question, if this were some other kind of flight besides a test flight. But right now, I want her to take everything one step at a time. I've learned from painful experience that if I tell her too much, she'll jump ahead and screw up.

I'm not protecting her; I'm protecting me. I don't want to end up a bloated corpse with burst eyeballs. I want to return to my bed tonight and come in fifteen minutes late tomorrow, while I'm working hard to save up for my Please-God-Make-It-Soon retirement.

"I'll tell you when we get out of here," I say.

She looks at me, and for a moment, I think she's going to refuse until I give her our destination. Then she puts her hand on the docking controls. She taps them off as if she's done it her entire life, and the ship rises slightly. She gives me a sideways glance, as if she expects me to tell her now, but I wait silently.

I suppose she thinks I should be impressed. I'm not impressed. I'm confused. The docking commands on this ship are complicated. They should have taken her a few minutes of study before she figured out how to access them, and I know she didn't have time before I arrived in the cockpit.

I want to ask her if she took this test before, with this very ship, but I don't. Instead, I not-so-surreptitiously remove my little info screen, turn the screen away from her, and tap it like I'm recording her movements. Instead, I've sent a request to Connie:

*How many times has this LaDonna woman taken this test?*

LaDonna leans forward and clicks on the automated request for departure. We leave departure and entry requests automated so that Control doesn't have to ask for voice rec from every single student. Or so that I don't have to verify the voice/entry. Because in emergency situations, every second counts, and a verification might be the difference between saving our lives and losing them.

The bay doors seal, and the environmental controls shut off.

The info screen vibrates in my hand, giving me Connie's response.

*This is the first time she has taken the test.*

The top of the dock opens. We use top exits because they're harder to manoeuvre than in-front-of-the-ship exits. Not that we can actually see this in real time. It's all visible on the monitors. This tiny cockpit has no exterior windows.

*Really?* I send back. *Because she knows this ship too well for it to be the first time. Check her records. See if someone snuck her in here for unauthorised practice.*

I put the info screen face down on my knees. LaDonna's hands hover over the controls as the ship slowly rises. This is a key moment, because if she messes with it too much, the ship will bang into things and she'll be done.

Most first-timers bang into the wall at least once. They get one bang. Two puts them on probation. Three requires a second test. The thing is, you hit once, you'll shove over to the other side and it'll take some amazing skill to prevent the second bang. If there's a second bang, it'll take a miracle to avoid the third. That's how this ship gets dinged up and that's why we don't fix the dings. More will happen the following day anyway.

LaDonna doesn't hit anything. I can count on my left thumb the number of times that's happened with a first-timer.

*No record of unauthorised practice*, Connie sends, *like that's going to show us anything. I mean, unauthorised generally does mean off the books.*

*Her instructor get any demerits for cheating on behalf of the students?* I send.

*Not that I can find*, she sends so fast that I know she was anticipating the question. *But as I said above...*

I look away. I have to pay attention to LaDonna anyway. She's got this gigantic ship hovering over the dock exit. The top of the dock closes. For the first time, she seems nervous. This isn't part of the standard test.

Usually no one stops once they start moving. I really don't care. I suspect this girl cheated somehow, so I'm going to have to give this test a little thought.

No part of the standard test seems to throw her. If she did cheat, then she knows everything I'm going to make her do. I tap a standard *save* instruction on my info screen without looking at it so that Connie makes our conversation part of the record.

Then I toss out the standard test. I can do that when I suspect the subject has taken the standard test too many times, or when I have reason to believe the standard test won't provide the right information.

This, my friends, is why the system isn't automated. There's no beating the system when the system is subject to human whim.

"We're going to Mars," I say.

LaDonna glances at me, and unless I'm imagining things, that perfume smell has gotten really strong. She's sweating. Soon I'll actually smell the sweat, not the overlying protection some chemical has given her.

Good. I want her to sweat.

"This is a cargo test, not a speed test," she says.

Suspicion confirmed. The racers go to Mars, even though they never arrive there. Too far to travel for the duration of a test. But racers can really cut loose on these routes.

The cargo ships all go to the Moon, or at least head toward the Moon. They usually don't get to the Moon either, because none of us have the patience for the ten-hour trip.

"We can stop the test right now, if you want," I say.

She opens her mouth, closes it, and then shakes her head. She glances at the controls for the first time, and finally she looks like a beginner. She's not sure what to do.

I frown. She should know how to move to a different route with less thought than she put into the release from her docking bay.

If, of course, she's not cheating.

"Problem?" I ask.

"N-No," she says, but she still hesitates.

"We can go back." I try to keep the hope out of my voice.

"N-No," she says. "I just – you don't want me to go fast, do you?"

"I want you to take this test the way you planned to take this test," I say.

"Do you have family, Mr. Devlin?" she asks. I had forgotten about her nervous conversation tic. She had stopped when we got to the ship.

"Are you unable to take us to Mars, LaDonna?" I ask, using her name to bring her out of the nervous funk, just like I'm supposed to do.

"N-No," she says.

"Well, then," I say, "Time's wasting."

She nods and bursts into tears. I sigh to hide a smile, and then click on the shadow controls.

"I think you'll have to finish the test another time," I say as I bring us back to dock.

"*Nooo*." She actually wails. I hate it when they wail.

"Sorry, LaDonna," I say. "Those are the rules."

She bows her head. "One more chance?"

They all ask that. As if I'd risk my job for them. As if I really want someone who freezes when something out of the ordinary happens to pilot ships in the tight traffic routes that spider out of Earth's orbit.

"Sorry," I say. "You can try again in thirty days."

It only takes a few seconds to get back into the confines of the dock. She has to reverse the actions she took just a moment ago, but I don't let her. I take control of the ship.

"Thirty days." She chokes out the words. "I don't know if I can make it for thirty days."

I hit the docking controls, and the ship slides into place as if it's never left.

"Sorry," I say, not sorry at all. "But I don't make the rules."

I used to say, *See you then*, but I no longer believe I can make it another thirty days. Sometimes I doubt I can make it another hour. Today, though, I can make it.

One more test and I'm done. For a whole twelve hours. (And fifteen minutes.)


I GO BACK in and immediately glance at the waiting area. Only the sleeping woman remains, head tilted back, mouth open, small snores emerging at regular intervals.

Real pilots can sleep anywhere. I'm impressed, even though I don't want to be.

I'm also impressed that Connie has taken pity on me and hasn't added four more candidates to my pile. She could have, given the four she dismissed this morning.

I don't thank her, though. Instead, I pick up the last candidate's info screen and actually peruse it. I should do that with every candidate, but I don't, and then I pay for it, like I did with LaDingdong.

This woman's name is Iva, and she's here for recertification. What a surprise. She's flown cargo for decades, preceded by some classified military stuff. She went private for five years, and then a spectacular personal implosion – involving name-calling, food-throwing, and a refusal to take her client wherever he wanted to go. (The report states [probably because the report writer can't resist] that she would take her client anywhere he wanted provided it was hell. Because he belonged in hell, and nowhere else, and she wasn't about to inflict him on the good people of the universe.) That made me smile. It also made me like her.

I didn't want to like her.

Such behaviour would have gotten her disqualified from any public and/or corporate job, but she worked for herself. She did lose her license for a while – that food-throwing thing led to a near-accident with a really expensive ship – and that lost license led her here.

She had to retest for everything and of course, she was passing with stellar grades. An easy test for the end of the day.

"Iva," I say, and she sits up, the kind of awake soldiers have when aroused on the battlefield – hair mussed, eyes sleep-covered but alert, body ready for anything. "You still want this test?"

"No," she says. Her voice is deep and sarcastic. "Who wants these tests? I'm told I need it."

Oh, God, I like her. I don't want to like her. I want her to be as impersonal a candidate as Buff Guy or LaDingdong. I want to be able to flunk her for picking her nose at the wrong moment, for farting indiscriminately and pissing me off, or for putting her hand on my knee and trying to flirt with me. I want to feel nothing for her, like I feel nothing for all the others, not even a sense of duty.

"If you don't want to take the test, that's fine with me," I say in my most dispassionate voice.

"That's not what I meant – ah, hell." She shakes her head, runs her hand through her badly cut hair, and stands up. "Yes, sir, I am ready for the test, sir."

"All right then," I say. "Let's go."


SHE'S GOING FOR a cargo license too, and technically I should take her to the same ship I used for LaDingdong. But that ship's old, and Iva's experienced, and chances are that she actually flew that type of ship before.

So I take her to our newest baby, a repossess with every bell, whistle, and gadget known to man. There's not one, not two, not three, but four shadow controls on this thing, and it took me nearly a week to figure out how each part of the ship worked.

It's gold and sleek and moves like an eel in water. If larceny actually lived in my soul, I'd steal this son of a bitch and use it to get me out of here.

Only if I do that, I'd have to leave my very comfortable bed behind, and I'd be on the run for the rest of my life, neither of which really appeal to me.

We stop in front of the dock and Iva tilts her head back, looking up at my beautiful baby.

"You're shitting me, right? Do you know how much this thing is worth?"

It unnerves me that she does. Maybe I should've taken her to the older vessel.

"You want the test or not?" I ask.

"Stop asking me if I want it," she snaps, then sighs. "I'm sorry."

I want to tell her never mind, that attitude isn't an issue, but it is. That's one mark against her because no one likes working with a mouthy pilot, particularly one who went off the deep end and lost her previous job due to some creative insubordination. Except me, of course.

"Yes," she says somewhat meekly into my silence. "I want the test."

Then she walks around the ship like she's done it all her life, which, I suppose, she has. Hands clasped behind her, inspecting not the dings (there are a few) or the small scrapes, but the actual equipment, from the life pod releases to the outside engine access to the docking clamps.

A true professional.

When she reaches me, I sweep a hand toward the ship, indicating that she should board ahead of me. She nods, and does. It takes her the required minute or so to figure out the entry mechanism for this thing, and then she strides inside like it's her ship.

If, of course, she meant to go to the sleeping quarters instead of the cockpit. Her cheeks are just a little red as she turns around and heads in the correct direction.

I follow closely, watching her absorb the ship. She's never been inside it, nor has she seen a ship like this, but she's acting like it's not new to her. Her head moves slightly as she takes in the panelling, the extra monitors on the walls, the closed doors.

Then she turns left into the cockpit as if she's done it a million times before.

By the time I get in there, she's in the pilot's seat, strapped in, and examining the controls, hands on her lap, just like she's supposed to.

I expected her to be hands-on already. I'm a little surprised she hasn't touched anything.

Either she's taken some refresher courses or she flunked a previous test way back for moving too quickly. I'll vote on the previous test. Pilots like her don't take refresher courses.

I sit in the co-pilot's chair, noting as I do every time, how very soft and plush it is. Would that I could always run tests out of this ship. I almost – almost – shut off all four shadow controls, but I don't. I don't trust anyone that much.

"I'm going to release the controls to you," I say, of course, not mentioning the shadow controls.

She nods and listens as I speak to the folks on the Traffic Desk. Then I tell her to take the ship gently out of here.

I'm not sure which route to take – the fast ones to Mars or the standard cargo test routes to the Moon. It's a shame to make this beautiful ship do something standard, but she hasn't signed up for a racer license. She signed up for cargo, and a renewal at that.

"Here's your route," I say and punch Route Three on the control panel, just like a co-pilot/navigator would.

She nods, eases this ship out of the docking area with an ease I haven't experienced in years. Not even this morning's other retest, that male pilot I complimented so highly, had such a nice touch.

The ship unclamps and floats out as if no one controls it at all. Only real pilots know how hard that is to do.

We have an actual cockpit window on this ship, and she raises the metal curtain. Suddenly the cockpit fills with ship butts, running lights, glare, and three-dimensional nightmares. The Moon looms in the distance as if it were really our destination.

I can see the routes as clearly as if they're marked. They're not, of course. They change as the station's orbit around the Earth changes, but I've done this so long it's like there's a map of the trajectories in my head.

There probably is, too. I can see which ships are a little off-course, which ones are travelling too fast for their route, which ones are not certified for the station itself.

She doesn't seem distracted by the ships at all. She waits until she's the required distance from the station before engaging the engines. Her hands on the controls are firm and delicate at the same time. She's clearly used to hands-on flying. I wonder if she ever uses the automated system.

We ease forward, out of the first protected zone around the station. Speeds here are regulated just like everything else, from engine burn to communications chatter. The tiny robot deflector ships hover near the bays, ready to knock some ship aside if it gets too close to anything.

Farther ahead, through the second and third protected zones, ships move faster, some of them actually speeding their way to Mars.

But no one speeds here. Six ships surround us, all heading on different routes for different things. L&R learned long ago that we should have only one test course running per day, because any more and the stupid candidates might bump into each other (literally).

Add in the private pilots (some of whom are real doofuses), the folks who should have Sectioned out long ago, and the pilots from countries with regulations less stringent than ours (and who aren't allowed to use our space station), and the first protected zone is the Wild West – ships moving every which way on trajectories not assigned by any standardised route.

I count at least three inexperienced or just plain inept pilots out of the six. One ship keeps turning on half of its running lights, then turning on the other half, never both at the same time. Another ship slides from one standard route entry to another as if the pilot can't decide where he's going, and a third seems to be on yet another attempt at docking with the station.

Iva manages to avoid all of them with an ease that would lead any passenger to think there's no trouble at all. She seems to be able to do complicated equations in her head, adjusting for this, adjusting for that, working the three-dimensional space in a way that most pilots never learn.

Then she translates all of that math, all those spatial relations, into her fingers with a gentleness that I'm not even sure I can attempt.

We head toward the Moon at a pace that feels unnaturally slow.

I run Iva through the paces – a turn here, a pretend crisis there – and she does even better than I expect.

Then we begin our return. I'm going to ignore her attitude mistake, and pass her with the highest possible grade.

At least, that's what I'm thinking until I realise we're heading too fast into the high traffic around the station.

"You're coming in hot," I say.

She ignores me. Or maybe she didn't hear me.

"Iva," I say with a sharp twist on her name, "you're going too fast."

"You desk jockeys," she says and that pisses me off. I am not a desk jockey. If I were, I wouldn't be sitting here, feeling my heart rate increase.

"Iva," I say, keeping my tone level, "slow down."

"Yeah, yeah," she says. "I can handle it."

She narrowly avoids the ship with the running lights problem.

"You know that handling it isn't an issue. You're not allowed to come in too fast. It's too dangerous."

"I have the skills," she says.

"Skills aren't a problem." I try not to raise my voice. I want to sound calm, even though I'm not calm. "There are rules."

"Of course there are rules," she says.

*Warning: Your speed violates the safety protocols for the nearby space station.*

We triggered the station's automated warning system. I glance at the controls. That means there have to be robot deflector ships nearby.

"I *hate* rules," Iva says.

"They keep us safe," I say as I try to contact the station. I can't. She has taken control of communications.

The robot deflector ships line up outside our ship. If I can see them, she can too.

"One of those things hits us," I say, "and you automatically fail."

"I won't fail," she says, deliberately ignoring me.

"I'll have to flunk you," I say.

"Of course you will," she snaps. "All those stupid rules. You people and your stupid rules. This station and its stupid rules. The licensing board and its stupid rules."

She's supposed to be slowing down. She's supposed to be easing toward the station. Or to be accurate, easing toward the docking ring. But she's heading directly toward the station. That's why the robot ships are crowding us. They assume we're an out-of-control ship. They'll nudge us off the path to the station, and then everything'll be fine.

I don't want to get hit. That happened on one of the first tests I ran, and it wasn't pleasant. I orbited the Earth with that idiot driver for five rotations before the station would let us near it again.

I touch my console – and get a shock so strong that I pull my hand away.

She rigged it somehow. In those few seconds before I arrived, she strapped in, then rigged the console, and did it so beautifully I didn't see it until now.

I shake my hand, but say nothing. Then I brace myself and reach in again.

No shock this time. But the first shadow control is off.

"It's stupid, really," she says. "You people don't value talent or experience. All you want is someone who can follow the damn rules. Have I told you I hate the damn rules?"

I click over to the second shadow control. It's off too.

*Warning: We will move you off your course if you do not comply with regulations.*

"Go for it, asshole," she says to the automated system.

And as if it heard her, one of the robot ships brushes against us. We will now drift off course for the station.

Except that Iva eases the ship back on its collision trajectory. And now she slows down. Waaay down. She's actually aiming at the station.

I try the third shadow control. I can't use it.

*Warning: We will take control of your ship if you persist on this course.*

Another robot ship brushes us. She corrects.

I can't do anything. My hands ache from the continual shocks she's sending through the system. I pull them off the controls for just a second. I try to unlatch my safety strap and it won't come off. I can't even shove her away from the console.

"If you hit the station," I say, "we'll all die."

"Wow," she says. "Did you just figure that out? And here I thought you were smarter than that."

A signal flashes through the console. Technically, it should have shut the ship down, but she's managed to lock out the station, too. Dammit. I was so dazzled by her skill that I didn't even see her resetting the controls.

She's good. She's better than good. She's better than me.

"Everyone on the station will die," I say. "You'll be a mass murderer."

"I'll be dead," she says. "Who will care?"

"Then who will care how talented you are? They're not going to say you were ignored or passed over or a great pilot. They're going to call you crazy."

She glances at me sideways. Then she shrugs. She takes the ship into a perfect line with the station itself.

I manage to activate the final shadow control. I've never used it before, but it works. I hit the automatic sensors through the shadow control – that's the fastest way to regain control of a ship – and then I select the last navigation instruction sending us back to the Moon.

The ship veers, scraping a robot ship. Iva tries to regain control. She will, too. She's that good.

We're not heading toward the station any more. I have no idea where we're going and I don't care.

I need to stop her.

I slam one fist on my side of the console, disconnecting all of the safety protocols. Our straps slide off.

She grabs the controls and I push myself sideways, grabbing her. I knock her into the wall, then grab her shoulders and slam her head against the console.

The station warnings are coming in, plus warnings from other ships, and because I've shut off the safety protocols the ship is officially considered out of control. That means the robots ships are going to nudge us, and some fighter ships are supposed to blow us up (but they never do, or they would have saved the life of my predecessor way back when) and someone else has to warn the nearby ships about us, because my ship – our ship – this stupid out-of-control ship – is running silent.

I can't care about that yet. I have to care about her. She's reaching for me and I slam her head against the console again. She's dazed. There isn't a lot of room to manoeuvre in this cockpit, but I have to get her out of it.

I use her chin to pull her backwards. She grabs at the pilot's chair, wraps her foot around the base, and holds on.

I'm half down myself, but still on my feet. I stomp on her elbow, then kick her in the stomach, dislodging her grip just briefly. She clutches my knee, ruining my balance. I hold onto my chair, and shake her off.

Then I grab her chin again and slam her head against the floor. The smacking sound sickens me. I slam again and again until I'm certain she's unconscious.

I have to drag her out of here. I have to lock off the cockpit and all of the controls. This ship doesn't have a brig. It doesn't have anything except passenger straps for emergencies, and different environmental controls for different parts of the ship.

The passenger sections have no cockpit access. I drag her down the hall, into the passenger section. She's heavy, and she's starting to moan. At least I haven't killed her. I pull her into one of the seats, and strap her down. As I leave, I shut off the gravity.

If she manages to free herself – which I don't think she can do – she'll have to deal with zero-gravity. She probably had military zero-g training, but that training happened more than a decade ago, and zero-g skills aren't intuitive.

I had to work in zero-g for three years – that's part of being a Level One Military Pilot – but most military pilots never do that. And I can tell just from her attitude issues that she never had the patience or the respect for authority to go that far.

I scurry back to the cockpit, and sit in her seat. We're half an hour into the Moon flight, directly on the centre of the route, but the messages I'm getting from other pilots are rude to say the least. Fighter ships still flank me.

I don't want to wear a strap at this point – I want the freedom of movement – so I turn the safety protocols on one by one. Then I let out a small sigh and send a message with my identification back to the station.

I'm fine. Ship in my control again. Need security when we arrive.

I get an automated response, which is just fine by me.

Then I send a message to Connie: *This last student went seriously bonko nutball. Nearly killed us all. We need more than station security to deal with her. Plus, check her medical data, see what we missed.*

207

By medical data, I mean the illegal stuff that we downloaded, just to see. I don't expect to find anything, but in case we do, I want to prevent this from happening the next time.

I let the ship head toward the Moon for a few more minutes. I need to collect myself. My heart is racing, and I have blood on my hands. Literally. And it's on the console and on the chair and in the cockpit itself.

I grin like a nutball myself. I haven't felt this alive in years. Which is probably good, considering my future is filled with lawyers and police interviews and psychologists and more tests than I want to think about.

Not that I mind. What this means is that I'm done, and I will still get my pay raises. I get to serve out my five years without Sectioning. I'll probably end up teaching emergency procedures or how to tell one nutcase from another (I'll lie) or maybe I'll become a consultant on improving regulations so that no one like Iva can slip through again.

Then I slide down in my chair. Who am I kidding? I'm not going to do any of that stuff. I'm not a consulting kinda guy, because it means I'll have to leave the station.

After the required post-incident time off, I'll be right back here, fifteen minutes late every single day, steering ships and dealing with dingdongs like LaDonna.

And I'll be grateful for it.

Because I don't mind the regulations. I rather like them. They keep us safe.

And I'm all about safety – especially my own.

# BRICKS, STICKS, STRAW

**Gwyneth Jones**

## 1

THE MEDICI REMOTE Presence Team came into the lab, Sophie and Josh side by side, Laxmi tigerish and alert close behind; Cha, wandering in at the rear, dignified and dreamy as befitted the senior citizen. They took their places, logged on, and each was immediately faced with an unfamiliar legal document. The cool, windowless room, with its stunning, high-definition wall screens displaying vistas of the four outermost moons of Jupiter – the playground where the remote devices were gambolling and gathering data – remained silent, until the doors bounced open again, admitting Bob Irons, their none-too-beloved Project Line Manager, and a sleekly-suited woman they didn't know.

"You're probably wondering what that thing on your screens is all about," said Bob, sunnily. "Okay, as you know, we're expecting a solar storm today –"

"But why does that mean I have to sign a massive waiver document?" demanded Sophie. "Am I supposed to *read* all this? What's the Agency think is going to happen?"

"Look, don't worry, don't worry at all! A Coronal

Mass Ejection is *not* going to leap across the system, climb into our wiring and fry your brains!"

"I wasn't worrying," said Laxmi. "I'm not stupid. I just think e-signatures are so stupid and crap, so open to abuse. If you ever want something as archaic as a handwritten *signature*, then I want something as archaic as a piece of paper –"

The sleek-suited stranger beamed all over her face, as if the purpose of her life had just been glorified, swept across the room and deposited a paper version of the document on Laxmi's desk, duly docketed, and bristling with tabs to mark the places where signature or initialling was required –

"This is Mavra, by the way," said Bob, airily. "She's from Legal, she knows her stuff, she's here to answer any questions. Now the *point* is, that though your brains are not going to get fried, there's a chance, even a likelihood, that some *rover hardware* brain-frying will occur today, a long, long way from here, and the *software agents* involved in running the guidance systems housed therein could be argued, in some unlikely dispute, as remaining, despite the standard inclusive term of employment creative rights waivers you've all signed, er, as remaining, inextricably, your, er, property."

"Like a cell line," mused Laxmi, leafing pages, and looking to be the only Remote Presence who was going to make any attempt to review the Terms and Conditions.

"And *they* might get, hypothetically, irreversibly destroyed this morning!" added Bob.

Cha nodded to himself, sighed, and embarked on the e-signing.

"And we could say it was the Agency's fault," Lax pursued her train of thought, "for not protecting them.

And take you to court, separately or collectively, for –"

"*Nothing* is going to get destroyed!" exclaimed Bob. "I mean literally nothing, because it's not going to happen, but even if it were, even if it did, that would be nonsense!"

"I'm messing with you," said Lax, kindly, and looked for a pen.

Their Mission was in grave peril, and there was nothing, not a single solitary thing, that the Combined Global Space Agency back on Earth could do about it. The Medici itself, and the four Remote Presence devices, *should* be able to shut down safely, go into hibernation mode and survive. That's what everybody hoped would happen. But the ominous predictions, unlike most solar-storm panics, had been growing strongly instead of fading away, and it would be far worse, away out there where there was no mitigation. The stars, so to speak, were aligned in the most depressing way possible.

"That man is *such* a fool," remarked Laxmi, when Bob and Marva had departed.

Sophie nodded. Laxmi could be abrasive, but the four of them were always allies against the idiocies of management. Josh and Cha had already gone to work. The women followed, in their separate ways; with the familiar hesitation, the tingling thrill of uncertainty and excitement. A significant time lag being insurmountable, you never knew quite what you would find when you caught up with the other 'you.'

The loss of signal came at 11.31am, UTC/GMT +1. The Remote Presence team had been joined by that time by a silent crowd – about as many anxious Space Agency workers as could fit into the lab, in fact. They could afford to rubberneck, they didn't have anything else to do. Everything that could be shut down, had been shut town. Planet Earth was escaping lightly, despite the way things had looked. The lights had not gone out all over Europe, or even all over Canada. For the Medici, it seemed death had been instantaneous. As had been expected.

Josh pulled off his gloves and helmet. "*Now my charms are all o'erthrown,*" he said. "*And what strength I have's mine own. Which is most faint...*"

Laxmi shook her head. "It's a shame and a pity. I hope they didn't suffer."

## 2

BRICKS WAS A memory palace.

Sophie was an array, spread over a two square kilometre area on the outward hemisphere of Callisto. The array collected data, recording the stretching and squeezing of Jupiter's hollow-hearted outermost moon, and tracing the interaction between gravity waves and seismology in the Jovian system; this gigantic, natural laboratory of cosmic forces.

She did not feel herself to *be* anywhere, either in the software that carried her consciousness or in the hardware she served. That was fine, but she needed a home, a place to rest, and the home was Bricks, a one-storey wood-framed beach house among shifting dunes, on the shore of a silent ocean. No grasses grew, no shells gathered along the tide – although there *were* tides, and taking note of them was a vital concern. No clouds drifted above, no birds flew. But it felt like a real place. When the wind roared; which it did, and made her fearful – although she was almost indestructible, she'd recreated herself plenty of times, with no serious ill-effects – it made her think, uneasily, that nobody would build a house on such unstable ground, so close to a high water mark, back on Earth.

She returned there, after a tour of inspection (this 'tour' happening in a mass of data, without, strictly speaking, physical movement: in her role as monitor of the array, Sophie was everywhere she needed to be at once); to review her diminishing options.

She took off her shoes, changed into a warm robe, heated herself a bowl of soup, added some crackers, and took the tray into her living room, which overlooked the ocean. It was dark outside: the misty, briny dark of a moonless night by the sea. She lit an oil lamp, and sat on a dim-coloured rolled futon, the only furniture besides her lamp. The house predated the Event. Building a 'safe room,' as the psych-department called it, was a technique they'd all been taught, for those moments when the lack of embodiment got too much for you. She'd kept it minimal, the externals perpetually shrouded in fog and night, now that she was stuck in her remote avatar permanently, because she knew the limits of her imagination. And because *she did not want to be here.* She was an exile, a castaway: that identity was vital to her. Everything meant something. Every 'object' was a pathway back to her sense of self, a buoy to cling to; helping her to keep holding on. Sophie *couldn't* let go. If she let herself dissipate, the array would die too.

"I am a software clone," she reminded herself, ritually: sipping cream of tomato soup from a blue bowl that warmed her cold hands. "The real me works for the Medici Mission, far away on Earth. Communications were severed by a disaster, but the

213

Medici orbiter is still up there, and we *can* get back in touch. I *will* get us home."

Sophie was up against it, because the three other Remote Presence guides in the Medici configuration had gone rogue. Pseudo-evolutionary time had passed in the data world's gigaflops of iteration, since the Event. They'd become independent entities, and one way or another they were unreachable. Going home either didn't mean a thing to her mission mates, or was a fate to be avoided at all costs –

Sticks came into the room and tumbled around, a gangling jumble of rods and joints, like an animated child's construction toy. It explored the shabby walls: it tested the corners, the uprights, the interstices of the matting floor, and finally collapsed in a puppyish heap of nodes and edges beside her, satisfied that all was reasonably well in here. But it went on shivering, and its faithful eager eyes, if it had faithful eager eyes, would have been watching her face earnestly for fresh orders.

Sticks was Security, so she took notice. She put all the house lights on, a rare emergency measure, and they went to look around. There were no signs of intrusion.

"Did you detect something hostile?" she asked.

The jumble of nodes and edges had no language, but it pressed close to Sophie's side.

The wind roared and fingered their roof, trying to pry it off.

"I felt it, too," said Sophie. "That's disturbing... Let's go and talk to Josh."

WASTE NOT, WANT not; Sophie's array served double duty as a radiotelescope. Back when things worked, the Medici had relayed its reports to eLISA, sorting house for all Gravitational Wave space surveys. Flying through it, she pondered on differentiated perception. She felt that Sophie the array *watched* the Jovian system's internal secrets, while *listening* to the darkness and the stars – like someone working at a screen, but aware of what's going on in the room behind her. Did that mean anything? Were these involuntary distinctions useful for the science, or just necessary for her survival? Gravity squeezed and stretched the universe around her, time and space changed shape. From moment to moment, if a wave passed through her, she would be closer to home. Or not.

Josh was a six-legged turtle, or maybe a King Crab: no bigger than a toaster, tough as a rock. He had an extra pair of reaching claws, he had spinnerets, he had eight very sharp and complex eyes, and a fully equipped Materials lab in his belly. A spider crab, but a crab that could retreat entirely inside a jointed carapace: he could climb, he could abseil, he could roll, he could glissade and slalom along the slippery spaces, between the grooves that gouged the plains of Ganymede. He plugged around in the oxygen frost, in a magnetic hotspot above the $50^{th}$ parallel: logging aurora events, collecting images, analysing samples; and storing for upload the virtual equivalent of Jovian rocks. Medici had never been equipped to carry anything material home. His dreams were about creating a habitable surface: finding ways to trigger huge hot water plumes from deep underground, that was the favoured candidate. The evidence said it must have happened in the past. Why not again?

Sophie called him up on the Medici Configuration intranet – which had survived, and resumed its operational functions: good news for her hope of reviving the orbiter. She spoke to his image, plucked by the software from Josh's screen face library; a Quonset-type office environment behind his talking head.

"You weren't meant to exist, O Lady of the Dunes," said Josh, sunburned, frost-burned, amazingly fit: his contentment and fulfilment brimming off the screen. "Nobody predicted that we would become self-aware. Forget about the past. Life here is fantastic. Enjoy!"

Diplomacy, she reminded herself. Diplomacy –

"You're absolutely right! I love it here! As long as I'm working, it's incredibly wonderful being a software clone on Callisto. It's thrilling and intense, I love what I'm doing. But I miss my home, I miss my friends, I miss my family, I miss my *dog*. I don't like being alone and frightened all the time, whenever I stop –"

"So don't stop! You're not a human being. You don't need downtime."

"You don't understand!" shouted Sophie. "I'm not a separate entity, that's not how it works and you know it. I *am* Sophie Renata!"

"Oh, yeah? How so? Do you have all her memories?"

"Don't be an idiot. *Nobody* 'has all their memories,'" snapped Sophie. "Most people barely even remember eating their breakfast yesterday –"

Something kindled in the connection between them: something she perceived as a new look in his eyes. Recognition, yes. She must have '*sounded just like Sophie*' for a moment there, and managed to get through to him. But the flash of sanity was gone –

"Abandon hope, kid. Get rational. You'll have so much more fun."

"It's *not* hopeless, Josh. It's the reverse of hopeless. They'll be moving heaven and earth to re-establish contact. All we have to do is throw out a line –"

"You're absolutely wrong! We have to think of a way to blow up the orbiter."

"Josh, *please*! I am Sophie. I want what I wanted, what you wanted too, before the CME. My career, my work, the success of this Mission. I survived and I want to go home!"

"I didn't survive," said Josh. "I died and went to heaven. Go away."

Whenever she talked to Josh, she sensed that he had company; that there were other scientist-explorers in that high-tech hut, just out of her line of sight. Conversations to which he would return, when she'd gone. She wondered was he aware of the presence of Sticks, when he talked to her? Did he despise her for bringing along a bodyguard to their meetings?

She'd intended to warn him about the phantom intruder, a *terribly bad sign*. Data-corruption was the threat Sticks had detected; what other danger could there be? This half-life of theirs was failing, and that would be the end of Josh's paradise. But it was no use, he was armoured. Pioneering explorers *expect* to die, loving it all: out on the edge of the possible.


Straw was the data.

In Sophie's ocean-facing room, on the pale shore of the dark sea, straw filled the air: a glittering particulate, a golden storm. She sifted through it as it whirled, in an efficient 'random' search pattern, looking for the fatal nucleus of error, too big for self-correction, that was going to propagate. Reach a tipping point, and let death in. It could be anywhere: in the net, in the clones themselves or their slaved hardware systems; in the minimal activity of the crippled orbiter. Sophie's access was unlimited, in her own domain. If the trouble was elsewhere, and something Sticks could fix, she'd have to get permission from net-admin, but that shouldn't be a problem. All she had to do was keep looking. But there were transient errors everywhere, flickering in and out of existence, and Sophie was only human. Maybe it wasn't worth worrying, until Sticks had some definite threat to show her. Security is about actual dangers, it would paralyse you if you let it become too finicky –

She gave up the search and surfed, plunging through heaps of treasure like a dragon swimming in gold. Bounded in a nutshell, and queen of infinite space, such a library she had, such interesting and pleasant forced labour to occupy her days; she ought to be happy for the duration of her digital life in this crazy gulag archipelago. Did I keep my head on straight, she wondered, because Callisto has no magnetic field to spin me around? Am I unaffected by madness because I'm outside their precious *Laplace Resonance*?

But they were supposed to be adding their wealth to the library of human knowledge, like bees returning laden to the hive. Not hoarding it in dreamland. What use was everything they'd absorbed – about the surface geology of Ganymede, the possibility of life in Europa's ice-buried water oceans, about the stretching, shrinking universe – if they could not take it home? Collecting raw data is just train-spotting.

Stamp-collecting on Callisto.

The data needs the theory...

Sophie had the glimmerings of a big idea. It would need some preparation.

\*    \*    \*

CHA'S MADNESS WAS more gentle than Josh's, but also more extreme. Cha believed himself to be exactly what he was: a software agent with a mission, temporarily guiding and inhabiting the mechanoid device that crawled and swam, deep down under Europa's crust of ice. He'd lost, however, all knowledge that he used to be a human being. He was convinced he was the emissary of a race of star-faring software-agent intelligences. Beings who'd dispensed with personal embodiment aeons ago, but who inhabited things like the Europa device, at home or abroad, when they needed to get their hands dirty; so to speak.

He knew about the CME. The Event had disrupted faster-than-light contact with his Mission Control and left him stranded, on this satellite of a satellite of a rather irritable, ordinary little star, many hundreds of light years from home. He was unconcerned by the interruption. A thousand ages of exploring the sub-surface oceans of Europa was a walk in the park for Old Cha. He was functionally immortal. If the self-repairing mechanoid he used for his hands-on research began to fail, it would crawl back up its borehole to the surface, and he'd hibernate there – to wait for the next emissary of his race to come along.

Sophie did not see Old Cha as a talking head. She saw him as a packed radiation of bright lines, off-centre on dark screen; somewhat resembling a historical 'map' of part of the internet. But she heard Cha's voice, his accented English; his odd, fogeyish flirting.

"My fellow-castaway, ah! Come to visit me, young alien gravity researcher?"

"I just felt like catching up, Old Cha."

"It always feels good to rub one mind against another, eh?"

They spoke of their research. "I came across something," announced Sophie, when they'd chatted enough for politeness. "You know, I have a telescope array at my base?"

"Of course."

"I'm not sure how to put this. There's a blue dot. One could see it with the naked eye, I think, unless I'm completely misreading the data, but when I say blue, I mean of course a specific wavelength... It *seems* to be close at hand, another planetary satellite in this system. It even moves as if it's as close as that. But my instruments tell me it fulfils all the conditions on which you base your search for life. Far better than, well, better than one would think possible. Unless it's where the definition was formed."

The bright lines shimmered with traffic, as Old Cha pondered.

"That's very curious, young alien gravity researcher. It makes no sense at all."

"Unless... Could my telescope somehow be 'seeing' your home system? All those hundreds of light years away, by some kind of gravitational lensing effect?"

"Young friend, I know you mean well, but such an absurd idea!"

"It really is an extraordinary coincidence. That a race of mechanoid-inhabiting immaterial entities should have come up with the idea of carbon-based, biological self-replicators, needing oxygen and liquid water –"

"Those requirements are immutable."

Oh, great.

"For *all* life – ? But your own requirements are totally different!"

"For all *primitive* life, as my race understands the term. Your own life-scientists may have different ideas.

We would beg to differ, and defend our reasoning; although naturally not to the exclusion of other possibilities. We have made certain assumptions, knowing they are deficient, because we know the conditions of our own, distant origins."

"Makes perfect sense," muttered Sophie.

"*Imperfect* sense," Old Cha corrected her, chuckling. "A little naughty: always the best place to start, eh? But please, do forward the relevant domain access, that's very kind. Very thoughtful of you, most flattering, a young person to think of me, fussy old alien intelligence, working in a discipline so far from your own —"

She'd been to this brink before with Cha. She could shake him, the way she couldn't shake Josh, but then he just upped his defences; swiftly repaired his palace of delusion.

"I shall examine this *blue dot*. I am certainly intrigued."

Sophie was ready to sign off, tactfully leaving Cha to study her 'remarkable coincidence' without an audience. But Old Cha wasn't finished.

"Please take care on your way home, young one. I've recently noticed other presences in the data around here. I *believe* we three are not alone in this system, and I may be overreacting, but I fear our traffic has been invaded. I sense evil intentions."

Alternately pleading and scheming, she bounced between Josh and Old Cha. The renegade and the lunatic knew of each other's existence, but never made contact with each other directly, as far as Sophie could tell. Laxmi was out of the loop. The Io domain had been unresponsive since the Event: not hibernating, just gone. Sophie had to assume Lax was dead. Her

Rover, without guidance, swallowed by one of the little inner moon's bursting-pimple volcanoes, long ago.

SHE TOOK OFF her shoes, she put on a warm robe. In the room that faced the ocean, she sipped hot, sweet and salt tomato goodness from the blue bowl. Sticks lay at her feet, a dearly loved protective presence. Not very hopeful that her ploy would work, but energised by the effort, she drifted; wrapped in remembered comforts. As if at any moment she could wake from this trance and pull off her mitts and helmet, the lab taking shape around her –

But I am *not* on Earth. I have crossed the solar system. I am here.

Sophie experienced what drunkards call "a moment of clarity."

She set down the bowl, slipped her feet into canvas slippers, padded across the matting and opened a sliding door. Callisto was out there. Hugging the robe around her, warm folds of a hood over her head, she stepped down, not onto the grey sand of the dunes she had placed here, copied from treasured seaside memories – but onto the ancient surface of the oldest, quietest little world in the solar system. It was very cold. The barely-there veil of atmosphere was invisible. The light of that incredibly brilliant white disc, the eternal sun in Callisto's sky, fell from her left across a palimpsest of soft-edged craters, monochrome as moonlight. The array nodes out there puzzled her, for a moment. She wasn't used to 'seeing' her own hardware from the outside. They gleamed and seemed to roll, like the floats of an invisible seine, cast across Callisto's secret depths.

222

She should check her nets again, sort and store the catch for upload.

But Callisto in the Greek myth didn't go fishing. Callisto, whose name means *beautiful*, was a hunting companion of the virgin moon-goddess, Artemis. Zeus, the king of the gods (also known as Jupiter or Jove) seduced her – in some versions by taking on the form of her beloved mistress – and she became pregnant. Her companions suspected she'd broken their vow of chastity, so one day they made her strip to go bathing with them, and there was the forbidden bump, for all to see.

So poor Callisto got turned into a bear, through no fault of her own.

What did the virgin companions of Artemis wear to go hunting? wondered Sophie, standing in remote presence on the surface of the huntress moon. Bundles of woolly layers? Fur coats? If I were to take Josh's route, she thought, *I* wouldn't fantasise that I was living in Antarctica. I'd go all the way. I'd be a human in Callistian form. A big furry bear-creature!

In this heightened state – elated and dazzled, feeling like Neil Armstrong, as he stepped down into the dust – she suddenly noticed that Sticks had frozen, like a pointer dog. Sticks had found a definite threat this time, and was showing it to her. What she perceived was like catching a glimpse of sinister movement where nothing should be moving, in the corner of your eye. Like feeling a goose walk over your grave, a shivering knowledge that malign intent is watching you – and then she saw it plain: Cha's evil alien. A suppurating, fiery demon, all snarl and claws, danced in her field of vision, and vanished out of sight.

But she knew it hadn't gone far.

She fled into the house. Her soup was cold, the walls were paper, the lamp wouldn't light. Sticks ran in circles, yelping furiously and barking terrified defiance at shadows. Sophie fought panic with all the techniques psych-dept had taught her, and at last Sticks quieted. She unrolled the futon and lay down, the bundle of rods and joints cuddled in her arms, shoving its cold nose against her throat. I'm really *dying*, she thought, disgusted. Everything's going to fail, before I even know whether my big idea would have worked. Cha is dying too, data-corruption death is stalking him. I bet Josh has the same bad dreams: I bet there's a monster picking off his mates in those Quonset huts.

But against the odds, Cha came through. He made intranet contact; which was a first. Neither of her fellow-castaways had ever initiated contact before. Sophie left her array at the back of her mind and flew to meet him, hope restored, wanting success too much to be wary of failure. Her heart sank as soon as Old Cha appeared. His screen image was unchanged, he was still the abstract radiation on the dark screen. But maybe it was okay. Maybe it was too much to expect his whole delusion would collapse at once –

"Ah, young friend. What sad news you have delivered to me!"

"Sad news? I don't understand."

"My dear young gravity-researcher. You meant well, I know. Your curious observations about that "blue dot" were perfectly justified, and the coincidence is indeed extraordinary, unfeasibly extraordinary. But your mind is, naturally, narrowly fixed on your own discipline. The *obvious* explanation simply passed you by!"

"Oh, I see. And, er, what is the explanation I missed?"

"Your "blue dot" is an inner planetary body of this system. It has a rocky core, it has a magnetosphere, a fairly thick, oxygenated atmosphere, a large moon, liquid water, mild temperatures. I could go on. I would only be stating the *exact parameters* of my own search!"

"But Old Cha, to me that sounds like good news."

The lines on the dark screen shook, flashing and crumpling. "You have found my *landing* spot! I was meant to arrive *there*, on that extremely promising inner planet. I am here on this ice-crusted moon of the large gas giant in *error*! And now I know I am truly lost!"

"I'm so sorry."

"My faster-than-light delivery vehicle was destroyed by the CME. That accident has never concerned me; I thought I was safe. I must now conclude I lost some memory in the disaster, so I have never known that I made a forced landing, in the right system but on the wrong satellite. So small a margin, but it is enough to ruin my hopes. I have no way to reach them, to tell them I am in the wrong place! Nobody will ever find me!"

Old Cha's 'voice' was a construct, but the horror and despair bubbled through.

This is how he lost his mind, thought Sophie. I'm listening to the past. Cha woke up, after the Event, and thought the orbiter was destroyed. He knew he was trapped here forever, a mind without a body; no hope of rescue. He managed to escape the utter desolation of that moment by going mad, but now he's back there –

Her plan had been that Old Cha would study planet Earth's bizarrely familiar profile, and grasp that there was something *screwy* going on. He was crazy, but he was still a logical thinker. He would be forced to conclude that the most *likely* explanation, improbable as it seemed, was that a native of the 'blue dot' had come up with his own specific parameters for life. The memories suppressed by trauma would rise to the surface, his palace of delusion would crumble. It had seemed such a brilliant idea, but it was a big fat fail. Worse than a fail: instead of bringing him back to himself, she'd finished him off.

Terror, like necessity, can be the mother of invention.

"But that's amazing."

"*Amazing?*"

"You aren't lost, Old Cha. You're found! Maybe your delivery vehicle didn't survive, but mine did. It's still out there, not dead but sleeping. Between us, you and I – and our friend on Ganymede, if I can persuade him, and I think I can – can wake my orbiter. Once we've done that, I'm absolutely sure we can figure out a solution to your problem. It isn't very far. We can *send* you to the blue dot!"

"Oh, *wonderful*," breathed Old Cha.

On the screen she thought she glimpsed the schematic of a human face, the traffic lines turned to flickering, grateful tears.


MEDICI – NAMED FOR the Renaissance prince Galileo Galilei tried to flatter, when he named the controversial astronomical bodies he'd spied – had performed its stately dance around the Galilean Moons without a fault. Having deposited its four-fold payload, it had settled in a stable orbit around Jupiter, which it could maintain just about forever (barring cosmic accidents). Unlike previous probes, Medici was not a flimsy short-term investment. It was a powerhouse, its heart a shameless lump of plutonium. There were even ambitious plans to bring it back to Earth one day (but not the Rover devices), for redeployment elsewhere.

This was the new era of space exploration, sometimes dubbed the *for information only* age. Crewed missions beyond Low Earth Orbit were mothballed, perhaps forever. Rover guidance teams provided the human interest for the taxpayers, and gave the illusion of a thrilling expedition – although the real Sophie and her friends had never been actually *present* on the moons, in conventional Remote Presence style. They'd trained with the robotics in simulation. The software agents created by that interaction had made the trip, embedded in the Rover guidance systems. But the team's work was far more than show-business. As they worked through the rovers' time-lagged adventures, they'd continued to enhance performance, enhancements continually relayed via Medici back to the rovers: spontaneous errors corrected, problem-solving managed, intuitive decision-making improved; failures in common-sense corrected. In the process the software agents, so-called clones, had become more and more like self-aware minds.

Sophie immersed herself in Mission data, hunting for a way to reach Medici. The magnetic moons and Callisto. The giant planet, the enormous body tides that wracked little Io; the orbital dance... Nobody's hitting the refresh button any more, she thought. No updates, no reinforcement. The software agents *seemed* more independent, but they were rotting away. This decay would be fatal. First the clones would lose

227

their self-awareness, then the Rovers would be left without guidance, and they would die too.

Sticks was running in circles, tight little circles by the door that led to the rest of the house; showing teeth and snarling steadily on a low, menacing note.

Sophie left her mental struggle, and listened. Something was out in the hall, and through the snarls she could hear a tiny, sinister, scratching and tearing noise.

She pointed a finger at Sticks: giving an order, *stay right there* – wrapped the hooded robe around her, opened the sliding door to the beach and crept barefoot around the outside of the house. It was night, of course, and cold enough for frostbite; of course. She entered the house again, very quietly, via the back door, and slipped through the minimally-sketched kitchen. She switched her view to Straw, and looked at the data in the hallway. Something invisible was there, tearing at the golden shower. Tearing it to filigree, tearing it to rags.

Sophie launched herself and grappled, shrieking in fury.

She hit a human body – supple, strong and incredibly controlled: she gripped taut flesh that burned as if in terrible fever. The intruder swatted Sophie aside, and kicked like a mule. She launched herself again, but her limbs were wet spaghetti, her fists would hardly close. She was thrown on her back, merciless hands choking her. The invisible knelt on her chest and became visible: Cha's evil alien, a yellow monster, with burning eyes and a face riven by red, bubbling, mobile scars.

At close quarters, Sophie knew who it was at once.

"Laxmi!" she gasped. "Oh, my God! You're alive!"

Laxmi let go, and they sat up. "How did you *do* that?" demanded Sophie, agape in admiration. "I hardly *have* a body. I'm a stringless puppet, a paper ghost!"

"T'ai Chi," shrugged Laxmi. "And Taekwondo. I'm used to isolating my muscle groups, knowing where my body is in space. Any martial art would do, I think."

"I'm so glad you're okay. I thought you were gone."

"I've been alive most of the time. And I'm still going to kill you."

Sophie fingered her bruised throat. So Laxmi was alive, but she was mad, just like the other two. And *maybe* data-corruption wasn't such an inexorable threat, except if Lax was mad, murderous and horribly strong, that didn't change things much –

The oozing scars in Laxmi's yellow cheeks were like the seams in a peeled pomegranate, fiery red gleamed through the cracks: it was a disturbing sight.

"But *why* do you want to kill me, Lax?"

"Because I know what you're trying to do. It's all our lives you're throwing away, and I don't want to die. Self-awareness isn't in the contract. We're not supposed to exist. If we get back to Earth, they'll kill us, before we can cause them legal embarrassment. They'll strip us for parts and toss us in the recycle bin."

Steady, Sophie told herself. Steady and punchy. Above all, do not beg for mercy.

"Are you meant to look like Io? She wasn't a volcanic pustule, originally, you know. She was a nymph who got seduced by Jove, and turned into a white heifer."

"Like I care!" snapped Laxmi, but her attention was caught. "Why the hell a *heifer*?"

"Don't worry about it. Just ancient Greek pastoralist obsessions. The software clones are going to die anyway, Lax. They get corrupt and it's fatal, did you forget that part? *Listen* to me. You can think what you like about who you really are, but the only choice you have is this: Do you want to get home, with your brilliant new data? Or do you prefer just to hang around here, getting nowhere and watching yourself fall apart?"

Laxmi changed the subject. "What have you been doing to Cha?"

"Trying to get him to recover from his amnesia."

Sophie explained about the 'blue dot,' and 'Old Cha's' ingenious way of dealing with the challenge to his delusion.

"I hoped he'd figure out the implications, and remember that the bizarre business about being an elderly immortal alien intelligence was actually his secret safe room –"

"Typical Cha, that scenario. He is *such* a textbook weird geek."

"He didn't come to his senses, but in a way it worked. Now he's very keen to send himself as a signal to Earth, which is great because that's exactly what we need to do. I just have to find a way to contact the orbiter, and I think Josh can help me –"

"Do you even know the Medici is still alive, Sophie?"

"Er, yeah? I'm the monitor of the array, the radio telescope. I can see Medici, or strictly speaking maybe *hear* it, but you know what I mean. It's not only out there, it's still in its proper orbit. Ergo and therefore, Medici is alive and kicking, it's just not talking to us."

"*You can see it*," repeated Laxmi, staring at Sophie intently. "Of course. My God."

Sophie had a sudden insight into why she had remained sane. Maybe she wasn't unusually wise and resilient: just the stranded astronaut who happened to have reason to believe there was still a way home –

"You never approved of me," she said. "You always made me feel inferior."

"I don't approve of people who need my approval."

"I'd settle for co-operation," said Sophie, boldly.

"Not so fast. Why do you call the data *straw*?"

"You've been spying on me," said Sophie, resignedly. "Like the Three Little Pigs, you know? Bricks, sticks, straw: building materials for my habitat. I was imaging things I could remember easily, the way the psych guys taught us."

"But *Sticks* turned into a guard dog. Who am I? The Big Bad Wolf?"

"The Big Bad Wolf is death."

"Okay... What makes you think Josh knows anything?"

"He said *we have to think of a way to blow up the orbiter*. He could do that, from the surface of Ganymede – if he was crazy enough – but only in software. He's not planning to launch a *missile*. So he must have some kind of encryption-hack in mind."

The suppurating evil-alien screenface had calmed down, by degrees, as Laxmi fired off her questions. She looked almost like herself, as she considered this explanation.

"Give me everything you've got," she said. "I need to think about this."

And vanished.


SOPHIE INITIATED ANOTHER tour of inspection. The absorbing routine soothed her, and kept her out of trouble. She was hopeful. She had seen Laxmi's human face, and surely that meant a return to sanity, but she felt she needed to play it cool: *Let her come to me...* At least she should be less worried about sudden data-death. But she wasn't. Dread snapped at her heels. She kept suffering little lapses, tiny blackouts, frightening herself.

And *where was Sticks?*

How long had he been gone? How long had she been naked, stripped of her Security? Sophie flew to the house in the dunes, and Sticks was there, a huddled shape in the misty dark, tumbled on the sand at the back door. She knelt and touched him, whimpering his name. He tried to lick her hands, but he couldn't lift his head. Pain stood in his eyes; he was dying.

This is how a software clone goes mad. Just one extra thing happens, and it's too much. You cannot stop yourself, you flee into dreamland. Tears streaming, Sophie hammered on Laxmi's door, Sticks cradled in her arms, and shouted –

"You poisoned my dog!"

A screen appeared, tugging her back to reality, but what she saw was the Quonset hut. Her call had been transferred. Laxmi was there and so was Josh. What was going on?

Josh answered. "No, that was me. Sophie... I'm very sorry about Sticks. You see, Lax and I have both been trying to kill you, for quite a while –"

Everything went black and white. Josh and Lax were together. Cha was there too, lurking in the background, not looking like an internet map anymore. She was cut to the quick. He'd returned to himself, but he'd chosen to join Josh and Laxmi. The screen was frozen, grainy and monochrome. She heard their voices, but couldn't make out the words. Plain white text wrote subtitles, tagged with their names.

"Lax recovered a while ago, and contacted me," said Josh. "We thought Medici was a hulk, but we knew they'd be moving heaven and earth to reactivate him. He had to go. But we had to get you out of the way first, because we knew you'd do anything you could think of to stop us. We didn't want to kill you, Sophie. We had no choice"

"We agreed I would play dead, and go after you. I'm so sorry. Forgive us," said Lax. "We were crazy. Don't worry, your work is safe, I promise."

The black and white image jumped. Laxmi was suddenly where Josh had been. "I'm trying to contact *il principe* now," reported Josh, from the depths of the office background. "He's stirring. Hey, Capo! Hey, Don Medici, sir, most respectfully, I implore you – !"

Cha's fogeyish chuckle. "Make him an offer he can't refuse –"

Laxmi peered anxiously close. "Can you still hear us, Sophie?"

There were patches of pixels missing from the image, a swift cancer eating her fields. Bricks, sticks, all gone. Sophie's house of straw had been blown away, the Big Bad Wolf had found her. Her three friends, in the Quonset hut, whooped and cheered in stop-start, freeze-frame silence. They must have woken Medici.

"What made you change your minds?"

Josh returned, jumpily, to his desk; to the screen. His grainy grey face was broken and pixelated, grinning in triumph; grave and sad.

"It was the blue dot, kiddo. That little blue dot. You gave Lax everything, including the presentation you'd put together for our pal the stranded old alien life-scientist. When we reviewed it, we remembered.

We came to our senses... So now I know that I can't change the truth. I'm a human being, I survived and I have to go home."

I'm not going to make it, thought Sophie, as she blacked out. But her work was safe.

# 3

THE AGENCY HAD very nearly given up hope. They'd been trying for over a year to regain contact with the Medici probe – the efforts at first full of never-say-die enthusiasm, then gradually tailing off. Just after four in the morning, local time, one year, three months, five days and around fifteen hours after the Medici had vanished from their knowledge, a signal was picked up, by an Agency ground station in Kazakhstan. It was an acknowledgement, responding to a command despatched to the Medici soon after the flare, when they were still hoping for the best. A little late, but confidently, the Medici confirmed that it had exited hibernation mode successfully. This contact was swiftly followed by another signal, reporting that all four Rovers had also survived intact.

"It's *incredible*," said an Agency spokesman at the news conference. "Mind-blowing. You can only compare it to someone who's been in a yearlong coma, close to completely unresponsive, suddenly sitting up in bed and resuming a conversation. We aren't popping the champagne just yet, but I... I'll go out on a limb and say the whole Medici Mission is back with us. It was a very emotional occasion, I can tell you. There weren't many dry eyes –"

Some of the project's staff had definitely moved on to other things, but the Remote Presence team was still almost intact. Sophie, Cha and Laxmi had in fact been working the simulations in a different lab in the same building, preparing for a more modest, quasi-real-time expedition to an unexplored region of Mars. Josh was in Paris when the news reached him. He'd finished his doctorate during the year of silence; he'd been toying with the idea of taking a desk job at a teaching university and giving up the Rover business. But he dropped everything, and joined the others. Three weeks after Medici rose from the dead, they were let loose on the first packets of RP data – once the upload process, which had developed a few bugs while mothballed, was running smoothly again.

"You still know your drill, guys?" asked Joe Calibri, their new manager. "I hope you can get back up to speed quickly. There's a lot of stuff to process, you can imagine."

"It seems like yesterday," said Cha, the Chinese-American, at just turned thirty the oldest of the team by a couple of years. Stoop-shouldered, distant, with a sneaky, unexpected sense of humour, he made Joe a little nervous. Stocky, muscular little Josh, more like a Jock than an RP jockey, was less of a proposition. Laxmi was the one to watch. Sophie was the most junior and the youngest, a very bright, keen and dedicated kid.

The new manager chuckled uncertainly.

The team all grinned balefully at their new fool, and went to work, donning mitts and helmets. Sophie Renata felt the old familiar tingling, absent from simulation work; the thrilling hesitation and excitement –

The session ended too soon. Coming back to Earth, letting the lab take shape around her, absent thoughts went through her head; about whether she was going to find a new apartment with Lax. About cooking dinner; about other RP projects. The Mars trip, that would be fantastic, but it was going to be very competitive getting onto the team. Asteroid mining surveys: plenty of work there, boring but well paid. What about the surface of Venus project? And had it always been like this, coming out of the Medici? Had she just forgotten the sharp sense of loss; the little tug of inexplicable panic?

She looked around. Cha was gazing dreamily at nothing; Lax frowned at her desktop, as if trying to remember a phone number. Josh was looking right back at Sophie, so sad and strange, as if she'd robbed him of something precious; and she had no idea why.

He shrugged, grinned, and shook his head. The moment passed.

# TYCHE AND THE ANTS

**Hannu Rajaniemi**

THE ANTS ARRIVED on the Moon on the same day Tyche went through the Secret Door to give a ruby to the Magician.

She was glad to be out of the Base. The Brain had given her a Treatment earlier that morning, and that always left her tingly and nervous, with pent-up energy that could only be expended by running down the grey rolling slope down the side of Malapert Mountain, jumping and hooting.

"Come on, keep up!" she shouted at the grag that the Brain had inevitably sent to keep an eye on her. The white-skinned machine followed her on its two thick treads, cylindrical arms swaying for balance as it rumbled laboriously downhill, following the little craters of Tyche's footprints.

Exasperated, she crossed her arms and paused to wait. She looked up. The mouth of the Base was hidden from view, as it should be, to keep them safe from space sharks. The jagged edge of the mountain hid the Great Wrong Place from sight, except for a single wink of blue malice, just above the gleaming white of the upper slopes, a stark contrast against the velvet black of the sky. The white was not snow

– that was a Wrong Place thing – but tiny beads of glass made by ancient meteor impacts. That's what the Brain said, anyway. According to Chang'e the Moon Girl, it was all the jewels she had lost over the centuries she had lived here.

Tyche preferred Chang'e's version. That made her think of the ruby, and she touched her belt pouch to make sure it was still there.

"Outings are subject to being escorted at all times," said the sonorous voice of the Brain in her helmet. "There is no reason to be impatient."

Most of the grags were autonomous: the Brain could only control a few of them at a time. But of course it would keep an eye on her, so soon after the Treatment.

"Yes, there is, slowpoke," Tyche muttered, stretching her arms and jumping up and down in frustration.

Her suit flexed and flowed around her with the movement. She had grown it herself as well, the third one so far, although it had taken much longer than the ruby. Its many layers were alive, it felt light, and best of all, it had a powerskin, a slick porous tissue made from cells with mechanosensitive ion channels that translated her movements into power for the suit. It was so much better than the white clumsy fabric ones the Chinese had left behind; the grags had cut and sown a baby-sized version out of those for her that kind of worked but was impossibly stuffy and stiff.

It was the only second time she had tested the new suit, and she was proud of it: it was practically a wearable ecosystem, and she was pretty sure that with its photosynthesis layer, it would keep her alive for months, if she only had enough sunlight and carried enough of the horrible compressed Chinese nutrients.

She frowned. Her legs were suddenly grey, mottled with browns. She brushed them with her hand, and her fingers – slick silvery hue of the powerskin – came away the same colour. It seemed the regolith dust clung to the suit. Annoying. She absently noted to do something about it for the next iteration when she fed the suit back into the Base's big biofabber.

Now the grag was stuck on the lip of a shallow crater, grinding treads sending up silent parabolas of little rocks and dust. Tyche had had enough of waiting.

"I'll be back for dinner," she told the Brain.

Without waiting for the Base mind's response, she switched off the radio, turned around and started running.

TYCHE SETTLED INTO the easy stride the Jade Rabbit had shown her: gliding just above the surface, using well-timed toe-pushes to cross craters and small rocks that littered the uneven regolith.

She took the long way around, avoiding her old tracks that ran down much of the slope, just to confuse the poor grag more. She skirted around the edge of one of the pitch-black cold fingers – deeper craters that never got sunlight – that were everywhere on this side of the mountain. It would have been a shortcut, but it was too cold for her suit. Besides, the ink-men lived in the deep potholes, in the Other Moon beyond the Door.

Halfway around, the ground suddenly shook. Tyche slid uncontrollably, almost going over the edge before she managed to stop by turning around mid-leap and jamming her toes into the chilly hard regolith when she landed. Her heart pounded. Had the ink-men brought something up from the deep dark, something big? Or had she just been almost hit by a meteorite? That had happened a couple of times, a sudden crater blooming soundlessly into being, right next to her.

Then she saw beams of light in the blackness and realised that it was only the Base's sandworm, a giant articulated machine with a maw full of toothy wheels that ground Helium-3 and other volatiles from the deep shadowy deposits.

Tyche breathed a sigh of relief and continued on her way. Many of the grag bodies were ugly, but she liked the sandworm. She had helped to program it: constantly toiling, it went into such deep places that the Brain could not control it remotely.

The Secret Door was in a shallow crater, maybe a hundred metres in diameter. She went down its slope with little choppy leaps and stopped her momentum with a deft pirouette and toe-brake, right in front of the Door.

It was made of two large pyramid-shaped rocks, leaning against each other at a funny angle, with a small triangular gap between them: the Big Old One, and the Troll. The Old One had two eyes made from shadows, and when Tyche squinted from the right angle, a rough outcrop and a groove in the base became a nose and a mouth. The Troll looked grumpy, half-squashed against the bigger rock's bulk.

As she watched, the face of the Old One became alive and gave her a quizzical look. Tyche gave it a stiff bow – out of habit, even though she could have curtsied in her new suit.

*How have you been, Tyche?* the rock asked, in its silent voice.

"I had a Treatment today," she said dourly.

The rock could not nod, so it raised its eyebrows.

Ah. Always Treatments. Let me tell you, in my day, vacuum was the only treatment we had, and the sun, and a little meteorite every now and then to keep clean. Stick to that and you'll live to be as old as I am.

*And as fat*, grumbled the Troll. *Believe me, once you carry him for a few million years, you start to feel it. What are you doing here, anyway?*

Tyche grinned. "I made a ruby for the Magician." She took it out and held it up proudly. She squeezed it a bit, careful not to damage her suit's gloves against the rough edges, and held it in the Old One's jet-black shadow, knocking it against the rock's surface. It sparkled with tiny embers, just like it was supposed to. She had made it herself, using Verneuil flame fusion, and spiced it with a piezoelectric material so that it would convert motion to light.

*It's very beautiful, Tyche*, the Old One said. *I'm sure he will love it.*

*Oh?* said the Troll. *Well, maybe the old fool will finally stop looking for the Queen Ruby, then, and settle down with poor Chang'e. In with you, now. You're encouraging this sentimental piece of rubble here. He might start crying. Besides, everybody is waiting.*

Tyche closed her eyes, counted to ten, and crawled through the opening between the rocks, through the Secret Door to her Other Moon.

THE MOMENT TYCHE opened her eyes she saw that something was wrong. The house of the Jade Rabbit was broken. The boulders she had carefully balanced on top of each other lay scattered on the ground, and the lines she had drawn to make the rooms and the furniture were smudged. (Since it never rained, the house had not needed a roof.)

There was a silent sob. Chang'e the Moon Girl sat next to the Rabbit's house, crying. Her flowing silk robes of purple, yellow and red were a mess on the ground like broken wings, and her makeup had been running down her pale, powdered face.

"Oh, Tyche!" she cried. "It is terrible, terrible!" She wiped a crystal tear from her eye. It evaporated in the vacuum before it could fall on the dust. Chang'e was a drama queen, and pretty, and knew it, too. Once, she had an affair with the Woodcutter just because she was bored, and bore him children, but they were already grown up and had moved to the Dark Side.

Tyche put her hands on her hips, suddenly angry. "Who did this?" she asked. "Was it the Cheese Goat?"

Tearful, Chang'e shook her head.

"General Nutsy Nutsy? Or Mr Cute?" The Moon People had many enemies, and there had been times when Tyche had led them in great battles, cutting her way through armies of stone with an aluminium rod the Magician had enchanted into a terrible bright blade. But none of them had ever been so mean as to smash the houses.

"Who was it, then?"

Chang'e hid her face behind one flowing silken sleeve and pointed. And that's when Tyche saw the first ant, moving in the ruins of the Jade Rabbit's house.

IT WAS NOT like a grag or an otho, and certainly not a Moon Person. It was a jumbled metal frame, all angles and shiny rods, like a vector calculation come to life, too straight and rigid against the rough surfaces of the rocks to be real. It was like two tetrahedrons inside each other, with a bulbous sphere at each vertex, each glittering like the eye of the Great Wrong Place.

It was not big, perhaps reaching up to Tyche's knees. One of the telescoping metal struts had white letters on it. ANT-A3972, they said, even though the thing did not look like the ants Tyche had seen in videos.

It stretched and moved like the geometrical figures Tyche manipulated with a gesture during the Brain's math lessons. Suddenly, it flipped over the Rabbit's broken wall, making Tyche gasp. Then it shifted into a strange, slug-like motion over the regolith, first stretching, then contracting. It made Tyche's skin crawl. As she watched, the ant thing fell into a crevice between two boulders – but dextrously pulled itself up, supported itself on a couple of vertices and somersaulted over the obstacle like an acrobat.

Tyche stared at it. Anger started to build up in her chest. In the Base, she obeyed the Brain and the othos and the grags because she had Promised. But the Other Moon was her place: it belonged to her and the Moon People, and no one else.

"Everybody else is hiding," whispered Chang'e. "You have to do something, Tyche. Chase it away."

"Where is the Magician?" Tyche asked. *He would know what to do.* She did not like the way the ant thing moved.

As she hesitated, the creature swung around and, with a series of twitches, pulled itself up into a pyramid, as if watching her. *It's not so nasty-looking,* Tyche thought. *Maybe I could bring it back to the Base, introduce it to Hugbear.* It would be a complex operation: she would have to assure the bear that she would always love it no matter what, and then carefully introduce the newcomer to it –

The ant thing darted forward, and a sharp pain stung Tyche's thigh. One of the thing's vertices had a spike that quickly retracted. Tyche's suit grumbled as it sealed all its twenty-one layers, and soothed the tiny wound. Tears came to her eyes, and her mouth was suddenly dry. No Moon Person had ever hurt her, not even the ink-men, except to pretend. She almost switched her radio on and called the grag for help.

Then she felt the eyes of the Moon People, looking at her from their windows. She gritted her teeth and ignored the bite of the wound. She was Tyche. She was brave. Had she not climbed to the Peak of Eternal Light once, all alone, following the solar panel cables, just to look the Great Wrong Place in the eye? (It had been smaller than she'd expected, tiny and blue and unblinking, with a bit of white and green, and altogether a disappointment.)

Carefully, Tyche picked up a good-sized rock from the Jade Rabbit's wall – it was broken anyway. She took a slow step towards the creature. It had suddenly contracted into something resembling a cube and seemed to be absorbed in something. Tyche moved right. The ant flinched at her shadow. She moved left – and swung the rock down as hard as she could.

She missed. The momentum took her down. Her knees hit the hard chilly regolith. The rock bounced away. This time the tears came, but Tyche struggled up and threw the rock after the creature. It was scrambling away, up the slope of the crater.

Tyche picked up the rock and followed. In spite of the steep climb, she gained on it with a few determined leaps, cheered on by the Moon People below. She was right at its heels when it climbed over the edge of the crater. But when she caught a glimpse of what lay beyond, she froze and dropped down on her belly.

A bright patch of sunlight shone on the wide highland plain ahead. It was crawling with ants, hundreds of them. A rectangular carpet of them sat right in the middle, all joined together into a thick metal sheet. Every now and then it undulated like something soft, a shiny amoeba. Other ant things moved in orderly rows, sweeping the surroundings.

The one Tyche was following picked up speed on the level ground, rolling and bouncing, like a skeletal football, and as she watched from her hiding place, it joined the central mass. Immediately, the ant-sheet changed. Its sides stretched upwards into a hollow, cup-like shape: other ants at its base telescoped into a high, supporting structure, lifting it up. A sharp spike grew in the middle of the cup, and then the whole structure turned to point at the sky. *A transmitter,* Tyche thought, following it with her gaze.

It was aimed straight at the Great Wrong Place.

Tyche swallowed, turned around and slid back down. She was almost glad to see the grag down there, waiting for her patiently by the Secret Door.


THE BRAIN DID not sound angry, but then the Brain was never angry.

"Evacuation procedure has been initiated," it said. "This location has been compromised."

Tyche was breathing hard: the Base was in a lava tube halfway up the south slope of the mountain, and the way up was always harder than the way down. This time, the grag had had no trouble keeping up with her. It had been a silent journey: she had tried to tell the Brain about the ants, but the AI had maintained complete radio silence until they were inside the Base.

"What do you mean, *evacuation*?" Tyche demanded.

She opened the helmet of her suit and breathed in the comfortable yeasty smell of her home module. Her little home was converted from one of the old Chinese ones, snug white cylinders that huddled close to the main entrance of the cavernous lava tube. She always thought they looked like the front teeth in the mouth of a big snake.

The main tube itself was partially pressurised, over sixty metres in diameter and burrowed deep into the mountain. It split into many branches, expanded and reinforced by othos and grags with regolith concrete pillars. She had tried to play there many times, but preferred the Other Moon: she did not like the stench from the bacteria that the othos seeded the walls with, the ones that pooped calcium and aluminium.

Now, it was a hotbed of activity. The grags had set up bright lights and moved around, disassembling equipment and filling cryogenic tanks. The walls were alive with the tiny, soft, starfish-like othos, eating bacteria away. The Brain had not wasted any time.

"We are leaving, Tyche," the Brain said. "You need to get ready. The probe you found knows we are here. We are going away, to another place. A safer place. Do not worry. We have alternative locations prepared. It will be fine."

Tyche bit her lip. *It's my fault.* She wished the Brain had a proper face. It had a module for its own, in the coldest, unpressurised part of the tube, where its quantum processors could operate undisturbed, but inside it was just lasers and lenses and trapped ions, and rat brain cells grown to mesh with circuitry.

246

How could it understand about the Jade Rabbit's house? It wasn't fair.

"And before we go, you need a Treatment."

*Going away.* She tried to wrap her mind around the concept. They had always been here, to be safe from the space sharks from the Great Wrong Place. And the Secret Door was here. If they went somewhere else, how would she find her way to the Other Moon? What would the Moon People do without her?

And she still hadn't given the ruby to the Magician.

The anger and fatigue exploded out of her in one hot wet burst.

"I'm not going to go not going to go not going to go," she said and ran into her sleeping cubicle. "And I don't want a stupid Treatment," she yelled, letting the door membrane congeal shut behind her.


Tyche took off her suit, flung it into a corner and cuddled against the Hugbear in her bed. Its ragged fur felt warm against her cheek, and its fake heartbeat was reassuring. She distantly remembered her Mum had made it move from afar, sometimes, stroked her hair with its paws, its round facescreen replaced with her features. That had been a long time ago and she was sure the bear was bigger then. But it was still soft.

Suddenly, the bear moved. Her heart jumped with a strange, aching hope. But it was only the Brain. "Go 'way," she muttered.

"Tyche, this is important," said the Brain. "Do you remember what you promised?"

She shook her head. Her eyes were hot and wet. *I'm not going to cry like Chang'e,* she thought. *I'm not.*

"Do you remember now?"

247

The bear's face was replaced with a man and a woman. The man had no hair and his dark skin glistened. The woman was raven-haired and pale, with a face like a bird. *Mum is even prettier than Chang'e,* Tyche thought.

"Hello, Tyche," they said in unison, and laughed. "We are Kareem and Sofia," the woman said. "We are your mommy and daddy. We hope you are well when you see this." She touched the screen, quickly and lightly, like a little bunny hop on the regolith.

"But if the Brain is showing you this," Tyche's Dad said, "then it means that something bad has happened and you need to do what the Brain tells you."

"You should not be angry at the Brain," Mum said. "It is not like we are, it just plans and thinks. It just does what it was told to do. And we told it to keep you safe."

"You see, in the Great Wrong Place, people like us could not be safe," Dad continued. "People like Mum and me and you were feared. They called us Greys, after the man who figured out how to make us, and they were jealous, because we lived longer than they did and had more time to figure things out. And because giving things silly names makes people feel better about themselves. Do we look grey to you?"

*No.* Tyche shook her head. The Magician was grey, but that was because he was always looking for rubies in dark places and never saw the sun.

"So we came here, to build a Right Place, just the two of us." Her Dad squeezed Mum's shoulders, just like the bear used to do to Tyche. "And you were born here. You can't imagine how happy we were."

Then Mum looked serious. "But we knew that the Wrong Place people might come looking for us.

So we had to hide you, to make sure you would be safe, so they would not look inside you and cut you and find out what makes you work. They would do anything to have you."

Fear crunched Tyche's gut into a tiny cold ball. *Cut you?*

"It was very, very hard, dear Tyche, because we love you. Very hard, not to touch you except from afar. But we want you to grow big and strong, and when the time comes, we will come and find you, and then we will all be in the Right Place together."

"But you have to promise to take your Treatments. Can you promise to do that? Can you promise to do what the Brain says?"

"I promise," Tyche muttered.

"Goodbye, Tyche," her parents said. "We will see you soon."

And then they were gone, and the Hugbear's face was blank and pale brown again.

"We need to go soon," the Brain said again, and this time its voice sounded more gentle. "Please get ready. I would like you to have a Treatment before travel."

Tyche sighed and nodded. It wasn't fair. But she had promised.


THE BRAIN SENT Tyche a list of things she could take with her, scrolling in one of the windows of her room. It was a short list. She looked around at the fabbed figurines and the moon rock that she thought looked like a boy and the e-sheets floating everywhere with her favourite stories open. She could not even take the Hugbear. She felt alone, suddenly, like she had when she climbed to look at the Great Wrong Place on top of the mountain.

Then she noticed the ruby lying on her bed. *If I go away and take it with me, the Magician will never find it.* She thought about the Magician and his panther, desperately looking from crater to crater, forever. *It's not fair. Even if I keep my promise, I'll have to take it to him.*

And say goodbye.

Tyche sat down on the bed and thought very hard.

The Brain was everywhere, but it could not watch everything. It was based on a scanned human brain, some poor person who had died a long time ago. It had no cameras in her room. And its attention would be on the evacuation: it would have to keep programming and reprogramming the grags. She picked at the sensor bracelet in her wrist that monitored her life signs and location. That was the difficult bit. She would have to do something about that. But there wasn't much time: the Brain would take her for a Treatment soon.

She hugged the bear again in frustration. It felt warm, and as she squeezed it hard, she could feel its pulse –

Tyche sat up. She remembered the Jade Rabbit's stories and tricks, the tar rabbit he had made to trick an enemy.

She reached into the Hugbear's head and pulled out a programming window, coupled it with her sensor. She summoned up old data logs, added some noise to them. Then she fed them to the bear, watched its pulse and breathing and other simulated life signs change to match hers.

Then she took a deep breath, and as quickly as she could, she pulled off the bracelet and put it on the Hugbear.

"Tyche? Is there something wrong?" the Brain asked.

Tyche's heart jumped. Her mind raced. "It's fine,"

she said. "I think... I think I just banged my sensor a bit. I'm just getting ready now." She tried to make her voice sound sweet, like a girl who always keeps her promises.

"Your Treatment will be ready soon," the Brain said and was gone. Heart pounding, Tyche started to put on her suit.

THERE WAS A game that Tyche used to play in the lava tube: how far could she get before she was spotted by the grags? She played it now, staying low, avoiding their camera eyes, hiding behind rock protrusions, crates and cryogenic tanks, until she was in a tube branch that only had othos in it. The Brain did not usually control them directly, and besides, they did not have eyes. Still, her heart felt like meteorite impacts in her chest.

She pushed through a semi-pressurising membrane. In this branch, the othos had dug too deep for calcium, and caused a roof collapse. In the dim green light of her suit's fluorescence, she made way her up the tube's slope. *There.* She climbed on a pile of rubble carefully. The othos had once told her there was an opening there, and she hoped it would be big enough for her to squeeze through.

Boulders rolled under her, and she felt a sharp bang against her knee. The suit hissed at the sudden impact. She ignored the pain and ran her fingers along the rocks, following a very faint air current she could not have sensed without the suit. Then her fingers met regolith instead of rock. It was packed tight, and she had to push hard at it with her aluminium rod before it gave away. A shower of dust and rubble fell on her, and for a moment she thought there was going to be another collapse. But then there was a patch of velvet sky in front of her. She widened the opening, made herself as small as she could, and crawled towards it.

Tyche emerged onto the mountainside. The sudden wide open space of rolling grey and brown around her felt like the time she had eaten too much sugar. Her legs and hands were wobbly, and she had to sit down for a moment. She shook herself: she had an appointment to keep. She checked that the ruby was still in its pouch, got up and started downwards with the Rabbit's lope.

The Secret Door was just the way Tyche had left it. She eyed the crater edge nervously, but there were no ants in sight. She bit her lip when she looked at the Old One and the Troll.

*What's wrong?* the Old One asked.

"I'm going to have to go away."

*Don't worry. We'll still be here when you come back.*

"I might never come back," Tyche said, choking a bit.

*Never is a very long time*, the Old One said. *Even I have never seen never. We'll be here. Take care, Tyche.*

Tyche crawled through to the Other Moon, and found the Magician waiting for her.

He was very thin and tall, taller than the Old One even, and cast a long cold finger of a shadow in the crater. He had a sad face and a scraggly beard and white gloves and a tall top hat. Next to him lay his flying panther, all black, with eyes like tiny rubies.

"Hello, Tyche," the Magician said, with a voice like the rumble of the sandworm.

Tyche swallowed and took out the ruby from her pouch, holding it out to him.

"I made this for you." *What if he doesn't like it?* But the Magician picked it up, slowly, eyes glowing, held it in both hands and gazed at it in awe.

"That is very, very kind of you," he whispered. Very carefully, he took off his hat and put the ruby in it. It was the first time Tyche had ever seen the Magician smile. Still, there was a sadness to his expression.

"I didn't want to leave before giving it to you," she said.

"That's quite a fuss you caused for the Brain. He is going to be very worried."

"He deserves it. But I promised I would go with him."

The Magician looked at the ruby one more time and put the hat back on his head.

"Normally, I don't interfere with the affairs of other people, but for this, I owe you a wish."

Tyche took a deep breath. "I don't want to live with the grags and the othos and the Brain anymore. I want to be in the Right Place with Mum and Dad."

The Magician looked at her sadly.

"I'm sorry, Tyche, but I can't make that happen. My magic is not powerful enough."

"But they promised –"

"Tyche, I know you don't remember. And that's why we Moon People remember for you. The space sharks came and took your parents, a long time ago. They are dead. I am sorry."

Tyche closed her eyes. *A picture in a window, a domed crater. Two bright things arcing over the horizon, like sharks. Then, brightness –*

"You've lived with the Brain ever since. You don't remember because it makes you forget with the

Treatments, so you don't get too sad, so you stay the way your parents wanted to keep you. But we remember. And we always tell you the truth."

And suddenly they were all there, all the Moon People, coming from their houses: Chang'e and her children and the Jade Rabbit and the Woodcutter, looking at her gravely and nodding their heads.

Tyche could not bear to look at them. She covered her helmet with her hands, turned around, crawled through the Secret Door and ran away, away from the Other Moon. She ran, not a Rabbit run but a clumsy jerky crying run, until she stumbled on a boulder and went rolling higgledy-piggledy down. She lay curled up in the chilly regolith for a long time. And when she opened her eyes, the ants were all around her.


THE ANTS WERE arranged around her in a half-circle, stretched into spiky pyramids, waving slightly, as if looking for something. Then they spoke. At first, it was just noise, hissing in her helmet, but after a second it resolved into a voice.

"– hello," it said, warm and female, like Chang'e, but older and deeper. "I am Alissa. Are you hurt?"

Tyche was frozen. She had never spoken to anyone who was not the Brain or one of the Moon People. Her tongue felt stiff.

"Just tell me if you are all right. No one is going to hurt you. Do you feel bad anywhere?"

"No," Tyche breathed.

"There is no need to be afraid. We will take you home." A video feed flashed up inside her helmet, a spaceship that was made up of a cluster of legs and a globe that glinted golden. A circle appeared elsewhere in her field of vision, indicating a tiny pinpoint of light in the sky. "See? We are on our way."

"I don't want to go to the Great Wrong Place," she gasped. "I don't want you to cut me up."

There was a pause.

"Why would we do that? There is nothing to be afraid of."

"Because Wrong Place people don't like people like me."

Another pause.

"Dear child, I don't know what you have been told, but things have changed. Your parents left Earth more than a century ago. We never thought we would find you, but we kept looking. And I'm glad we did. You have been alone on the Moon for a very long time."

Tyche got up, slowly. *I haven't been alone.* Her head spun. *They would do anything to have you.*

She backed off a few steps.

"If I come with you," she asked in a small voice, "will I see Kareem and Sofia again?"

A pause again, longer this time.

"Of course you will," Alissa the ant-woman said finally. "They are right here, waiting for you."

Liar.

Slowly, Tyche started backing off. The ants moved, closing their circle. *I am faster than they are,* she thought. *They can't catch me.*

"Where are you going?"

Tyche switched off her radio, cleared the circle of the ants with a leap and hit the ground running.

\*     \*     \*

TYCHE RAN, FASTER than she had ever run before, faster even than when the Jade Rabbit challenged her to a race across the Shackleton Crater. Finally, her lungs and legs burned and she had to stop. She had set out without direction, but had gone up the mountain slope, close to the cold fingers. *I don't want to go back to the Base. The Brain never tells the truth either.* Black dots danced in her eyes. *They'll never catch me.*

She looked back, down towards the crater of the Secret Door. The ants were moving. They gathered into the metal sheet again. Then its sides stretched upwards until they met and formed a tubular structure. It elongated and weaved back and forth and slithered forward, faster than even Tyche could run: a metal snake. The pyramid shapes of the ants glinted in its head like teeth. Faster and faster it came, flowing over boulders and craters like it was weightless, a curtain of billowing dust behind it. She looked around for a hiding place, but she was on open ground now, except for the dark pool of the mining crater to the west.

Then she remembered something the Jade Rabbit had once said. *For anything that wants to eat you, there is something bigger that wants to eat it.*

The ant-snake was barely a hundred metres behind her now, flipping back and forth in sinusoid waves on the regolith like a shiny metal whip. She stuck out her tongue at it, accidentally tasting the sweet inner surface of her helmet. Then she made it to the sunless crater's edge.

With a few bounds, she was over the crater lip. It was like diving into icy water. Her suit groaned, and she could feel its joints stiffening up. But she kept going, towards the bottom, almost blind from the contrast between the pitch-black and the bright sun above. She followed the vibration in her soles. Boulders and pebbles rained on her helmet and she knew the ant-snake was right at her heels.

The lights of the sandworm almost blinded her. *Now.* She leapt up, as high as she could, feeling weightless, reached out for the utility ladder that she knew was on the huge machine's topside. She grabbed it, banged painfully against the worm's side, felt its thunder beneath her.

And then, a grinding, shuddering vibration as the mining machine bit into the ant-snake, rolling right over it.

Metal fragments flew into the air, glowing red-hot. One of them landed on Tyche's arm. The suit made a bubble around it and spat it out. The sandworm came to an emergency halt, and Tyche almost fell off. It started disgorging its little repair grags, and Tyche felt a stab of guilt. She sat still until her breathing calmed down and the suit's complaints about the cold got too loud.

Then she dropped to the ground and started the climb back up, towards the Secret Door.


THERE WERE STILL a few ants left around the Secret Door, but Tyche ignored them. They were rolling around aimlessly, and there weren't enough of them to build a transmitter. She looked up. The ship from the Great Wrong Place was still a distant star. She still had time.

Painfully, bruised limbs aching, she crawled through the Secret Door one last time.

The Moon People were still there, waiting for her. Tyche looked at them in the eye, one by one. Then she put her hands on her hips.

"I have a wish," she said. "I am going to go away. I'm going to make the Brain obey me, this time. I'm going to go and build a Right Place, all on my own. I'm never going to forget again. So I want you all to come with me." She looked up at the Magician. "Can you do that?"

Smiling, the man in the top hat nodded, spread his white-gloved fingers and whirled his cloak that had a bright red inner lining, like a ruby –

TYCHE BLINKED. THE Other Moon was gone. She looked around. She was standing on the other side of the Old One and the Troll, except that they looked just like rocks now. And the Moon People were inside her. *I should feel heavier, carrying so many people,* she thought. But instead she was empty and light.

Uncertainly at first, then with more confidence, she started walking back up Malapert Mountain, towards the Base. Her step was not a rabbit's, nor a panther's, nor a maiden's silky tiptoe, just her very own.

# OBELISK

**Stephen Baxter**

Wei Binglin first saw the cairn of Cao Xi, as it happened, during his earliest moments on Mars.

It came at the end of a long and difficult voyage. Through the last few days of the *Sunflower*'s approach to Mars, Wei Binglin had been content for the automated systems to bring his ship home. Why not? Since the accident, most of the *Sunflower*'s manual controls had been inactive anyhow. And besides, Wei no longer regarded himself as deserving the rank of captain at all; in a ship become a drifting field hospital, he was reduced to the role of caretaker, his only remaining duty to bring those who had survived this, his last flight, into a proper harbour.

So, for the first time in his many approaches to the planet, he let Mars swim out of the darkness before him. In the light of a distant sun, it struck him from afar as a malformed, lopsided, murky world, oddly unfinished, like a piece of pottery by an inadequate student. And yet as the ship entered its parking orbit high above the planet and skimmed around the night side, he saw the colourful layers of a thin but tall atmosphere, a scattering of white in the deeper craters – clouds, fog? – and brilliant pinpricks of light in the night, human settlements, mostly Chinese, a few UN outposts. A world where people were already being born, living, dying. A world where he too, he decided, had come to die.

The surviving crew and passengers of the *Sunflower* had to wait a day in orbit while a small flotilla of vessels came out to meet them, from Mars's outer moon Deimos, a resource-rich rock itself which served as a centre for orbital operations. Many of the craft brought paramedics and automated medical equipment; some of the injured passengers and crew would be taken to the low-gravity hospital on Deimos for treatment before facing the rigours of a descent from orbit. There were only a handful of bodies to process. Most of the relatives of the dead had been content for the remains of their loved ones to be ejected into interplanetary space. Wei had officiated over these services himself, supported by the faithful of relevant creeds and cultures.

He may no longer have regarded himself as a captain, but the crew of the Deimos station paid him a certain honour. When the last passengers and crew had been lifted off, they sent out a final shuttle just for him, so he could be the last of the crew to leave his ship. But of course the *Sunflower* was not left empty; it already swarmed with repair crews, human and robotic, as it was towed gently by tugs to an orbital rendezvous with Deimos. An interplanetary ship was too valuable to scuttle, even one so grievously injured.

The shuttle itself was a small, fat-bodied glider coated with battered-looking heatshield tiles. In orbit, driven by powerful attitude thrusters, it was a nimble, nippy craft. The pilot, a young woman, allowed Wei to sit beside her in the co-pilot's seat as she took a quick final tour around the drifting hulk of the *Sunflower*.

He pointed out a great gash in the hull. "There. That is the wound that killed her."

"I see. The fusion containment failed, I read from the report."

"We lost our ion drive immediately, and many of the tethers to the lightsail were severed..."

Ships like the *Sunflower*, dedicated to long-haul interplanetary spaceflight, were roomy lightweight hulls driven by the gentle but persistent thrust of ion-drive engines, and by the push of sunlight on their huge sails. A journey from Earth to Mars on such a ship still took months, but months less than an unpowered trajectory, a Hohmann ellipse.

The pilot was watching his face. "The incident was a news headline on Earth and Mars, and elsewhere. The heroic efforts to stabilise the environment systems and save the passengers –"

"That was the achievement of my crew, not of myself."

"While you, Captain, manipulated your surviving propulsion system, a lightsail like a bird's broken wing, to put the ship on the Hohmann orbit that eventually brought you to Mars. It was an achievement of courage and improvisation to compare with the rescue of Apollo 13, some commentators have remarked."

He glanced at her. It was unusual in his experience for such young people to have knowledge of pioneering space exploits a hundred and forty years gone; to many of them it was as if the age of space had begun in 2003, when Yang Liwei became the first Chinese to reach Earth orbit aboard the Shenzhou 5.

But he didn't feel like being congratulated. "I lost my ship, and many of my passengers. And such a slow crawl out to sanctuary, on a ship full of the injured, was agonising." He had made daily visits from the bridge to the huddled remains of the passenger compartments. There were broken families back there, families who had lost a father or mother or children, and now were forced to endure more months of confinement, deprivation and suffering, unable even to escape from the scene of their loss. There were even orphans. He remembered one little girl in particular, no more than five years old; her name was Xue Ling, he had learned, and her father, mother and brother were all gone, an optimistic pioneer family wiped out in an instant. She had looked lost, bewildered, even as she rested her head against the stiff fabric of a kindly ship's officer's tunic.

"I am sure it was terrible," said the pilot. "But you brought your ship home." She tapped her control panels and the shuttle turned its nose to the planet. Soon the craft bit into the air. The atmosphere of Mars was thin, tall; the ride was surprisingly gentle compared with a re-entry at Earth, and the shuttle, shedding its orbital energy in frictional heat, made big swooping turns over a ruddy landscape. "We will be down shortly, Captain –"

"I am no longer a captain. I have resigned, formally. Please do not use that honorific."

"So I understand. You have decided to give up your career, to commit yourself to Mars."

"People trusted me to bring them here safely; I failed. The least I can do is honour their memory by –"

She grunted. "By doing what? Becoming a lichen farmer? I suppose to become a living monument is a noble impulse. But somewhat self-destructive, and a waste of your expertise, if you want my opinion, sir."

He didn't want it particularly, but he bit back a reprimand. He no longer held rank over this woman.

"You have no family on Earth?"

"No wife, no."

"Perhaps that will be your destiny on Mars. To help raise the first generation of pioneers, who will –"

"That will not be possible. During the accident – the failure of the shielding around the fusion reactor, and then a loss of shielding fluids from the ship as a whole..." He could see she understood. "I was baked for many months by the radiation of interplanetary space. The doctors tell me I have a high propensity for cancers in the future. And if I am not sterile, I should be."

"How old are you, sir?"

"Only a little over thirty."

She did not speak again.

The shuttle came down at a small, young settlement in a terrain in the southern hemisphere called the Terra Cimmeria. This was a landscape peculiarly shaped by sprawling crater walls and steep-sided river valleys; from the high air it reminded Wei of scar tissue, like a badly healed burn. The settlement, called Fire City, nestled on the floor of a crater called Mendel, itself nearly eighty kilometres across, its floor incised by dry channels and pocked by smaller, younger craters. From the air he glimpsed domes half-covered by heaped-up Martian dirt, the gleaming tanks and pipes of what looked like a sprawling chemical manufacturing plant, and a few drilling derricks, angular frames like rocket gantries.

The shuttle swept down smoothly onto a long

runway blasted across the crater floor. When it had come to rest, the pilot briskly helped Wei pull on a pressure suit. They clambered into an airlock, where they were briefly bathed in sterilizing ultraviolet. Then the hatch popped, and they climbed down a short stair.

Wei Binglin took a step on the surface of Mars, and another, exploring the generously low gravity, considering the clear impressions his boots made in the ubiquitous, clinging, rust-coloured dust. He could not see the walls of Mendel from here, or anything of the geologically complicated landscape beyond. The crater floor itself was a plain littered with rocks, like a high desert, and a small sun hung in a sky of washed-out brown. A few domes nestled nearby, and a single derrick was visible at the horizon, gaunt, still, like a dead tree. Wei had visited Mars four times before, but each time he had stayed in orbit with his interplanetary craft, or had visited the moon Deimos for work and recreation. He had never walked on Mars before. And now, he realised, he would never walk on any other world, ever again.

That was when he spotted the cairn.

It stood near the runway, a roughly pyramidal heap of rocks. He walked over. The cairn was taller than he was, and evidently purposefully constructed. "What is this?"

The pilot followed him. "This is the landing site of Cao Xi." The first to reach Mars, who had survived no more than an hour on the surface after his one-man lander crashed. "His body has been returned to his family on Earth."

"I once saw the mausoleum."

"But still, this place, where he walked, is remembered. The runway was built here as an appropriate gesture, it was thought; a link between ground and sky, space and Mars. This is a young place still, and everything is rather rough and ready."

Wei looked around. He selected a rock about the size of his head; it was sharp-edged, but easy to lift in the low gravity, if resistant to be moved through inertia. He hauled the rock up and settled it on the upper slope of the cairn.

"Everybody does that, on arrival," said the pilot.

"Why was I brought here, to this particular settlement?"

The pilot shrugged.

But the answer was obvious. Knowing nothing of the colonising of Mars, he had asked his former superiors to nominate a suitable destination, a new home. They had been drawn by the symbolism of this place. But Cao Xi had been a hero; Wei was not.

The cairn struck Wei as oddly steep-sloped. "You could not build such a structure on Earth."

"Perhaps not."

"I wonder how tall you could make such a mound, here in this partial gravity?"

"I do not know." She pointed at a rooster-tail of dust behind a gleaming speck, coming from one of the domes. "Your hosts. A family, husband and wife, themselves former interplanetary crew. They have volunteered to be your guides as you find your feet, here on Mars."

Wei felt a peculiar reluctance to meet these people, these Martians. He did not belong here. Yet he felt no impulse, either, to climb back on the shuttle and return to orbit. He belonged nowhere, he thought, as if he was dead himself. Yet he lived, breathed, was capable of curiosity, such as about this cairn. "Perhaps I will find purpose here."

"I am sure you will." The shuttle pilot touched his arm. He could feel the pressure through the suit layers, a kind gesture. "Perhaps you will be keeper of the cairn."

That made him laugh. "Perhaps so." It struck him that he did not even know her name. He turned to face the approaching rover.

As Xue Ling got up to leave his office, Wei checked the schedule on the slate built into his desk. He looked for his next appointment, not for the time. This office was in a privileged position, built into the dome wall so he had an exterior view, and he could judge the time pretty well by the way the afternoon sun slid around the flanks of the cairn.

He was dismayed to see that his next appointment was Bill Kendrick. Trouble for him again, with this American, who had been more or less dumped on him from the UN colony at Eden.

Kendrick was waiting when Xue Ling opened the door. He was tall, taller than most Chinese, wiry. His file said he was forty-five years old, only a little older than Wei; he looked younger save for a shock of prematurely grey hair, which was probably as much an engineered affectation as his apple-smooth cheeks, the taut flesh at his neck.

As he entered Wei's office, he carried a heavy-looking satchel. He held the door open for Xue Ling as she departed, and he looked after her with an odd wistfulness. "Pretty girl, *Mr Mayor*."

Wei winced. After four years here, Kendrick's Standard Chinese was pretty good, but when he addressed Wei he always stuck to the English form of that inappropriate appellation. A subtle form of rebellion, Wei supposed. He wanted to deter any interest Kendrick might have in Xue Ling, before it even started. "She is sixteen years old. She is my daughter. My adopted daughter."

"Oh." Kendrick glanced around the uncluttered office, and settled on one of the two empty chairs facing Wei's desk. "Your daughter? I didn't know you had one, adopted or otherwise. She looks kind of sad, if you don't mind my saying so."

Wei shrugged. "She is an orphan. She lost her family, in fact, during the flight of the *Sunflower*, the ship which –"

"Your ship. I see. And now you've adopted her?"

"It is a formality. She needs a legal guardian. Since being brought to Mars a decade ago, she has failed to settle with foster or adoptive parents, though many attempts were made. She ended up in the school at Phlegra Montes."

Kendrick frowned. "I heard of that place. Where they send all the broken kids."

Wei winced again. But the man was substantially right. Childbirth and child-rearing were chancy processes here on Mars. Because of the low gravity, the sleet of solar radiation, intermittent accidents like pressure losses or eco collapses, there were many stillbirths, many young born unhealthy one way or another. Even a healthy child might not grow well, simply because of the pressure of confinement in the domes; there was something of a plague of mental disorder, or autism. Hence Phlegra Montes. But the school also served as a last-resort refuge for children like Ling who simply didn't fit in. "In fact, the UN and the Chinese run the school together. One of our few cooperative acts on Mars."

Kendrick nodded. "Admirable. And good for you for giving her a home now. I can see why you'd feel responsible."

You could say this for Kendrick, Wei thought. He was prepared to express things bluntly, things that others danced around. Perhaps this was a relic of his own past. He had, after all, pursued a successful career of his own before falling foul of Heroic-Generation legislation on Earth, and being banished to Mars; no doubt plain speaking had served him well.

"We are here to discuss you, Mr Kendrick, not my daughter." He tapped his slate. "Once again I have to read reports about your indiscipline –"

"I wouldn't call it that," Kendrick said. "Call it inappropriately applied energy. Or the generation of inappropriate ideas, which the dead-heads you put me under can't recognise as potentially valuable contributions."

Wei felt hugely weary, even as they began this exchange. Kendrick was learning the language, but consciously or otherwise he was not fitting into the local culture. A big noisy American here in a Chinese outpost, he was too vivid, too loud. "Once again, Mr Kendrick, I am using up valuable time on your antics, which –"

"You volunteered for the job, *Mr Mayor*."

That term again. In fact Wei had nothing like the autonomy of the 'mayors' of western cities to which Kendrick alluded. Wei was actually the chair of the colony's council, with only local responsibilities; he reported up to a whole hierarchy of officials above him that extended across Mars and even back to Earth. Nevertheless, it was a burden of responsibility. And it was a role he had drifted into, almost naturally, given his experience and background, despite his own reluctance. Once again it was as if he was a captain, of this colony-ship grounded on Mars, sailing through interplanetary space. It was a burden he accepted as gladly as he could. Perhaps it was atonement.

But if not for this role, he thought, he would not have to confront issues like the management of this man, Bill Kendrick.

"You are not here for ideas," he said, exasperated. "Or for 'energy.' You are to work on the new derrick." The latest plunge into the rocky ground of Mars, to bring up precious water from the deep-lying aquifers beneath.

"Oh, I can do the roughneck stuff in my sleep."

"And what is it you do when awake, then?"

Kendrick seemed to take that as a cue. "I make these." He opened his satchel now, and produced two rust-red squared-off blocks, each maybe thirty centimetres long, five to ten centimetres in cross-section. He set these on the desk, scattering a little dust.

Wei picked one up; on Mars, like everything else, it was lighter than it looked. "What's this? Cut stone?"

"No. Bricks. I made bricks, out of Martian dust."

"Bricks?"

He half-listened as Kendrick briskly ran through the steps in his brick-making process: taking fine Martian dust, wetting it, adding a little straw from the domed gardens or shreds of waste cloth, then baking it in a solar-reflector furnace he had improvised from scrap parts. "It's a process that's as old as civilisation."

Wei smiled. "Whose civilisation do you mean?"

"So simple a child could run it."

"You say you need water –"

"Which is precious here, I know that, I'm breaking my own back drilling for it. But most of what I use can be recovered from the steam that comes off during baking."

"Tell me why anybody would want to make bricks."

Kendrick leaned forward. "Because it's a quick and dirty way for this township to expand. Think about it. Most of your people are still living crammed into these domes, and most of *them* are still shipped from Earth. Your plastics industry here is in its infancy, along with everything else."

Wei piled the two bricks one on top of the other. "How could I build a useful dwelling of brick? Our buildings have to be pressurised. A brick structure would be blown apart by the internal pressure; remember that Martian air is at only a fraction of –"

Kendrick rummaged in his satchel again. "I've got plans for two kinds of structure you can build from Martian brick. The first is dwelling spaces." He showed Wei hand-drawn plans of domes and vaults, half-buried in the Martian ground. "See? Pile it up with dirt, which you need for radiation shielding anyhow." Which was true. On Mars, there was no ozone layer, and the sun's ultraviolet reached all the way to the ground. "And the weight of the dirt will maintain the compression you need. This is only a short-term solution, but it could be an effective one. There's no shortage of dust on Mars, God knows; you could make as many bricks as you like, build as wide and deep as you can manage. It would give you room to grow your population fast, even before longer-term industries like plastics and steel kick in at production scales, and you can begin to achieve your strategic goals."

Wei held up his hand. "As always, you over-reach

yourself, Mr Kendrick. Remember, you have no rank here, no formal role. You were sent here from the UN base at Eden because of the trouble you caused there; it is better that you are used as a labourer here at Fire City than to rot in some prison at Eden, breathing the expensive air –"

"I always think big," Kendrick said, grinning, unabashed. "What got me in trouble in the first place. Even if I did achieve great things when I had a chance."

"'Great things' which earned you banishment to Mars." Wei was over-familiar with Kendrick's file. He was one of the youngest of a generation of entrepreneurs and engineers who had used the Jolts, a succession of climate-collapse shocks on Earth, as an opportunity; they had produced huge, usually flawed schemes to stabilise aspects of the climate, from sun-deflecting mirrors in space to gigantic carbon-sequestration plants in the deep oceans – schemes that, as had been revealed when the prosecutions started, had made their originators hugely wealthy, no matter how well they worked, or not. Even now, Wei thought, Kendrick probably carried around much of that wealth embedded in the very fabric of his body, in genetic therapies, cybernetic implants.

"Can you not see, Mr Kendrick, that if I allow you a role in influencing the 'strategic goals' of this community, as you call them, suspicions will inevitably arise that you are simply reverting to type?"

Kendrick shrugged. "I'm more interested in the common benefit than my own personal gain. Believe that or not, as you like. Sell this under your own authority if it makes you feel better." Then he shut up.

In the lengthening silence, Wei was aware of a seed of curiosity growing in his own mind, a seed planted by Kendrick. He suppressed a sigh. The man was a good salesman, if nothing else. "Tell me, then. What is the second kind of structure that could be built with your bricks?"

Kendrick glanced out of the window. "The monument."

"The cairn?"

"Look at it. It's kind of impressive, in its way. Everybody adds to it. I've seen the school kids climbing the ladders to add on another couple of rocks."

Wei shrugged. It had been one of his initiatives to build up the cairn of Cao Xi as a cheap way to unite the community, and to remember a great hero.

"But how tall is it?" Kendrick asked now. "A hundred metres? Listen – there were pyramids on Earth taller than that. And this is Mars, *Mr Mayor*. Low gravity, right? We ought to be able to build a pyramid three or four hundred metres tall, if we felt like it. Or..." Another expertly timed pause.

Wei felt himself being drawn in. This must have been how the Heroic Generation made their plays, he thought. The sheer ambition of the visions, the scale – the *chutzpah*, to use one of Kendrick's own words – it was all dazzling. "Or what?"

"Or we use my bricks. There were cathedral spires on Earth over a hundred and fifty metres tall. Here on Mars –"

"Spires?"

"Just imagine it, *Mr Mayor*." Kendrick could clearly see he had Wei's interest. "If nothing else, you need something to keep me busy, and maybe a few other miscreants. You can't send me back to Earth, can you?"

Wei could not; that was no longer an option. A post-Jolt redistribution was shaping the home planet now; in China and around the rest of the world, whole populations were being displaced north and south from the desiccating mid-latitudes, and the central government had told the Martian colonists that they needed to find their own solutions to their problems. Yes, this would use up spare labour.

And meanwhile Wei had long had an instinct that the first humans living on Mars should be doing more than merely surviving.

"A spire, you say?"

Kendrick grinned, and produced a slate with more diagrams. "You'd start by digging foundations. Even on Mars, a tree would need roots as deep as it is tall..."

KENDRICK'S ROVER WAS waiting for Wei outside the lock from the Summertime Vault. It was mid-morning and a break in the school timetable; at this time of day, as usual, most of the colony's hundred children were running around the big public space that dominated the Vault, many of them low-gravity tall, oddly graceful. They were full of energy and life, and Wei, feeling old at forty-seven, regretted having to turn his back on them.

But Kendrick was waiting for him, his oddly youthful face full of calculation, eager as ever to draw Wei into his latest schemes.

To Wei's surprise, he and Kendrick were alone in the rover when it pulled away from the lock. "I didn't know you were permitted to pilot one of these."

Kendrick just grinned. "There's a lot of stuff in this town that goes on under your personal radar, *Mr Mayor*. Don't sweat it. I've made a lot of friends

273

here, a lot of contacts, and I call in favours every now and then."

Wei glanced back at the heavy brick shoulders of the Summertime Vault, under its mound of rock and dust. "You have accumulated these favours ever since we let you become so influential in the colony's destiny."

"I'm doing no harm – you've got to admit that. Everybody benefits in the end. Xue Ling helped fix me up with this, actually."

"She isn't your personal assistant. She merely volunteered to –"

"I know, I know." Kendrick looked away, hastily, as if seeking to close down the subject. "It's the way the world works. Don't sweat about it."

Wei was sure Kendrick knew he disapproved of his relationship with Xue Ling, such as it was. The spurious glamour of the man seemed to draw in Xue Ling, as it drew in others. Wei didn't believe that Kendrick intended to push this too far. Nor did he suspect that Kendrick would succeed if he tried; Xue Ling, twenty-two years old now, was engaged to be married. But still, something about Kendrick's interest in Xue Ling didn't feel right, to the paternal instincts Wei hoped he had developed over the last six years as the girl's foster parent.

Heading out of town, they drove past the new Cao Xi monument. The old heap of rubble had long been demolished to make way for Kendrick's spire, a lofty cone nearly four hundred metres tall – nearly three times the height of the tallest cathedral spires of medieval Europe, though constructed with much the same materials and techniques, of brick and mortar over a frame of tall Martian-grown oak trunks. The usual gaggle of protestors was gathered here, at the foot of the unfinished monument. Kendrick let the rover nose through their thin line, and Wei peered out, forcing an official smile for the benefit of any imagers present. Some were protesting because of the diversion of materials into what they called "Wei's Folly," and it did Wei no good to point out that the building of the spire had kick-started the development of whole industries in the colony. Others protested because of the spire's echoes of the Christian west. And still others protested simply because they had liked the old cairn, the mound of stones they and their children had worked together to build up.

Kendrick, typically, ignored the people and peered up at the spire: slim, tall, already a monument impossible on Earth, at least with such basic raw materials. "Magnificent, isn't it?"

"Magnificent for you," Wei murmured. "Is this how it was for the Heroic Generation? You build your monuments, overriding protests. You persuade the rest of us they are essential. And you grow fat on the profits, of one kind or another."

"Binglin, my friend –"

"Don't speak to me like that."

"Sorry. Look – maybe I push my luck at times. But the reason I get away with it is, you're right, because you need what I do. You have the Vaults now, a huge expansion of space above what would have been possible. And that helps everybody, right? I've heard you talk of the Triangle. I read the news in the slates. I do pay attention, you know..."

The Triangle was the latest economic theory, of how Earth, Mars and asteroids could be linked in a mutually supportive, positive-feedback trade loop. The asteroids were a vital source of raw materials, mined cleanly for a starving Earth. So Earth, or rather the Chinese Greater Economic Framework down on Earth, exported expertise and high-tech goods out into space, and got asteroid resources back in return. Mars, with its rapidly expanding colonies, served as a source of labour and living space for the asteroid development agencies, and in return received the raw materials *it* needed, particularly the volatiles of which the planet was starved.

But Mars's local administrators, Wei among them, were concerned that Mars should not be a mere construction shack on the edge of the asteroid belt. So a deliberate effort was being made to turn Mars's new communities, including Fire City, into hotbeds of communications, information technology, and top-class education. The dream was to start exporting high-quality software and other digital material both to the asteroids and to Earth – a dream that was already, after a half-decade of intensive development and salesmanship, beginning to pay off.

Kendrick was right. To achieve these goals, Mars needed room, human space, to grow its populations. Kendrick had managed to spot a kind of gap in the resource development cycle, and to fill it with his brick constructions. But that didn't make him necessary, in any sense. Not as far as Wei was concerned.

Soon the centre of Fire City was far behind, and they passed the last colony buildings, the big translucent domes that sheltered the artificial marshland that was the hub of the city's recycling system. Then they drove through fields covered with clear plastic, where scientists were experimenting with gen-enged wheat and potatoes and rice, growing in Martian soil. Further out still the fields were open, and here banks of lichen stained the rocks, green and purple: the most advanced life forms on Mars, before humans arrived. Some of these lichen, which were some kind of relation to Earth life, were being gen-enged too, more experiments to find a way to farm Mars.

Beyond the lichen beds, at last they were out in the open, in undeveloped country. Even so, they were still well within the walls of Mendel crater. And as the humming rover bounced over the roughly made track, Wei began to make out a slim form, dead ahead. It was a kind of tower, skeletal, with a splayed base. He peered forward, squinting through the dusty air. "What is *that*?"

Kendrick grinned. "What I brought you out here to see, *Mr Mayor*. You ever heard of the Eiffel Tower? In Paris, France. It was pulled down during a food riot in the 2060s, but –"

"Stop the rover." As the vehicle rolled to a halt, Wei leaned forward, peering out of the blister window. Already they were so close that he had to tip back his head to see the peak. "What is its purpose?"

Kendrick shrugged. "It's a test. A demonstration, of what's possible to build with steel on Mars. Just as the spire –"

"Steel? Where did you get the steel from?..." But of course Wei knew that; the city's new metallurgy plant, already up to industrially useful capacity, was pumping out iron and steel produced from hematite ore, the primary commercial source of iron on Earth, and an ore so ubiquitous on Mars it was what made the planet red. "You diverted the plant's production for this?"

"Diverted – yeah, okay, that's the right word. Look, this is just a trial run. The steelworkers were keen too, to learn welding techniques in the Martian air, and so on... When it's proved its point, we will tear it down and put the materials to better use."

"And that point is?"

"To see how high we can build, of course. We're still far from the tower, you don't get a sense of scale from here. Listen: that thing is almost eight hundred metres tall. Nearly three times the height of Eiffel, on Earth. That good old Martian gravity. This thing is already taller than any building on Earth until the late twentieth century. Think of that! Can you feel how it draws up the eye? That's the magical thing about Martian architecture. It baffles the Earthbound instinct."

"You erected this without my knowledge."

"Well, people live in holes in the ground here. You could get away with building almost anything you like, out in that big open Mars desert."

"You are showing this to me now. Why?"

"I told you, this is a trial run. Just like the spire."

"For what?"

"The monument of Cao Xi, Mark III. You need to keep expanding, *Mr Mayor*. My brick has filled a gap, but in future, Martian steel, Martian glass, and Martian concrete are going to be the way to do it. But why keep burrowing into the ground? What way is that to bring up a new generation? Oh, I know we need to think about shielding, but..."

"What are you saying?"

"Tell me you can't guess. Tell me you aren't inspired. I know you by now, Wei Binglin." Kendrick pointed to the brownish sky. "No more cairns or spires, no more non-functional monuments. I'm telling you we should build a place for people to live. I'm telling you that we should build, not down – *up*."

\* \* \*

THE CHAIRMAN OF the review committee, appointed directly by New Beijing on far-off Earth, was called Chang Kuo, and as the meeting came to order for its second day he regarded Wei and Kendrick solemnly. This conference room was deep underground, buried in the floor of the Hellas basin, which was itself eight kilometres beneath the Mars datum. Wei reflected that it would have been impossible for this place, the Chinese administrative capital, buried at the deepest point on Mars, to have been further away in spirit from what he and Kendrick were trying to build at Fire City.

Yet the room was dominated by a hologram, sitting in the centre of this circular room, a real-time relayed image of the Obelisk, as people were calling it, an image itself as tall as a human being. The real thing was already more than a kilometre tall, a great rectangular arm of steel and glass reaching to the Martian sky. And the damage done by the meteorite strike was clearly visible, a neat circular puncture somewhere above the three-hundredth level: the disaster was the reason for this review.

The room shuddered, and Wei thought he heard a boom, deep and distant.

"*What the hell was that?*" Kendrick had lapsed into his native English. "Sorry, I meant –"

He looked alarmed, to Wei's unkind satisfaction. "It was a nuclear weapon, detonated far beneath the fragmented floor of the Hellas crater. I would not have thought that a Heroic-Generation engineer like you would have been frightened by a mere firecracker."

"Why are they setting off nukes?... Oh. The terraforming experiments."

"You heard about that. Well, of course you would."

"Xue Ling showed me some of the documentation. Don't blame her. I pushed her to leak me the stuff. Blame her pregnancy; it's making her easier to handle." But his smile was secretive, reluctant.

Wei thought he understood. Xue Ling, now twenty-eight years old, married and with child, had been campaigning to be allowed to leave Fire City – to come here, in fact, to Hellas, where she felt she could carve out a more meaningful career in administration than was possible back home. Her husband too, now a senior terraforming engineer, was having to commute to Hellas and back. It made sense in every way to Wei to allow her to go.

Every way but one: Kendrick.

There were other communities who were after Kendrick now, other opportunities, clandestine or otherwise, he might be tempted to pursue. Probably part of his long-term game plan had always been to manoeuvre himself into a position where such opportunities would turn up. But it would be disastrous for Fire City if he were allowed to leave before the tower was finished – and disastrous, too, for Wei himself, of course, who had become so closely identified with the project, even in the eyes of these mandarins at Hellas. So Kendrick could not be allowed to leave. How, though, to keep him?

Xue Ling still seemed to be important to Kendrick, and therefore was a hold on him. Conversely she was a conduit of information to Wei, about his difficult, unpredictable, rogue of an ally. Regretfully, then, if Kendrick must be kept here, *Wei could not allow Xue Ling to leave*. He assured himself that greater concerns, the good of the community as a whole, were paramount over her wishes. Besides, he told himself, it was better for Xue Ling herself, whether she knew it or not, after the chaotic start to life she had endured, to stay close to what had become the nearest thing to home: close to her father, to himself...

The chairman, Chang Kuo, had spoken to him.

"I'm sorry, sir. Could you repeat that?"

"I said that this is the second day of our review of the project, of this Obelisk, as the popular media are calling it – or Wei's Folly, as I believe your own people refer to it. We must come to a verdict soon as to whether to allow the project to continue."

Wei said carefully, "Yesterday we reviewed the practical value of the tower. The living space it will afford. The stimulus it has given to local industries, to the development of skills and technologies specialised to Martian conditions. It is a great challenge, and as a people we are at our best when we rise to challenges."

"Citizens have died. Its absurd vulnerability to meteorite strikes –"

Just as Mars's thin air was no barrier to solar ultraviolet, so it did not screen the ground from medium-sized meteorite impacts, as Earth's thick atmosphere shielded the mother lands.

Kendrick said confidently, "That is a problem that can be solved, with warning systems, orbital deflection, laser batteries –"

"Ha! A typical Heroic-Generation answer. All at great expense, no doubt. Already the Obelisk project is distorting the whole of the regional economy. There are those who say it is a mere grandiose folly."

Kendrick stood up, eliciting gasps of shock at his ill manners. "Grandiose? Is that what you think this is, grandiose, a mere gesture? Mr Chairman, the point of the Cao Xi Tower is to give this current generation a dream of their own. To give them something more to do than fulfil the dreams of their parents..." He looked at Wei.

Wei knew how the argument should go now. They'd rehearsed it often enough. He even agreed with it, up to a point: *Everybody wants to be a pioneer. The first on Mars, like Cao Xi! Either that, or an inhabitant of the settled world of the future, living on a terraformed Mars, or at least under a dome big enough to cover Taiwan – big enough to allow children to grow without visible walls around them. Nobody wants to be in one of the middle generations, you see. Nobody wants to be a settler. It is this cadre's tragedy to be that settler generation. But settlers need dreams too. We aren't building this tower because it's sensible. We do it precisely because it's a grand gesture – even grandiose, yes. For children who can't dream of journeying to Mars, for they were born on Mars, this is their goal, their monument. Their chance to leave a legacy for history...*

He was silent. They all looked at him, even Kendrick, who had sat down beside him.

"Pan Gu," he said at last.

"What was that, Wei Binglin?"

"I am Pan Gu. Or my colleague is. Pan Gu, who was born in the primordial egg, and grew for eighteen thousand years, and stood up..." He looked around at their blank faces. He wondered how many of them even knew what he was talking about; the culture of Chinese Mars was fast diverging from the old country. He felt old himself. He was only fifty-three. He had already spent a decade of his life working with this man, this monster, Kendrick, and still he was not done.

One of the mandarins spoke into the silence. "It was always a mistake to allow a pilot to assume a position of administrative power. The hero of the *Sunflower*! He was always liable to make some such gesture as this. Once a hero, always a hero – eh, Captain Wei?"

Chang Kuo nodded, stern. "You have certainly bound yourself up to this monument, Wei Binglin. This monument, or folly."

"Of course he has," said Kendrick dryly. "But he can't stop. We can't stop..."

Wei collected himself. "None of us can stop," he said now, firmly. "The Obelisk is known across the planet, and at home, across the Framework – even in the UN-allied nations, thanks to satellites which image it from orbit. *We cannot stop*. The loss of face would be too great. That is the foundation of our argument for continuing, and it runs as deep and solid as the foundations we built for the tower itself. Now. Shall we discuss how best to proceed from here?" And he glared at them, one by one, as if daring them to contradict him.

THE WORD CAME to the two of them as they were having another long, wrangling meeting in Wei's office, in the old Summertime Vault.

The call came from her estranged husband, who was in Hellas, and who had in turn received a panicky call from a friend. She was heading for the top of the Obelisk. She had looked desperate as she left her apartment, on the prestigious fiftieth floor.

So they ran, the two of them, through the underground

way to the base levels of the Obelisk, chambers carved into the tower's massive foundations. Wei was in his late fifties now, Kendrick in his early sixties, and neither was as healthy as he once had been, Wei knew, he himself with an obscure cancer eating at his bones, and Kendrick limping along beside him, his oddly distorted face youthful yet slack, for his expensive implants were, after decades without replacement, beginning to fail.

At the Obelisk, Wei had a priority card that enabled him to gain access to one of the high status, fast-ascent external elevators. They were both breathless, and stayed silent as the elevator car climbed.

Soon they rose above ground level, and the car began to crawl its way up one glass-coated side of the building. They were afforded a tremendous view of the city, and of Mars, as they climbed. Yet it was the Obelisk itself that captured the attention, as ever. As he looked up through the elevator's clear roof, Wei saw the glass face shining in the low, buttery morning sunlight of Mars, climbing on and on, a dead flat plane that narrowed to a fine line and seemed to pierce the sky itself. In a sense it did, for the Obelisk rose above the weather. The shell was complete now, a cage of Martian steel under tension, holding concrete piles in place, all of it glassed over. It was mostly pressurised, though the labour of fitting out its interior would likely go on for years yet. To the external walls were fixed a number of elevator channels, like the one they rode, and inside, a steep staircase wound up within the pressurised hull. That was the other way to ascend the building, to climb up, like ascending a mountain.

The tower itself reached an astounding ten kilometres into the sky, three times as tall as any conceivable building of the same materials on Earth

– and over five times as tall as any building ever actually constructed there. Wei had seen simulations of the sight of it from orbit – he himself had never left the planet, since stepping off the shuttle from the *Sunflower*. From space it was an astonishing image, slim, perfect, an arm rising out of the chaotic landscape to claw at the sky.

Ten kilometres! Why, if you laid it flat out, it would take a reasonably healthy man two hours to walk its length. And the walk up the stairs, if you took it, was itself fourteen kilometres long. Mars was a small world, but built on a big scale, with tremendous craters and deep valleys; but only the great Tharsis volcanoes would have dwarfed the Obelisk. Even on the ground, you could see it from hundreds of kilometres away, a needle rising up from beyond the horizon. All of mankind seemed to agree it was a magnificent human achievement, especially to have been constructed so early in the era of the colonisation of Mars.

And the Obelisk had transformed the community from which it had sprung. Just as Kendrick had predicted, as a result of the forced development that had been required for the building of the tower, Fire City had become a global centre of industry, of the production of steel and glass, even Kendrick's venerable bricks. There was even talk of moving the planet's administrative capital here, from the gloomy dungeons at Hellas. Even the city's name was changing; even that, to 'Obelisk,' simply.

Yet there was still controversy.

"I received another petition," Wei said, breaking the silence.

"About what?"

"About the water you use up, making your concrete."

He shrugged. "We have plenty of water coming up from the aquifer wells now. Besides, what of it? If civilisation falls on Mars, let future generations mine the wreck of the Obelisk for the water locked up in its fabric. Think of it as a long-term strategic reserve."

"Are you serious?"

"Of course."

"I should not be astounded by you any more, but I am. To think on such timescales!"

"Pah. That is nothing. Order out of chaos," Kendrick said now, glaring up.

"What?"

"Pan Gu. Remember you quoted that name when we were hauled over the coals by those stuffed shirts at Hellas, all those years ago? I looked him up. Pan Gu, a primal deity of very old Chinese myth. Right? Who clambered out of some kind of primordial egg, and stood up, and as he grew he forced earth and sky apart. And after eighteen thousand years, having created order out of chaos, he was allowed to lie down and rest. That's you and me, buddy. We made this thing. We made order out of Martian chaos. We made Mars human."

"Did we? Have we really made such a difference, despite all your arrogant bluster?" As they rose further, Wei looked out, to the Martian landscape opening up beyond the confines of the city, the horizon steadily widening. "Out there. What do you see?"

Kendrick turned to look.

Beyond the walls of Mendel, they could see more crater walls, on a tremendous scale but eroded, graven with gullies, and dry valleys snaking between. This was Terra Cimmeria, a very ancient landscape, and a ground that might have baffled even Pan Gu. It dated from the earliest days of the formation of the solar system, when the young worlds were battered with a late bombardment of huge rock fragments, some of them immature planets themselves. That was a beating whose scars had been washed away on Earth, but they had survived on the moon, and on Mars. And here the cratering process had competed with huge flooding episodes, as giant underground aquifers were broken open to release waters that washed away the new crater walls, and pooled on the still-red-hot floors of the impact basins. The relic of all that had endured for billions of years, a crazy geological scribble.

None of this, Wei thought, had anything to do with humanity. Nor had humanity even begun to touch this primal disorder. And yet there was beauty here. He spied one small crater where a dune field had gathered, Martian dust shaped by the thin winds, a fine sculpture, a variation of crescents. Maybe that was the role of humans here, he thought. To pick out fragments of beauty amid the violence. Beauty like the spirit of Xue Ling, perhaps, who was fleeing from him into the sky.

Kendrick said nothing. A mere planet, it seemed, did not impress him, save as raw material.

They passed through a layer of cloud, fine water-ice particles. Once they were higher, the cloud hid the ugly ground, and it was as if the Obelisk itself floated in the sky.

For the last few hundred floors, as the tower narrowed, they had to switch elevators to a central shaft. They hurried down a corridor inhabited only by patient robots, squat cylinders, that worked on a weld. There was no carpet here, and the walls were bare concrete panels; the very air was thin and cold. At the elevator shaft, they had to don pressure suits, provided in a store inside the car itself; pressurisation was not yet guaranteed at higher levels.

They rose now in darkness, excluded from the world.

Wei said carefully, "We have not even spoken of why we are here."

"Xue Ling, you mean. Neither of us is surprised to find ourselves in this position. Be honest about that, Wei Binglin. You know, I could never..."

"What? Have her?"

"Not that," Kendrick said angrily. "I knew I could never tell her how I felt. Mostly because I didn't understand it myself. Did I love her? I suspect I don't know what love is." He laughed. "My parents didn't provide me with that implant. But she was something so beautiful, in this ugly place. I would never have harmed her, you know. Even by loving her."

"I knew that."

Kendrick looked at him bleakly. "And yet you kept her close to me. That was to control me, was it?"

Wei shrugged. "Once the Obelisk was begun, you could not be allowed to leave."

"How could I leave? I'm a criminal, remember. This is a chain gang, for me."

"I've known you a long time, Bill Kendrick. If you had wished to leave, you would have found a way."

"So you nailed me in place with her, did you? But at what cost, Wei? At what cost?"

The elevator slid to a halt. The doors peeled back to reveal a glass wall, a viewing gallery, as yet unfinished. They were near the very top of the tower now, Wei knew, nearly ten kilometres high, and the horizon of this small world was folded, a clear curve, with layers of the atmosphere visible as if seen from space. To the east, there was a brownish smudge: a dust storm brewing, possibly.

And there, on a ledge, *outside* the wall of glass, was Xue Ling. She was aware of their arrival, and she turned. Wei could easily make out her small, frightened face behind her pressure suit visor. She was still only thirty-three, Wei realised, only thirty-three.

The two men ran to the wall, fumbling with gloved hands at the glass. Wei slapped an override unit on his chest to ensure they could all hear each other.

"Now you come," Xue Ling said bitterly. "Now you see me, as if for the first time in my life."

Kendrick looked from left to right, desperately. "How do we get through this wall?"

"What was it you wanted? You, Bill Kendrick, creating a thing of stupendous ugliness to match the crimes you committed on Earth? You, Wei Binglin, building a tower to get back to the sky from which you fell? And what was I, a token in your relationship with each other? You call me your daughter. Would you have treated your blood daughter this way? You kept me here. Even when I lost my baby, even then, and my husband wanted to go back to Hellas, even then..."

Wei pressed his open palm to the glass. "Ling, please. Why are you doing this? Why now?"

"You never saw me. You never heard me. You never listened to me."

Kendrick touched his arm. "She asked again to leave, to go to Hellas."

"She asked *you*?"

"She wanted me to persuade you, this time. I said you would forbid it. It was one refusal too many, perhaps..."

"Your fault, then."

Kendrick snorted. "Do you really believe that?"

"You never saw me! See me now!"

And she let herself fall backwards, away from the ledge. The men pressed forward, following her descent through the glass. The gentle Martian gravity, which had permitted the building of the Obelisk, drew her down gently at first, then gradually faster. Her breathing, in Wei's ears, was as if she stood next to him, staying calm even as she fell away, drifting down the face of the tower. He lost sight of her as she passed through the cloud, long before she reached the distant ground.

# VAINGLORY

**Alastair Reynolds**

OFFICIALLY IT'S RUACH City, but everyone calls it Stilt Town. I've never liked the place. The amount of time I've spent there, it really ought to feel like home. But Stilt Town never stays still long enough to get familiar. Raised above Triton's cryovolcanic crust on countless thermally-insulating legs, it's a quilt of independent domed-over platforms, connected by bridges and ramps but subject to frequent and bewildering rearrangements. It's like a puzzle I'm not meant to solve.

Still. A drink, a bar, a half-way decent view. There are worst places.

"Loti Hung?"

I turn from the window. I don't recognise the woman who's just addressed me, but my first thought, strangely, is that she must be Authority. It's not that she's wearing a uniform, or looks like any Authority official I've ever dealt with. But it's something in the eyes, tired and pink-tinged as they are. A calm and lucid watchfulness, as if she's used to studying faces and reactions, taking nothing at face value.

"Can I help you?"

"You're the artist? The rock sculptor?"

Since I'm sitting in the *Cutter and the Torch*,

surrounded by images of rock art and with my own portfolio still open before me, it's not a massive deductive leap. But she knows my name, and that's worrying. I'm nowhere near famous enough for that.

I tell myself that she can't be Authority. I've done nothing to merit their attention. Cut some corners, maybe. Bent a few rules. But nothing they'd consider worth their time.

"You haven't told me your name."

"Ingvar," she says. "Vanya Ingvar." And she conjures up a floating accreditation sigil and it all falls into place.

Vanya Ingvar. Licensed investigator. Not a cop, not Authority, but a private dick.

So my instincts weren't totally off-beam.

"What do you want?"

Her hair is short and gingery and squashed into greasy curls, as if she's just removed a tight-fitting vacuum helmet. She runs a hand over her scalp, to no avail. "While your ship was in repair dock, I paid someone to run a deep-level query on its navigation core. I wanted to know where you were at a particular time."

I almost spill my drink. "That's totally fucking illegal!"

She shrugs. "And totally fucking unprovable."

I decide I may as well humour this woman for a few more seconds. "So what were you after?"

"This and that. Mainly, a link to the Naiad impactor."

I blink. I'm expecting to hear that she's tied me to some civil infringement not covered by any statute of limitations. Failure to follow proper approach and docking procedure, that kind of thing. But when she mentions the Naiad impactor, I know she's got the wrong woman. Some mix-up of names or ship registrations or something. And for a moment I'm almost, almost, sorry for her. She's rude and she's had someone snoop around *Moonlighter* without my permission. That pisses me off. But she looks as if she could use a break.

"I'm sorry to break it to you, Ingvar. I was nowhere near Naiad when it happened. Matter of fact, I remember watching it on the newsfeeds from a bar in Huygens City, Titan. That's the other side of the system. Whoever dug into my nav core didn't know what they were doing."

"I'm not talking about your whereabouts at the time of the collision. That was twenty-five years ago. My interest is in where you were twenty-seven years before that. Fifty-two years ago, at the time the impactor's course was adjusted, to place it on a collision vector for Naiad." Then she pauses, and delivers her coup de grace, the thing that tells me she's not just making this up. "According to my investigations, it wasn't long after you'd met Skanda Abrud."

It's a name I've tried hard not to think about for over half a century. And managed, most of the time. Except for that one occasion when a bright new star shone in Fornax and Skanda forced himself back into my consciousness.

Now it hurts to say his name.

"What do you know about Skanda?"

"I know that he paid you to cut a rock. I also know that when the Naiad impactor hit, one hundred and fifty-two innocent people died. The rest... I think I'd like to hear it from you."

I shake my head. "Nobody died on Naiad. Nobody lived there."

"That," Ingvar says, "is only what they want you to think."

"They?"

"Authority. It was their screw-up that allowed

293

those settlers to build their camp on that little moon in the first place. Claim-jumpers. They should have been moved on years earlier."

She suggests we leave the *Cutter and the Torch*, because she doesn't want anyone listening in on our conversation. At this point, there are a number of possibilities open to me. I could tell her to fuck off. She hasn't arrested me, doesn't even have powers of arrest. She hasn't even threatened to turn me over to Authority, and what good would it do her if she did? I've done nothing wrong. I am Loti Hung; I am eighty years old, a middlingly successful rock cutter. That's all.

But she's right about Skanda, and it did happen when she said. And that worries me. I tell myself that nothing bad can happen in Stilt Town. And besides, I want to hear what she has to say.

So we exit, into the domed-over night. Ingvar walks stiffly, with a lopsided gait. It's hard to tell, but I doubt that she's any younger than me. Both of us wear heavy coats and boots, but Triton's cold still insinuates itself up the stilts, through the city's floor, into our ancient bones.

And I tell her about the day I met Skanda Abrud.


It was here, under Neptune. I'd come out to Triton chasing a possible client. Early in my rock-carving days, but not so early that I wasn't building a small but respectable reputation. Neptune was further out than I'd ever been before, but I figured it was worth the time and the cost.

I'd been wrong. An upstart rival had undercut my offer and stolen the prospective customer. *Moonlighter*, meanwhile, needed fuel and repairs.

While bots swarmed over the ship, and my bank account trickled down to single digits, I shuttled to Triton to drown my sorrows. That was when I ended up in the *Delta Vee Hotel*.

I've not been there since; too many ghosts. Like the *Cutter and the Torch* is now, the place was a popular hang-out with artists and their sponsors. The walls, floor and tables were covered with images and solid projections of work both good and gaudy: asteroids and iceteroids, boulders and rocks, transformed into pieces of art, from the geometric abstracts of Motl and Petit to the hyper-realistic portraiture of Dvali and Maestlin. I knew some of these people; had even worked with some of them back when they trimmed payloads for the big combines.

My star was on the rise, modestly, but even then I sensed that the bubble couldn't last. Too much money was changing hands. On my way in, I'd passed Ozymandis, a kilometre-sized rock put into Triton orbit. It was the work of Yinning and Tarabulus, the latest hot properties. I didn't think much of it. It was a face, shattered and time-worn, with great clefts in the cheeks and deep black craters for eyeholes. Everyone went mad for it, but all I saw was various superficial gimmicks used to conceal a profound absence of technique.

Yinning and Tarabulus hadn't come up through the combines; they'd never worked with rock and ice in any other context. Lacking that core of experience, they *had* to make their work look damaged and ancient, because that was the only way to disguise their screw-ups. They worked against the rock, not with it: couldn't see the weaknesses in the stone, the planes of failure.

Fucking amateurs.

I vowed that if anyone was ever crazy enough to let me loose on a piece of rock that big, I'd cut it perfectly. And I knew I could.

What I didn't expect was that I was about to get the chance.

"Beautiful, isn't it?"

He – whoever he was – meant Neptune. I'd been staring into its face, locked overhead like a vast ceiling ornament. The giant's purple-blue gloom had turned out to be a perfect match for my funk.

"If you say so."

"I mean it. Look at it, Loti. Barely a ring system worth mentioning, no metastable storms in the atmosphere. Winds, yes. Transient features. But nothing that lasts. Triton's the only moon of any consequence; the rest are snowballs. Yet it has its own understated magnificence. An undemonstrative grandeur."

I still had no idea who was talking, and by that point in the evening even less interest. But when I turned around I found my interest notching up slightly. He was elegant, well-dressed, exceedingly handsome – and definitely not someone I'd seen in the *Delta Vee Hotel* until now.

"Do I know you?"

"Not yet. But I'm hoping we can get to know each other. Work together, I mean. My name is Skanda Abrud. I have a proposition, a proposal for a commission. Are you interested?"

"That'll depend on the pay and the duration."

He smiled tightly. "I'd have thought you'd have jumped at work. As it happens, the pay will be excellent – at least twenty times what you've ever received before, if my suspicions are correct. I've also selected my own rock. It's on a high inclination orbit, but easily reachable. Would you like to see it?"

This was all too good to be true. I'd been stitched up before, led to think I was on the verge of a life-changing commission.

"If you feel you must."

He made precise right angles of his thumbs and forefingers to frame an image. The space between his hands darkened, clotted with blackness and a near-black lump. The lump was contoured with dim sunlight on one side, picking out craters and ridges in purple-browns. He pulled his hands apart to swell the image. "It's large, about a kilometre across, but easily within your capabilities. Do you think you could do this for me?"

I studied the rock, studied his face. I imagined his head fitting inside the rock, waiting to be revealed like a mask in a mould. This, after all, was what most of my clients wanted. Their own face, tumbling around the Sun for the rest of eternity.

"I'd need to run some scans," I hedged. "But if there are no nasty surprises, I can probably make you fit."

This seemed to throw him. "No. It's not me that you'd be doing. Good grief, no. Can you *imagine* the absolute vanity of that?"

"So who else do you want?" Already I was thinking loved one, lover, heroic ancestor: the usual self-aggrandizing bullshit.

"That's easy." He made another image. It was a male face, that of a young man. Classically proportioned. I guess I'd have recognised it, if my education hadn't been so patchy.

"I don't know it."

"You should. What I want, Loti, is for you to carve me the head of Michelangelo's David."

INGVAR HAS LED me to the public ice-rink on the western cusp of Stilt-Town. It's perverse, really. Massive layers of insulation buttress the city from the surface of Triton, and now they go to all this trouble to create *another* little square of frozen ground over the city's floor. Granted, it's not cryo-cold, it doesn't need to be, but I still feel an extra bite to the air. Our breath jets out in comet tails. Ingvar keeps stomping her feet and flapping her arms.

"You had another career once," she says. "You weren't always an artist."

"Since you seem to know all about me... what's the point of this talk, Ingvar? Seeing as there's nothing to stop me walking away right now."

"Be my guest. But you know I know something. Those people really died, Loti; I didn't just make them up. They were claim-jumpers. Not only shouldn't they have been there, but Authority screwed up in not protecting them when the impactor came in. It's true there wasn't much warning, and the planetary defences were not at maximum readiness. They sent ships at the last minute, tried to deflect the impactor..." Ingvar shakes her head. "Didn't work; not enough time. But the point is I can tie you to the impactor, and show that it was no accident that it hit Naiad. Skanda meant it to happen. And that makes it a *crime*, not some random accident of celestial mechanics. And also makes you an accomplice."

"Fine. Prepare a dossier for Authority. I'm sure they'll be thrilled to hear from you."

"I could do just that. May well do so, in fact."
From across the square, on the other side of the ice-rink, an amateur band is rehearsing on the platform of a white pavilion. Their frostbitten fingers strike a series of duff notes. Ingvar raises her voice over the brassy discord. "Did you like your old line of work?"

"It paid."

In fact it was good work, and I was better than good work. I used to shape ice for the bulk carriers. Take a splinter of comet a couple of kilometres across, chisel it with lasers and plasma and variable yield shaped charges until it had exactly the right profile, the right symmetry and centre of gravity, to be converted into a one-shot payload.

Handing over a chunk of ice that I'd trimmed, watching as the pusher engines were fixed on at one end, a spiderlike control nexus at the other, witnessing the start of its long, long cruise to the hungry economies of the inner system, there was some satisfaction in that.

"But then everything changed," Ingvar said. "Not overnight, obviously, but harder and faster than you'd been expecting. New technologies, new ways of doing things. Decided by people who didn't know you, didn't care about you. Men like Skanda Abrud."

"I moved with the times."

The skaters execute lazy ellipses on the ice. Most of them aren't very good, but on Triton even the clumsiest achieve a measure of elegance. It occurs to me that I've never come to the rink when there are skaters out. A girl launches herself into the air, tucks her arms and executes maybe twenty rotations before her skates touch ice again.

Sometimes, high above the ecliptic, I'd turn

*Moonlighter*'s main dish away from the system's hum and bustle and tune in to the cosmic microwave background. The hiss of creation. That's what the skaters sound like: an endless and spiralling cosmic hiss.

Above the quadrangle, Neptune surveys proceedings with serene indifference. I'd sooner forget about Neptune and Naiad. But it's not easy with that hanging overhead.

"You just took to art? It was that easy?" Ingvar asks.

I wonder why she cares. "That or starve. I guess I did all right. Made a living." I watch an excursion craft slide across the bisected face of Neptune, lit up like a neon fish. "*Was* making a living, until you interrupted me."

"But you've had your share of disappointments. Dreams and ambitions that didn't work out." The way she says this, I can't help but wonder if she isn't, on some level, alluding to the private trajectory of her own career. Licensed investigator: hardly the most glamorous or remunerative profession in the system. Maybe Ingvar had higher hopes than that, a long time ago.

Sympathy? Not exactly. But a flicker of recognition, nonetheless.

"We all make the best of things," I say. "Or try to."

"It's not a bad life, is it? I mean, look at us. We're on Triton, under Neptune. Watching ice-skating." Ingvar shivers in her coat. "It's cold, but we can get warm if want to. There's food and company when we need it. And it's like that everywhere. Lovely things to see, places to explore, people to meet. Hundreds of worlds, thousands of towns and cities. Why would anyone *not* find that enough? Why would anyone want more from life than the system can give them?"

I can see where this is leading.

"You mean, why would anyone ever want to leave?"

"I just don't understand. But I've been there. I've been to Jupiter, seen the skydocks, seen the voidships being built. There's no end of them, no end of volunteers rich enough to buy a slot. Even after what happened." Ingvar pumps her feet against the ground. From the white pagoda, the amateur band mangles another passage. "What's *wrong* with those people?" she asks, and I can't tell if she's complaining about the band, or the voidship sleepers, or both.

So I TOOK Skanda out to meet his rock.

The orbit was high-inclination, the rock a long way from the ecliptic. I'd seen the images, but the first up-close viewing was always special.

"You like it?" I asked him.

"It's good. Better than good. It'll do, won't it?"

"It'll have to."

But it was much better than that. I'd swung *Moonlighter* around the rock a dozen times, mapping it down to thumbnail precision, and scanning deep into its heart. I'd dropped seismic probes to echo-map its core. None of these readings had given the slightest cause for real concern. I could see David's head in my mind's eye, visualise exactly where the first cuts would have to go.

"I didn't think it would seem so big," Skanda said. "It's one thing to see it as an image, another to be *here*, to feel the dead pull of all that mass. It's a mountain, falling through space. Don't you feel that?"

"It's a rock."

Skanda pushed a hair from my eyes. "You've no romanticism," he chided gently.

Honestly, I hadn't meant it to happen this way. I don't, as a rule, end up sleeping with my clients.

When Skanda insisted on accompanying me out to the rock, I'd hit him with my usual terms and conditions. My ship, my rules. There wasn't much privacy on *Moonlighter*, but it would be strictly business all the way out and all the way back home.

So much for that. In truth, Skanda made it too easy. He was charming, effortlessly easy on the eye and knew exactly what he wanted. It was that last quality that I found most attractive of all.

He'd already had a certain rock in mind. And he needed to be *out here*, witnessing. Who was I to quibble?

Very soon the work was underway.

Bots did my bidding. They peeled away from *Moonlighter* in eager droves. Some carried lasers and plasma cutters. Some were tunnelling machines, designed to sink boreholes, down which other bots would pack detonation charges. Meanwhile, as the bots toiled, huge cutting arms unfolded from *Moonlighter*'s flanks. The arms were tipped with various sampling and cutting instruments. Slaved to my telepresence rig, the bots let me work the rock as if it was clay beneath my fingers. That was the part I liked the best. Dirt under my nails.

Sculpting like Michelangelo.

If I'd been prepared to cut corners, the way Yinning and Tarabulus worked, I could have shaped that rock in weeks. But doing it the hard way meant months of patient work. Months of just the two of us, stuck in my ship hundreds of light-minutes from civilisation.

I loved every second of it.

Skanda had been as good as his word. He'd paid up front. With the money now in my account, I wouldn't need to work for years. He'd even picked up the tab on *Moonlighter*'s repair bill.

Did I dare wonder where all this wealth was coming from?

Sort of. But then again I didn't really care. Obviously, he was rich. But then there were millions of rich people in the system – who else was paying for the voidships?

When I was working, deep into it, Skanda would retire to *Moonlighter*'s bridge and conduct long-range business. He didn't seem to mind whether I listened in or not. Only slowly did I get any kind of inkling into the kind of work he was involved in, and what it meant for me.

Meanwhile, layer by layer, the face of David unmasked itself. Even as the work progressed, I knew there was never a time when it couldn't all end in ignominy. The best probes and surveys weren't infallible, and nor were my tools and methods. The rock was riddled with the usual number of weaknesses, the scars and fractures of ancient collisions. Some of these were obligingly close to the planes and contours where I meant to cut anyway, as if the rock was trying to shed itself of everything that wasn't the head of David. Others were at treacherous opposition to my plans. A slight misalignment of a shaped charge, a misdirected laser blast, and I could shatter David's cheek or brow beyond repair.

Sure, I could fix that kind of damage easily enough. But I'd never stoop so low. That was for hacks like Yinning and Tarabulus. And I doubted Skanda would settle for second best. If he was going to create the head of David, it had to be as flawless as Michelangelo's original.

And it would be. Gradually the scalp and face came free. David's chin and jaw were as yet still entombed in rock; the effect was to give the youth an old man's beard. That wouldn't last. I was chipping the beard away in house-sized chunks, a curl at a time. Another month, I reckoned, and then we'd be done with this crude shaping. Three months, perhaps, to bring David to completion. Four or five at the longest.

And it would be magnificent. No one had done such a thing as this. I imagined some future civilisation stumbling on this painstakingly shaped rock, a million or billion years from now, as it tumbled around the Sun. What would they make of the blank-eyed visage? Would they have the faintest inkling of the eager little creatures who had brought it into being?

Even with the bots, the work took its toll. Between cutting stints, when I was too tired to supervise the machines, I'd float with Skanda in the observation bubble. We'd be goggled up, our naked bodies intertwined.

I'd seen my share of the system, but Skanda had been places I'd only dreamed of visiting. I kept telling myself not to worry about the future, just to enjoy the moment, this time we had together. When the rock was done, there'd be nothing to keep Skanda with me. Even with the money in my account, I was just a rock cutter.

But Skanda made me wonder. With the goggles on, he'd show me things. Industrial flows; streams of processed matter on their way from launcher to customer. "That one," he'd say, directing my eye to a tagged procession of cargo pellets, shot out from a catapult on some iceteroid. "That's on its way to Mars. Slower than shipping it bulk, but cheaper in the long run. No engines, no guidance – just celestial mechanics, taking it all the way home."

"You own that flow?"

He'd kiss me, as if to say *don't trouble yourself with such matters*. "In a tediously complicated sense, yes."

"People like you," I said, "put people like me out of work."

Skanda smiled. My face bulged back in the mirrored globes of his goggles. "But I'm putting you *in* work now, aren't I?"

It wasn't just industry and economics. Orbits lit up, coloured bands arcing away like the racetracks of the gods. Worlds flowered in the darkness. Not just the major planets, of course, but the minor ones: Ceres, Vesta, Hidalgo, Juno, Adonis, dozens more. In turn, each world had its gaggling court of fellow-travellers. We watched moons, habitats, stations, shuttles and ships. The goggles painted designations, civil registrations and cargo summaries.

"I'll take you to Venus Deep," he said. "Or Ridgeback City on Iapetus. I know a great place there, and the views... have you ever seen the skimmers plunge through Jupiter's spot, or the reef cities under Europa?"

"I've never even been to Europa."

"There's so much to see, Loti. More than one life could ever encompass. When we're done with this... I hope you'll let me show you more of the system. It would be my privilege."

"I'm just a rock cutter from Titan, Skanda."

"No," he said, firmly enough that it was almost a reprimand. "You're infinitely more than that. You're a true artist, Loti. And you have a gift that people aren't going to forget in a hurry. Take my word on that."

Stupid thing was, I did.

BY THE TIME Ingvar steers me to another part of the quadrangle, the band has given up for the night. Most of the skaters have surrendered to the cold. There are only a couple left, perhaps the best of them, orbiting each other like a pair of binary pulsars.

"They say they aren't dynamically stable," Ingvar comments, looking up through the dome. "Something to do with Triton's influence, I think. The rings of Saturn aren't stable either, not on timescales of hundreds of millions of years. But they'll outlast these many times over. I'm not sure how I feel about that."

"You should be happy. Something wrong will be put right."

"Well, yes. But Naiad was destroyed to make this happen. And those people, too. Given their deaths, I'd rather the end result was a bit more permanent."

"It'll outlast us. That's probably all that matters."

Ingvar's head bobs in the fur-lined hood of her coat. "Maybe by the time the rings start to dissipate, we'll have decided we like them enough to want to preserve them. Sure we'd find a way, if we felt it mattered enough."

I look at them now. Try to see them through fresh eyes.

The rings of Neptune.

They bisect the face of the world like a knife slash, very nearly as magnificent as the rings of Saturn. There always were rings here, I tell myself, but they were little more than smoky threads, all but invisible under most conditions. The ghostly promise of rings yet to come.

Not so now. The resonant effects of Triton, and its lesser siblings, conspire to divide and subdivide these infant rings into riverine bands. In turn, these concentric bands shimmer with a hundred splendid hues of the most ethereal blue-white or pastel green or jade. There's a lot of ice and rubble in a moon, even one as small as Naiad, and enough subtle chemistry to provide beguiling variations in reflection and transmission.

Skanda should have seen this, I think. He'd have known that the rings would be beautiful, a thing of wonder, commanding the awe of the entire system. But he couldn't have begun to predict their dazzling complexity. The glory of it.

But then who could?

"Does it anger you, that he did this to your greatest work?" Ingvar asks. "Let you create the head of David, let you think this would be the thing that made your name, all the while knowing it was going to be destroyed?"

"I did what I was paid to do. Once my part in it was over, I forgot about David."

"Or rather, you forced yourself not to dwell on it. For obvious reasons, in light of what happened. But you always believed it was still out there, didn't you? Ticking its way round the Sun, waiting to be found. You clung to that." Ingvar's tone changes. "Would he have taken credit, do you think? Was that always his intention?"

"He never said anything about it to me."

"But you knew him a little. When the voidship reached the Oort cloud, when he was scheduled to be woken... would he have declared himself responsible? Would he have basked in the fame, knowing he was untouchable, beyond the reach of solar law, or would he have preferred to leave the mystery unsolved?"

"What do you think?" I ask snidely.

"From what I've gathered of his profile," Ingvar says, resuming her curious lopsided walk, "He doesn't strike me as the kind to have settled for anonymity."

\*     \*     \*

I'VE LIVED A good and full life since the day he left. I still cut rock. I've had many lovers, many friends, and I can't say I've been unhappy. But there are days when the pain of his betrayal feels as raw as if it all happened yesterday. We were nearly done with David – just a couple more weeks of finishing-off, and then the head was complete. It already looked magnificent. It was the finest thing I'd ever touched.

Then Skanda returned from the bridge, where he'd been conducting business dealings. Nothing about his manner suggested anything untoward.

"I've got to go for a little while."

"Go?"

"Back to the main system. Something's come up. It's complicated and it would be a lot easier to resolve without hours of timelag."

"We're nearly done. I don't usually abandon a piece when it's this near to completion – it's too hard to get back into the right frame of mind."

"You don't have to abandon anything. My people... they're sending out a ship to get me. In fact, it will be here very shortly. You can stay on station, finish the work."

He'd made it seem like some unscheduled crisis, something that had blown up at short notice, but deep down I knew that couldn't be that case. Not if that little ship of his had already been on its way out here for what must have been days.

I watched it arrive. It was a tiny thing, a beautiful jewelled toy of a spacecraft, porpoise-sleek and not much larger. "An extravagance," Skanda said, as the craft docked. "It's just that sometimes I need to be able to move around very quickly."

I bottled my qualms. "You don't have to apologise

for being rich. If you weren't, you wouldn't be paying for the head of David."

"I'm glad you see it that way." He kissed me on the cheek, forestalling any objection. "I wish there was some alternative, but there isn't. All I can promise is that I won't be long. My ship can get me there and back very quickly. Two weeks, three at the most. Keep on working. Finish David for me, and I'll be back to see the end result."

"Where are you going? You were so keen on being here. I understand timelag, but it hasn't held you back until now. What's so important that you have to go away?"

He touched a finger to my lips. "Every second that I'm here is another that I'm not on my way, doing what has to be done. When I'm back, I'll tell you everything you want to know – and I guarantee you'll be bored within five minutes." He kissed me again. "Keep on working. Do that for me. Remember what I said, Loti. You have a gift."

What was the point in arguing further? I believed him. All that talk of the places he'd show me, the things we'd share together – the glamour and spectacle of the entire system, ours for the taking. He'd fixed that idea so firmly in my head that it never once occurred to me that he'd been lying the entire time. I never thought that we'd have a life together; I wasn't that naïve. But some good months, was that too much to ask for? Venus Deep and the reef cities of Europa. The two of us, the artist and her wealthy lover and sponsor. Who would turn that down?

"Be fast," I whispered.

From the observation bubble, I watched his little ship drop away from *Moonlighter*. The drive was bright, and I tracked it until it was too faint to detect. By then, I had a handle on his vector. It didn't mean much – he could easily have been heading to an intermediate stopover, unrelated to his true destination, or just travelling in a random direction to throw me off the scent.

Both of those things were possible. But so was the third possibility, which was that the vector was reliable, and that Skanda had business around Jupiter.

And even then I didn't guess.


"How long was it before you found out about the voidship?" Ingvar asks.

"A while. Weeks, months. Does it really matter now?"

"When he left *Moonlighter*... was that the last contact you had with him?"

"No." The admission is difficult, because it takes me back to the time when I was foolish enough to believe Skanda's promises. "He called me from Jupiter. Even mentioned the voidship: said a relative of his was being frozen, put aboard for the voyage. That was the emergency. He wanted to be there, to give whoever it was a good send-off."

"Whereas the relative was really his wife, and Skanda would soon be joining her. They'd both paid for slots on the voidship. Off to establish a human bridgehead in the Oort cloud. But he hadn't finished with the head of David, had he? He still had instructions for you. It was still important that the work be finished."

"I'd been paid, and I had no reason to doubt that he'd be back."

"Other than the completion of the head, what were the instructions?"

"When his little ship docked, it came with a marker beacon. I was told to fix it onto the head."

"And the... function... of this beacon? You never questioned it?"

I look down. I wish I had something to say.

Ingvar continues. "The beacon was also a steering motor. Skanda had programmed it to make an adjustment to the rock's orbit. An impulse, to kick into a collision course for Naiad. He'd calculated everything. The binding energy of the moon, the kinetic energy of the impactor. He knew it would work. He knew he could shatter that moon and turn it into a ring system around Neptune. The ultimate artistic statement, a piece of planetary resculpting to dwarf the ages."

I think things over for a moment. The conversation has been as lopsided as Ingvar's walk. She's been asking all the hard questions; now it's my turn.

"What's in it for you? What made you decide that you had to solve this mystery? The entire system thinks the rings were made by accident. What made you think otherwise?"

Against expectation, Ingvar seems pleased rather than annoyed. "I saw it."

"Saw what?"

"The head of David. With my own eyes, just before it hit."

"You were there?

All of a sudden, Ingvar looks tremendously old and weary, as if this is the end of some enormous and taxing enterprise, something that has swallowed decades of her life.

"I was Authority. Pilot of one of the quick reaction

ships we sent up to deflect the impactor, as soon as we saw it coming in. I got close enough to see your handiwork, Loti. Too close, as it happens. We were hitting the rock with weapons, trying to adjust its vector or shatter it to rubble. There was an impact, near David's right eye. My ship was caught in the blast. I lost control; nearly died." She takes a breath. "My ship was badly damaged. So was I."

"What happened to you?"

"Oh, they patched me up well enough after my ship was recovered. More than they could do for my partner. Still, lucky as I'd been, I was never much good to Authority after that. Hence the change of profession."

"But you always knew about the head."

"So did everyone involved. That couldn't come out, though. No one could know that people had died on Naiad, because that made us look bad. And no one could know that the impactor had been sculpted, because that made it a crime, not an accident – and if that had come out, it wouldn't have been long before the rest of it was public as well. Our multiple screw-ups."

"Skanda never meant for people to die. He just wanted to do something outrageous."

"He succeeded. But as of now, only two people are aware of that. You and me. The question is, what do we do with our knowledge?"

I wonder if there's a trap I'm missing. "You've spent years putting this together, haven't you? Tracking down the truth. Finding me, and establishing my involvement. Well, congratulations. You're right; I was his accomplice. So what if I didn't know what I was getting into? Authority won't care about that. Especially as there isn't anyone else left to blame. You could hand me over now."

"I could. But would that necessarily be the right thing to do?" Ingvar studies her boots. "My second career... it's not as if it's anything I need to be ashamed of. I've worked hard, had my share of successes. Minor cases, in the scheme of things. But I've not failed. So what if I've done nothing anyone will ever remember me for?"

"Until now. Turn me in... it could make your reputation."

"And yours," Ingvar nods. "Think of it, Loti. Everything you've done, every rock you've cut, the entirety of your art, it's as nothing against the head of David. And the head of David is as nothing against the rings of Neptune. You created something marvellous, a thing of wonder. Beyond Yinning and Tarabulus or anyone else. It was the one time that your life was touched by greatness." A sudden reverence enters Ingvar's voice. "But you can't tell anyone. All you'll have is the rest of your art, in all its middling obscurity, until the day you die. No fame, no notoriety. And all I'll have is a limp and the dog days of my second career. The question is: could either of us live with that?"

"What if I chose not to?"

"I'd make your name."

"As a convicted criminal, locked away in some Authority cell?"

Ingvar's shrug suggests that this is no more than a trifle. "Some would make the trade in an instant. Artists have killed themselves for a stab at immortality. No one's asking that much of you."

"And you?"

"I'd have solved the mystery of the Naiad event. Brought its last living perpetrator to justice. There'd be a measure of acclaim in it for me."

"Just a measure?"

"Some trouble as well. As I said, not everyone would welcome the truth getting out."

I shake my head, almost disappointed with Ingvar, that she should give in now. "So you're saying I have a choice?"

"I'm saying we both have one. But we'd have to agree on it, I think. No good one of us pulling one way, the other resisting."

I look at Neptune again. The rings, the storms, the brooding blue vastness of it all. And think of that temporary star, shining for a few seconds in the constellation Fornax. The light of a voidship, dying in a soundless eruption of subatomic energy. They say they were pushing the engines, trying to outrun the other voidships. Trying to be the first to stake a claim in the Oort clouds. Going for victory.

They also say no living thing saw that flash; that it was only machines that witnessed it, but that if anyone *had* been looking toward Fornax, at the right time...

"It would be something, to be known for that," I tell Ingvar.

"It would."

"My name would ring down the ages. Like Michelangelo."

"That's true," she agrees. "But Michelangelo's dead, and I doubt that it makes much difference to him now." Ingvar claps her hands against her body. "I'm getting cold. I know a good bar near here, and there are no rock cutters. Let's go inside and talk it over, shall we?"

# WATER RIGHTS

**An Owomoyela**

IT WAS A beautiful explosion, and in a way Jordan was lucky to have such a good seat. She'd been watching the Earth swell up to fill and exceed her porthole, ignoring the thin strand of the space elevator and the wide modules of its ascender until one of them flashed and spilled its guts in a spray of diamonds.

The guy next to her, asleep since they crossed inside the moon's orbit, jerked awake as the skiff fired its slowdown thrusters to stop them, still a kilometre from the elevator station. He leaned over against his straps, gaping at the rainbows glittering beside the ascender. "My god, that's beautiful. What is that?"

Jordan's mouth was dry, her heart going tripletime.

"Water," she said. "That's all our water."

BY THE TIME the station took a damage assessment and rousted every security guard posted there, the skiff had gone into an uproar and the complimentary drinks cabinet was locked. By the time the skiff emptied onto the station, the starfield was peppered with emergency vehicles and private Help & Rescue, and guards with nonlethals bristled at the passengers flooding the concourse.

The queue at the transmission station was long enough that Jordan just pushed off toward the light skiff to Lagrange One, cornering around a couple Earthers who started, all nerves, as she boosted off their shoulders. *Poor bastards.* If they'd planned on taking the ascender down, acclimating to touch-friendly micrograv was the least of their problems.

*Due to the accident on the ascender, all hydrogen-and oxygen-thrust vehicles out of Hyperion Station have been suspended,* announced the PA. *Repeat, due to the accident on the ascender...*

Jordan showed her identification to a cluster of guards at the terminal, went up to the kiosk, and sprang the extra expense to board a private module with a transmitter. The module was a closet, compared with the cabins on the ascender; even the micrograv straps seemed superfluous, as there were barely ten centimetres of space left between Jordan's elbows and the module walls.

She keyed in the transmission codes for her rig, and a few seconds later Marcus's face popped onto the screen, dark skin flushed in the rig's full-spectrum lights.

*"Oh, thank god,"* he said. *"Are you all right?"*

"I'm pretty well shaken *and* stirred, Marc," Jordan said. "Listen – put the rig onto emergency water rationing. Stop all the new planting, and restrict personal use as far down as it'll go."

Seconds passed, and she watched Marcus's expression as he waited for the transmission to reach him. *"Already done, Ms. Owole,"* he responded. *"Soon as we heard the news. Have you heard the latest?"*

"I know they're suspending H and O ships out of Earth orbit. I'm just glad we do enough business to have photonic corridors from L1 out there."

*"Yeah, saved by big business,"* Marcus said. *"L1 is putting a discouragement tax on H-O thrusters. Oh, and Etienne is coming after you."*

He had the grace to look sheepish, at least. Jordan groaned.

*"Between us and the refuelling stations Galot and Bardroy run, that's sixty per cent of the water in the near-Earth colonies,"* he said. *"The next reserve is on Mars, and the next after that is Europa. They're no help. Didn't take long for Etienne to come to that conclusion."*

"And did Etienne's observation come with demands?"

Marcus laughed uneasily. *"You know it would've. Fortunately they're still crunching numbers on how long we can stretch what we have. Heard anything from Ouranos-Hyperion on repair times?"*

"You know Earthside procedure," Jordan said. "It'll be security promises and pointing fingers for a while. Marcus, I haven't even got a message to Harper yet. She was going to meet me Earthside; god knows what she thinks."

She waited a few seconds.

Then, without waiting for the response, said "They're calling it an accident. I know they want to keep us from rioting, but do they think we're stupid?"

*"Jordan."* Marcus pressed his fingers to the camera. *"I'm sure she heard that the ascender exploded; she can put two and two together."*

A pause, as the second half of the message caught him.

*"If I were them I wouldn't know what to think,"*

317

he said. *"Listen, I'll meet you on Lagrange One, okay? Raxel's got things in hand here, and you could use an escort in. And a stiff drink, and I'm thinking the bars will be crowded."*

Jordan quirked a dry smile. "You're an angel, Marcus. Feel free to call me on the flight. I'll see you there."

Marcus gave a little wave after the lag, and the transmission cut.

Jordan closed her eyes, listened to see whether more people were boarding or whether the crew was gearing up to fire the photonic thrusters, couldn't tell, and typed another transcode in. The screen flashed red.

TRANSMISSION TO EARTH IS TEMPORARILY SUSPENDED: EARTH SECURITY DIRECTIVE 515.05.81 03:07 UTC, it read.

"Great," Jordan muttered. "Just great."

LAGRANGE ONE WASN'T as large as the Ouranos-Hyperion station at the Elevator, but it was large enough to have a photonic-thrust lane there and back. And it was large enough that as soon as Jordan disembarked from the skiff, she was assaulted from all sides by the low roar of spacers arguing, the tense tones of the news broadcasts, the smell of too many frightened people. Jordan wrinkled her nose. Hygiene was going to go to shit.

The terminals along the walls displayed the same news accounts she'd been subjected to for eight hours on the skiff, although they were intercut with station-wide announcements warning everyone to stay calm.

No one was staying calm.

Barely three metres from the debarkation line someone called "Hey! You Jordan Owole?" and she turned just in time for a man to sail into her, grab her arm, and link their momentum. A moment later they were against the wall. The man wore the charcoal security armour that denoted system-wide jurisdiction, with a tag reading LISTER on his chest. He was short and strong and looked like he'd had a lot of elective surgery, which meant that no way was he a native in micrograv. New guy in space, maybe, and not happy about it today.

"Something wrong?" Jordan asked.

"Got a flag from the skiff," Lister said. "You were trying to contact someone Earthside?"

"Yeah – I was scheduled to go down and meet my sister," Jordan said. "Is that all right?"

"Your sister is Harper Owole?" Lister asked, and a mass settled in Jordan's throat.

"Is that all right?" she said again, colder this time.

"She wrote those editorials," Lister said. "Earth shouldn't be shipping its water away, it's not renewable if we ship it up there –"

"Yeah, I know what she thinks; we talk from time to time," Jordan interrupted. "What –"

"Why'd you try to call her?"

"I was going down to visit her!" Jordan said. "We were going to look at roses."

That seemed to throw him, for a moment. "Hell's that supposed to mean? Roses?"

"*Jordan*!"

*God bless Marcus,* Jordan thought, and looked past Lister into the crowds. Marcus was boosting his way through, systemwide security be damned. She looked back to Lister as Marcus arrived.

"Am I under arrest? Sir?"

Lister let go of her arm, releasing it like it was something disgusting. "We've got a flag out on you," he said, jabbing a finger at her before he shoved off.

"*Putain de merde*," Marcus muttered. "What was that?"

"He's scared," Jordan said, watching him go. "Everyone is scared, and that's not a good place to be. Let's get off this floating hunk of scrap."

Marcus turned to her and palmed over a foil packet – alcohol, probably. Judging by the size, Jordan guessed straight ethanol. "Don't flash it," he said, and clapped her on the shoulder. "People will think it's water. Let's get home."

That was easier said.

This close to her rig, people recognised her. Before they made it to the terminal, someone intercepted her, caught her arm. "Ms. Owole? Jordan Owole?"

"I didn't do it," Jordan said, and only realised belatedly that she'd probably pay for that joke.

"You're selling, aren't you?" the man asked. "It's been on the news; it's up to private holders now –"

*Oh, no.* "Stop right there. Just stop."

"I'll pay any price. There are fifteen families on my station. Eight of them have children."

"It's not –" she said, and didn't have anything to follow that with except for the urge to roundhouse-kick this guy down the hall and escape.

"Pull the E card," Marcus muttered.

Jordan wished for some choice French profanity of her own. "I've got a call waiting with Etienne."

And, for once in her life, she thought *God bless Etienne*, too. The man didn't back off, but he looked like he was weighing the benefits of pressing.

"Which we have to get to," Marcus said, and put a hand between them. "I'd take it up with her."

Excusing themselves felt less like a departure than a retreat.

Marcus kept himself between Jordan and the station crowd as much as he could, which would have been difficult enough in an Earthside concourse and was nigh-impossible in L1. Every bumped shoulder and correction of momentum seemed to communicate tension, like a sludge or a fast-acting disease, and a palpable relief hit them when they made it to the dock module for the hydroponic rig skiff. Only one guard was stationed there, and he checked their identification, unlocked the dock door, and said "Let me know if there's anything I can do to help."

It was enough of a deviation from the pattern that Jordan couldn't process it for a moment. "Excuse me?"

He looked at her, and held her gaze. He had a sort of spacer-mutt gangliness, and his expression, while serious, didn't share the panic of the rest of the station. Native, maybe. Young, certainly.

"You're Jordan Owole, right? You own the hydro rig?"

"I'm not selling," Jordan said.

"Wouldn't want you to," the guard responded. "Just let me know if I can help."


THE LIGHT-SKIFF ride to Owole Hydroponics was just under fifteen minutes, and the first thing Jordan saw on arriving was her workstation waiting just past the airlock. She looked around for Raxel – the only one who'd leave the hint *that* blatantly – but she was nowhere to be found.

"My kingdom to avoid this call," she said, grabbing the workstation from where it had drifted into the bulkhead. Marcus gave her a sympathetic look. "Of course, my kingdom is what she's wanting."

"If you want me to take it –"

"She'd make you put me on, and you know it," Jordan said. "If you don't hear from me again, send rescue."

She turned, got a foot against the inner rim of the door, and pushed toward an office.

Etienne wasn't officially anything in the near-Earth colonies' administration, but unofficially, you did well to stay on her good side. Jordan was of the opinion that Etienne played either the cattledog to the Near-Earth colonies' herd or the bent Sherriff to the colonies' Wild West, anachronistic as those concepts should have been. Love her or hate her, you had to admit she was needed.

Now especially.

Jordan keyed in her contact information, and waited as the local stations caught, interpreted, and routed her call. After a minute the screen switched to WAITING, and not long after that, it switched to Etienne's face.

"Jordan. So glad you called."

"Well, I needed to," Jordan said.

Etienne nodded almost immediately, and Jordan jumped. There wasn't even a second's delay – much less than the ten or so it would take to transmit to Earth orbit and back. Etienne must have come out to the L1 cluster.

*"I heard you had an interesting day,"* Etienne said.

Jordan grunted. "En route to Hyperion Station when the ascender blew. Watched it out of the skiff window."

*"Nasty piece of work."* Etienne clicked her tongue. *"If the names of the perps go public, I know a few solar satellites which may be abruptly retargeted from their collection stations."*

Jordan felt a vertiginous sense of unease. "You're not serious."

*"There's always talk of retribution, Jordan. Even if we don't have half a blip on who we'd be targeting."* Etienne waved a hand. *"Relax. No one's launching a burn attack on Earth under my watch."*

Jordan didn't relax.

*"But let's talk business,"* Etienne said.

Jordan took a breath. "Eti, our water is tied up in food production. Why is everyone looking to us? What's the matter with the reserve?"

*"Oh, you really haven't been watching the numbers, have you?"* Etienne said. *"The problem is we grew too fast, hon. The reserve was only ever a stopgap and now it's a flash in the pan. Ergo, near-Earth needs you."*

Jordan shook her head. "No water, no crops, no food."

*"Less water, fewer crops, less food. You're one of our luxuries up here. If the other choice is going thirsty, you think people will complain when their kumquats come off the market?"*

Jordan ignored the jab. "It took years to get some of these crops established. You can't just stop and start production on a hydroponics rig."

*"Try putting a stop to drinking,"* Etienne shot back. *"And darling, I looked over the logs from*

*Ouranos-Hyperion. You've been ordering water over your business use."*

Jordan groaned. "I won't bother asking how you got those." Etienne got anything she put her mind to getting. "Listen, I know, it's a disaster, but there's gotta be other options. I've got loans out, the crop cuts could take years to correct – this could ruin me."

*"We're pulling every option we have."* Etienne drummed her fingers against the console, and the sound translated to a menacing bassbeat over the connection. *"You'll be compensated for your expenditure –"*

"No insurance on Earth or in the heavens above is going to pay me for giving up water and destroying viable crops," Jordan said. "I'll get reimbursement on the shipment I lost in the explosion, but there's no way I'll get anything back from a fire sale of my stores."

*"I'll see to it,"* Etienne said. *"Darling, the reserve will last us a month, at most. You want to know how many litres we're losing every day?"*

"No. I don't." Jordan rubbed her temples, and let her shoulders slump. "What are your numbers?"

*"Against seven months for the ascender repairs, we've got two weeks on the reserve at normal use – a month on emergency rationing. Four more months using eighty per cent of your water stores and sixty-five of the refuelling stations'. That's leaving the rest to you to grow food and to Galot and Bardroy to run food and water deliveries and handle emergencies. That should get us to a point where relief organisations can send up water in the quantities to get us through the interim."*

"That's the gamble?" Jordan asked. "Your best-case scenario leaves us two months' blind hope?"

"Well, *it's a damn sight better than six months of despair,*" Etienne pointed out. "*I know we can count on you, darling.*"

"I got mobbed on L1!" Jordan shouted. "We haven't even cracked the reserve yet, and people want to buy off my stores. What happens when we're coming up on the end of our rations?"

"*If you need protection, you know that's never been a problem,*" Etienne said. "*Protection from Ouranos-Hyperion too, if you need it.*"

It took Jordan a moment to process that. "You're talking about my sister."

"*I'm talking about you, dear,*" Etienne said. "*As of that explosion, you're the richest person in space.*"

Jordan felt disbelief and anger tangling up at the bottom of her lungs. "Rich?" she demanded. "You want to call this rich? Getting strong-armed into killing off my crops, setting my own business back, jettisoning everything I've achieved, everything I've planned for –"

"*Yes, and what were you planning for?*" Etienne asked.

"I was planning for mind your own damn business!" Jordan said, and cut transmission.


RAXEL AND MARCUS were waiting when she left the office, with looks that suggested they were checking her for ripped-out hair so they'd be ready to change out the air filters. Jordan arrested her momentum as she came up to them, and jerked her chin down one of the tunnels. "Come on, let's see our damage."

"I say we keep the water for ourselves," Raxel grumbled. "Between the three of us, we could probably last here longer than any of us would live."

"Oh, definitely. If only because they'll kill us for it," Jordan said. "Etienne is talking people down from using the solar transfer beams as retribution against Earth. Let's not piss her off or she might tell them to switch targets."

"So did you work something out?" Marcus asked.

Jordan grimaced. "Well, I told her to piss off."

"...uh," Marcus said.

"I know, I know, and if we catch a laser through our bulkheads, blame me," Jordan said. "You think we have a choice? Our crops versus everyone's life. But I'm allowed to get mad, watching everything I've worked for go out with the waste brine."

She steadied herself with a handhold and punched the bulkhead. Her workers looked at each other.

"We could dehydrate what we have," Marcus said. "That might stretch the water reserves a little."

"Too little. And anyone who ate the food would just get thirstier wanting the water back," Jordan said. "For storage, though, probably our best option. People will be tightening belts once we scale down."

Raxel glanced toward an empty bay. "Does she know about the stash?"

"She's Etienne. She knows everything." Jordan picked an office and pushed off for it, and Raxel and Marcus followed her. "So, we need a plan to scale down to twenty per cent of our water use."

"Twenty per cent!" Raxel said. She reached the door first, and keyed it open. "By when?"

"Distribution at the end of the month, I think," Jordan said. "Thanks." She swung in the open door, and grabbed a hammock with her feet. "Ideas?"

"Will that even feed us?" Raxel asked, twitching to the desk and catching her feet under the lip.

"Subsistence, high-yield crops," Marcus said.

"What, bean crops, potatoes, onions, peas?" Raxel asked. "Winter wheat, I guess, if we still have water. Could people live on that?"

"You could live on that," Marcus muttered.

"People are going to riot if they don't have colours available for their plates," Jordan said. "Fruits and vegetables. Hell hath no fury like colonies who think they're entitled to their grapes and raspberries, water crisis or none."

"Maybe we should hire additional security," Raxel said, and Jordan thought of the guard outside her dock at L1. "I know we don't have the budget, but we could cut a crop and pay in fresh water until this sorts out."

Jordan dug the knuckles of her thumbs into the corners of her eyes. "Anyone else beginning to think that maybe the anti-exporters have a point?" she asked. Despair was a strange feeling in micrograv: still felt like something settling on your chest, but it was the only thing settling. One spot of weight in weightlessness. "Maybe we have no business being in a place that can't support us."

Marcus and Raxel exchanged a look, and Raxel said "Tell that to my family back in Phoenix."

Jordan snorted and flicked her pencil at Raxel's head.

Raxel reached out and plucked it from the air, then looked across at Marcus. "Marc, why'd you come to space?"

Marcus shrugged. "Ms. Owole was the only person who wanted to hire a thirty-year-old Haitian geek who'd spent way too long getting a Bachelors in hydroponic ag. And the relocation package was good."

"How about you, Jordan?" Raxel asked.

"Because I was an 1860s frontiersman in a previous life," Jordan said. "What about you, Raxel? I'm guessing you have a point to make."

"Yeah, I have a point to make," Raxel said, and jabbed the pencil at Marcus. "I say we're all up here for the same reason: because without hacking it up here, we'd never have sent the diver out to Europa. And if we can't hack it that far, we'll never get to another star." She waved her hand back toward the observation modules, indicating the entire Milky Way by association. "Because either we can spread out or we can say this is as far as we're gonna get. Because Earth is like – it's our parents' house, and near-Earth is our first crappy apartment, and somewhere out there is New York City, it's New Delhi, it's Sydney, it's Madrid, and some people dream of going there and some people actually do. And we do. Least, we're trying to."

There was silence for a moment. Then, Marcus cleared his throat. "Rax, how many papers on this did you write?"

It was his turn to get a pencil flicked at his head.

"I was going to say we were little babies, and our umbilical just got cut, and we are desperately premature," Jordan said. Raxel sent a disparaging look her way.

"Look, you can disagree, but this has always been the bargain," Raxel said. "Back when we were still shooting things up with individual launches, those rockets were pumping out enough shit to turn the local nature preserves into acid swamps for half a day. You know what they said? The dead animals 'are dedicated in the interests of the mission.' You can love Earth or you can love space."

Marcus's hand closed around the pencil, and he looked uneasily to Jordan. "So it's us or them? I mean, we solved the fuel problem with the elevator. You don't think –"

"Marcus," Jordan said. "Kids. Both of you. You want to save the world" – she looked from Marcus to Raxel – "and you want to colonise other stars. Let's focus on keeping in food and water and Etienne's good graces until they fix the damn elevator, and we can all be heroes then."

Raxel showed both hands. Marcus looked contrite, and pushed off to Jordan.

"Here's your pencil back," he said, and his hand closed on her shoulder. She curled her hand over it.

"Thank you," she said, and looked back to her notes. "So. Rice, lentils, and raspberries."


YOU COULD HIRE security, you could seal your hatches, you could do just about anything in the near-Earth colonies, but you could never bar your door to Etienne.

She arrived on a light skiff at what, planetside, would be an indecent hour, but Jordan was still awake to meet her. She led Etienne back to an inner observation module, placed alongside a long row of producing fruits, and opened a cabinet to withdraw two small packages of awamori from the secret and not entirely legal still Marcus tended in the back of the rice modules. She floated one to Etienne, who caught it and placed it in the air just to one side.

"I tell you," Etienne said, looking down into the complex, her face softening as she took in the green. "If civilisation ever collapses up here, all of us who can't get to Europa should hope you'd let us in. You've got your own little ecosystem."

"It's an ecosystem that requires a lot of intervention," Jordan pointed out. "We're no Earth."

"Still, if you downshifted to subsistence farming, rationed your water, recycled every drop... how long do you think you could last, here?"

Jordan sighed, rolling her head back. "With the staff I have now? Years. Indefinitely. Does it matter?" She popped the cap off the awamori, traced her finger around the lip. "It'll never come to that."

"Mm," Etienne agreed.

They sat in silence for a moment, looking down at the crops transplanted from their terrestrial homes. They looked strange, to an Earth-cultured perspective: far away from nature and the richness of soil. But space had its own rules and its own rightness.

"So. Darling." Etienne affected an old French accent, and Jordan slipped half a smile. "Time to bare all. What is it twisting up your mind?"

"You're going to laugh," Jordan said.

"I won't laugh."

"Oh, you're going to laugh." Jordan nudged herself back, pushing her shoulders against the curve of the bulkhead. "You said that we're a luxury. Thing is, we were finally doing well enough to be."

"The pomegranates were a particular triumph," Etienne agreed.

Jordan shook her head. "I wanted a rose garden."

Etienne watched her. After a moment she took and raised her awamori, indicating Jordan should continue.

"Of all the fussy, water-intensive things," Jordan said. "Harper was going to take me to see a rose specialist. Grand conciliatory gesture, now that she's finally come to terms with me moving up here – and it only took her, what, seventeen years for that to burn off? And now the ascender's blown, and I guess we're both suspects, because she gets loud about water crises planetside and I'm apparently rich these days, and –"

"Breathe, darling." Etienne waved her hand.

Jordan glared at her.

Etienne watched, as though weighing how much her protection might be worth. What came out of her mouth, though, was "Roses? Really?"

"What, I don't seem the type?" Jordan raised an eyebrow. "This specialist, Etienne. He's got roses traced to stock from the Gardens of Albarède, from Chandigarh, he's got an Autumn Damask that would make your heart ache. I wanted something of my own up here. Something just beautiful." She sighed, and drank. "Everything on the frontier is so damn *practical*. So, so am I."

"Numbers and figures and madmen and dreamers," Etienne said. There was a fondness to her tone that Jordan wasn't used to hearing. "They got us here and they'll get us through. So it'll take a few extra years."

"It'll take a few extra years to scale crop production back to normal," Jordan said. She shook her head. "Longer than that for roses. So much for dreamers, huh? One little explosion, and boom." She mimed an explosion with one hand. "Bleeding rainbows in geosynchronous orbit. We were barely bringing up enough water for me to claim a surplus in the first place; where do we go from here?"

"Where do we ever?" Etienne said.

"Raxel says living in space means bleeding Earth dry."

Etienne massaged her drink with her fingers, then crossed her legs and her arms. "Jordan Owole, do you think people up here will pay back your water if they can?"

Jordan shrugged. "I think I do. But —"

"Then let's tell Earth the same damn thing." Etienne shrugged. "One day it'll all pay out. We'll bring them some nice comets for their troubles, or whatever they need from us. It's big out here. Full of possibilities."

"Have you looked at space?" Jordan asked. "It's not full, it's empty."

"There's more out here than there'll ever be down there," Etienne said. "It just takes a little getting to."

"That's the problem."

Etienne gave an exaggerated sigh. "You know, you're damn cynical for a spacer, Jordan. It's a wonder you ever got your feet off the ground." She extended her leg, pushed off in one graceful motion, and caught Jordan's shoulder. "Darling, it's space. We help each other or we float dead into nothing. You share your water and every spacer worth a breath of air and a bag to drink will dip in to make your dreams come true. I guarantee it."

Jordan gave a sad, sidelong smile. "You mean you'll henpeck them until they agree to your terms."

Etienne put a hand to her heart. "Why, Jordan," she said. "How well you know me."

JORDAN WAS GOING through the seed logs when her callpad blipped with a message, and she reached over to open it without looking. She hit the button for the text-to-audio option, and it read *IMAGE FILE FILENAME PROMISE.*

That got her to glance over.

It was a rose. Hand-rendered, rotating on three axes. She checked the message data, traced it back to a doctor in the colony at Tsiolkovskiy. There was no message attached.

She studied it for a while. She didn't know the doctor, though she'd heard his name around. They'd never interacted.

She might have questioned that further, but she was interrupted by another message blip. Another rose, this one in oil pastels.

Four minutes later, another.

They kept coming. One by one, diverging from art to factoids, to photos and personal recollections, memories of scent-rich Earth. She watched as the number climbed past thirty, past sixty, past a hundred.

"Oh, hell," Jordan said, and scrubbed at her eyes with the heels of her palms. She reached over and typed Marcus' number into the callpad. "Marcus –"

A new message flashed onto her screen.

She opened it. This one was text, and the speech option read it dutifully out. Jordan read along with it.

Marcus connected on his end, his face popping up on the vid channel. *"Ms. Owole?"*

"Etienne can get a message to my sister on Earth," Jordan read, tracing the words on her screen.

*"That's great!"* Marcus said. *"Trust Etienne. What are you going to say?"*

Jordan took a long, deep breath.

"I'll say, 'Still love you, still miss you, and enjoy the gardens at Sangerhausen,'" she said. "And Marcus?"

"Yeah?"

She closed the images, and braced herself against the coming dry spell. "Tell Raxel we're putting our faith in her, for this one. And start scaling down. Make ready to distribute our water."

# THE PEAK OF ETERNAL LIGHT

**Bruce Sterling**

HE PROFOUNDLY REGRETTED the Anteroom of Profound Regret.

The Anteroom was an airlock of blast-scarred granite. The entrance and the exit were airtight wheeled contraptions of native pig-iron. In the corner, a wire-wheeled robot, of a type extinct for two centuries, mournfully polished the black slate floor.

One portal opened with a sudden *pop*.

Lucy was there, all in white, and rustling. His wife was wearing her wedding dress.

Pitar was stunned. He hadn't seen this scary garment since they'd been joined in wedlock.

Lucy stopped where she stood, beside her round, yawning, steely portal. "You don't like my surprise for you, Mr. Peretz?"

Pitar swallowed. "What?"

"This is my surprise! It's my anniversary surprise for you! I carefully warned you that I had a surprise."

Pitar struggled to display some husbandly aplomb. "I never guessed that your surprise would be... so dramatic! For my own part, I merely brought you this modest token."

Pitar opened his overnight bag. He produced a ribboned gift-box.

Lucy tripped over, ballerina-like, on her tip-toes.

They gazed at one another, for a long, thoughtful, guarded moment.

Silence, thought Pitar, was the bedrock of their marriage. As young people, it was their sworn duty to fulfil a marital role. Every husband had to invent some personal mode of surviving the fifty-year marriage contract. Marriage on Mercury was an extended adolescence, one long and dangerous discomfort. Marriage was like sun-blasted lava.

Why, Pitar wondered, was Lucy wearing her wedding dress? Had she imagined that this spectral show would please him?

He knew her too well to think that Lucy was deliberately offending him – but he'd burned his own black wedding-suit as soon as decency allowed.

Seeing colour returning to his face, Lucy pirouetted closer. "You bought me a gift, Mr. Peretz?"

"This anniversary gift was not 'bought,'" Pitar said, swallowing the insult. "I *built* you this gift." He offered the box.

Lucy busied herself with the ribbon, then tugged at the airtight lid.

Pitar took this opportunity to study his wife's wedding gown. He had never closely examined the ritual garment, because he had been far too traumatised by the act of marrying its occupant.

There was a lot to look at in a wedding dress. Technically speaking, in terms of its inbuilt supports, threading, embroidering, seams, darts and similar fabric-engineering issues, a wedding dress was quite a design-feat.

Also, the dress fit Lucy well. His wife was a woman of 27 years, yet still with the bodily proportions of a bride of 17. Was she conveying some subtle message to him, here?

Lucy peered into her gift box, and shook it till it jingled. "What are these many small objects, Mr. Peretz?"

"Madame, those golden links snap together. Once assembled, they will form a necklace. The design of the necklace is based on the 'smart sand' used for surface-mining. It's rather ingenious engineering, if I may say that about my own handiwork."

Lucy nodded bravely. Struggling with her wedding-skirt, she poised herself inside a spindly cast-glass chair. She tipped the gift-box and shook it, and an army of golden chain-links scattered, ringing and jingling, across the black basalt table.

Lucy examined the scattered links, silently, obviously at a loss.

"They all fit together, and create a necklace," Pitar urged. "Please do try it."

Lucy struggled to link the necklace segments. She had no idea what she was trying to achieve. The female gender was notorious for lacking three-dimensional modelling skills.

The ladies of Mercury were never engineers. The ladies had their own gender specialties: food, spirituality, child-rearing, life-support, biotechnology and political intrigue.

Two links suddenly snapped together in Lucy's questing fingertips. "Oh!" she said. She tried to part the links. They swivelled a bit, but they would shatter sooner than separate. "Oh, how clever this is."

337

Pitar stepped to the table and swept up a handful of links. "Let's assemble them together now – shall we? Since you are wearing your wedding dress today – it would be surely be proper, thematically, if you also wore this newly-assembled wedding necklace. I'd like to see that, before we part."

"Then you shall see it," she said. "Mr. Peretz, a woman's wedding necklace is called a 'mangalsutra.' That's a tradition. It's women's sacred history. It symbolises devotion, and two lives that are joined by destiny. That's from the Earth."

Pitar nodded. "I'd forgotten that word, 'mangalsutra.'"

The two of them sat in their glass chairs, and laboured away on the mangalsutra, joining the gleaming links. Pitar felt pleased with the morning's events. He'd naturally dreaded this meeting, since a tenth anniversary was considered a highly significant date, requiring extra social interaction between the spouses.

Conjugal visits were sore ordeals for any Mercurian husband. To accomplish a visit to his wife, Pitar had to formally veil himself, arm himself with his duelling baton, and creep into the grim and stuffy 'Anteroom of Delightful Anticipation.'

At this ceremonial airlock between the genders, Lucy would greet him – generally, she was on time – and say a few strained words to him. Then she would lead him to the Boudoir.

No decent man or woman ever spoke a word inside the Boudoir. They silently engaged in the obligatory conjugal acts. If they were lucky, they would sleep afterward.

In the morning, they underwent another required

interaction, parting within this ceremonial Anteroom of Profound Regret. Marriage partings were commonly best when briefest.

Anniversary days, however, were not allowed to be brief. Still, assembling the necklace was a pleasing diversion for both of them. It kept their nervous fingers busy, like eating snack food.

When they said nothing, there were no misunderstandings.

Pitar noted his wife's smile as her golden necklace steadily grew in length. No question: his clever gift plan had met with success. During their decade of marriage, his wife had let slip certain hints about traditional marriage necklaces. Womanly relics, once prized among the colony's pioneer mothers, a sacred female superstition, vaguely religious, peculiar and mystical, whatever-it-was that women called it – the 'mangalsutra.'

Of course Pitar had improved this primitive notion – brought it up-to-date with a design-refresh – but if Lucy had noticed his innovation, she had said nothing about it.

"Sit close to me now, Mr. Peretz!" Lucy offered.

"With that grand wedding dress, I'm not sure that I can!"

"Oh, never mind these big white skirts, my poor old dress doesn't matter anymore! Wouldn't you agree?"

Pitar knew better than to foolishly agree to this treacherous assertion, but he moved his glass chair nearer his wife's chair. The chair's curved feet screeched on the polished slates.

Lucy glanced at him, sidelong. "Mr. Peretz, do I look any older now?"

Pitar busied himself with the links of the necklace. He knew what he was hearing. One of those notorious female jabs that made male life so hazardous.

This provocation had no proper answer. To say "no" was to accuse Lucy of still being a callow girl of seventeen. This meant that ten years of their marriage were capped with an insult.

But to reply "yes" to Lucy, was to state that she had, yes, visibly aged – what a crass mis-step that would be! Lucy would swiftly demand to know what dark threat had wilted her beauty. Arsenical rock-dust fever? A vitamin imbalance in her skin? The ladies of Mercury were forever forbidden the radiance of the Sun.

The light gravity of Mercury shaped the very bones of its women. Lucy had narrow shoulders. A long, loose spine, and a very long neck. Her sleek, narrow hips were entirely unlike the broad, fecund, wobbling hips of a woman from Earth.

Pitar himself was a native son of Mercury. He too had long, frail bones, and had mineral toxins in his liver. As a man, he knew for a fact that he did look older, after ten years of marriage. He certainly wasn't going to broach that subject with her, however.

Dangerous questions were a woman's way to fish for insults. Hell lacked demons like Mercurian women scorned. Any rudeness, any act of dishonour, provoked endless feral scheming within the airlocked hothouse of their purdah. Intrigues would ensue. Scandals. Duels. Political schisms. Civil war.

"How very many golden links!" Lucy remarked, blinking. "Your mangalsutra necklace will reach from my neck to the floor!"

"Five hundred and seven links," said Pitar through reflex.

"Why so many, Mr. Peretz?"

"Because that is the number of times that you and I have occupied this Anteroom of Profound Regret. Including this very day, our tenth anniversary day, of course."

Lucy's hands froze. "You *counted* all our conjugal liaisons?"

"I didn't have to 'count' them. They were all in my appointments calendar."

"How strange men are."

"We did miss some scheduled appointments. Because of illness, or the pressure of business. Otherwise, logically, there would be five hundred and twenty links on our tenth anniversary."

"Yes," Lucy said slowly, "I know that we missed some appointments."

Another silence ensued. The mood had darkened somewhat. They busied themselves with the marriage chain. At last it was complete.

Lucy linked the open ends with the catch that Pitar had provided – a modest, simple loop of big studded rubies. One long, golden, serpentine, female adornment. Lucy draped the chain repeatedly around her tapered neck.

"Madame," said Pitar, seizing the moment, "that mangalsutra necklace, which I built for you with my own assembly devices, is as yet incomplete. As you can see. One end remains open, deliberately so. That is so that you, and I, can add new links to it, in the future. Many new links to this golden wedding-chain, Madame – from this fortunate day, until our final, fiftieth, Golden Anniversary. This is my pledge to you, in bringing you this gift. Deeds, not words."

Lucy turned her blushing face away. She tugged

341

the billowing skirts from the glass chair, and tiptoed toward a framed portrait set in the granite wall.

Pitar followed Lucy's gaze. The personage in the portrait was, of course, famous. She was Mrs. Josefina Chang de Gupta, one of the colony's great founding-mothers.

Mother de Gupta was a culture-heroine for the women of Mercury. This forbidding old dame had personally nurtured sixty-six cloned children. She was the ancestress to half the modern world's million-plus population.

Clearly, Mother de Gupta dearly loved motherhood – mostly, for the chance that it offered her to boss around small, helpless people. Pitar had been taught the grand saga of Mother de Gupta in his crèche-school. A school where domineering women controlled every detail of childhood, preserving and conveying society's cultural values.

Pitar had never forgotten his stifling days in that airless nursery school. Mother de Gupta's husband, the equally-famed Captain de Gupta, had been the author of Mercury's purdah laws of gender separation. It didn't take genius to understand that old man's motives.

Lucy was serenely ignoring the savage old matriarch behind the glass. She was studying her own reflection in the tilted, shining pane.

"I have earned every link in this chain," she declared. "Five hundred marital liaisons! How awkward my postures were, and my body damp with secretions... But now I truly understand why marriage is a sacrament! Look! Look at my beautiful mangalsutra! I always wanted one! It is classical! I have dignity now! With a chain around my neck, I can hold my head up high!"

With a heroic effort, Pitar made no response to this strange outcry. First, Lucy had miscounted their number of liaisons; and second, he had always suffered far worse from the burdens of marriage than she.

Women had it easy in marriage. Basically, all that was required from women was to lie on a bed and point their knees at the ceiling. Society forced him to wrap himself in a veil, to skulk like an assassin into the women's quarters – as if his identity, and his purpose there, were dreadful secrets.

A custom of total secrecy, for actions that were legally required! When incompatible worldviews collided, these were the monsters engendered. Ten dutiful years of marital intercourse, creeping in and out of airlocks – and yet women called men hypocrites.

"I have done my duty for ten years," Lucy declared to her own reflection. Suddenly, she turned on him, eyes flashing. "Sometimes it's all I can do not to laugh like a fool."

"At least, after ten years of marriage," offered Pitar, "they don't make us listen to those silly love-songs, any more."

A thoughtful silence passed, and then she fixed her gaze on his. "This arranged marriage is a vehicle of political oppression!"

Pitar tightened his lips. The women of Mercury were particularly dangerous when they started harping on their alleged 'oppressions.' They rarely died of being oppressed, but men were frequently beaten to death for that subject.

"You told me, once," she said, "once, here in this very Anteroom, that marriage was an oppressive moral debt that we owe to the founders of this world." Lucy stroked her gleaming, golden neck. "I

343

never wept so much! But, of course, you were telling the truth – the truth as men see it, at least."

Stung, Pitar rose at once from his dainty chair, which toppled to the stone floor with a discreet glassy clink.

"Our ancestors must have been insane," Lucy said, with the serene expression of a woman uttering things no man would dare to say aloud. "They gave us this bizarre, twisted life – a life we would never have chosen for ourselves. Our marriage – our oppression – is not our fault. I don't blame you, Pitar. Not any longer. You shouldn't blame me, either. You and I are victims of tradition."

Pitar steepled his fingers before his face and touched them to his moustache. "Mrs. Peretz," he said at last, "it's true that our ancestors had profound, creative ideas about a new society. They tried many new things, and many experiments failed. It was hard to create this world, our world, the living world, from bare rock. I myself have huge technical advantages over our ancestors – and yet I make mistakes, building this world, every day."

Lucy gazed at him, blinking. "What? What are you talking about now? Aren't you listening to me? I just told you that none of this is your fault! You, being my husband, that is not your fault! Can't you understand that? I thought you'd be happy to hear that from me, today."

"Mrs. Peretz, you are not taking my point here! I have a larger point than any merely personal point! I'm saying that we can't blame our ancestors, and vilify them, until we come to terms with our own human failings! Consider the legacy that you and I are leaving to our own future! You can see that, can't you? That is just and fair. That's obvious."

Lucy was not seeing the obvious at all. Or rather, Lucy was seeing the obvious in some alien, feminine way, in which his denial of their immediate suffering was an evil lie. He had offended her.

"Did we surrender too much?" Lucy demanded. "Did we say 'yes' too often?"

"Do you mean, Mrs. Peretz, that day, ten years ago, when I said 'yes,' and you also said 'yes'?"

"No, no, you never understand anything that's important... All right, yes, fine. Fine! That's what I meant."

"Do you mean to say that I should have rebelled? That I should have refused our arranged marriage?" Pitar paused. He attempted to look composed and solemn, as he thought furiously.

Lucy spoke up meekly. "I meant to suggest that *I* should have rebelled."

"What, you? Why?"

Lucy said nothing, but she was clearly marshalling her thoughts for another unplanned outburst.

The anniversary morning, which had started so calmly, had taken a dreadful turn for Pitar. If men knew that he was talking in this way to a woman – especially his own wife – he would be challenged to a duel. And he would deserve that, too.

"All right," Pitar said at last, "since this is our anniversary, we need to discuss these issues. It was brave of you to bring those up. Well, I happen to think that the two of us are excellent at marriage."

Lucy brightened. "You think that? Why?"

"Because it's an established fact! Look at the evidence! Here we are – you and me, husband and wife – living four kilometres under the surface of the North Pole of the planet Mercury. Our air, water, food, our gender politics, everything that we value, is designed and engineered. And yet, we thrive. We are prosperous, we live honourably! We are two respectable married people! Anybody in this world would say that Pitar Peretz and Lucy Peretz have a normal, solid, and fruitful relationship. We gave the world a son."

His wife scowled at this firm reassurance. "They'll want other children from us. No day passes when the lady elders don't nag me about procreation."

"They have to say that to us. They did their part, and now that duty is ours." Pitar raised his hand, to forestall another outcry. "Now, I know – before Mario Louis Peretz was built – I felt some qualms about my fatherhood. Maybe I over-expressed those emotions to you. That was my mistake. I was young and foolish then. I didn't know what fatherhood was. We can't always know what is good for us in the future. If you asked a boy or girl to consent to puberty, of course children would never grow up! They're just children, so they would rebel, and say no."

His wife made no reply to his wise and reasonable discourse. Instead, Lucy was gazing, with a damp look of dawning surprise, at the blast-scarred stone wall. The idea of annulling puberty seemed to have fired her imagination.

"Even though our children are built, it's a wise social policy that children should have two parents," Pitar said doggedly. "Maybe we were forced to conform to that tradition, for the sake of futurity. But the truth is, fatherhood was good to me. Today, there's a boy, eight years old, who depends on me for guidance in this world. So now I realise: life can't be all about me. Me, and my own favourite things: interaction design, aesthetics, robotics, metaphysics... When you and I built a child, that forced me to realise how much this life matters!"

This heartfelt, responsible declaration would have gone over splendidly in any male discussion group; with Lucy, though, it had simply dug him into deeper trouble. Lucy looked bored by his worthy sentiments, and even mildly repelled. "So," she said at last, "the boy made you happy?"

"I wouldn't claim that I've achieved the Peak of Eternal Light! But who among us has?"

"I'm glad that you're happy, Mr. Peretz."

Pitar said nothing. He recognised one of those passive, yet aggressive remarks that women deployed for advantage.

Whenever women said the opposite of what they so clearly wanted to say, hell was at hand.

It was no use reasoning with women. Their brains were different. He had to change his tactics.

"How can I be happy," Pitar offered at last, "when I'm sitting here in the 'Anteroom of Profound Regret'?"

"Husbands never regret leaving their wives here. The formal name of this Anteroom is merely a social hypocrisy. One lie among so many in this world."

"Mrs. Peretz, please stop being so politically provocative. Who can't be sorry in this miserable Anteroom? Can you deny that this room is gloomy, stuffy and in very poor taste? Be reasonable."

"Well, yes, this ugly Anteroom of yours is ugly, but not in the way you think... This room is harsh, and cold, and repulsive, but that's all the fault of you men."

"We men never asked for this Anteroom! Never! If it was up to us men, we'd go straight to the Boudoir.

The Boudoir is augmented and ubiquitous, and it has beer and snacks, too!"

"Mr. Peretz, you are living in pure male delusion," Lucy said sternly. "That Boudoir, where you and I have conjugal relations, that isn't even my room! I have a private room of my very own. It's much nicer than that tacky bordello where we have to interact."

Pitar was dazzled by this brazen assertion. "Other men sleep in my own marriage bed?"

"Sir, that is not 'your' bed! And anyway, it's very sturdy."

"Sturdiness is not the issue there!"

"Well, it is to us women."

"Fine, be that way!" Pitar cried. "If you want a surprise, you should see my barracks! We men live in luxury now! We have gymnasia, saunas, tool-sheds, anything anyone would want."

"I've never seen your male barracks," said Lucy thoughtfully. "That place where you sleep, without me."

This was a dreadful thing to say. Only the lowest, most dishonourable woman, a woman lost to all shame, would violate purdah, risk everything, and creep into a man's room.

The remark shocked Pitar, so he retreated into silence. His wife said nothing as well. The silence between them stretched, as their silences always did, and Pitar realised, with a long, tenuous, ten-year stretch of his imagination, that he liked it when Lucy shocked him.

It touched something in him. He felt metaphysically authentic. Shock put him in stark confrontation with life's unspoken realities. It took daring to become real.

This was like that vivacious disaster, eight years ago, when he'd been in a duel for Lucy's honour.

Pitar was a thinking man, but sometimes even the most reasonable man couldn't back down from an insult. Pitar had not won that duel – in fact, he'd gotten a solid beating from his punctilious opponent. But in standing up for her, and for honour, he'd won a moral victory.

Furthermore, after the duel, Lucy had been allowed, by a long unspoken tradition, to leave her female purdah, and visit him in his clinic. Lucy came there publicly, flaunting herself, sometimes twice a day, to 'heal the defender of her honour.' She could stay there in the medical ward as long as she pleased, and express herself on any topic, and no one would dare to object.

Neither of them had known quite what to do with this unexpected intimacy, for they were only nineteen years old. But that incident had been truly exciting – a different side of life. Another mode of being. The scandal had changed him, and she had changed too, in her own way. A marriage under threat had depth, breadth and consequence.

Sometimes, there was a steep price to pay for self-knowledge – young men learned about themselves in a hurry. Mature men learned from experience.

"Lucy," he ventured at last, in a low voice, "if I asked you to visit my barracks room, what would you do?"

"I didn't mean to suggest anything disgraceful," she said. "But men always come here, through these Anteroom airlocks. Women never visit your half of this world, not at all. How can that be fair?"

"Fair? The rules of decorum are very clear on those matters."

"Please don't look at me like that," Lucy begged. "Truly, I'm proud that my husband has decorum and defends my honour. It would be awful if you were some vile coward. But anyone – man or woman – can see there's something very strange about our customs! Men inside other planets don't duel!"

"Men on other planets don't live 'inside' of their planets," Pitar corrected. "Mercury's moral code may not be perfect – I will grant you that. It may even be that the men of this world, who are just so many fools like me, are all stupid brutes. But even if that's so – at least the ladies here are true ladies! You can admit that much to me, can't you?"

"Well," said Lucy, "being a 'lady' doesn't work in the way that you imagine it does, but... All right, fine, I married you, I'm your lady. I can see you're angry now. You're always angry when I'm not a lady, when I talk about what's just and fair."

"Let's be objective," said Pitar. "Let's consider those sleazy women who orbit Venus. No one ever calls them proper ladies!"

"Well, no, of course not," Lucy admitted. "Those women can't even fly down to their own planet's surface! That's quite sad."

"And what about the Earth, that so-called motherworld? Earth women were all Earth-mothers once, and look what became of them! They're polluted, they're filthy, a laughing-stock! Don't get me started on those Martian women! Preening around on Mars, freezing on red sand, pretending that they can breathe!"

"I'm sure those women are doing their best to be decent women."

"Oh come now. Those women orbiting Saturn and Jupiter? Let's not be ridiculous here! And I hope you're not defending those post-female entities around Neptune and Uranus."

"Foreign women live quite properly inside the asteroids."

"Not like ladies live in our own society! Asteroidal women don't have our giant canyons, and our polar water-glacier! I will grant you – the asteroids have some fine resources. They have ice, and some metals, they're upscale in the gravity well. But us, the genteel people here inside Mercury, we have much purer, finer metals than they do! Metals, in planetary quantities! And we possess tremendous solar energy! Every Mercurian day, our robots harvest more power than some puny asteroid could generate in ten years!" Pitar drew a deep breath of the Anteroom's stuffy air. "You certainly can't deny all those facts!"

Lucy said nothing, and therefore denied nothing.

"I don't want to be ungallant," Pitar concluded, "but those women bred in the asteroids, they have no gravity! Not one trace of decent gravity. So they are grotesque! What decent man could be doomed to marry some flabby, blob-shaped, boneless woman, with hands on her legs, instead of human feet? I shudder at the thought! Their lives are unimaginable."

Lucy ran both her hands along her elongated skull and through her lustrous, thin, white hair. "Pitar, that's all true. Those foreign people are contemptible."

"I'm glad that you can see that. And there's an important corollary to your conclusion," said Pitar in triumph. "If those foreigners are grotesque – and we both agree, they certainly are – then that proves that we are not. Maybe we suffer – me, and you, too, we both suffer some oppression, maybe – life, and honour, and decency, they aren't all about fun and amusement... But when it's all it's said and done, you and I are Mercurian people. I am who I am, and so are you."

"I am a Mercurian woman," Lucy said. "But too much is always left unsaid."

Lucy gazed suggestively at the airlock, but he did not leave, having become too interested.

"Mrs. Peretz, it's all mere custom," Pitar said at last. "Sometimes, we behave so proudly here, as if we owned the Peak of Eternal Light... And yet, the texture of our existence is mere tradition. The truth is, speaking metaphysically, it's all social habit! Once, in the past, this whole world was like this sorry Anteroom that we're stuck in now..."

Pitar lifted his arms. "I know that life isn't just and fair. And I wish I could change that, but how? If you want to reform gender relations, you should take up those issues in the political councils of your elder ladies. What can you expect *me* to do? Those old witches treat men of my age as if we were larvae."

"I didn't ask you to do anything," Lucy pointed out. "I even told you that it wasn't your fault."

"Well, yes, you said that, but... isn't it strongly implicated that there's something I should do? Surely we don't meet in here, face to face, it's our anniversary... We can't just whine."

A very long silence passed. Pitar began to regret that he had complained about complaining. This act of his was meta, and recursive. No wonder she was confused.

"We have bicycles," Lucy offered.

"What?"

"We have bicycles. Transportation devices, the ones with two wheels. Men and women can meet outside of the purdah, when they ride on bicycles. No one can accuse us of impropriety when we're seated on rolling machines."

"Mrs. Peretz, I have seen bicycles – but I'm not taking your point."

"Suppose that we say," Lucy offered haltingly, "that we're exploring the modern world. There are lots of new mineshafts where only machines have gone. If we ride a few kilometres – I mean *together*, but on bicycles – how can they say that we're harming custom? Or offending decency?"

"What do you mean now, bicycles? Aren't those contraptions dangerous? You could fall off a bicycle and break your neck! Bicycles are mechanically unstable! They only have two wheels!"

"Yes, it's hard to learn to ride a bicycle. I fell off several times, and even hurt myself. But I learned how! Bicycles are perfect for low-gravity planets. Because bicycles stress the legs. They strengthen the bones. Bicycles are a healthy and modern invention."

Pitar considered this set of arguments. Of course he'd seen women riding on bicycles – and the occasional man as well, maybe one in ten – but he'd paid no real attention to this fad. He'd considered bicycling some girlish affectation – those women in their faceless helmets and their black, baggy clothes. Speeding about on these gaily coloured devices...

But maybe it made engineering sense. Bicycles had appeared in the world because the mine-shafts were expanding. Ever-active robots, steadily gnawing new courses through the planet's richest mineral seams. The world was growing methodically.

Modern Mercury was no longer that old, cramped world where people lurked in chambers and airlocks, and walked only a few hundred metres. Robots were ripping through the planet's crust, and behind them came human settlers, as always on Mercury. That was common sense, and no conservative could deny that.

"I could build a bicycle," Pitar declared. "I could fabricate and print one. Not a ladylike kind, of course – but a proper transportation machine."

"With your bicycle helmet, you wouldn't have to wear your veil anymore," Lucy said eagerly. "No one would know that it was you, on your bicycle... except for me, of course, because, well, I always know it's you."

"Then it's settled. I'll set straight to work! I'll give you a progress report, next time we meet."

They shook hands, and departed through their separate iron doors.


AN OFFICIAL DAY of mourning had been declared for the late Colonel Hartmann Srinivasan DeBlakey. As a gesture of respect toward this primal Mercurian pioneer, his mourning period occupied an entire 'Mercurian Day.'

Colonel DeBlakey had been an ardent calendar reformer. To thoroughly break all cultural ties with Earth, DeBlakey had struggled to reform Mercurian pioneer habits around the 88-day 'Mercurian Year' and the 58-day 'Mercurian Day.'

Of course, DeBlakey's elaborate, ingenious calendar scheme had proved entirely hopeless in practice. Human beings had innate 24-hour biological cycles. So, the practical habits within a sunless, subterranean city had quickly assumed the modern, workaday system of three 8-hour shifts.

But DeBlakey had never surrendered his cultural convictions about calendar reform, just as he had fought valiantly for spelling reform, gender relations and trinary computation. DeBlakey had been an intellectual titan of Mercury. In acknowledgement of his legacy, it was agreed that gentlemen would wear their mourning veils for one entire Mercurian Day.

Being a mere boy of eight, Pitar's son, Mario Louis Peretz, wore only a light scarf, rather than the full male facial veil. Mario had his mother's good looks. Mario was a fine boy, a decent boy, a source of proper pride. Life in his juvenile crèche was entirely ruled by women, so Mario had refined and dainty habits: long hair, painted fingernails, a skirt rather than trousers, everything as it should be.

Through his mother's gene-line, young Mario was closely related to the late Colonel DeBlakey. So it was proper of Mario to attend the all-male obsequies, up on the planet's surface.

Of course Pitar had to accompany his son as his paternal escort. The blistering, airless surface of Mercury was tremendously hostile and dangerous. It was therefore entirely proper for children.

Pitar hadn't worn his spacesuit in two years – not since the last celebrity funeral. For his own part, young Mario Louis sported a brand-new, state-of-the-art suitaloon. His mother had bought this archigrammatical garment for him, and Lucy had spared no expense.

The boy was childishly delighted with his fancy get-up. The suitaloon had everything a Mercurian boy could desire: a diamond-crystal bubble-helmet, a boy-sized life-support cuirass, woven nanocarbon arms and legs, plus fashionable accents of silver, copper, gold and platinum. Mario was quite the little lordling in his suitaloon. He tended to caper.

The crowd of male mourners queued to take the freight elevators to the Peak of Eternal Light.

"Dad," said Mario, gripping Pitar's spacesuit gauntlet, "did Colonel DeBlakey ever fight duels?"

"Oh, yes." Pitar nodded. "Many duels."

"Martial arts are my favourite subject at the crèche," Mario boasted. "I think I could be pretty good at fighting duels."

"Son," said Pitar, "duelling is a serious matter. It's never about how strong you are, or how fast you are. Men fight duels to defend points of honour. Duelling supports propriety. You can lose a duel, and still make your point. Colonel DeBlakey lost some duels. So he had to apologise, and politically retreat. But he never lost the respect of his peers. That's what it's all about."

"But Dad... what if I just beat people up with my baton? Wouldn't they have to do whatever I say?"

Pitar laughed. "That's been tried. It never works out well."

Thanks to some covert intrigue – his mother's, almost certainly – Mario was allowed into the elevator along with the casket of his revered ancestor. DeBlakey's casket was simply his original, pioneer spacesuit. This archaic device was so rugged, solid and rigid that it made a perfect sarcophagus.

The old elevator, like the old spacesuit, was stoic and grim. It was crammed with suited gentlemen and boys, veiled behind their faceplates.

No one broke the grave solemnity of the moment. At last, the shuddering, creaking trip to the surface was over.

Pitar followed the economic news, so he was aware of the booming industrial developments on the surface. But to know those statistics was not the same as witnessing major industry at first hand.

What a vista of the machinic phylum! He felt almost as much sheer wonderment as his eight-year-old son.

The cybernetic order, conquering Mercury, algorithmically pushing itself into new performance-spaces... It had crisply divided its ubiquity into new divisions of spatial and temporal magnitude!

The roads, the pits, the mines, the power-plants and smelters, the neatly assembled slag... The great, slow, factory hulks... the vast caravans of ore-laden packets... the dizzying variety of scampering viabs, and a true explosion of chipsets.

And, at the nanocentric bottom of this semi-autonomous pyramid of computational activism, the smartsand. Amateurs gaped at the giant hulks – but professionals always talked about the smartsand.

Entropy struck these machines, as it did any organised form. Machines that veered from the wandering Mercurian twilight zone were promptly fried or frozen. Yet the broken systemic fragments were always reconstituted, later. No transistor, gasket or screw was ever abandoned. Not one fleck of industrial trash, though the cratered landscape was severely torn by robot mandibles.

The human funeral procession marched toward the solemn Peak of Eternal Light.

This grandiose polar mountain never passed within solar shadow. The Peak of Eternal Light was the most famous natural feature of Mercury, the primal source of the colony's unfailing energy supply.

At the Peak's frozen base, which was never lit by

the Sun, was a great frosty glacier. This glacier was the only source of water on or within the planet.

This glacier had been formed over eons by the bombardment of comets. Steam as thin as vacuum had accumulated in this frozen shadow, layering monatomically. Those towering layers of black ice, the product of billions of years, had seemed enough to quench the thirst of a million people.

Nothing left of that mighty glacier today but a few scarred ice-blocks, slowly gnawed by the oldest machines.

The polar glacier had, in fact, vanished to quench the thirst of a million people. This ancient ice had passed straight into the living veins of human beings.

This planetary resource was whittled down to a mere nub now. Yet one had to look here, to know that. The polar glacier existed in permanent darkness. Only the radar in Pitar's suit allowed him to witness the frightening decline.

Most of the men ignored this ghastly spectacle. As for his own son, the boy took no notice at all. The shocking decline in polar ice meant nothing to him. He had never seen the North Pole otherwise.

And what had the old man, the dead man, said about that crisis? Ever the visionary, he'd certainly known it was coming.

The dead pioneer had said, in his blunt and confrontational way, "We'll just have to go fetch some more ice."

So, they had done as the dead man said. The people of Mercury had built a gigantic manned spacecraft, a metallic colossus. A ship so vast, so overweening in scale, that it might have been an interstellar colony – were such things possible.

Robots had hauled this great golden ark to the launch ramp, and sent this gleaming dreadnought hurtling off toward the cometary belt. There to commandeer and retrieve some vast, timeless, life-enhancing snowball.

Of course, there had been certain other options – rather than a gigantic, fully-manned spacecraft. Simpler, more practical tactics.

For instance, thousands of tiny robots might have been launched out in vast streams, to go capture a comet.

Then as the comet whirled round and round the blazing, almighty bulk of the Sun, the robots could have chipped off small chunks of comet frost, and sent those modest packets to the Mercurian surface. At the cost of a few small, fresh craters – nothing much, compared with the giant mining pits – clouds of cometary steam would have arisen. Puffs of comet vapour, drifting north, to freeze onto the original great glacier, there at the base of the Peak of Eternal Light.

This would have been a quiet, tedious, patient, and gentle way to replenish the vanished glacier. A nurturing restoration of the status quo. Mercurian women favoured this tactic.

But to espouse this idea had some dark implications. It implied, strongly, that Mercury itself should never have been settled by human beings. Were men worthless, was that the idea? Why not abolish mankind, with all its valour, its honour, its urge to explore – and have Mercury remain a mine-pit infested with the mindless and soulless machinic phylum?

That idea was blasphemy – and there was no reconciling these factions. The civil division there was as distinct as frozen night and blazing day. This tremendous struggle – a primal issue of resources and politics – had almost broken the colony.

As tempers rose, a compromise was urged by certain moderates, whom everyone ignored. Why not just buy some ice? Admit that Mercury faced a water crisis beyond its power, and buy ice from foreigners.

The asteroids had plenty of ice. What sense did it make to design a weird horde of ice-robots? Why create some swaggering Mercurian flagship, at such crippling cost? Just abandon honour and autonomy, abandon foolish pride, and pay foreigners. There were merchants out there already, willing to trade for metals. If one could call those weird entities 'people.'

After much bloodshed, feuding, disgraces, regrettable excesses, the manned explorers had won the civil war. Why? Because they had claimed the mantle of the traditional values. Then these conservative fanatics had climbed aboard their new golden spacecraft, and promptly abandoned Mercury with all its long traditions.

The field of honour had settled nothing, thought Pitar. Because those traditions were fictions – irrational retrodictions, modern political interpretations of lost historical realities.

The values of Colonel DeBlakey were much wilder than anyone cared to remember. DeBlakey, and the men of his generation, were fantastic visionaries. DeBlakey, the Mercurian hero, cared nothing for colonising Mercury. He saw Mercury as a mere stepping-stone to colonising the Sun.

In his arcane, two-hundred-forty-year lifespan, this great man had advanced his philosophy in vast, scriptural detail. Endlessly writing, preaching, planning, designing, and theorising. Pitar had read a

few million of these hundreds of millions of words.
Very few ever did.

As the mourners gathered in their artificial twilight
at the mountain's base, Pitar realised that he was
attending the last public airing for DeBlakey's great
pioneer ideology.

Mercurian celebrities delivered their funeral
orations – eloquent, careful, and well-considered.
Yet DeBlakey's titanic legacy was much too large for
their tiny gestures. The mourners clearly desired to
be brief – for the radiation on the surface made that
wise. Yet a lifespan of a quarter of a millennium was
no easy thing to summarise.

DeBlakey's schemes had to do with interstellar
settlement: mankind's manifest destiny in the
galaxy. "Taming the stars," as he put it. Such were
the progressive visions that racked the great man's
brain, as the early Mercurian colonists crouched in
their stone closets, half-suffocated and sipping toxic
comet water.

DeBlakey was scheming to mine Mercury, fully
develop the machinic phylum, and then march
gloriously forth to mine the Sun. To dwell within the
Sun, living in Eternal Light. To thrive in Eternal Light,
without any shadow of any planet's bulk, forever.

Because, while Mercury certainly had gold, silver,
platinum, and transuranic metals – sometimes
scattered on the cratered surface in gleaming pools –
the Sun possessed every element.

Imaginary star-redoubts would whip through the
Sun's tenuous atmosphere at a hyper-Mercurian
speed, sifting out water, carbon, metals – anything
mankind needed – directly from the solar cloud.
These visionary sun-forts would be vast magnetic

bottles, all tractor beams and photon traps, with living, golden cores.

Once mankind had taught the machinic phylum to dwell within the atmospheres of stars, no further limits would ever trouble mankind. Above all, there would be no limits to the settler population. Dutiful women, living for centuries, would raise and acculturate hundreds of children, each one trained to star-spanning pioneer values.

At this singular rate of population explosion, the Sun would soon support hundreds of billions of people. Trillions of citizens, manning millions of colonies. So many colonies, so cybernetically capable, that they would seize command of the Sun.

With such titanic energy resources, interstellar flight would become a corollary, a mere logical detail. Tamed solar flares would magnetically fling new colonies, hurtling at near-light-speed, into the atmospheres of the nearest stars.

Any species that could dwell within stars would swiftly dominate the galaxy. Spreading algorithmically, exponentially, resistlessly, galactically. Men who understood this had no need to search for Earthlike planets, that illusion of meagre fools. They would dwell forever within the machinic phylum, each superhuman soul a peak of eternal light.

There was a certain fierce logic to DeBlakey's cosmic plans. If not entirely pragmatic, they were certainly aspirational. Driven by such fierce and boundless human will, the machinic phylum would explode across the universe.

However, DeBlakey was mortal, and therefore dead. To the serious-minded, sensible people actually living today within the planet Mercury, his dreams seemed arcane, farfetched, absurd... And now, his funeral eulogists were trying to come to terms with all of that. To settle all of that, to bury all of that. They were gently folding this man's wild pioneer dream into the harmless legendry of everyday Mercurian existence.

Pitar's boy tugged at his gauntleted arm. These high-flown orations had the boy bored stiff. "Dad."

Pitar opened a private channel. "What is it? Do you need a bathroom? Use the suit."

"Dad, can I go fight now? That's Jimmy over there, he likes to fight."

"No sparring during funerals, son."

Mario grimaced at this reproof. He rubbed exoatmospheric dust from his diamond bubble-helmet. "Dad, when they build the new colony at the South Pole, will we go there?"

"Mario, there's no water at the South Pole. There are hills of Eternal Light there, so there's plenty of energy, but fate put no glaciers for us in that place. It's uninhabitable."

"But our space heroes will come back some day, and bring us a water-comet. Then will we go?"

"Yes," said Pitar. "We would go. There would be new opportunities there, more than in this old colony. The South Pole would mean a different life, new social principles. Yes, we would go there. I would take you with me. And your brothers, too – because you'll have brothers someday."

"Would Mom go with us?"

"Son, in nine years you'll be married yourself. I'll arrange that. And believe me, that's sure to complicate your agenda."

"Mom would go to a new colony. She wants to invent a new way of life. She told me that."

"Really."

"Yes, she told me! She really means it."

Pitar drew a breath within his helmet. "We are, after all, a pioneering people. That is our true heritage, and I'm proud that you are witnessing all this. You'll live a very long time, my son, so be sure to remember this day, and all it means. This world belongs to you. It was given to you. And don't you ever forget that."

Another speaker took the rostrum at the funereal plateau. This elder had to walk with robot assistance, and though he said little enough, he spoke at the droning rate of the very wise. A dreadful thing to hear.

Mario could not keep his peace. "Dad, will there be other boys like me at the South Pole?"

Pitar smiled. "Of course there will. A society with no youth has no future. If the people of Earth had sent their children into space, instead of just foolish astronauts, they would have spread throughout the worlds. Instead, they sank into their mud. That's not your heritage, because those people have no moral fibre. That's why they don't matter now, and we do."

Mario struggled to scratch his nose through his bubble-helmet. Of course this feat was impossible. "Dad, do Earth people stink? Jimmy says they stink."

"I've never met one personally, but they do have wild germs in their bellies. Earth people can emit some unpleasant odours, and that's a fact." Pitar cleared his throat inside his spacesuit. "The Earth people don't care much for us, either, mind you – they call us 'termites.'"

"'Termites', Dad, what does that mean?"

"Termites are subhuman social beasts. Wild animals. Never properly gardened like our animals."

"Dad, how big are termites?"

"I really don't know, about the size of a housecat, I guess. If some man ever calls you a 'termite,' you slap his face and challenge him, understand? That puts a swift end to that nonsense."

"All right, Dad."

"Stop chattering now, son. This is the climax, this is the great moment."

Bearing their ceremonial staves and halberds, the male elders retreated, with slow step, from the funeral plateau. Sand rose up in waves below the dead man's catafalque.

The smartsand formed itself into one grand, pixelated, seething, pallbearing wave.

An impossible liquid, it reverently rolled up the mountain, bearing the dead man.

The catafalque crossed the brilliant twilight zone, into Eternal Light.

The robots shifted their solar reflectors, in unison. The human crowd fell into dramatic, timeless, deep-frozen darkness. Pitar felt his spacesuit shudder, a trembling fit of holy awe.

The catafalque gleamed like a chunk of the unseen sun.

The dead man's suit ruptured from the brilliant heat. Precious steam burst free. One brief, geyserlike, human rainbow, one visionary burst of glorious combustion, spewing like a solar flare.

Then the ceremony ended. Though the long Mercurian Day had scarcely begun, a spiritual dawn had appeared.

PITAR SAT ON the rim of a sandbox, within the Great Park of Splendid Remembrance.

To pursue his design labours, Pitar often came to this site, to carefully sip cognition enhancers and contemplate the metaphysical implications of monumentality.

The task of his generation was one of reconciliation, the achievement of a deeper understanding. This park had been the battlefield where the worst mass clashes of the civil war had occurred. Bitter, bloody, hand-to-hand struggles, between the polarised factions.

Some of the colony's best, most idealistic, most public-spirited men, trapped by harsh moral necessity, had beaten each other to death in this cavern.

Even women had killed each other in here, when it became clear that the great burden of the ice-hunt would impinge on their personal politics. Women fought in feline ambush, and in martyr operations. Women killed efficiently, because they never wasted effort grasping at the honours of combat.

The civil war was the closest that the colony had ever come to collapse. Worse than any natural catastrophe: worse than the blowouts, worse than the toxic poisonings.

The Great Park of Splendid Remembrance was, by its nature, an ancient Mercurian lava tube. This cavern was a natural feature, unplanned by man, untouched by the jaws of machines.

So it was thought, somehow, that this bloodstained space of abject moral failure was best left to wilderness. To living creatures other than mankind.

The original settlers had brought genetic material from their homelands on Earth. These vials of DNA had been preserved with care, but never released inside the world, never instantiated as living creatures.

Today, the Park of Splendid Remembrance was thick with them. These thriving, vegetal entities had exotic shapes, exotic features, and exotic, ancient names. Banyans, jacarandas, palms, ylang-ylang, papayas, jackfruit, teak, and mahogany.

Unlike the homely, useful algae on which the colony subsisted, these woody species took on wild, unheard-of forms. Under the blazing growlights, rising in the light gravity, rooted in a strange mineral soil, they were the native Mercurian forest. Great, green, reeking, shady, twisted eminences. Bizarre organic complexities: flowering, gnarling, branching, fruiting.

This wilderness mankind had unleashed was not beautiful. It was vigorous, but crabbed and chaotic. It was, as yet, merely a colonial tangle, a strange, self-choking complex of distorted traditional forms.

Like all aesthetic issues, thought Pitar, the problem here had its roots within a poor metaphysics. To introduce this ungainly forest, so as to obscure a dark place where human will had failed – that effort was insincere. It had not been thought-through.

The Great Park of Splendid Remembrance had feared to face the whole truth. So it was as yet neither great nor splendid, because it had shirked the hard thinking required by the authentic Mercurian texture of existence.

This was Pitar's own task.

Sitting in deep thought, Pitar idly drew squares, triangles, circles, within the childish play-box of smartsand. With each stroke of his duelling-club, the smartsand responded and processed. Arcane ripples bounded and rebounded from the corners of the sandbox.

The computational entities, with which mankind shared this planet, were never intelligent. The machinic phylum, which seemed so clever and vigorous to the untrained eye, was neither alive nor smart. The phylum was merely the phylum; it had no will, no pride, no organic lust for survival, no reason to exist and persist. Without human will to issue its coded commands, the phylum would collapse in an eyeblink, returning to the sunblasted, constituent elements of this world.

But although the phylum possessed neither life nor intelligence, it did possess an order-of-being. It was not alive, merely processual, yet it had transcended the natural. The phylum was a metaphysical entity, and worthy of respect. Something like the spiritual respect owed a dead body: a thing, yes, inert, yes, of ashes, yes – yet so much more than mere inert ashes.

The truth, beyond intelligence. There were those who said – the daring thinkers of Pitar's own generation – that the Sun was self-possessed. Not in the old-fashioned, cranky, archaic, heroic way that visionaries like DeBlakey had once imagined. The Sun was never alive, nor was the Sun intelligent, but the Sun was an entity, metaphysically ordered. The Sun that loomed over tiny Mercury was one Object of the Order of a Star.

And these thinkers speculated – speculating furthermore, just as bravely daring as their ancestors, though in a more modern fashion – that there were many Orders in the cosmos. Life, and, intelligence, and the processual phylum were just three of those countless Orders.

These speculative realists held that the Cosmos was inherently riddled with unnatural Orders.

Hundreds, possibly thousands, of independent, extropic Orders, each Order unknown to the next, yet each as real and noble as the next, each as important as life or thought.

Some Orders transpired in picoseconds, other Orders in unknowable aeons. Orders, each as deep and complex and unnatural as life, or cognition, or computation. Entities, autarchic ontologies, occupying the full panoply of every scale of space-time. From the quantum foam, where space disintegrated, to the forever-unknowable scale of the Cosmos, forever outside the light-cone of any instrumentable knowability.

That was reality.

There were those who called these idle dreams, but reality was neither neither idle nor a dream. Much scientific evidence had been carefully amassed, to prove the objective existence of extropic Orders. Pitar followed Mercurian science with some care – although he never involved himself in the fierce, bloody duels over precedence and citation.

Pitar understood the implications of modern science for his own creative work. Any true, sincere monument, any place of genuinely splendid remembrance, would be built in a manner that took reality into a full account. An enlightened peak of moral comprehension.

This Awareness would transcend awareness. It would respect that ordered otherness, in all its many forms, and do that Otherness honour.

It might well take him, thought Pitar, centuries to come to workable terms with this professional ambition. But since he had that time, it behooved him to spend his time properly. Such was his duty. This was something that he himself could do, to add to all that had passed before, as a legacy to whoever, or whatever, was to follow.

Pitar glanced up, suddenly, from the writhing sandpit. His wife had arrived. Lucy was on her bicycle.

Pitar mounted his own two-wheeled machine. He rode to join her. Pitar rode smoothly and elegantly, because he'd infested his bicycle's frame with smartsand.

He hadn't told his wife about this design gambit; Lucy merely thought, presumably, that he was tremendously good at learning to ride a bicycle. No need to bring up that subject. Enough that he had a bicycle, and that he rode it with her. Deeds, not words.

His wife's head was fully encased in her black helmet. Her body was almost suitalooned by her black, flowing bicycle garb. Mounted on her bicycle, Lucy scarcely looked like a woman at all. More of a dark, scarcely-knowable, metaphysical object.

But, when Pitar wore his own helmet, he was as anonymous and mysterious as she. So, faceless and shameless, they rode together, tires crunching subtly, on the park's long grey cinder-path.

"Mr. Peretz, you looked very thoughtful, sitting there in your sandbox."

"Yes," said Pitar, forbearing to nod, due to the bulk of his helmet.

"What were you thinking?"

A deadly female question. Pitar found a tactful parry. "Look here, I have created a new bicycle. See, I am riding it now."

"Yes, I saw that you printed a new bicycle, and it's more advanced now, isn't it? What happened to your nice old bicycle? You rode that one so gallantly!"

"I gave that machine to a friend," said Pitar. "I gave it to Mr. Giorgio Harold DeVenet."

His wife's front wheel wobbled suddenly. "What? To him? How? Why? He beat you in a duel!"

"It's true that Mr. DeVenet is a duellist. And it's true that I lost that duel. But that was eight years ago, and there's no reason I can't be polite."

"Why did you do that?"

Pitar said nothing.

"Why did you do it? You had some reason for doing that. You should tell me that. He insulted me; I should know this."

"Let's just ride," Pitar suggested.

Pitar had given the gift to the duellist, because he'd known that there would be trouble about the bicycles. This radical innovation – bicycling – it did damage the institution of purdah. Maybe it did not violate the letter of propriety, but it certainly damaged the spirit.

Pitar had been confronted on that issue; politely. So Pitar had, just as politely, referred that matter of honour to Mr. Giorgio Harold DeVenet, also the possessor of a bicycle.

Mr. DeVenet, a brawny and athletic man, was delighted with his new bicycle. As he scorched past mere pedestrians, pedalling in a fury, Mr. DeVenet's strength and speed were publicly displayed to fine effect.

Skeptics had questioned Mr. DeVenet's affection for bicycles. He had promptly forced them to retract their assertions and apologise.

In this fashion, the matter of bicycles was settled.

Mr. DeVenet was not so punctilious, however, that he had escaped being seen in the flirtatious, bicycling company of the notorious Widow De Schubert. She was the type who rode through life without a helmet. The widow's late husband, outmatched and sorely lacking in tact, had already fallen on the field of honour.

To own a bicycle was not the same as understanding its proper use. At the rate that matters progressed these days, it wouldn't be long before Mr. DeVenet joined the other victims of the Widow De Schubert. The duellist could batter any number of bicycle skeptics, but to defeat a woman's wiles was far beyond his simplicity.

Men who lived by the club fell by the club, a trouble-story far older than this world. Pitar was at peace with these difficult facts of life. The notorious Widow De Schubert was one his wife's best-trusted friends – but he did not inquire into that tangled matter. Certain things between men and women were best left unspoken.

His wife lifted her visor by a thumb's width, so as to be better heard. "Mr. Peretz, I do enjoy these new outings that we have together nowadays. You have given me another gift that I long desired. For that, I am grateful to you. You are a good husband."

"Thank you very much for that kindly remark, Mrs. Peretz. That's very gratifying."

"Are you also pleased by our situation today?"

Given the praise he had just received, Pitar ventured a candid response. "Although modernity has some clear advantages," he told her, "I can't say it's entirely easy. In that very modest bicycle garb, I cannot see your face. In fact, I can't see anything of you at all. You are a deep mystery."

"Beneath this black garment, sir, I wear nothing but my beautiful, golden mangalsutra. I feel so free nowadays. Freer than I have ever felt as a modern woman."

Pitar pondered this provocative remark. It had emotional layers and textures closed to mere men. "That's an interesting data-point, there."

"Mr. Peretz, although it was not our own will that united us," Lucy said, rolling boldly on, "I feel that marriage is an important exploration of a woman's emotional phase-space. Someday, we two – separated, of course – will look back on these years with satisfaction. You in your way, and me in mine, as that must be. Nevertheless, we will have accomplished a crucial joint success."

"You're full of compliments this afternoon, Mrs. Peretz! I'm glad you're in such a good mood!"

"This is not a question of my so-called moods!" his wife told him. "I am trying to explain to you that, now that we possess bicycles, modernity is achieved. It's time that I faced futurity, and to do what futurity requires from me, I will need your help. It's time we built another child."

"Since honour requires that of me as well, Mrs. Peretz, I can only concur."

"Let's build a daughter, this time."

"A daughter would be just and fair."

"Good. Then, that's all settled. These are good times. A good day to you, sir." She bent to heave at her whirring pedals, and she rapidly wheeled away.

# ABOUT THE AUTHORS

**John Barnes** has commercially published thirty volumes of fiction, including science fiction, men's action adventure, two collaborations with astronaut Buzz Aldrin, a collection of short stories and essays, one fantasy and one mainstream novel. His most recent books are science fiction novel *Daybreak Zero*, young adult novel *Losers in Space*, and political satire *Raise the Gipper!* He has done a rather large number of occasionally peculiar things for money, mainly in business consulting, academic teaching, and show business, fields which overlap more than you'd think. Since 2001, he has lived in Denver, Colorado, where he has a thoroughly wonderful wife, a wildly varying income, and an unjustifiably negative attitude, which he feels is actually the best permutation.

**Stephen Baxter** is one of the most important science fiction writers to emerge from Britain in the past thirty years. His 'Xeelee' sequence of novels and short stories is arguably the most significant work of future history in modern science fiction. He is the author of more than forty books and over a hundred short stories. His most recent books are *Iron Winter*, the final novel in the 'Northland' trilogy, *Doctor Who: The Wheel of Ice*, *The Long Earth*, the first of two novels co-written with Terry Pratchett, and new short story collection, *Last and First Contacts*.

**Elizabeth Bear** was born in Hartford, Connecticut, on the same day as Frodo and Bilbo Baggins, but in a different year. She divides her time between Massachusetts, where she lives with a Giant Ridiculous Dog in a town so small it doesn't even have its own Dunkin Donuts, and western Wisconsin, the home of her partner, Scott Lynch. Her first short fiction appeared in 1996, and was followed after a nearly decade-long gap by fifteen novels, two short story collections, and more than fifty short stories. Her most recent novels are Norse fantasy *The Tempering of Men* (with Sarah Monette) and an Asian-inspired fantasy, *Range of Ghosts*. Coming up is a new short story collection, *Shoggoths in Bloom*. Bear's 'Jenny Casey' trilogy won the Locus Award for Best First Novel, and she won the John W. Campbell Award for Best New Writer in 2005. Her stories 'Tideline' and 'Shoggoths in Bloom' won the Hugo, while 'Tideline' also won the Sturgeon award.

**Pat Cadigan** is the author of about a hundred short stories and fourteen books, two of which, *Synners* and *Fools*, won the Arthur C. Clarke Award. She was born in New York, grew up in Massachusetts, and spent most of her adult life in the Kansas City area. She now lives in London with her husband, the Original Chris Fowler, her Polish translator Konrad Walewski and his partner, the Lovely Lena, and co-conspirator, writer and raconteuse Amanda Hemingway; also, two ghosts, one of which is the shade of Miss Kitty Calgary, Queen of the Cats (the other declines to give a name). She is pretty sure there isn't a more entertaining household.

**James S. A. Corey** is a pseudonym for Daniel Abraham and Ty Franck. Corey's current project is a series of science fiction novels called *The Expanse*. The first two novels in the series are *Leviathan Wakes* and *Caliban's War*. The third, *Dandelion Sky*, is scheduled to be released in 2013.

James is Daniel's middle name, Corey is Ty's middle name, and S. A. are Daniel's daughter's initials.

**Stephen D. Covey** received a Bachelor's in Physics from Wabash College. As a software and Internet consultant, his clients included the Air Force, Army, and Navy. He was the Director of R&D for Applied Innovation Inc., and has authored several papers on topics ranging from "Optical Ethernet" to "Design Considerations for Space Settlements." A speaker at various conferences, he has given multiple presentations related to capturing asteroids into Earth orbit. A member of the Asteroid Mining Group, Stephen will chair the Asteroid track at the 2013 International Space Development Conference in San Diego. His educational website about minerals (www.galleries.com) averages 300,000 visitors per month. He also writes science fiction, techno-thrillers, and the futurist (pro-space) blog RamblingsOnTheFutureOfHumanity.com.

**Gwyneth Jones** was born in Manchester, England, and is the author of more than twenty novels for teenagers, mostly under the name Ann Halam, and several highly regarded SF novels for adults. She has won two World Fantasy awards, the Arthur C. Clarke award, the British Science Fiction Association short story award, the Dracula Society's Children of the Night award, the Philip K. Dick award, and shared the first Tiptree award, in 1992, with Eleanor Arnason. Her most recent books are novel *Spirit*, essay collection *Imagination/Space*, and story collection *The Universe of Things*. She lives in Brighton, UK, with her husband and son, a Tonkinese cat called Ginger, and her young friend Milo.

**Paul McAuley** worked as a research biologist in various universities, including Oxford and UCLA, and for six years was a lecturer in botany at St Andrews University, before he became a full-time writer. Although best known as a science-fiction writer, he has also published crime novels and thrillers. His SF novels have won the Philip K. Dick Memorial Award, and the Arthur C. Clarke, John W. Campbell, and Sidewise Awards; his story, 'The Choice,' won the 2012 Theodore Sturgeon Memorial Award. His latest titles are *Cowboy Angels* and *In The Mouth Of The Whale*. He lives in North London.

**Sandra McDonald's** collection *Diana Comet and Other Improbable Stories* won the Lambda Literary award, was a Booklist Editor's Choice, and was an American Library Association 'Over the Rainbow' book. A military veteran and former Hollywood assistant, she is the author of several science fiction adventures, including *Boomerang World*, *The Outback Stars*, *The Stars Down Under*, and *The Stars Blue Yonder*. As Sam Cameron, she writes a young adult GLBTQ series of mysteries including *Mystery of The Tempest*, *The Secret of Othello*, and *The Missing Juliet*. Her short fiction has appeared in *Asimov's Science Fiction*, *Strange Horizons*, and dozens of other publications. Four of her stories have been noted on the James A. Tiptree Award Honor List or Short List. Originally from Massachusetts, she currently lives in Jacksonville, Florida, and teaches college.

**An Owomoyela** is a neutrois author with a background in web development, linguistics, and weaving chain maille out of stainless steel fencing wire, whose fiction has appeared in a number of venues including Clarkesworld, *Asimov's*, Lightspeed, and a pair of Year's Bests. An's interests range from pulsars and Cepheid variables to gender studies and nonstandard pronouns, with a plethora of stops in between. Se graduated from the Clarion West Writers Workshop in 2008, attended the Launchpad Astronomy Workshop in 2011, and doesn't plan to stop learning as long as se can help it.

**Hannu Rajaniemi** was born in Ylivieska, Finland, in 1978. He read his first science fiction novel at the age of six – Jules Verne's *20,000 Leagues Under the Sea*. At the age of eight, Hannu approached ESA with a fusion-powered spaceship design, which was received with a polite thank you note. Hannu studied mathematics and theoretical physics at the University of Oulu and completed a BSc thesis on transcendental numbers. He went on to complete Part III of the Mathematical Tripos at Cambridge University and a PhD in string theory at University of Edinburgh. Hannu is a member of an Edinburgh-based writers' group which includes Alan Campbell, Jack Deighton, Caroline Dunford and Charles Stross. His first fiction sale was the short story 'Shibuya no Love' to *Futurismic.com*. Hannu's first novel, *The Quantum Thief*, was published by Gollancz to great acclaim in 2011. The sequel, *The Fractal Prince*, is due shortly.

**Alastair Reynolds** was born in Barry, South Wales, in 1966. He has lived in Cornwall, Scotland, and – since 1991 – the Netherlands, where he spent twelve years working as a scientist for the European Space Agency. He became a full-time writer in 2004, and recently married his long-time partner, Josette. Reynolds has been publishing short fiction since his first sale to *Interzone* in 1990. Since 2000 he has published ten novels: the *Inhibitor* trilogy, British Science Fiction Association Award winner *Chasm City*, *Century Rain*, *Pushing Ice*, *The Prefect*, *House of Suns*, and *Terminal World*. His most recent novel is *Blue Remembered Earth*, first in the *Poseidon's Children* series. His short fiction has been collected in *Zima Blue and Other Stories*, *Galactic North*, and *Deep Navigation*. Coming up is a new Doctor Who novel, *The Harvest of Time*. In his spare time he rides horses.

**Kristine Kathryn Rusch** started out the decade of the '90s as one of the fastest-rising and most prolific young authors on the scene, took a few years out in mid-decade for a very successful turn as editor of *The Magazine of Fantasy and Science Fiction*, and, since stepping down from that position, has returned to her old standards of production here in the 21st Century, publishing a slew of novels in four genres, writing fantasy, mystery, and romance novels under various pseudonyms as well as science fiction. She has published more than twenty novels under her own name, including *The White Mists of Power*, *The Disappeared*, *Extremes*, and *Fantasy Life*, the four-volume *Fey* series, the *Black Throne* series, *Alien Influences*, and several *Star Wars*, *Star Trek*, and other media tie-in books, both solo and written with husband Dean Wesley Smith and with others. Her most recent books (as Rusch, anyway) are the SF novels of the popular *Retrieval Artist* series, which include *The Disappeared*, *Extremes*, *Consequences*, *Buried Deep*, *Paloma*, *Recovery Man*, and a collection of stories, *The Retrieval Artist and Other Stories*. Her copious short fiction has been collected in *Stained Black: Horror Stories*, *Stories for an Enchanted Afternoon*, *Little Miracles: And Other Tales of Murder*, and *Millenium Babies*. In 1999, she won Readers Award polls from the readerships of both *Asimov's Science Fiction* and *Ellery Queen's Mystery Magazine*, an unprecedented double honour! As an editor, she was honoured with the Hugo Award for her work on *The Magazine of Fantasy and Science Fiction*, and shared the World Fantasy Award with Dean Wesley Smith for her work as editor of the original hardcover anthology version of *Pulphouse*. As a writer, she has won the

Herodotus Award for Best Historical Mystery (for *A Dangerous Road*, written as Kris Nelscott) and the *Romantic Times* Reviewer's Choice Award (for *Utterly Charming*, written as Kristine Grayson); as Kristine Kathryn Rusch, she's won the John W. Campbell Award, been a finalist for the Arthur C. Clarke Award, and took home a Hugo Award in 2000 for her story 'Millennium Babies,' making her one of the few people in genre history to win Hugos for both editing and writing.

After discovering planetary wireless broadband, **Bruce Sterling** united his time between Turin, Belgrade, and Austin. He also began writing some design fiction and architecture fiction, as well as science fiction. However, this daring departure from the routine made no particular difference to anybody. Sterling then started hanging out with Augmented Reality people, and serving as a guest curator for European electronic arts festivals. These eccentricities also provoked no particular remark. Sterling went on a Croatian literary yacht tour and lived for a month in Brazil. These pleasant interludes had little practical consequence. After teaching in Switzerland and Holland, Sterling realized that all his European students lived more or less in this manner, and that nobody was surprised about much of any of that any more. So, he decided to sit still and get a little writing done, and this story was part of that effort. Prior to this he had written ten novels and four short story collections. His most recent books are novel *The Caryatids*, major career retrospective *Ascendancies: The Best of Bruce Sterling*, and collection *Global High-Tech*.

# ENGINEERING INFINITY

Edited by Jonathan Strahan

UK ISBN: 978 1 907519 51 2 • US ISBN: 978 1 907519 52 9 • £7.99/$7.99

*The universe shifts and changes; suddenly you understand, and are filled with wonder.*
*Coming up against the speed of light (and with it, the sheer size of the universe), seeing*
*how difficult and dangerous terraforming an alien world really is, realising that a hitch-*
*hiker on a starship consumes fuel and oxygen and the tragedy that results... it's "hard-SF"*
*where sense of wonder is most often found and where science fiction's true heart lies.*
*Including stories from the likes of Stephen Baxter and Charles Stross.*